When Perfect Ain't Possible

When Perfect Ain't Possible

Suzette D. Harrison

sepia

★BET BOOKS

BET Publications, LLC
http://www.bet.com

SEPIA BOOKS are published by

BET Publications, LLC
c/o BET BOOKS
One BET Plaza
1900 W Place NE
Washington, DC 20018-1211

All Kensington Titles, Imprints, and Distributed Lines are available at special quantity discounts for bulk purchases for sales promotions, premiums, fund-raising, and educational or institutional use. Special book excerpts or customized printings can also be created to fit specific needs. For details, write or phone the office of the Kensington special sales manager: Kensington Publishing Corp., 850 Third Avenue, New York, NY 10022, attn: Special Sales Department, Phone: 1-800-221-2647.

ISBN: 1-58314-257-6

First Printing: August 2003
10 9 8 7 6 5 4 3 2 1

Printed in the United States of America

I dedicate this book to my mother, LaVada Ann Kelley, and her fellow unsung heroines better known as mothers, for the matchless, countless sacrifices made in the name of love for your children. I rise up and call you blessed.

This book is also dedicated to my one and only sweetheart of a husband, Dr. Milmon F. Harrison, and every other Black Prince who knows how to love a woman through thick and thin. I salute you.

IMANI EVANS

Imani had seen comb-overs before, but a comb-up was an entirely new breed of foul. So was his breath.

"Sweetheart, call me Moses 'cause I'm inspired by the *red* I *see*," the stranger with the patchwork hairdo declared, his laser-like gaze rolling across Imani's red silk-clad bosom, down to her shapely hips and then up again.

Thirty-four-year-old Imani Evans bit her lip to keep from flipping wicked in the middle of the mall. No matter that his lusty comments and interest were unwanted, or that his breath was enough to ignite the moisturizing oil in her virgin hair. And so what if the man was one of the last members of the jheri curl club, and had brushed forward and plastered down the unusually long hair clinging to the rim of his skull in an attempt to cover his otherwise bald head.

He's still one of God's critters . . . I mean creatures, Imani reminded herself, wanting to shield her eyes from the glare of his bright blue velveteen sweat suit.

Her attempt at a smile was so tight that her river-deep dimples failed to appear in the smooth chocolate of her face, Imani calmly advised, "Excuse me, but I'm in a hurry," before stepping past the man in her path.

"Baby, baby, baby you gonna melt all that sweet stuff rushing like that," the man called, undaunted by Imani's hasty departure. He easily caught up with and found his stride beside her. "What's your name, love?"

Worn out from the rush and crush of an extremely tedious day, Imani really did not want to be bothered, especially not by a fire-breathing, Smurf-suited brother wasting her last nerve. "My name is Joyce." *Lord, forgive me,* Imani silently repented. "And I really can't talk right now."

"Juicy Joyce, you walk and I'll talk. I'm Herb. I just resituated from Mobile and I'm tryna' find my way 'bout Sacramento," he explained. "Would you be my own personal and private tour guide? Wherever you lead me, girl, I'll follow," he vowed, placing a hand over his heart for emphasis.

Imani whirled around as her customary restraint and reserve gave way to something unpleasant. She opened her mouth ready to say something, anything guaranteed to eject the irritating individual from her presence. Instead, memory of her pastor's most recent message pierced Imani's plans.

Be careful how you treat people, especially strangers, because they could be angels in disguise.

If heaven was missing a Daddy Mack monster Imani knew where he could be found.

The thought pulled unexpected amusement from somewhere deep beneath her annoyance and fatigue so that Imani found herself laughing at the idea of Herb being an angel in disguise.

Bewildered by Imani's response, Herb tried to say something sobering, something convincing. But the more he talked, the harder Imani laughed. Herb stood rooted in the middle of the walkway looking confused. His immobility granted Imani a golden opportunity. Quickly, she escaped.

A thick odor of incense invaded Imani's nostrils as she stepped into Culture Corner, a Black-owned establishment offering clothing, art, greeting cards, books, collectible figurines and more. A bell chimed, announcing her entrance so that an employee behind the register looked up and called a greeting. Dabbing away laughter-induced tears with a tissue pulled from her purse and feeling a twinge of guilt for having laughed in her pursuer's face, Imani returned the employee's greeting before quickly examining the shopping list she held.

Nylons. Choker or scarf to match dress. Sympathy card for Vickie. And at the bottom in big, block letters: *GROCERIES.*

Imani sighed. It was almost nine o'clock in the evening and still her day was not over. Wasn't it enough that she hopped out of bed at 6:00 A.M., dropped her daughter off at school and the clothes at the cleaners, then ended her work day by taking the car in for an oil change and servicing? Then it was back to the cleaners to pick up the clothes, home to pack for her business trip to Phoenix, off to the salon for a manicure and pedicure, and finally this mad dash to the mall just minutes before it closed. And she still had to stop by the grocery store. When it was all over, said, and done, Imani could flop into her empty bed to snatch a moment's rest before bouncing up tomorrow morning in time enough to bathe, dress, and make the drive from Tahoe Park to Sacramento Metro Airport to run its gamut of security checks before her 7:20 A.M. flight.

As lead coordinator of Training and Development for Daystar Communications Imani rarely traveled, but rather organized and facilitated in-house training for new and existing employees at the home office in Sacramento. But as of yesterday, Vickie, the trainer assigned to the Phoenix site, was out on bereavement leave due to the sudden passing of her mother. And with another trainer out on maternity leave and one more on an extended assignment at Daystar's Dallas locale, Imani was short-staffed. Opening ahead of schedule, the Phoenix site was not yet fully equipped to handle its own training demands. So out of necessity, Imani was required to step up to the plate and cover the gap.

Daystar Communications, the rapidly growing company where Imani had been employed since college graduation, had expanded its territory yet again. Its sprawling new Phoenix location would house a new state-of-the-art call center that would comfortably hold over one hundred customer service specialists alone, making it Daystar's largest call center yet. Due to a relatively small pool of in-house applicants requesting transfers to Phoenix, there existed an influx of new hires resulting in the need for on-going and extensive training even after this initial session was complete.

Passing quickly through the aisles and gathering what she needed, Imani chewed her lower lip. She had a sneaking suspicion that this mission to Phoenix might prove a precursor of things to come.

Her sigh was tinged with weariness and dissatisfaction.

Her life was good, overall. Her job was a blessing. Daystar had done right by her these past ten years, allowing Imani to work her way up from an entry-level post to hold various jobs within the company so that she now enjoyed the privileges of her upper level position. She owned company stock, earned a decent salary, had a nice office, excellent benefits, and agreeable rapport with fellow employees. Still, Imani found herself falling out of love with her current situation. After a decade of devoted service to Daystar, Imani was drained. She did not want to be promoted upward or moved laterally. Imani wanted out.

Perhaps it *was* time for Imani to do what *she wanted* to.

So many years had passed that Imani had difficulty remembering the last time she visited her dream of becoming an entrepreneur. The dream of establishing her very own clothing boutique provided warmth during the winter of her marriage, and gave Imani a semblance of hope and comfort while struggling to mother her young child and earn a college degree. Out of necessity, Imani became a realist, long ago accepting the fact that actualizing her plan to move to the Big Apple and pursue a career in fashion was highly unlikely. Still the dream was resilient, transforming like a chameleon in her mind's eye so that right then and there, surrounded by the lovely wares in Culture Corner, Imani imagined success as a clothier in Sacramento.

"Are you finding everything okay?"

She glanced up and saw the salesperson busy tidying the store in preparation for closing.

"Actually, I'm looking for either a choker or scarf to accessorize an outfit," Imani advised, before following the woman to a glass-enclosed display case in the center of the store. Immediately, her sight fell on a three-strand choker made of pale wooden beads with a brown and ivory cameo featuring the regal profile of a woman of African descent. It suited Imani's Afrocentric sensibilities perfectly.

"May I see that?" Imani requested. Accepting the choker, she turned to stand before a full-length mirror encompassing the wall between two tiny fitting rooms as the salesperson moved on to continue her nightly tasks. The pale beads glowed against the dark skin of Imani's long throat as she held them in place. She imagined the jewelry would contrast nicely with the new mocha-colored, knit dress she planned to wear to the Friday night after party.

Hosting a social mixer for new employees and their significant others at the end of a training session was just one example of why Daystar Communications, an innovative leader in its field, was dubbed "the caring company." And while Imani did not relish the thought of fly-ing solo at a couples' function, she rather enjoyed the idea of letting her hair down for a change.

Satisfied with her selection, Imani removed the choker only to pause at her image reflected in the floor-to-ceiling mirror.

She was pretty decent, she decided, for a thirty-four-year-old di-vorcee who would never fit into a size six as she had before becoming pregnant with her fourteen-year-old daughter, Nia. Her deep, almond-shaped eyes were bright, her complexion clear, her natural hair hung in loose tendrils about her shoulders. At five-foot-eight-inches and one hundred and forty-nine pounds Imani's physique was . . . well . . . *sisterish*. Some days Imani needed a girdle to remind her hips that they wore a size ten not twelve. And her considerable breasts refused to stand at attention without the aid of a maximum-support bra. Her feather-smooth brows inching upward as she twisted left then right, Imani inwardly concluded that even if she didn't have it going on at least she was still going.

"Will the necklace work for you?"

"I'll take the entire set," Imani advised, placing the choker atop the counter with her other selections to watch as the saleswoman wrapped it and the matching earrings and bracelet in tissue paper. After pay-ing for her purchases and while en route to the exit, Imani noticed an assortment of cookie jars resting on a tall display fixture. After receiv-ing a cookie jar shaped like a jazz saxophonist as a house-warming gift five years prior, Imani continued collecting Black memorabilia so that the ledge between her kitchen cupboards and the ceiling were lined with glazed porcelain canisters depicting various facets of African American life. She was tempted to browse for an addition to her col-lection, but the lights at the rear of the store faded to black, remind-ing Imani of the lateness of the hour. Besides, she'd already spent far too much money on the new dress and jewelry.

That was an investment in your future. You have to be ready in case Mo's prediction pans out, Imani reasoned, remembering her crazy cousin's recent "spirit reading" that she would soon stumble into the arms of her true love. *Yeah, right! Mo is about as psychic as I am Jewish,* Imani mused, stepping onto the near empty concourse outside the store.

An announcement crackled over the public address system that the mall would be closing in five minutes. Imani hurried toward the near-est exit.

"Joyce! 'Ey, Joyce!"

At first the frantic calls failed to penetrate Imani's consciousness until the memory of her earlier falsification was triggered. Glancing over her shoulder, Imani saw the man named Herb in hot pursuit on her heels. She did what she could. She clutched her bags and ran.

Imani was still breathless and grinning as she headed north on Sixty-fifth Expressway in the direction of her quaint two-story home in Sacramento's Tahoe Park. For the most part, the homes in Tahoe Park were older as were Imani's neighbors, but the streets were quiet and the neighborhood was safe. Imani cherished her home, not because it was lavish or grand, but because it was hers. Granted, her parents had loaned her the money for the down payment after her divorce, but she made good on their loan and repaid every penny so that her sense of pride and ownership were intact.

The house will be so quiet without Nia, Imani thought as she approached a red light. Where that notion came from, she was uncertain. Her baby was only fourteen and had at least three years before even beginning the college application process. Still the idea persisted until Imani found herself wiping an unexpected tear from her eye.

There would be no more adolescent chatter, incessant telephone calls, loud music, or mother-daughter tug-of-war over issues large and small. Imani would miss Nia, her only child and constant companion over the years. But she would somehow adjust. And unlike her own mother, when the time came, Imani would support Nia's college choice rather than dictate her decision.

Who knew? If Imani had obtained her bachelor degree in fashion design from the Academy of Art College in San Francisco before relocating to New York as initially planned, rather than placating her mother by matriculating at Howard University, she might not have met and married Nigel Evans. That was one particular torment she could have done without, Imani thought, easing her car forward as the signal light changed in her favor. But then again, without Nigel there would be no Nia. Lord knew their daughter was the only blessing to come out of the two-year marriage destined for disaster from the start.

Imani lowered her car window as if the cool March air could help whisk away irksome memories of her ill-fated marriage.

Good Lord, how simple and silly she was back in the day.

Nigel—her newfound love, fellow Howard U. student and budding thespian two years her senior—charmed Imani out of her panties and into position faster than Maurice Green could run the one hundred meter dash. Calling home and breaking the news of her pregnancy to her mother and stepfather had been sheer torture. True to form, Eunetta McGee Carmichael promptly recovered from a case of the vapors to articulate her *utter* disappointment before demanding an audience with the "no-count, nasty Negro responsible for knocking up" her only child who had evidently gone to college and lost her mind. When finally they did meet, Imani's mother fell victim to Nigel's oily charm while Ray, her stepfather, remained leery at best. Still Eunetta insisted Imani marry Nigel despite Imani's protestations that she was not ready for such a big step. "If you're ready to spread your legs then you're ready to wed," her mother had snapped, making it clear that no grandchild of hers would be born "a miscellaneous bastard."

I guess one per family was enough, Imani flatly concluded, concentrating on the road ahead and considering her own entry into the world as a fatherless child.

The privilege of meeting or knowing her biological father had never been hers. At the age of seventeen, Imani's mother fell for an older man who made off with her heart and left her with his seed, marking Imani with his chocolate skin and dazzling dimples, but not his loving care. Not once in her thirty-four years had Imani's father made an attempt to contact her, leaving her mother's husband to fill the paternal gap. Imani was a high school senior when Ray met and married Eunetta so that Imani's longing for paternal love was not quite the same as it had been during childhood. At least Nia benefited greatly from the love of both her paternal and maternal grandparents and the powerful example of their intact marriages, which was more than Imani could offer.

A sudden beeping jarred Imani from her less than sweet reverie. With one hand on the steering wheel, Imani reached over with the other to extract her Palm Pilot from her purse. Glancing at the illuminated faceplate Imani read the reminder: *MISS P.*

"Oh, Lord!" she exclaimed, realizing she had completely forgotten about Nia's "baby"—an antiquated, overweight Cocker Spaniel with a bladder the size of a dime. Imani had exactly five minutes to make it home to let Miss P. out or a puddle or pile of unmentionable matter might be waiting to welcome her home. The grocery store could wait.

The upstairs lights were on when Imani pulled into the driveway.

Nia was home. Apparently Dr. Morton, the band director, had cut practice short tonight which was a good thing considering how re-hearsal hours would be extended over the next week as the students polished up and prepared to enter a local competition that could lead to other more advanced opportunities.

"Nia?" Imani called, as she unlocked the front door and stepped in-side.

There was no reply.

Imani called again and still encountered silence.

Except for the lit entryway, the lower level was dark. Imani made her way up the stairs where lights appeared to be on in practically every room. Yet there was no sign that her daughter was home, and nothing appeared out of the ordinary until Imani entered her own bedroom.

The door of her walk-in closet was ajar and clothing was strewn across her bed, creating the only disarray in the otherwise immacu-late room. Sighing, Imani placed her packages atop the cherry wood dresser, irritated by the sight of chaos in her quarters.

Just then the cordless telephone rang. Imani answered it after checking the incoming telephone number on the caller I.D. feature.

"Hey, Mo," she half-heartedly greeted the caller on the other line.

"Hey, 'Mani. I just left your house," advised Monique St. James, Imani's favorite cousin and sister in spirit.

"Obviously. What did you steal this time?"

"I *borrowed* your white crocheted skirt," Monique admitted, her so-prano voice snapping lively across the phone.

"Good! That skirt is a size ten and you wear an eight. I hope you look like a walking doily especially since I told you before that your borrowing days are over until you return my suede boots. Sound fa-miliar?"

"I don't have your boots," Monique contested.

"Yeah, right. I'll be sure to send you this month's electricity bill see-ing as how you left every light on upstairs," Imani fussed, transporting garments from her bed back to the closet to hang them neatly in their proper places. Imani's closet was better organized than most people's lives. Cedar shoe racks lined the bottom of the closet all along its perimeter. Neatly folded sweaters rested in nooks built on top of the racks. Above were pants, skirts, blouses, jackets, suits, and dresses: all hung in neat categorical clusters, ordered by color from light to dark.

"Did you let Miss Pitman out to do her business while you were here?"

"Oops," was Monique's response.

"Oops, what?"

"I forgot her in the backyard, but I did remember to put your mail on the kitchen counter."

"Mo!"

Imani sighed. Nia would have a cow and its calf if she knew her dog had been left outdoors unattended for any amount of time.

"Earth to Imani, that dog is a dog and they *belong* outdoors," Monique trilled, causing Imani to laugh despite her aggravation.

"I'm sorry, Mo. I'm tired and you know how your goddaughter is about that mutt of hers." Imani inhaled deeply. "So, why were you shopping through my clothes tonight?"

"I needed something for my blind date," Monique answered excitedly.

"Try a neon warning that a brother's about to be broke," Imani teased, her tone much lighter than before. Her clothing restored to proper order, Imani surveyed her room to ensure that nothing was out of place, her eyes straying to her wide, empty bed. The eggplant bed linens on the four-poster king-sized bed seemed utterly inviting, but Imani knew if she dared to rest even a moment she was prone to fall asleep. Instead, she kicked off her shoes and padded across the pearl-gray carpet to open her bedroom window. A soft spring breeze kissed her face, stroked her hair with a lover's caress while whisking wide the curtains to grant entry to the silver dust of the March moon. The scent of honeysuckle and the overgrown rose bushes two stories below drifted upward to tickle her nostrils. Tonight nature held a gentle tranquility Imani would have thoroughly appreciated but for the woman interrupting her peace.

"You are so off the wall with that broke brother nonsense!" Monique returned sharply, causing Imani's ears to ring.

"Hello, it's me, your girl you're talking to so let's keep it real, Mo. You always bleed a man dry on a first date."

"I resent that, 'Mani! When I go out with a man for the first time I test him to see if he's funny with money. That's all!" Monique said, defending herself. "So don't make it sound as if I'm a gold-digging skoochie. Even the Bible says if a man won't part with his change then his love is strange."

Imani rolled her eyes and leaned against the windowsill.

"Mo, stop lying on God."

"I'm not lying," Monique protested. "The scripture reads 'For where your treasure is there will your heart be also.' So said the good Lord and I'm not one to disagree."

"Okay, Miss anti-organized religion, don't use Jesus to justify your craziness." Imani frowned. "And what is a skoochie?"

"Girl, I don't know. Ask your child. I heard her say it the other day. Probably a cross between a skeezer and a hoochie."

"That Nia and her mouth are too much. A skeezer and a hoochie equal skoochie, huh?" Imani surmised with a shake of the head. "I guess it's a half-breed hybrid like you."

"Who you calling 'hybrid'? Like your one hundred percent Mandika warrior genes haven't been diluted over time."

Her dimples flashed with her smile as Imani jested, "Better diluted than polluted."

"I'm telling Daddy you said that," Monique threatened with a bell-like laugh.

"Uncle Matt knows he's my favorite Anglo Saxon uncle," Imani stated, in reference to Monique's father married some thirty-eight years to Imani's aunt.

"Daddy's your *only* white uncle."

"Precisely! I want my skirt laundered and returned by the time I get home Saturday afternoon," Imani warned, as she left the cool embrace of the open window to sit, momentarily, on the lavender and gray wing-back chair and absently finger the spines of the books resting on the small reading table beside it. Her favorite novel lay beneath her daily devotional Bible for women of color. Imani whisked dust from its cover thinking that at the rate she was reading God's word, it might as well have been a yearly journal.

There was a challenge in Monique's tone when she responded, "And if I don't return your funky little skirt by then?"

"I'll drop a dime on you and inform your Grass Circle that you slipped up and had some turkey neck with those collard greens Mama made last week," Imani threatened, referring to the vegetarian support group to which Monique belonged.

"That's the *Garden Society*," her cousin corrected. "Not the Grass Circle, goofy. Speaking of which, when're you coming to one of our gatherings?"

"When God stops making bacon," Imani deadpanned. She loved Monique like the sibling she never had. And granted they'd endured many storms together, surviving Imani's divorce, Monique's false breast cancer scare, and a host of other life experiences. But she had to draw the line somewhere. Imani was not interested in sitting barefoot on a bamboo mat smoking a peace pipe, inhaling incense and squawking *Kumbaya* with her cousin and the ham haters.

"See, that's why the death rate for African Americans is disproportionately higher than that of Whites with regards to hypertension and heart disease! We're dining on and dying from bad food choices," Monique passionately declared.

"You're only half Black so your risk balances out."

" 'Mani, have you ever thought about being a comedienne?"

"No."

"Good, 'cause that dry wit of yours could start a fire."

Their laughter was easy, light.

"So, has Spirit's message been realized? Have you stumbled into love?"

Imani rolled her eyes. The family psychic was about to take center stage.

Since early adolescence, Monique had exhibited a certain propensity for the mystical and mysterious, claiming she sensed and saw things that others obviously missed. But it wasn't until after her breast cancer scare several years ago that Monique's paranormal proclivities became more pronounced. Having survived the false scare and obtaining a clean bill of health, in her relief, Monique turned to deeper spiritual pursuits, stopped eating meat, gathered with other higher minded individuals and fully tapped into her psychic abilities so that she now "received messages" from a higher source she reverently referred to as "Spirit." Granted, Monique's "visions" were sometimes on point, but more often they were far out in left field.

Imani debated as to whether or not she should tell her cousin about the close encounter at the mall, but she didn't want to bust Monique's psychic bubble. But then again Monique would find the situation humorous and not proof of her psychic inabilities. Imani opened her mouth to speak, but Monique's excited whisper gave her pause.

"He's here!"

"Who?"

"My date. Took him long enough. He called three times saying he was having trouble finding my street," Monique complained. "And he called me *Monica* instead of Monique."

"Mo, why are we whispering and why are you letting a perfect stranger come to your home?" Imani wondered while examining her freshly painted toenails. "You should have arranged to meet him someplace neutral."

" 'Mani, please," Monique retorted, resuming her normal, high-pitched tones. "I'm not going to drive somewhere and waste my good gas on an obviously bootsy brother."

"But you're still going out with him, bootsy or not."

"That's right. I'm starving."

Lord, deliver me from the nuts in my family tree, Imani silently implored before asking, "So how does he look?"

"I'm peeking out the window, but the street light's a little dim. Okay, he's getting closer," Monique breathed. "Ooh, he has flowers. Eww, and a box of chocolates."

"Drop the candy off over here," Imani half-jested.

"I'll save it for you. Gotta go, he's ringing the doorbell. Tell my god-child I'll see her tomorrow."

"Okay. Hey, Mo!" Imani called.

"Yes?"

"Take your pepper spray just in case," Imani cautioned.

"It's in my purse along with the handcuffs and whipped cream and . . . Oops! I just opened my front closet to get my jacket and guess what?" Monique giggled. "I found your suede boots! Well, have fun in Phoenix, and remember love is out there waiting for you."

The phone clicked in Imani's ear before she had a chance to respond.

"I knew you had my boots, you little klepto," Imani told the air.

Placing the phone on the arm of the chair, Imani decided that there was nothing to get excited about. Monique was about as clairvoyant as a pancake. No tall, dark, delectable brother awaited her in Phoenix. And even if he did, what would Imani do? She couldn't indulge in love on the run and fornicate in Phoenix. There were too many whackos and diseases to worry about. Besides, didn't she have an obligation to God to keep her temple holy?

Attempting to explore her own developing interest in spiritual matters, Imani recently began attending a nondenominational, multicultural church with her parents. Her attendance was sporadic at first, but gradually increased as Imani expressed a deeper longing and curiosity for the things of God. She'd never "gone to the altar" or "given her life" to Christ, but Imani often felt as if her heart was being pulled in that direction. Having joined the *Saved & Single Ministry* at church Imani heard repeated teachings that her body as God's temple was to be kept clean from sexual immorality and, philosophically speaking, the idea appealed to her sense of self-worth and self-respect. But did that really mean living a sexless, loveless existence?

"What does it matter seeing as my life doesn't leave time for love?" Imani blandly inquired of the empty room.

She had grown accustomed to leaving herself for last. Everything and everyone seemed to take precedence over Imani and her needs: Nia, the house, church, work, and family. Being a divorced and devoted mother of a fourteen-year-old who thought she was grown but yet required Imani's guidance and attention often made loneliness the norm. Imani accepted her reality. She gladly made sacrifices— personal and financial—for the sake of her child. And that was fine by Imani. Usually. But Monique's newest romantic rendezvous had Imani wondering if indeed her Black prince would come before she settled for the troll beneath the bridge.

Chuckling, Imani eased up from the too comfortable chair to add the items purchased that night to the luggage waiting outside her bedroom door. Stretching to ease the fatigue from her back, Imani decided the groceries could wait. Nia would be staying with Monique while she was away so there really was no need to rush out again. Plus Nia usually ate with members of the school band before practice so even her dinner was taken care of. Groceries now a non-issue, Imani padded into the master bathroom. She was too tired for even a bath. Instead, Imani cleansed her face then stripped and slipped into her nightshirt. Smoothing the purple fabric over her hips Imani revisited her former train of thought.

She hadn't had a rendezvous—romantic or otherwise—in so long she wanted to ask God if her sexual organs came with a lifetime warranty? If so, was there a clause guaranteeing replacement in the event of atrophy due to lack of use? Shaking her head at the thought, Imani doused the bathroom lights and headed downstairs.

No matter how long Imani stood in the modest daffodil and white kitchen holding the refrigerator door open and staring into its near empty confines, the refrigerator refused to offer a miracle. As it was, Imani could have her pick of condiments, a loaf of nearly petrified bread, some gray-looking cold cuts, and other items she could no longer easily identify.

Not enticed, Imani searched the shelves in the small pantry for specific ingredients. "You're never too tired for cookies," she asserted, feeling victorious upon finding a bag of semi-sweet chocolate morsels. Seeing she had practically everything she needed, Imani returned to the refrigerator only to find there was no butter or eggs. "Dog it!" *Dog? Miss Pitman!* "Oh, goodness!"

Grabbing the unopened mail from the kitchen counter, Imani headed toward the back of the house. She opened the sliding glass door and in came a fat ball of black fur hobbling on stiff legs.

Laughing, Imani bent down to scoop up the insulted beast that sniffed indignantly. Scratching behinds its ears, she cooed, "I'm sorry Mo left you out in the cold. But you have to excuse her. She's special."

Imani closed and locked the sliding door before turning on her stereo so that the sounds of Christian jazz flowed into the family room. Imani dropped onto the oversized armchair and propped her feet on the matching black and tan-striped ottoman. With the dog on her lap, she closed her eyes and leaned back against the soft, thick cushions.

It was serene there in the room at the back of the house. The unlit vanilla candles atop the fireplace mantel scented the air as recessed ceiling lights glowed dimly. The walls were lined with framed African American movie posters, African statues graced the coffee table, and an entertainment center stood flush against a wall complete with built-in bookshelves. With the addition of the matching sofa, Imani's plethora of potted aloe vera plants and ficus trees, the family room was compact, but comfortable. Imani deeply inhaled the comfort and the quiet only to remember the mail in her hands.

There was nothing of interest: just a utility bill, a reminder from Dr. Yasuda's office regarding Nia's upcoming dentist appointment, a flier with a coupon for a free pint of chow mein from a new Chinese restaurant nearby, and a postcard addressed to Nigel Evans.

And just when her stress levels had decreased.

How many times did Imani have to tell that man that she was not his personal postal worker and to stop using her mailing address as his own? Annoyed, Imani started to snatch up the cordless phone resting on the coffee table and speed dial the deadbeat. Just as suddenly, she stopped. Nigel was out of town, but even if he weren't, she didn't feel like dealing with his no-money-thickheaded-narcissistic self. Not tonight.

Imani frowned at the thought of Nigel trying to smooth her into submission.

Ah, Butter, don't be mad at your baby's daddy. You don't want me to miss an important piece of mail while I'm out here trying to make it in Hollywood do you?

Like she cared.

The only mail Nigel needed was a demand letter from the district attorney stating that his child support and alimony payments were now many years in arrears. But Imani had yet to report his errant ways. Turning the small card over in her hand, Imani painfully admitted that she never did. Instead, she covered for him, bearing the full burden of ensuring that Nia lacked for nothing. Imani understood that as an up-and-coming actor, Nigel was often on the go and sometimes strapped for money. Still it hurt too much to admit it to anyone that she had assumed the role of damage control by giving Nia gifts in her father's name when he failed to come through on Christmas or her birthday. Now, Imani was covering Nigel's half of their daughter's allowance, her health insurance, school and band supplies and everything else in between. Knowing firsthand the pain of growing up with no father to call her own, Imani tolerated Nigel's inconsistencies. She would do whatever she deemed necessary to give her child some semblance of paternal love. Imani could only hope that her good intentions never backfired.

Dropping the mail on the coffee table, Imani stroked the dog's soft fur, and willed her mind to a place of peace.

"Hey, Miss Pitman, we have graham crackers in the pantry. You want some?"

The dog wagged its stub of a tail in reply to the offer of its favorite treat.

"I'll give you some, but if you tell Nia, you'll be Pet Partner's newest dog of the week," Imani threatened, referring to the local animal adoption agency from which they adopted the canine. Miss Pitman—named by her former owners for whom only God knew—bared her teeth. Imani chuckled. "Let me just have a minute and I'll go get the crackers," she promised with a yawn, easing deeper into the large chair, crossing her long legs at the ankles and tugging the hem of the purple nightshirt over her thick thighs. She just needed to rest if only but for one moment.

The sound of the front door opening and closing with a bang jarred Imani from her too brief sleep.

"Mom, where are you? Mom? *Yo, Mama!*"

"I'm in the family room, Nia," Imani answered, feeling groggy and listless.

Miss Pitman confirmed their whereabouts with a loud bark.

Imani stretched and rubbed her eyes as a bubble of adolescent energy burst into the room. Nia rushed forward, her face full of excitement as she carefully leaned her clarinet case against a wall before plopping down onto the ottoman barely missing Imani's feet in the process.

"Mommy, you gotta peep this," Nia bubbled, her long thick hair swinging over her shoulders as she removed her backpack and rummaged through its various compartments until finding what she needed. "Your snookie bookie is off the hiz-zookie!" Nia sang. "Here, read the proof."

Imani took the envelope Nia thrust at her. She sat back and crossed her arms, shaking her head clear of Nia's youthful jargon.

"Can a mama get some love here?"

Nia planted a dutiful kiss on her mother's forehead.

Imani smiled and looked at her daughter. Nia frightened her sometimes, the child was growing so fast. Nia would probably be taller than she within a year's time. Nia had inherited Imani's chocolate skin and river-deep dimples, her father's jet-black hair, wide eyes, and reed thin physique that had begun to give way to a few curves here and there. The girl was gorgeous. Apparently, some of Nia's snot-nosed, pimple-popping schoolmates were of the same opinion, particularly one named Clarence, who called Imani's house with all that

fake bravado and bass in his little man-like voice talking about, "Yeah,
is Nia in?"

*Yes, she's in and she's going to stay in so I can keep your nasty little humpty
dumpty—*

"Mom, stop staring at me and read it already. Please! Yo, Miss P.
How're things in the K-9 quarter?" Nia asked, nuzzling her beloved
Spaniel curled up in her mother's lap. The dog licked Nia's face affectionately. "Mom didn't feed you anything not on your diet, did
she?"

Imani suppressed a smile thinking back on her plans to do just that
and busied herself with extracting and unfolding the document she
held.

"That's a good girl," Nia cooed and scratched the dog's muzzle.
"Are you finished reading yet, Mom?"

The enthusiasm in Nia's voice propelled Imani to read faster.
When she finished, Imani lowered the paper to flash her child a brilliant smile.

"Nia, this is wonderful!"

"I know! You have to be in band at least three semesters before you
can audition for orchestra. I'm an "insignificant" freshman and they
want *me* to audition for the orchestra *and* the jazz ensemble. Am I not
da' bomb diggity?" Nia chimed while doing a little shoulder bounce.
"Go 'head, Mom, say it loud and say it proud."

Imani laughed and switched from her normally low contralto to a
childish falsetto to chirp, "Mommy is so proud of her little snookie
bookie wookie woo." She pinched Nia's cheeks for good measure.

"Mother, get a hold of yourself."

"How about I get a hold of you?" she said, hugging her daughter
briefly. "Well, what's next, girlie? The Philharmonic Symphony?
Carnegie Hall?"

Nia ran her fingers through her hair and turned up her already
pert nose.

"I'll play them during my down time when I'm not busy in my vet-
erinary practice."

"Well, all right then, Miss Evans. Go on with your good self. What's
this?" Imani asked, barely glancing at the papers Nia provided.

"The first is a permission slip for the freshman class trip to Marine
World next Saturday, and the second is a consent form for my audition," Nia hurried to explain. "You have to sign a consent form be-

cause this is only my second semester, and because orchestra and ensemble practice two hours more than band each week."

Imani nodded.

"I see. Well, you have my consent provided your grades don't suffer. If your grades drop even a fraction then you don't do orchestra or ensemble or band. Agreed?"

"Agreed," Nia readily responded.

"Good. I need a pen."

Nia hurried to extract one from her backpack.

Imani quickly signed and returned the forms to her daughter. "Here's your pen, and get your little mutt off of my lap."

Nia complied, scooping the fur ball into her arms.

Imani stood and stretched a cramp out of her right leg. She had not visited the gym since last week and she felt stiff from inactivity. The closest she had come to exercise was her mad dash from the man in the mall. It was time to resume her routine.

"So, when's your audition?" she questioned, turning off the stereo and dousing the lights before exiting the family room with Nia at her heels, the dog in one arm, her belongings in the other. Imani checked the front door to make sure it was locked before engaging the security system and mounting the stairs as Nia provided her with details regarding her audition date and time, and the music selections she was considering.

"Maybe I'll just embellish *Bootylicious* with a few riffs. Naw, Dr. Morton would kick me out for being too krunk," Nia joked as they reached the top landing.

Imani shook her head, amazed at how her daughter effortlessly segued between proper English and slang, from using words like "embellish" to "krunk." Whatever that meant.

"Why don't you look through my CDs or ask your father if you can borrow some of his, since his jazz collection is larger than mine," Imani suggested, noting the slightly sour look that swiftly passed over Nia's face before her daughter swiveled in the direction of her bedroom.

"He's still in LA," Nia called over her shoulder, her voice odd and hollow.

Imani followed Nia into her room, pausing as she always did whenever entering her daughter's domain. Imani was the first to admit that she was something of a neat freak. She liked order and the proper placement and alignment of things. Nia obviously had no such pref-erence. Nia claimed her room boasted a "free style décor." It looked more like a natural disaster motif to Imani. But now was not the time to scold Nia for her questionable cleanliness or taste. Imani sensed that something was amiss.

"You have the key to his apartment, Nia. We can go by there if you want to browse through his music collection. Just call and let him know. He won't mind," Imani soothed, remembering her surprise when Nigel relocated from DC to Sacramento four years ago to be closer to his daughter, or so he said. Nigel spent most of his time in Los Angeles chasing fame and fortune.

Imani watched as Nia gently deposited Miss Pitman at the foot of her bed before undressing and tossing her clothing atop her already overflowing clothes hamper.

"He's been in LA a week and hasn't called me to tell me which hotel he's at, and he's not answering his cell phone."

Imani's heart lurched with her child's pain so evident in her voice and in her eyes.

"Maybe your grandparents have the hotel information," Imani softly suggested.

"It's no big deal." Nia shrugged. There was a bitter note in her voice. "I can get by without him."

Imani bit her bottom lip. She wanted to slap Nigel Evans into next week and beyond. He could screw her over by not paying alimony or child support, but messing over her child made him a candidate for a rub down with hot grits.

"Nia, what's really going on?"

Nia silently considered Imani before extracting a newspaper clip-ping from her backpack and handing it to her mother.

It was a page from Sacramento's premier Black-owned newspaper featuring a photo of Nigel, smiling like he didn't have a care in the world. The caption beneath read LOCAL ACTOR WOOS HOLLYWOOD.

More like local louse woos dimwit number ninety-nine, Imani thought, looking at the woman in the photograph with Nigel and understand-ing the source of Nia's vexation. From her flawless smile to her flow-ing hair and hourglass figure, Nigel's companion-of-the-week reeked perfection. Imani knew Nigel was a camera hog, but this publicity campaign of his was insensitive to say the least. Every time he ap-peared in the press, the woman on his arm changed. It was no secret that their daughter harbored a desire to see her parents reconcile. It would never happen as long as Imani was sane, but still Nigel could show some sensitivity for Nia's feelings.

"Mom, what are you doing?"

"Huh?"

Nia snickered.

"You're folding dirty clothes."

Imani glanced down, realizing she had returned the paper to Nia only to snatch dirty garments off the floor and proceed to neatly fold them in her agitated state.

"Oh. I'm sorry if that photo disturbed you, Nia, but your father is somewhat of a public figure so this is just par for the course and has nothing to do with his love for you."

Nia's reply was a noncommittal shrug.

Imani knew not to press the issue. Instead, she let the matter rest and pushed aside a pile of clothing to sit on Nia's bed as Nia shamelessly unhooked her bra and tossed the pink undergarment over the back of her desk chair.

"Woo, Lord, someone's finally getting some boobie doobies."

Nia rolled her eyes and pulled a green and white knee-length nightshirt over her head.

"Mother, I have breasts, not boobs," Nia proudly stated.

"Exc-c-cuse me." Imani smiled. "I remember when I got my first training bra. Your Grammy told everyone in sight and even wanted me to pull up my top and show my bra to an elderly white lady at the bank."

"That sounds like Grammy. Oh, Mom, I forgot to tell you that the answering machine's jacking up the incoming messages."

"I know." Imani sighed. "It's on my list of things to repair right along with the lawn mower, the downstairs bathroom sink and anything else around here that needs fixing."

"You can add my computer to your list. My zip drive is doing weird things and the CD-ROM is acting up," Nia announced, plunking down and stretching out on her bed.

Yawning, Imani stood and headed for the door. "Okey dokey, artichokey."

"I'm hungry," Nia suddenly announced.

"You didn't eat dinner before band practice?" Imani asked, pausing in the doorway.

"I just kicked it at school until rehearsal time. Mrs. Ramirez offered to stop and get me and Krista something on the way home, but I didn't want anything then," Nia said, referring to the neighbor with whom Imani rotated carpooling their daughters to and from practice and school.

"And I suppose you do now."

"I could eat one of Miss P.'s dog biscuits."

"You just might have to," Imani said before explaining, "I still haven't made it to the grocery store."

"That's okay, Mom. Let's go out!"

"Now? Nia, it's after nine o'clock and we have to get up early tomorrow so I can get you to Mo's en route to the airport, *and* we're both in our pajamas."

"Just put on a jacket and we can do take-out. Hey, why not drop me off at Aunt Mo's tonight to save time in the morning?"

"She's out."

"Well, just leave me here. I can get up for school on my own," Nia asserted.

"Hah! Do you have homework?" Imani asked, fingering a crystal teddy bear atop Nia's cluttered desk.

"Done. And it'll only take me a few minutes to pack my clothes for Aunt Mo's so let's go eat before I faint. Look," Nia said, extending a trembling hand, "I'm shaking with hunger."

Imani grinned and turned away.

"What do you want?"

"Chinese food," came Nia's muffled reply, as she pulled a sweat-shirt over her sleepwear.

"There's a coupon in the family room. One of us has to grab it on the way out."

Imani entered her room, its immaculate order a stark contrast to Nia's "free style," and pulled a pair of jeans, a sweater and slip-on loafers from her closet. She dressed quickly.

"Yo, Mom, can Miss P. ride?" Nia hollered across the hall.

"I don't care," Imani answered, grabbing her purse and keys and joining Nia in the hall. Together, they descended the stairs.

"What's on the menu?" Imani asked, when she finally backed the Volvo sedan down the drive and out onto the quiet street. The March sky was a sweet shade of blue, kissed by shimmering stars. Imani lowered her window to inhale the cool night air.

Nia turned on the car stereo, changing Imani's twenty-four hour Bay Area gospel station to tune into a local hip-hop channel before relaxing in her seat. She read the menu on the restaurant flier aloud by the overhead light in the car.

"Dinner A for two sounds good to me," Imani remarked, as Nia concluded.

"Me, too," Nia agreed, turning off the light.

"Look in my purse and find my cell phone to call ahead and order," Imani requested.

"Can we get a side of pot stickers, Mom?"

"Do you have a job?"

"Mom has jokes," Nia laughed and placed the call. "It'll be ready in ten minutes."

"Good. Hey, turn that up. I like that song," Imani chimed, bobbing her head to the beat of the music filling the car.

"That's *so* passé, Mom!" Nia protested.

"I still like it," Imani asserted and sang, "Who let the dogs out? Woof woof! Come on Miss Pitman, sing it with me," Imani told the dog standing on its hind legs in the back seat and looking out the window.

"Mom, have I told you lately that you're corny?"

"Nope. Have I told you lately that you're my favorite child?"

"I'm your only child."

"You're still my favorite," Imani said, as she headed toward Folsom Boulevard as Nia reluctantly joined in and Miss Pitman began to howl.

BRAXTON J. WADE

A brother cannot start a Monday morning dreaming about Vanessa Williams and have a bad day. Or so I thought.

That's how my day started with me sleep-freaking over one of God's loveliest creatures. That's sho' 'nuff not how it ended. I'll get to the end eventually. But have mercy on a man and just let me hang out at the beginning for a minute.

It went something like this . . .

There I was—every inch and ounce of my 6'1", 210-pound frame— sprawled carefree on a sparkling white beach just smooth chilling with all this pure azure water pushing against the shore. The sun was high. Sea gulls were sailing. I was rocking to the boss sounds of steel drums drifting over my head. Ray Bans kept the deep browns shaded while I sipped one of those exotic drinks in a coconut shell decorated with a paper umbrella. I was kicking it large. Then I just about choked when (as far as I'm concerned) the first *real* Miss America, Vanessa Williams, appeared out of nowhere to glide toward me across the sand, barefoot and naked except for the huge pink beach towel wrapped about her banging body. She stood over me, produced a bottle of oil and asked if she could rub me down. I noticed her lips were ruby red. Red is my color so I smiled. She smiled back. It was all good. Miss Williams unscrewed the top off the bottle of the seriously sweet-smelling oil and poured some onto her palm. She reached for me, and time stood still. I wanted to scream because her hands were huge! And ashy! I mean the nails were split and cracked and there were nappy balls of hair on her knuckles. I *knew* I was tripping until I glanced down. *What the heazy!* Her feet were even worse, looking like big, thick Fred Flintstone brontosaurus burgers with corns and bunions popping all over the place. Recoiling, I looked up. "I'm ready to rub you now, Monsieur," this deep baritone announced. It was that pro-wrestling-looking brother who played Debo in that flick *Friday* peeping at me with one eye and watching the ocean with the other.

I screamed like a pistol-whipped punk.

"Bring her back, Man!"

" 'Ey, get off of me!"

The struggle was on.

"Gimme back my queen," I hollered. "Where's Vanessa?"

"Brax. Yo, Kid, it's me. Brax. B., wake up!"

I did, only to realize I'd tackled my best friend and housemate of the past seven years and had him pinned on my bed in a headlock.

"Aw, dag, man. My bad," I rushed, relieved to know that it was only a dream and that an ashy Adonis-looking brother wasn't trying to lure me to hell. Releasing my hold on Terrance's neck, I half-yawned, half-laughed.

Terrance wasn't feeling my joy. He jumped up and clocked me in the arm. And you know that hurt because at 5'10" and 215 pounds, Terrance is built like a prizefighter.

" 'Ey, Cuddy! I said I was sorry."

Terrance just mean-mugged me with his face all twisted up as if my breath stank, which it probably did since I just woke up and had yet to brush or gargle.

I guess Terrance decided not to make good use of his combat skills learned on the streets of his native Inglewood to beat me down on my bed. Instead, he collected himself and swaggered over to my mirrored closet doors, all dignified, intent on smoothing the marks of our scuffle from his overpriced silk dress shirt and Versace slacks. That's Terrance Blackmon, attorney at law, for you. Only the costs-enough-to-feed-Al Sharpton-for-a-week kind of garments will do.

"Brax, I swear your imagination is straight gone." Meticulously examining his clothing and deciding it was all good and that he wouldn't have to sue me for damage to his personal property, T. began knotting the tie hanging loosely about his neck. "What were you fantasizing about now? And who's Vanessa?"

"Nobody. Wassup and what time is it?" I asked, lying down again.

"Five after six."

"What!" I jolted up in the bed and without the aid of my contacts, squinted at the clock on my nightstand just to make sure Terrance wasn't kidding. I live only fifteen minutes from work so I didn't have to leave the house until eight forty-five. The way I shower and dress and drive, I could have slept until eight-forty. Terrance had just robbed me of one hundred and fifty-five luscious minutes of uninterrupted dream time with the woman of the century. "I'm trying to get my sleep on and you're messing with me because . . . ?"

"Come on, Kid. I need a ride to the dealership," Terrance informed me, still flexing his image in the mirrored doors. I don't know why he wasted his time. T. was one of those high-end kind of brothers—you know, the bigger the price tag the better. From his thirty dollar haircut, to his manicured fingernails and butter-soft designer footwear. Despite the blade-thin, inch long battle scar marking his left jaw, Terrance was tight and he knew it.

"BMW never heard of shuttle service?"

"The shuttle service can't be here until 7:00 and I want to be at the lot *by* 7:00 to finish up the paperwork and pick up my car."

Terrance had just spent the equivalent of my annual salary as a high school guidance counselor on a brand new, tricked out 325Ci convertible. His ride did everything but cook a brother breakfast. I'm not a hater, but in my opinion, he'd spent way too much money.

"Back up off of my closets, Cuddy," I mumbled around another yawn. "You're fogging up my glass."

Terrance ignored me and took his time straightening his tie, smoothing the tiny waves in his red hair and finger-brushing the mustache beneath his freckled nose before smiling in self-approval.

Talk about transformations: Terrance Blackmon was the epitome of positive change. Maybe, in a way, we both were.

I met my boy T-Black, as he was known back then, during our sophomore year in college. I always planned to graduate from my native Indiana State University, but my parents shipped me out to California with quickness after I tried to elope with this shorty named Brandy after dating her for all of one week. But you can't blame a brother. Brandy was my first sexual conquest and *she* conquered *me*.

See, it *only* took until I was eighteen for my Dad's long, lean genes to kick in so that I finally stretched up instead of out. Until that time, I was a horn-rimmed, coke bottle eyeglass-wearing, acne-having, double-breasted-orange-sweater-with-white-piping-and-gold-buttons-across-the-fat-boy-belly sporting mess. Just goofy. Intelligent as heck, but goofy as you wanna be. And I was a virgin because fat, goofy guys with opaque glasses and last decade's fashions were not *en vogue*. So anyhow, when I turned eighteen and lost weight and gained some fashion sense (thanks to my older twin sisters, Cassondra and Alondra), Brandy was the first woman to get a taste of the new improved Braxton J. Wade. She tasted so good *I* had to marry her. And Moms had to hold Pops back from kicking my tail out of that wedding chapel and onto the next thing smoking for college in California, far from temptation and stupidity. I haven't seen Brandy since. . . .

But as I was saying, T. and I crossed paths during our second year at UCLA. Like me, T. was bused there against his will. He was a collegiate by court order.

Being one of eleven children with a father and mother who held down four jobs between them, which didn't leave them much time for hands-on parenting, T. fell in with the wrong crowd and got caught up in a little illegal activity in his junior year in high school. Miraculously, the juvenile court judge saw past Terrance's hardened exterior to recognize his inherent good and misguided energy. The judge sentenced T. to a two-year stint as an office assistant for the district attorney and four years in college. Terrance went kicking and screaming all the way, but the journey made such an impact on him, that he straightened up his act and graduated with an undergraduate degree in political science before enrolling in law school. He sends that old judge a Christmas card every year to express his gratitude.

"B., do you have any mouthwash? I'm all out."

I nodded, rubbing sleep from my eyes before lowering myself to the ground for my ritual morning crunches, deciding I might as well start my day.

"Under . . . the . . . sink," I puffed in between contracting and releasing my abs. Now that I'm fit, I strive not to revert to the blob I used to be. I started weight training in college, took up swimming, and even tried my hand at fencing. Okay, I went overboard with the fencing. Fighting off an opponent dressed in white and wearing a mask, bent on stabbing me was a bit much. The only thing missing was the burning cross. Still, without question, my California college experience was good and west side living got under my skin, so much so that I decided to stay here after graduating with my bachelors degree in psychology.

My mother was concerned that California would corrupt me, and that I would become superficial and start talking with a beach boy accent. I just laughed and assured her that I would remain true to who she and Pops raised me to be. But I did not return home except for the occasional visit. I love Indiana and my peeps are there, but the idea of going back to Gary and kicking it with my old gold-tooth-wearing, jheri-curl-dripping, Cadillac-cruising cuddies was not all that appealing. So, I stayed out west and went to graduate school, earning my Masters in psychology, school psychology to be exact.

Don't ask me why. Maybe it had something to do with how I had a crush on my eighth grade guidance counselor, or because even back in the day when I was too goofy to get a girl, females still liked me, and confided their problems in me because I was "such a good listener." Or it could be because, as my parents were quick to point out, I had the gift of empathy. Shoot, maybe I studied school psychology and became a high school guidance counselor just so I could revisit my youth, but this time as the big man in charge. Could be a combination of the above and then some. Whatever my reasons, I made it through grad school with reasonable success.

While I studied the psyche, Terrance pulled all nighters with his law books. T. became the brother I never had and we ended up sharing an apartment in student housing. After Terrance passed the bar exam a year after I received my Masters, he and I played with the idea of bouncing from southern Cal and finding a less expensive, less stressful, less polluted place to live.

That's how I ended up in Sacramento while Terrance camped out in Oakland for a minute until a great aunt on my Pops' side passed away and I purchased her house (way below market value) and invited "my brother" to share my dwelling. T. took me up on the offer because he liked Sac-town, but didn't want to commit to a mortgage before getting his feet wet as a resident here. Being from a big family, T. relished his newfound privacy, but I also think growing up accustomed to noise, he was afraid of feeling lonely by living on his own. So he moved in and found a spot with a prestigious law firm here in the city. That was seven years ago, right around the time my father died, and T. is still kicking it at my crib. We kind of settled into a comfortable living arrangement, somewhat like *The Odd Couple*—T. in his space, me in mine. I didn't mind my brother's being there with me. After Pops died, having Terrance around helped me to cope with the loss of my own personal hero.

". . . fifty-eight . . . fifty-nine . . ."

I only intended to do my usual fifty abdominal crunches before flipping over for push-ups, but sudden thoughts of my father had me going.

It's still hard and I still hurt when I think of how Pops put himself in the ground.

My father had over twenty years of service with the public transportation system back home in Indiana. And although he worked to put my mother, my two older sisters and myself through college, he never finished high school. He never would've admitted it but I think Pops was embarrassed by his lack of formal education. So—the way I psychoanalyze it—he worked like some old pack mule on Massa's farm to prove his worth, and to prove that he was anything but shiftless or ignorant. And he put himself in the grave by not following his doctor's orders, by not taking the medication meant to lower his cholesterol and regulate his blood pressure, and by working a double shift three months straight.

Intellectually, I understand that it is not God's fault that Pops checked out of here early because he didn't do right by his doctor or his family, and subsequently suffered a massive stroke. But I'm still mad at my maker for not getting Pops' full attention before it was too late. Seven years ago, I never planned to be twenty-five-years-old and putting my Pops in the ground.

". . . seventy-six . . . seventy-seven . . ."

I could smell my housemate's Cool Blue Mint Listerine breath from where he stood over me holding out a tiny white container.

"Mind if I take this dental floss?"

I shook my head.

"Thanks. I'm going to the store today so I'll replace it," he promised, a quizzical expression on his redboned face. "Hey, Brax, man, are you crying?"

What? I wasn't crying—

Oh, yes, I saw that I was as I paused to wipe hot moisture from my face with the back of one hand.

Terrance would understand if I told him, but I didn't feel like feeling all that old pain today.

"You all right, Brax?"

"I'm . . . straight," I huffed, all gruff and brave. "Just . . . sweating . . ."

"Good, 'cause I can't have your big butt getting all soft on me." Terrance looked at his Rolex. "Get a move on it, Kid, and go scrub off some of that grime before you make me late."

I collapsed onto my back and took a moment to catch my breath before jumping up to snatch open the mini blinds at my window, promising myself that I would slip in an extra set of push-ups tonight at the gym.

I shouldn't have bothered with the blinds. Even the sun knew it was too early to truly shine.

I suddenly felt irritable.

I gathered my attire for the day from the closet and tossed the black jeans and gray and white FUBU jersey across my bed, scratching my right buttock through the thin fabric of my red boxers all the while. *Whew!* I had a sudden itch that wouldn't quit.

"Need some Vagisil?" Terrance asked, dropping onto my recliner and cracking up at his own joke.

"You have any left over?" I shot.

Terrance chuckled, and finding the remote control on the floor by my chair, turned on the television. "Yo, Kid, get a new TV already," he ragged, tuning my ten-year-old television to CNN. So what if I sometimes had to hit the sides to improve the reception. My boob tube works and that's good enough for me. Besides, Terrance was just hating on my domain as usual.

Granted, I don't have pure Egyptian cotton bedspreads, imported Italian leather furnishings, fabric-lined dresser drawers and cedar wood hangers, or a suit valet in one corner and a serenity rock fountain and lotus plants in the other as found in T.'s "personal lodgings." And I don't freak if a film of dust coats my stuff. However, I am not living like a caveman with dinosaur doodoo on his heels.

I like my set-up. It is comfortable. It's me.

When I purchased this single-story ranch style house located in the Pocket area of south Sacramento from my great aunt's estate, it was in good condition. I'd like to think I've improved upon it. I had an opening cut between the master bedroom and an adjoining bedroom (which now serves as my media center) to increase my space. Floor-to-ceiling glass panels now occupy another wall complete with a sliding door that opens onto a brand new redwood deck outside. I don't like a lot of foo-foo decorating. Just my California king-sized bed and matching nightstands, my fish tank, stereo system and classic R&B collection, my Dad's favorite recliner, and my PC are sufficient. Okay, add a closet full of FUBU gear, Lugz, Nike, Kani and RL (i.e. Ralph Lauren) and I'm a man made the way I want to be. *Skip T.!* I swear he'd make a good queen if he weren't so straight, with his foo-foo-la-la land-having taste.

Ignoring my housemate's ragging, I padded off to my bathroom and got busy and felt better for it.

Thirty minutes later, my ivories were polished, I'd flossed and gargled, popped in my contact lenses, and showered—being careful to, as Pops used to say, hit the hot spots. Slicked the underarms with Mitchum, rubbed on a little of this aromatherapy lotion my oldest sister, Cassondra, gave me for Christmas (which happens to be two days before my birthday), and spritzed myself with Lagerfeld. I even managed to lather and shave the new stubble from my dome.

Okay, now wait: every brother can't sport a bald head just because. I've seen some skinned cats who needed to grow some hair like yesterday! I mean brothers with dents and hooks on their heads, looking like old beat up coffee cans. Then you have the hefty brothers with the Baptist preacher hot dog pack sitting at the back of their necks, or the brothers with keloids and crooked ears. Come on now . . . Anyhow, thanks to my gene pool, I have a nice symmetrical sphere. And I look all right—this from an ex-fat boy who attended his Junior Prom with his cross-eyed, bucktoothed, pigeon-toed cousin, Sharitha, because he couldn't get a date—with this hard-earned physique, neatly trimmed goatee, a nice smile, and the little gold hoop glittering from my left earlobe.

Terrance was still there, slumming I suppose, when I reentered my room to hop into my gear.

"Say, T., I know you're treating a brother to breakfast, right? I did get out of bed to play chauffeur to your no-car-having behind," I asserted while lacing up my Lugz.

Eyes still glued to CNN, he absently responded, "I have a deposition this morning so I need to get to the office after finishing up at the dealership. How about I spot you for lunch?"

"That'll work," I agreed, smoothing my jersey into place before grabbing my jacket and keys. "Let's bounce. I'm dropping your hitch-hiking self off at the lot and then I have a date with a couple of hot and sweet little honeys."

As in a half-dozen, fresh from the oven, Krispy Kreme glazed doughnuts.

I ate two en route to work and washed them down with a bottle of strawberry milk while listening to old school jams on my car stereo.

There's something to be said for hot doughnuts, cold milk, and soul music. I'm an old school jams kind of man, and my radio was tuned to the local classic soul station so that by the time I arrived at work and parked in the staff lot I no longer cared about my lost sleep or interrupted freak fest with my first real Miss America. I was hyped and practically skipped onto campus and down the halls toward my office. You know I was feeling good because I did the unspeakable and gave two of my remaining four Krispy Kremes to a fellow coun-selor, a sure sign that the world was about to rain weird on my parade.

I ate my last two doughnuts while reading a memorandum marked URGENT.

Some knuckleheads broke into the study lab over the weekend and destroyed four computers, two sets of speakers used in the foreign language listening stations, an overhead projector and, they actually stole a singing daisy plant that belonged to Mrs. Greer, the study lab monitor. I'm sorry, but I would have paid someone to drown Mrs. Greer's irritating, animated plastic flower myself. But trashing the study lab? That was wrong.

I sat, shaking my head, disgusted, as I read.

The memo ended with a promise to beef up security and a request that any knowledge regarding the perpetrator(s) be reported imme-diately to the principal.

I guess we could do that in between striking and picketing in front of the school because that's what I planned to do if the proposed in-surance hikes indicated in the next memo I read went into effect.

Give me a butt-cracking break!

Why should I care about the increasing costs of prenatal care, or the number of patients requiring a urologist's care? There was no need to "spread the inflation across the board." I did not need to ab-sorb a higher co-pay or increased deductions from my paycheck. I wasn't pregnant and my prostate was fine. Besides, knowing our school district officials, the hikes probably weren't even necessary or certainly not as a result of what they claimed. They were just picking on old men and pregnant women.

Lawd, today!

I tossed the notice in my express filing cabinet—that is, my waste-basket—and got on with my day. There were some student files that I needed to review in addition to preparations I had to make for the Career Choice class that meets every Tuesday and Thursday after-noon and is facilitated by yours truly. But before I could even get to that, I had a stack of parent conference notification letters that had to be signed and mailed after I got out of the standard make-you-hate-Monday-mornings staff meeting spearheaded by our fearless princi-pal who obviously still struggled with the concept of concise and to the point. Can I get some No-Doz please?

Thumbing through the stack of letters, my eyes landed on one in particular. It was addressed to the parents of Nia Evans.

I placed the missive on top of the pile and scratched my ear as I'm prone to do when perplexed, in deep thought, lost in space or just plain bored. This time it was a thoughtful scratch.

Nia was a good kid: a bright student in my Career Choice class, and very outgoing. Perhaps, according to two of her instructors, too out-going. Apparently, Nia had the gift of gab, or as her English teacher put it, she possessed a "motorized mouth fueled by the Energizer bunny." Even I'd had to check Nia once or twice for talking out of turn or clowning in class. Plus, her science teacher tells me he had to repri-mand Nia yet again, this time for putting a dissected frog on a paper plate with potato chips and an attached handmade sign reading TASTES LIKE CHICKEN! She was a good little shorty, but protocol is protocol and I was obligated to counsel the student as well as inform her parents. I was successful with the former, frustrated with the latter because de-spite my leaving several messages on their home answering machine, I had yet to hear from either of Nia's parents.

I swear disinterested parents make me sick! I'm about as fond of them as I am of hemorrhoids.

Laughing at my own warped humor, I grabbed my thirty-two ounce water bottle and went to fill up before heading for the conference room. I didn't mind drinking up and peeing like a puppy if it meant frequent breaks from the staff slumber party—I mean, meeting ahead. By the time the meeting adjourns, I'm sure I'll have mastered sleeping with my eyes open.

*   *   *

After lunch at El Novillero, my favorite Mexican restaurant, I was ready to curl up in the back seat of my car for a nap. And I might have, too, had my car been where I'd left it in the staff parking lot.

T. had picked me up in his brand new Beemer and we rolled to lunch profiling like two big macks from way back. So I left Pearl (that's what my Dad named his vintage Ford Mustang that I inherited when he passed) parked at school. Now you know a brother has certain things that you don't mess with. Don't bother his money, his food, his woman or his ride. My money is squirreled away in investments. I had way too much food at lunch. The last woman I hugged was T.'s grandmother, who lives in Oakland with his grandfather, three cats, a blind Doberman, and a one-armed monkey named Skippy. My car is all I have.

By the time the police arrived, you could have tied me to a tree and beaten me with a pillowcase filled with pickled pigs feet and I wouldn't have cared.

There was no evidence of forced entry. No broken glass or anything else conspicuous. It was too clean. The police suspected it might be a student prank.

Were the doors locked? (Yes). *Did I leave a key anywhere on the vehicle?* (No). *Was the vehicle insured?* (Absolutely). *Did I wish to press charges if the thieves were apprehended?* (Does Michael Jordan and his Washington Wizards need to disappear? That would be an affirmative).

First the study lab and now this. My car! The first car Pops purchased brand new off the showroom floor. The car I washed and waxed every Saturday because it was a symbol of and reward for my father's years of hard work was gone. And from the parking lot of what was supposed to be one of the premier high schools in the district. My day was jacked! I shouldn't have given away my Krispy Kremes. I shouldn't have eaten a three-item combo at lunch because now I was belching *chile verde* out of one end and was scared what might come out the other.

I was oblivious to students making their way to class, a few calling out as I passed. "Yo, Mister B." wasn't penetrating today. I was singing and marching, marching and singing down the hall en route to the administrative offices, a preliminary police report in hand.

"Swing low, sweet chariot, coming for to carry me home . . ."

Another habit of mine: singing Negro spirituals at inane times.

My paternal grandfather sang with a gospel quartet. I remember spending nights at my grandparents', hearing Big Pa (as we called him) and his group rehearsing Negro spirituals late into the evening until I fell asleep with the song of Black angels in my ears.

So I sang my way out of lunacy and did my best not to "ack a fewl" up in there. I filed an incident report, spoke with the principal at length and received her commiseration and reaffirmed promise to increase campus security and restore normalcy to our school, then locked myself in my office, called my mama and cried.

Just kidding. I didn't lock my door.

My mother is in a class all by herself. She can find a silver lining in the darkest storm, and something right even when it's all wrong. I felt somewhat better after ending our call—despite Moms dropping hints about how this wouldn't have happened if I were back home—knowing that "the Lord was going to get those thieving thieves with His holy hammer of justice." In the meantime, Moms and her intercessory prayer partners would be "waging war in the heavenlies." I had to laugh at the thought of my mother and her "prayer warriors" dressed in fatigues, drop kicking the devil for messing with Pops' car.

Pops and Moms. Moms and Pops. They had the kind of love I don't even dream of.

I haven't had a decent relationship since Brandy and our fiasco at the altar fourteen years ago. So, I'm not getting married. Not now. Maybe when I'm old and decrepit and want someone to share my Ben Gay I'll think about it. Okay, so, I won't wait that long but there'll be no "Wedding March" for me until at least age forty. When my father died, I told God I wouldn't marry until then. I need to test my longevity gene. I am not about to marry young like Pops and work myself into an early grave and forfeit my life, or deprive my wife and children of the husband and father they deserve. If I live that long then I promise I'll find me a good, big-boned churchwoman like my mother and settle down and raise some big, round-headed babies. Until then I'll settle for the casual date, nothing serious or expensive because I'm saving up for my dream trip of spending two years touring Africa. So I am not interested in women with children or bad credit because I don't spend money on pampers or Enfamil and I am not a loan officer. I have a continent to see.

* * *

I made good use of my self-imposed isolation and gathered materials for my class the following day, signed and deposited the parent conference letters in the outgoing mail, updated notes on a few student files, and cleared out the e-mail messages clogging my computer. And still I was angry and outdone thinking about some "thieving thieves" riding in my father's car. They'd better not change my radio station to some hip-hop, rap roaring mess . . .

"Mr. B., are you in there?"

Some little demon had the nerve to rattle my doorknob when I didn't hurry to answer the tap on my door.

I sat there and waited to see who was so bodacious as to help her little uninvited self into my domain.

My door opened and a head peeped around the jamb.

"I thought you were in here, Mr. B. Whatcha doing?"

"Hiding from you and your kind."

Nia Evans smacked her lips and bounced into my office to flounce down onto the chair opposite my desk as uninvited as she pleased.

"Come on in, Nia, and have a seat. Can I get you anything? A soda? A sandwich?" *A clue that I'm trying not to be bothered right now?*

"Dang, Mr. B." she giggled. "I just stopped by 'cause I wanted to know if you still need a student assistant?"

I leaned back in my chair. "Who did you have in mind?"

"Ohmygosh, like *moi*," she answered, looking indignant, a hand on her chest.

I pursed my lips and shook my head.

"Naw, girl, you're on my hit list."

"See that's not even fair, Mr. B.! I've been doing better since you chewed me out for talking in class and for my Kentucky-fried frog bit. For real!"

"So says you. On another note, can you tell me how best to reach your parents?"

"Why?" Nia asked, suddenly suspicious.

"Official school business," I casually replied, not about to let on that I needed to speak to her parents about her recent infractions.

"My Dad's in LA," she cautiously began, "and—"

"Your mother's in China studying silk worms."

Nia looked at me, her head cocked slightly to one side. Then she giggled, again.

"I was going to say that my mother's picking me up at 2:45 because

I have a dentist appointment. If she can get here earlier, can she come talk to you then?"

I rubbed the back of my head.

I was suddenly tired from my eventful day. I did not relish the idea of discussing a student's errant behavior with a nonchalant or defensive parent, which I assumed Mrs. Evans would be seeing as how she had not responded to any of my earlier attempts to contact her. Still, in all fairness to Nia, she was a good kid with great potential. And who knew? If her father frequently traveled perhaps she acted out for attention and affection and . . .

And perhaps I could pause on the psychoanalysis and just give the child a chance.

I pushed my phone toward her.

"Call your mother. If she can be here by 2:30, I can meet with her then."

Nia unzipped her backpack to retrieve her own cell phone.

Kids today! I watched as Nia depressed a button that obviously stored her mother's phone number. A minute later she ended her conversation with a smile. "My mother will be here by 2:30," she reported and slung her backpack over her shoulders. "I gotta go or I'll be late for math. See ya, Mr. B., and don't tell my mom anything nasty about me."

She bounced out of the room before I had a chance to reply.

Sheesh! Kids can make you weary. That's another benefit to my not having any until after I'm at least forty. That gives me a minimum of eight more years of unmolested peace.

IMANI

"**P**ardon me. Could you please direct me to the counseling office?"

Imani stood at the front desk and waited for the young woman who was busy fussing with a Xerox machine to acknowledge her presence.

Startled, the young woman whirled about.

"I'm sorry. I was so busy trying to get that blasted machine to work that I didn't even hear you approach," she apologized, a bright smile illuminating her pretty face. "Did you mention something about counseling?"

Imani nodded.

"I have a 2:30 appointment with a Mr. Wade," Imani confirmed, noting that according to her watch, she was already five minutes late. "I believe my daughter said he's in room C-5, but I'm having trouble finding it."

The young woman came from behind the reception counter, her stylish strawberry blond hair bouncing with every step.

"It is rather hard to find," she agreed. "The counseling offices are inside the Student Services building so you wouldn't have been able to see the room numbers from the outside, but I can show you a shortcut."

Imani followed the receptionist who ushered them through what seemed like a maze of corridors until they arrived in the center of a large room teeming with students and staff and their jovial chatter. There were inspirational posters, student body pictures, staff names and their assigned offices, as well as announcements for various school functions lining the walls. The room was brightly decorated and had a lively feel. The receptionist stopped abruptly and knocked on a closed door. Imani glanced up to see the room number C-5 stenciled in black above the door frame, the name BRAXTON J. WADE in gold letters across the smoked-glass paneled door.

"Come in," a deep male voice answered from the opposite side.

"Mr. B., your 2:30 is here," the receptionist informed the office occupant, as she opened his door and moved aside to allow Imani to enter.

"I appreciate your help," Imani smiled as the receptionist waved and headed back toward the labyrinth they'd just negotiated. Imani entered the office and stopped in her tracks.

The man standing and extending his hand to her across his desk could not be Nia's guidance counselor. *Mmm, but times have changed,* Imani thought recalling that her high school counselor, Mr. McAfree, smoked a pipe and picked his nose when he thought no one was looking and complained about the students being "hooligans with one-way tickets to Hades." The man holding her hand in a firm, warm grip was a tall drink of brown sugar water that she could slurp with or without a straw.

Get behind me Satan, Imani silently rebuked temptation, reminding herself that lust was a sin and that the reason for her visit had absolutely nothing to do with this sex-a-fabulous brother with his mighty bald head and luscious . . .

"Mrs. Evans, I'm Braxton Wade. I'm glad you were finally able to take the time to come in today. Have a seat."

There was something in his tone, something unidentifiable that sounded like a rebuke of some sort.

Imani lost all her lust and sat in the chair Mr. Wade indicated, placing her purse at her feet, crossing her legs and squaring her shoulders, unwittingly exuding an impervious air in the process.

"This meeting was arranged so that we could discuss your daughter, Nia."

Imani noticed the way the man glanced at his wristwatch as if to remind her of her tardy arrival.

"I apologize for being late. I—"

"Not a problem," he rudely interrupted, dismissing any possible explanation.

Imani arched her brow and bit the inside of her lip. Something was eating away at this Brown Sugar Bear. She did not know what it was and she could not really say she cared. She had enough overloading her mind as it was.

It wasn't bad enough that due to overbooking, Imani had been bumped off her flight home from Phoenix on Saturday, and was forced to extend her out-of-town stay an extra night, not arriving home until late Sunday evening. Tired, Imani had overslept, was late to work Monday morning, only to arrive and learn her presence was requested at an impromptu mandatory meeting with the company CEO. Five minutes after the meeting adjourned, the dentist's office called asking if she could bring Nia in at three-fifteen instead of four. Just when she felt as if someone was playing tug-of-war with her fraction of a last good nerve, Imani received another call from her insurance agent informing her that there was a problem processing her premium via electronic debit due to insufficient funds. Imani had apologized profusely. It was her oversight. She would take care of the matter without delay.

She was doing too much. How could she forget to transfer funds from her savings to her checking account to ensure that other unforeseen expenses didn't absorb monies earmarked for the insurance? Imani made a concerted effort to keep her finances in order to ensure her livelihood. This mishap was just a fluke, hopefully. Thank goodness Friday was payday because as of now her checking account was empty.

But her ears were just about full of this man's scolding.

". . . I've found that children often mirror in public what they see at home. Or in their powerlessness they act out because of familial discord or strife. Nia needs focus, and perhaps extra attention." He paused long enough to sigh. "Your daughter is essentially a wonderful student, but she could benefit from more parental involvement and—"

"Excuse me, Mr. Wade, but I really fail to see how any of this pertains to Nia becoming your student assistant." Imani uncrossed her legs and shifted forward in her seat. "And please believe me, I am fully invested and involved in my child's life." Imani did not mean to sound defensive, but she suddenly felt as if a weight had just been rudely and unjustly deposited on her shoulders. And what did this man mean by all that "what you see at home you do in public" psychobabble?

Nia's counselor sat back and rubbed a hand over his head as if exasperated.

"Mrs. Evans, you're obviously misinformed. I have no intention of making Nia my student assistant. We're here because Nia's been sent to my office on two different occasions by two different instructors as a result of her disruptive and disrespectful behavior in class," he explained before filling Imani in on the details of Nia's recent misbehavior culminating in her science room debacle.

Nia? Disruptive? Imani knew her child could out talk Larry King, but disruptive *and* disrespectful? Not her 3.75 GPA-having, bound-for-Harvard daughter. And putting a dead frog on a plate in science class as if it were food? This man had to be mistaken. Besides, Nia knew better than to show her tail at school or anywhere else. Imani believed in self-expression and allowing her daughter to enjoy life, but Imani would revert to something straight out of her grandmother's era and strip the bark off three switches, braid them together and secure the ends with rubber bands and beat Nia's fourteen-year-old carefree behind if she had to. Okay, maybe that was a little too *Mommy Dearest* for her. But still . . .

Imani cautioned herself to remain calm.

"I don't understand."

Imani swore she heard the man mumble "obviously" beneath his breath.

She told herself not to snatch the paperweight from his desk and smash his hand.

Instead, she quietly asked, "When did all of this occur and why am I only being notified of it now?"

"Ma'am, I left numerous messages on your home answering machine."

Imani shook her head. "I never received one."

Braxton Wade studied her a moment before coming from behind his desk to sit on its edge right in front of Imani, a case file in his large hands. He opened the tri-fold file and pointed to a sheet of paper secured to the first flap. The top of the page was marked: CHRONO. Guiding Imani's eyes with his finger to the left column in which recent dates were noted he read, "March first: left message requesting call back from parents. March third: left message requesting call. March seventh: left message. March tenth . . ." His voice trailed off.

Imani continued to peruse the notations. Braxton Wade's attempts to reach her over the past two weeks via phone were clearly documented. Her malfunctioning answering machine! That's probably why she never received his calls. She wondered why didn't he send a message via mail when his other attempts proved futile? Imani voiced her thoughts aloud.

Mr. Wade chuckled dryly. "Mrs. Evans, would that have done the trick? Would you have bothered to respond?"

Imani knew her right eye had to be twitching by now, and she could feel the muscles in her neck warming up for rotation. "Pardon?"

"You didn't respond to my calls, or the request I penned at the bottom of the notice you signed regarding Nia serving detention last Thursday because of her misbehavior. I assumed my personally writing on a form letter would convey my concern—"

His words were like a bucket of icy water on her rising ire.

"Detention? I-I signed n-no such notice," Imani stuttered. "Nia couldn't have been in detention hall because she has band practice on Thursdays," was her lame reply.

Words escaped her as Imani examined the document Nia's counselor extracted from the file and handed to her. There it was before her very eyes, the form with her signature acknowledging awareness of Nia's infractions and subsequent punishment. And just as he said, a handwritten note reading: *Please contact me at your earliest convenience to discuss this matter.*

Nia had lied. She had not attended band practice last week, but had been in detention hall instead. Imani was furious and embarrassed. That girl had much explaining to do. *Where was Nia?*

Probably out in front of the school waiting for Imani as planned.

Nia's dentist appointment! Imani glanced at her watch. She had less than twenty-five minutes to make it halfway across town.

"I'm truly sorry, but I must leave—"

"I'm not surprised." Braxton Wade dropped Nia's case file on his desk as if washing his hands of a truly irritating affair. "Sorry I interrupted your busy afternoon, Mrs. Evans," he dismissed her and moved as if to reopen his office door.

Imani stood, blocking his path, a curious blend of anger and disillusionment stirring in her chest.

"Rest assured . . . *sir* . . . that I will handle this problem with my child," Imani stated as evenly as possible. "But you . . . you really need to get a handle on your approach. You've been hostile since I walked in the door."

"You can pick up a complaint form on your way out," the counselor advised, looking down at her.

Imani stood open-mouthed before swinging about and marching toward the door, flinging it open only to pivot back toward him.

"Do you know what it's like being a parent in today's world? Do you even have children, Mr. Wade?"

There was no forthcoming reply, just a loaded stare.

"That's what I thought. Before you pass judgment on me, try walking a mile in my shoes," Imani blurted, vexed that she had allowed this man, this situation to openly shake her usual reserve and self-control.

Braxton Wade merely scratched his ear while glancing at the expensive looking pumps on Imani's feet. He smirked.

"Can't afford 'em. And, yes, I have children, Mrs. Evans," he answered, tapping the lateral file cabinet near the door. "Monday through Friday I have nearly three hundred kids to your one. I manage to keep up with all of mine. If you parents did the same, we wouldn't have vandalized study labs, singing daisies wouldn't be missing, and Pearl would be sitting pretty in the parking lot waiting for me when I get off work—"

Imani had absolutely no idea what the man was ranting about. She just stared at him, wondering if she would have to snatch her pepper spray and hose him down. Then she remembered that her purse still sat on the floor beside the chair.

"Thankfully, I don't depend on parental cooperation for job satisfaction," he continued as Imani eased over to retrieve her purse. Rifling through it, she moved toward the door pausing long enough to plop a small vial of dental floss on top of the lateral file cabinet.

"Try some the next time you schedule an after lunch meeting," Imani spat, before storming away to hurriedly retrace her steps to her vehicle, wanting to but managing not to scream, *And that's* Miss *Evans, you raving, attitudinal, green-onion-between-your-teeth, boxers-twisted-up-your-evil-crack-having sea urchin!*

* * *

Nia was on restriction. Or to hear her version of the facts, "lock-down for the criminally insane."

Imani could care less about her daughter's opinion of her punishment. As far as Imani was concerned, if Nia had the good sense the Lord gave a lampshade she would thank her heavenly Father that she wasn't chained to the chimney.

Detention. And forgery! Well, not quite, but Nia had gathered her signature under false pretenses.

Nia had "kicked it on campus" before last week's band practice instead of eating dinner with her friends all right. Kicked it right in detention hall. And the so-called parental consent form giving Nia permission to audition for the orchestra and jazz ensemble was actually a document required for Nia's files indicating that her parents were aware of the disciplinary action for her infractions—a document which Nia had confiscated from the mail when noting her counselor's name stamped above the school's return address on the envelope in which it arrived.

Imani acknowledged that she was at fault for not reading the document carefully. Okay, so she had not read it at all while celebrating her child's success.

"But, Mom, I was afraid that you wouldn't let me audition or go to Marine World with my freshmen class if you knew I had gotten in trouble. I wasn't trying to be deceitful. I just got scared."

"Yes, well, you have two whole weeks to get un-scared."

No television, stereo, telephone, PC, DVD, VCR, nothing for two weeks! Nia was to go to school, come home, complete her homework, and clean her room. That was it. No socializing, no frills, no thrills whatsoever. Nia could have bread and water or water and bread. Okay, and a multivitamin, but nothing fancy like those fruity chewables. And if Nia so much as looked at Imani wrong, used an unacceptable tone of voice, or acted as if her punishment were unreasonable the two-week time clock would start all over again. She was barred from the amusement park excursion and her audition. The only music Nia would play or hear was the harp of angels if she even messed with Imani's last good fraction of a nerve.

"But, Mommy, what am I supposed to do for entertainment?" she'd had the gall to ask.

"I don't know, Nia," Imani replied, noting her child's whiny use of

"Mommy" as if Imani could be swayed by a tender signifier. "Help God count the stars, teach Miss Pitman to tell time or talk or something. Just don't touch the telephone or television or anything else that wasn't invented before Jesus walked on water."

Whew, three days and counting, Imani mused as she sat at her desk reviewing her training evaluations from the recent Phoenix trip. It was only Thursday and Nia was putting on as if she had been locked in a cellar with a dead mouse for a toy, moping about the house, face all pitiful, barely eating. Imani grinned, recalling what her mother would say to her whenever, as a child, Imani chose to be finicky and refuse the food on her plate.

Go ahead and fast, child, it'll give you power.

It was then that Imani realized she had not spoken to her mother or stepfather since returning from her trip. She made a mental note to call and check on them that night provided she could track them down. When not busy with Miss McGee's—a unisex styling salon voted one of the finest full-service salons in the city by the Sacramento African American Business Association for the past five years— Eunetta McGee Carmichael and her husband, Ray, were always busy with some thing or some one. A church project, on an exotic vacation or cruise, planting a garden, or entertaining friends; they never stayed still for long.

Imani was glad that her mother was enjoying life and love with her husband of sixteen years. Lord knew she'd sacrificed plenty raising Imani alone. And even if Miss Eunetta—as she was affectionately dubbed by her customers—was "living high off the hog" now, Imani remembered times when money was funny and change was strange.

With little job skills and being too proud to seek public assistance, Eunetta honed her natural talent for styling hair to earn a living in order to support herself and her child. Her first "salon" was little more than the tiny kitchenette in their studio apartment, but Miss Eunetta developed a good reputation and gained loyal customers. She had style and grace and with her sewing skills always kept herself looking like something straight off the fashion pages of *Ebony* or *Jet*. She was solicitous toward her customers, offering them something cool to drink in the summer, something hot in winter, even allowing payment arrangements for those who had fallen on hard times. And when Imani's mother eventually earned her cosmetology license and went to work as an operator in a salon, her customers went with her. But after years spent working for others, Eunetta McGee decided it was time to do for herself. Now twenty-two years later, Miss McGee's was hopping, featuring a posh ambiance and some of the hottest stylists in the city.

Thanks, Mother, for being a good example, Imani thought, as she laid aside the evaluations and gently patted her bleary eyes so as not to mar her perfectly applied makeup.

Closing her eyes and leaning back in her chair, Imani's mind drifted to a time long ago.

Imani remembered the Sundays of her childhood when her mother's undivided attention was hers alone. The Monday through Saturday hustle and bustle created by her mother's stream of steady customers waiting to yield their hair to Miss Eunetta's magic touch, and the interruptions caused by Eunetta's evening "outings" with gentlemen callers ceased on Sunday. That one day each week was theirs exclusively to spend poring over magazines, selecting fashions that Imani's mother replicated to perfection on their second-hand sewing machine. Imani loved their creations almost as much as she relished the uninterrupted time spent basking in her mother's presence. But after Eunetta obtained her cosmetology license and moved her patrons from her makeshift salon to an available booth at a local beauty parlor, that cherished bonding time became limited. Much to Imani's dismay, those private hours ceased altogether when Imani's mother found Christianity and Sunday worship services, and eventually Ray Carmichael and blissful marriage.

Initially Imani continued in her clothing construction as if doing so could somehow sustain the broken bond between mother and daughter. Over time she realized she had a gift and a knack, but it wasn't until moving to Washington DC to attend Howard University that she caught a glimpse of the possibilities that gift might bring.

Wanting a part-time job to supplement the allowance her parents provided, Imani stumbled upon an apprentice position with a notable African American fashion designer whose wares were featured in exclusive upscale stores nationwide. Though eccentric and temperamental, he proved a fierce ally and staunch supporter, even encouraging Imani to defy her mother and leave Howard U. for the Fashion Institute of Technology in New York. But Imani met Nigel, became pregnant with Nia, got married and divorced, then returned to Sacramento to raise Nia with the help of her close-knit extended family. To her mother's delight, Imani eventually resumed her studies and graduated from the California State University, Sacramento with a "respectable" undergraduate degree in business administration.

Imani sighed and stared at the far wall of her small office.

They had their differences, but Imani gave her mother credit for instilling a strong work ethic in her, and for being a positive example of a Black woman in business.

The intercom device embedded in her telephone suddenly beeped.

"Excuse me, Imani, but are you available to speak with a Vanessa Taylor?" the department administrative assistant asked.

"Absolutely."

"She's holding on line two."

"Thanks, Rachel." Imani lifted the receiver and emitted a high-pitch screech that was promptly returned by the party on the opposite end. "Girl, my Alpha sister soror, I am too glad to hear from you. I haven't seen you since the Christmas Ball. How are you, Vanessa?" Imani asked.

"Engaged," Vanessa Taylor smoothly replied, her voice brimming with joy.

"No!"

"I did it, Imani. I bit the bait the brother was offering and," Vanessa affected a southern drawl, "went and got myself hitched."

"Must be one smooth brother because you said yourself that your marriage club card was declined by wedding chapels worldwide."

Vanessa snickered.

"Yes, my Boo is smooth. You'll meet him Saturday."

"Saturday?"

"See something told me to call and remind your busy butt about the Spring Fling this weekend. I'm on this year's planning committee. It's going to be good so you better be there. I even tossed my weight at KSAC to get us a little television coverage."

Imani pressed a palm to her forehead.

"Ooh, Vanessa, thank you. It's on my Palm Pilot calendar and it still almost slipped my mind," Imani admitted, thinking of the annual event her sorority sisters and their counterpart fraternity brothers held each year to raise money for worthy causes. This year's proceeds would be donated to Maternal Instincts, a non-profit organization that provided parenting classes, mentorship, financial assistance and other services to low-income women and their families. The aid Maternal Instincts offered was not a typical handout. Clients fulfilled a community service agreement and sponsored mothers new to the program in exchange for the services they received. This self-help philosophy was the primary reason why the organization was selected as the recipient of this year's proceeds. "Maybe you'd better call me an hour before it starts and remind me again. Better yet, come over and help me dress."

Vanessa laughed.

"Girl, I'm sorry but I'm not going to sprain my back helping you stuff all those breasts in a bra."

"My 38Cs will be fine. You just make sure you purchase an extra ticket for all that junk-in-the-trunk you call a behind."

Their laughter rang freely.

"How's Miss Nia?" Imani's sorority sister inquired.

"She turned fourteen on Valentine's Day and she's making my eyebrows gray."

"Oh, my. I'll remember y'all in my prayers. Hey, wasn't your birthday at the beginning of the month?"

"March first."

"Did you get the birthday card I sent you?" Vanessa questioned.

"No."

"That's because I didn't send one. Girl, I forgot. I'm sorry," Vanessa apologized before launching into a rousing rendition of "Happy Birthday."

Imani held the phone away from her ear and frowned. Vanessa was a highly skilled woman with many talents, but singing was not one of them. Imani pounded the number keys on the dial pad, causing a series of beeps to sound in Vanessa's ears.

"Hey!" Vanessa protested.

"I'm going deaf over here, screechy," Imani exclaimed.

"Skip you, Imani. Okay, be sure to be there Saturday. This year's Spring Fling is gonna be off the hook! Melvina Richardson has some special guests lined up," Vanessa advised, referring to this year's chairperson.

"Who?" Imani inquired, her interest piqued.

"It's a secret, but you know how Melvina is with her flashy self. I'm sure we'll have guests to remember."

"That's the truth," Imani replied. "Well, let's get off the phone and do whatever it is we do to keep America rolling."

"Right! Bye Imani, see you Saturday."

"Are vegetables on the menu?" Imani's "date" for the evening asked, as Imani maneuvered her sedan through the circular drive in front of the Capitol City Club. She brought the vehicle to a stop just beyond a booth marked VALET PARKING.

"Mo, I've told you already that I requested a vegetarian plate for you."

"Just making sure," Monique replied, flipping down the visor to examine her visage in its illuminated mirror. She applied a fresh coat of gloss to her already shiny lips. "I don't want anything that once squawked, mooed, or pooped on my plate."

"Trust me, your wheelbarrow is waiting," Imani tonelessly quipped as a uniformed attendant approached the car, greeting her and handing her a numbered card while opening the door to assist her from the vehicle. Imani thanked him and slipped the card into the tiny beaded silk purse she carried as she stepped onto the curb where her cousin waited. Monique was her best friend, blood cousin, spirit sister and more, but Imani experienced a sudden desire for male companionship. She had been alone for years, and for the most part, Imani took it in stride and immersed herself in matters other than the heart. She tried to avoid self-pity, but admittedly at times, her solitary existence was hard to handle. It might have been nice attending the Spring Fling with a brother instead of Monique's woman-self. Imani should have invited an old friend or one of the brothers from the Saved & Single Ministry at church or called Rent-A-Romeo or some other escort service and charged the expense to her credit card or—

Ease up, girl, Imani told herself as she did her best to squash the unexpected sensation of loneliness fluttering in her breast. It was a beautiful night, a worthwhile occasion. She was determined to have a good time.

"How do I look?" Monique asked, smoothing a hand over her upswept hair as she pivoted for Imani's inspection.

"Very nice," Imani complimented, surprised that her cousin had selected something other than her usual bohemian style of dress for the evening. Imani had to admit her cousin was working the heck out of the deep wine evening gown hugging her svelte form in a cocoon of soft silk that left little to the imagination. At five-feet-ten-inches, with her runway figure, café au lait complexion and bright auburn hair, Monique St. James was a sight for hungry male eyes. "And very available."

"Good. I'm on a mission that's far from impossible," Monique chirped, pulling Imani forward into the building.

They made their way to the Riverside Room where the soiree was being held. The smooth sounds of a live jazz band flowed out the open doors to greet them as they joined the line of guests waiting for entrance. There was an obvious air of excitement buzzing near the top of the line, but Imani was too far back to see what all the commotion was about.

Imani turned toward Monique. "Well?"

"Well, what?"

"How do *I* look?" Imani asked, extending her arms slightly and striking a pose.

" 'Mani, please, you always look good and you know it," Monique replied, giving her cousin the once-over. "You're slamming that dress to death. I like this across-the-arms organza wrap-thingy you have going on here. But if I had your boobage, I'd opt for a little more *décolleté*. Can't you lower this thing?" Monique asked, fiddling with the bodice of Imani's sleeveless dress.

Imani slapped Monique's hands. "Stop it," she whispered, readjusting the front of her dress that, in her opinion, was cut low enough to accentuate rather than advertise her endowment.

"Excuse me," Monique hissed in return. "And exactly what color is this fetching little number?"

"Starfire blue," Imani answered, resuming her normal tone of voice.

"Looks like navy with a touch of silver to me."

Imani shook her head and sighed. She extracted two tickets from her evening bag as they neared the top of the line. Looking up, her heart plummeted. There was the cause of the commotion. Seated at an elaborately decorated table beside an attractive woman was a slim man with jet-black hair that contrasted deeply with his nut-brown skin. He was Hollywood handsome. From his attitude to his flawless attire, everything about him reeked clean. Too clean.

"Good evening and welcome. May I have your names please?" the hostess politely requested, prepared to consult the guest list at her fingertips.

"That would be Evans, Imani Evans," the man supplied, flashing perfectly set pearly whites courtesy of a dentist.

As he stood and came from behind the table to greet them, Imani grudgingly admitted that on the outside the man was smooth. But she knew that what was on the inside could break a grown woman's heart.

"Monique, you're looking lovely as always," he oozed, hugging her cousin while casting a saccharin smile Imani's way. "Hey, Butter, you're looking . . . thick . . . and healthy," commented Nigel Evans, actor extraordinaire and ex-husband from hell, as he assessed her person, gripping Imani's elbow and attempting to turn her about for further inspection.

"And you look vaguely familiar," she responded, prying his fingers from her flesh and wanting to choke from his excessive cologne assaulting her nostrils. *Butter. Thick. Healthy.* Imani hated the sardonic way Nigel tossed such inferences at her. He apparently considered it his duty to remind Imani that she no longer wore a size six as she had when they first met. She had a mirror and a scale and a closet filled with size ten garments, some size twelve, to remind her of that fact. Imani did not require Nigel's help.

"Don't be flip with your baby's daddy," Nigel chided, as he embraced her as if love still existed between them.

"You can stop the show, Nigel, there're no cameras around," Imani returned, aware of the unwanted attention being directed at her, overhearing curious chatter as to the identity of the woman receiving such an effusive greeting from one of Sacramento's hottest up-and-coming stars.

Chuckling lightly, Nigel released Imani and stepped back to straighten his bow tie and pat his perfect hair.

"Why are you here?" she inquired, struggling to keep her blood pressure from rising.

"Signing autographs for now, saving something else for later. You know, just a little community service," Nigel preened. Noting Imani's lack of enthusiasm he added, "I'll be by to spend some time with Nia tomorrow before I return to LA."

"I'm sure she'll appreciate you fitting her into your schedule," Imani replied, wondering if Nigel had even bothered to inform Nia that he was in town. Before she could voice her curiosity the ticket-taker at the table spoke.

"Ma'am, if you and your guest would be so kind as to follow this usher, he'll escort you to Table Fifteen. Enjoy your evening."

"Thank you," Imani returned, moving forward.

"I'll see you later, Butter," Nigel said before returning to his post and his adoring fans.

"Not if I see you first," Imani murmured, feeling as if a perfectly good evening was on a slippery slope to disaster. But then things began to look up again.

Imani and Monique, quietly chattering about Nigel's unexpected and unwanted presence, arrived at their designated table to find a couple seated there.

"Good evening." Standing, the man smiled pleasantly and extended a hand. "I'm Jamal Williams and this is my wife, Reina."

The woman's smile was genuinely warm and friendly as Imani and Monique introduced themselves.

"We've met before," Reina Williams stated, squinting slightly as Imani sat and placed her wrap across the back of her chair.

"Are you a soror?" Imani asked, placing her tiny purse in her lap.

"No, but I sometimes attend your functions with my best friend, Vanessa Taylor and—"

"Reina! Vanessa's Reina?!" Imani exclaimed.

"I'd like to think she's my Reina," her husband playfully responded, lifting his wife's hand to his mouth and kissing it gently. Reina purred sweetly in reply.

"I'm sorry," Imani began to apologize, "I truly did not recognize you, Reina. You look wonderful! You've cut your hair. The last time I saw you you were—"

"Fat! Go ahead and say it." Reina smiled. "I can handle it."

"Now, see I was not going there. I was going to say you were single and I wasn't aware that you married. Congratulations to you both! Do you still sing?" Imani turned to Monique. "You have to hear Reina sing. The diva is fierce."

"Thank you, and yes I still sing."

"We'll all have the pleasure of hearing her tonight," Jamal Williams proudly announced.

"You're one of the secret guests? Wonderful!" Imani replied.

"How much weight did you lose?" Monique interrupted, causing Imani to toss her an incredulous stare for her rudeness. "What? I'm always interested in stories about lifestyle changes," she defended, explaining about her scare with breast cancer and how it provoked her to change her dietary habits.

"Praise God for your recovery," Reina remarked. "And as to how much weight I've lost, let's just say I'd need a U-haul because I couldn't pull mine in a little red wagon like Oprah."

"You just wait until I see that Vanessa. She didn't tell me you were married," Imani stated.

"Well, here she is," Jamal remarked, glancing toward the couple approaching their table. "You can inform her of her wicked ways."

Imani peered over her shoulder to see a cinnamon-brown skinned woman with topaz eyes and an athletic physique escorted by an ultra chocolate, handsome specimen of a man.

"What did I do now?" the woman asked.

"Vanessa!" Imani sang, standing to exchange hugs with her sorority sister. "You are too cute tonight in your little black dress. And thanks a lot for the ogre at the door," Imani muttered in her ear.

"Girl, that's Melvina's doing," Vanessa commiserated. "I had a hand in Reina's performing, but that's all. Surprise," Vanessa half-heartedly sang. "Can you make it through the night with Nigel on parade?"

Imani smiled brightly.

"I'm sure I'll survive. Now flash the ring," she instructed, grabbing Vanessa's hand and gazing at the diamond solitaire on her finger. "My, my, look at all the bling-bling."

"Mah-h-va-lous, isn't it," Vanessa sang, turning to the man behind her. "Imani Evans, this is my fiancé, Chris McCullen. Boo, Imani is one of my Alpha sisters and she's good people."

"So I gather," Chris McCullen replied, extending a hand in Imani's direction. "Pleasure."

"Vanessa, Chris, this is my cousin, Monique St. James."

The couple exchanged pleasantries with Monique before going around the table to embrace Reina and Jamal.

Conversation flowed with ease. The fellowship and the food were good. Only the hors d'oeuvres were served thus far, and the night was yet young, still Imani was enjoying herself immensely. For the first time in a long while, Imani's heart and her mind felt light. Free. She even managed to forget the fact that she was dealing with a pouting pubescent child and that her wretch of an ex was somewhere in the building as she savored the night. Attempting to make herself even more comfortable, she placed her wrap and tiny evening bag on one of the two empty chairs between herself and Chris McCullen.

"Mmm, that reminds me," Vanessa piped suddenly, as if prompted by Imani's actions. "Boo, I reserved those seats for the brothers I told you and Jamal about," she told her fiancé, nodding toward the remaining two seats. "I think they'd be good additions to your 100 Strong network. Hopefully they'll be here soon."

Some time later, Monique and Vanessa were engaged in a lively conversation about the health benefits of omitting meat and fat from the diet, as Chris and Jamal segued from one topic to another.

Only Imani and Reina were finished with their salads.

"Care to follow me to the restroom?" Reina quietly asked, leaning across the table.

"Absolutely," Imani replied.

Together, they excused themselves and left the table.

Moments later, they stood side-by-side before a mirror in the women's lounge, freshening their lipstick and chatting effortlessly.

"I always rush to the bathroom before I sing. Nerves," Reina explained.

"Reina, do you mind my asking how you lost your weight? I'm not trying to pry," Imani offered, "but I keep playing with ten or fifteen pounds, taking them off and putting them on, and I'm open to any advice you can offer."

"Girl, who would've ever thought I'd be in a position to say anything about weight loss. But," Reina shrugged, "God works in mysterious ways. I joined a weight management group through my HMO, and I take my Magic E pill five times a week."

Imani stopped fluffing her hair and turned toward Reina.

"Magic E pill?"

Reina smiled.

"Exercise."

"I thought you were selling something I was ready to buy. Well, that's still encouraging because I joined a gym a month ago so I'm hopeful."

"Good Imani, have faith. I know I used to hate it when I was a few pounds from my goal weight and folks who knew me when told me I looked good and to stop tripping, but Imani, you *do* look good. Still, go for your goal, sis."

Imani smiled and nodded. "I will."

"Now let's get out of here because I am 'ret ta eat . . . although I'm never able to eat much before I sing."

"Can you can get a doggie bag in this joint?" Imani jested.

"Only if it has a pedigree," Reina replied.

They laughed as Imani followed Reina from the lavatory and down a narrow corridor leading toward the Riverside Room. They neared the dimly lit area filled with delicious aromas, jovial chatter, and the sounds of jazz played by the band on a raised dais at the front of the lavishly decorated ballroom. But before they could enter, the sound of a male voice at Imani's back startled her. She whipped about only to find Nigel there, his pearly whites displayed for all to see.

"Hello again."

"Nigel."

"I don't think we've had the pleasure," he addressed Imani's companion, reaching for Reina's hand.

Imani made the necessary introductions.

Nigel was syrup and silk as he exchanged brief pleasantries with Reina before redirecting his attention to Imani.

"I need to speak to you."

Reina excused herself.

"What do you want, Nigel?" Imani asked, once Reina was out of earshot.

"Why the icicles, Butter? I'm not contagious. You know you look good for . . ." He let the unfinished sentence dangle in the air.

"For someone who's no longer your type?"

Over the years, Imani noticed Nigel's increased proclivity for women who fit a certain mode. He had become an exclusive light-bright brother, salivating over long and lean, fair complexioned Black women with abundant hair or wonderful weaves. Intellect was not a prerequisite. Nigel's women need only offer beauty, a body, and a bed for him to romp in. Nigel wanted a showpiece not a partner.

"Well . . . you know. But you do look good. I could even manage getting with you to help relieve . . . some tension . . . for old times sake," he suggested in a voice he considered seduction at its best.

A full laugh erupted from Imani's throat. Was she wearing a sign that read SIXTY SEXLESS YEARS AND COUNTING? Even if that were the case, Imani would sew it up before granting Nigel entry again. He was not her ideal lover, not her notion of a man. When the time was right, Imani wanted a man of substance: spiritually, mentally, *and* physically. She did not want some scrawny, scrappy, simpleton who thought he was a gift to whom God owed thanks. Nigel need not apply.

"There's not that much tension in the world, Nigel," Imani retorted, fire snapping from her eyes.

His eyes narrowed, but he said nothing. Nigel merely straightened his tuxedo jacket and patted his perfect hair.

"Listen, I'm headed to LA Sunday. I have a callback for this new daytime drama I auditioned for and I'm going to do some live readings for a playwright friend of mine in Redondo Beach," he happily reported. "So I'll be gone longer than usual. You think you can take Nia by my apartment so she can get my mail and water my plants?"

The pop-headed egomaniac and his gall were limitless.

"Will you be compensating me for my mileage and my time because our daughter can't remember to put the cap on the toothpaste, so I'm sure I'll be the one stuck with the chore of looking after your half-dead plants."

"Lower your voice," Nigel cautioned, glancing about them to ensure no one was nearby. "Let's not trip out and make a fuss over a small favor." His voice became sly, condescending as he rationalized, "I doubt it's an inconvenience for you. Or are you busy these days?"

"And since you brought up the subject of mail," Imani continued, ignoring Nigel's thinly veiled critique regarding her lack of a personal life, "make this the last time I have to ask you to *please* stop using my mailing address."

"Come on, Butter. Pause the drama and give your baby's daddy a—" Nigel looked up and stopped abruptly. Suddenly, all displeasure left his face as he touched his hair and ran his tongue over his teeth before exposing an award-winning smile. Nigel grabbed Imani's arm and pulled her to him, quietly threatening, "Don't blow this."

Imani's attempts to free herself from his grasp were in vain as a voice called, "We heard we could find you out here, Mr. Evans. Can we get a shot of you please?"

"Absolutely!" Nigel turned Imani so that she too faced the oncoming paparazzi. Camera flashes illuminated the anteroom where they stood.

Still clutching Imani to his side in an embrace far too intimate for her liking, Nigel whispered in her ear, "Smile, Butter, my adoring public requires it of you." The clicking of camera shutters filled the air. Imani felt trapped. Nigel seemed to swell in his element. "Do me a favor and open the windows in my apartment on occasion so it can air out when you go over," he quietly commanded.

"Can we get the young lady to smile, please?" a photographer called.

Nigel slid his hand down past her waist, allowing his palm to rest on her hip.

Imani stiffened and quietly warned him to remove his offending member.

"Butter, please. I've been here before," he snidely remarked, increasing the pressure on her hip for good measure.

"Remind me why I even bothered to marry you," she whispered, pinching his finger and forcing him to readjust his hold.

"Ma'am, a smile please," a cameraman called.

"Because you were pregnant," Nigel answered, a malicious tone coating his voice.

Imani dug the heel of her shoe in Nigel's foot and shifted so that his foot bore the brunt of her weight. Only when Nigel swallowed a yelp of pain did Imani flash a smile as wide as her dimples were deep.

Imani meant to bypass her companions and journey outdoors for a much-needed breath of fresh air. But from a distance, she noticed that the two missing guests who were soon to arrive had indeed done so. Drawing closer, she believed she recognized one in particular. Calling on memory to aid her, Imani stopped dead in her tracks. Soon could have been a century away and it still would have been too soon as far as Imani was concerned. There was no mistaking the brown sugar bald head resting on the broad shoulders of a most annoying man. It *was* Braxton Wade, Nia's cretin of a guidance counselor, seated there at *her* table devouring salad like a cow chewing cud. Imani felt her world shift and her blood pressure rise. First, Nigel and now *him!* It was too much.

Thank God she didn't own a gun.

BRAX

S ometimes I wonder about God's sense of humor.
It's Friday night. I've had a long week. My Ford Mustang was
stolen Monday and returned to the staff parking lot on Tuesday
minus the rear fender, the six-disc CD player installed two years ago,
and a dozen of my old school jams. It was bad enough stealing Pearl.
But my music? Some unknown perp wanted to be dipped in a mound
of maggots.

I called the police and informed them that my vehicle had been recovered. Of course they told me not to touch the car. It had to be im-
pounded until someone could dust for fingerprints.

I needed a rental car. I phoned my insurance agent to learn my policy allowed twenty-five dollars per day for a maximum of thirty days toward the rental cost.

I called the rental outfit. Sure, they had cars in that price range:
specks that make Yugos look like limos!

I was not about to fold myself into some tacky Tonka toy that shook
when I manually rolled down the window. So, I decided to get a car I
could actually fit in and absorb the price difference even if that
meant screwing up my monthly budget. But that's what incidentals
were all about: they were meant to catch you off guard.

So I inched to work in my ride that's a step up from a speck and prepared for parent conference week. When Friday finally rolled around, a brother was beat.

Then there's Terrance calling my office talking about "Yo, Kid, swing to this black tie gig with me tonight. A business associated invited us. I already have the tickets."

Reading between the lines: his latest honey did the backstroke on him.

The only black tie I wanted to see was the one securing my doo rag to my bald head when I got home and flopped back after a game of hoops at the gym, a stretch in the steam room listening to Mr. Feldman tell his nasty stories, and a trip to the video store. But of course T. assured me his little foo-foo party was going to be straight so I caved. I could eat a bowl of cheese 'corn and watch a rented copy of *America on Ice* any time.

There's something soothing about ice skating. I get into those triple flips and toe loops and double axels and lose track of time. The skaters make it look so easy that I think I can get out there with mad skills and I would too if the judges wouldn't mind me doing my routine to Teddy P.'s *Turn Off the Lights*.

But as I was saying, I was in need of a reprieve so I accepted my housemate's offer, advising him that he could wear a tux if he wanted, but I wasn't doing the penguin waddle. I elected to wear the black Armani that I purchased for my father's funeral. That was seven years ago, but believe me I plan to get every nickel's worth out of this suit that set me back three weeks salary. Besides, according to the salesperson, it was a classic cut that never went out of style.

So I showered and dressed and hopped into T.'s BMW and we slid off to this gig, my attitude much improved. Then she walked in, stalling the mood like that record that skipped, fouling up the groove and grind you were getting at that house party in somebody's basement, the air smelling like Fritos, hair grease, and cheap cologne back in the day.

I couldn't do a thing but choke on a piece of romaine lettuce lodged in my throat.

You really can't expel a leaf stuck in your gullet the way you would like to when dining at a high-priced social affair. You cannot hawk and spit and wheeze until your airways clear. So I just sat there gagging into my linen napkin as inconspicuously as I could before guzzling down the contents of my water goblet *and* T.'s.

I managed to breathe again as T.'s associate, this sister named Vanessa, introduced the woman rejoining our table after what I assumed was a trip to the powder room. The brothers at the table did the gentlemanly thing and stood as she sat. I was glad. The motion seemed to help the lettuce slide down my throat. It also gave me time to recover from the surprise of seeing Imani Evans again.

Normally, I would have thought God was smiling on me by placing me near a banging beauty like *Miss* Evans (day before yesterday I noticed the parents' status marked "divorced" in her daughter's file) but I wasn't *that* naïve. There she was, one seat removed from me, looking like something I want to dream about.

I can't lie. The woman is beautiful. She has this natural hair thing going on, and even pulled up on top of her head with all these tiny rhinestone doo-dads it still looks wild. I like it. She has gorgeous, deep brown eyes, teeth you can't even pay a dentist for, sexy dimples, and a body I wish I could freeze-dry and save for later. I'm a leg-hips-breasts brother, and babygirl has more than her fair share on all counts. That would be all good by me except she's acting cool, smiling tightly and politely, reminding me that we don't like the air each other breathes as T.'s associate introduces us, not knowing we've already met.

Two can play that game.

"*Miss* Evans." I nod, all debonair like Mr. French from *Family Affair*.

A strange gleam sparkled in her eyes before she returned my greeting then averted her gaze.

I think I actually hummed a few verses of "Jesus Keep Me Near the Cross," in my head, at least.

Okay, someone tell me how I am supposed to enjoy this hundred-dollar-a-plate dinner with this cool fountain one chair removed. I want a refund.

Oh, yeah, I'm here on T.'s c-note. Well then, I'll sit back and enjoy whatever the night has in store.

An hour has passed and I'm actually having a good time. The brothers at this table are real. I'm feeling them and the effortless conversations we've had. The food was excellent, the music is purring, and I'm not even minding this dizzy Monique chick who must be an animal rights activist because she's made enough disparaging remarks about the meat in the meals we've consumed that I should feel guilty enough to swallow a bottle of Ipecac. Minus Monique, I'm undisturbed.

Practically.

My eyes have an agenda of their own. From time to time, they stray to reregister *her* image in my mind.

Imani Evans has made it a point to, when not ignoring my presence altogether, be painfully polite toward me. Can we say passive aggressive? Why she just can't have a ghetto-fabulous attitude, smack her luscious lips and cut her eyes at me, or straight diss me like I'm sure she'd like to, I don't know. I hate to admit it, but I find her restraint . . . alluring, like the rest of her.

I am not usually attracted to women who make fun of my hygiene so I can't even explain this sudden curiosity. Maybe my dry spell has dried my mind and made me weak and susceptible. After all, my last date was at a sold-out M.C. Hammer concert. Okay, so I've dated since then. Still, I'm not a woman-a-week kind of brother. I take sabbaticals. So, I feel it is safe to conclude that Imani Evans can be classified as nothing more than friction. She was sent here to stir my dust, to make me think it might be time to rev my engine and get my swerve on. But I am not a glutton for punishment. Beneath all of this masculine brawn beats a heart and I'm not interested in having it crushed beneath her glass slippers. Besides, the woman looks expensive and my cash flow is hemmed up in my Tour of Africa savings and . . .

Whoa!

I don't know how I jumped from zero to sixty in two seconds flat, but Imani Evans is not interested in me and I'm not interested in her. Our contempt for one another is mutual so I can squash all this nonsense because it's messing with my good evening vibe.

"Coffee, sir?"

I was so lost in my thoughts that our server's offer startled me.

I declined. Coffee does things to me better left unsaid in mixed company. However, I did accept the sliver of white chocolate raspberry something on some fancy little dessert plate that looked like it would break if you breathed on it too hard.

"Good evening everyone, and welcome to the tenth annual Spring Fling."

On stage was the sister who'd taken tickets at the door. There was a round of applause. She went on to thank everyone for their patronage and support, acknowledged key figures responsible for tonight's festivities, noteworthy guests in the audience, blah-blah-blah.

"And now I'd like to introduce to some and present to others our emcee for the evening. Those of you who arrived early were fortunate enough to have met him already. The rest of you on CP time, this is your chance," she said, evoking laughter. "Without further ado, please welcome to the stage Sacramento's very own brother who's making it big in the land of angels . . . Mr. Nigel Evans!"

Folks were clapping like Jesus just showed up.

His name was somewhat familiar, but I didn't know the brother so I chewed my dessert and observed.

Okay, I admit I dislike perfect people, or those who try to front like their feet don't stink. I could tell from my seat a mile away that old boy fit the description. From his clipped speech to his Pepsodent smile, there was something arrogant and unreal about him. And the way he kept droning on and on about his career! I couldn't even front like I cared. Instead, I zoned out until I heard the words "door prize." Even I like a freebie so I paid attention to the emcee as he asked the woman who'd collected tickets at the door to rejoin him on the platform to randomly draw those tickets from a humongous glass bowl.

They gave away passes to an art museum, theatre tickets, gift certificates for some overpriced department store, and an outrageous gift basket filled with everything from gourmet coffee, fruit and cheeses to who knew what else. Then came the big bang. I was hyped thinking it was something like a sports utility vehicle or a wide screen television with surround sound, but it was a steak dinner for two aboard a cruise ship sailing from Sacramento to San Francisco. That works, too, I guess.

". . . and the cruise goes to . . . Monique St. James."

Miss Veggie USA jumped up like she'd just won a trip to nirvana; gushing and cooing like a straight idiot as she hurried to collect her prize. Mr. Perfect was effusive, hugging homegirl all tight as camera flashes popped everywhere while he handed her the winning envelope, which she passed off to Nia's mom when rejoining our table.

"Here, girl, I don't want this," Monique announced. "I just wanted to get my picture in the paper."

I had to laugh along with everyone else at the table.

Mr. Emcee thanked the sponsors for donating the goods, reported the amount of proceeds being donated to some charity (impressive), then found some ludicrous way to segue back onto his career for another self-aggrandizing moment. I was about to practice my newfound skill of sleeping with my eyes open until the brother introduced the band and its special guest.

The wife of one of the brothers at our table crossed to center stage to position herself before a microphone as the lights dimmed and a spotlight washed over her. I realized then that she had excused herself from the table right before dessert but never returned. There she was, changed into some glittery dress singing like she knew her business.

Whoa! The sister had smoke in her throat. I mean she was caressing that song like nobody's business. I was impressed, moved really. Looking at her husband, so was he. Judging by their response, so was the rest of the crowd. She sang several tunes, each time setting the place on fire and receiving effusive praise, until she ended the set with "My Funny Valentine."

I think I saw Imani Evans wipe a tear from her eye when the sister chanteuse finally made her way through the standing ovation to return to the table. Shoot, I think I might have wiped one away, too.

The band continued playing as the evening mellowed. An area was cleared in front of the stage so people could dance. I wanted to take my mellow mood on home. Maybe I'd take Pearl out for a long drive or watch *America on Ice* after all. T. didn't have to ask me twice if I was ready to go when he made that move an hour later.

"Chris, Jamal, I'll roll through the next 100 Strong meeting," I promised, shaking hands with the brothers who schooled me on 100 Strong, a non-profit community based organization that primarily partnered with young men of color to provide mentoring, tutoring, job readiness and other life application skills. The organization appeared to be something I could and should get with, so I promised to look it up. "Vanessa, Monique, it was good meeting you. Mrs. Williams, I'll be one of the first in line when your CD drops on the shelves." She laughed and promised to autograph the cover for me. Then there *she* was. I could ignore her, but I felt smooth enough to be generous.

Up saying his good-byes to our party, T. no longer occupied the now empty chair between us. We were one-on-one.

"Miss Evans, tell Nia I said hi and I hope she's not suffering too much during house arrest."

For the first time that night, Nia's mom actually spoke directly to me. "Nia told you about her being on restriction?"

I nodded and chuckled deeply. "She came to school the other day telling me I'd sold her out and that I was responsible for her 'cruel and unusual punishment.' "

"That child of mine. What was your response?"

"I told her to stop whining then drop and give me ten."

Imani Evans actually laughed.

"No, really," I paused, recalling my statement. "I told Nia that in my opinion her mother was fair and just, and that I admire any parent who cares enough about her child to discipline her properly."

I wasn't lying. That is exactly what I said. And had I known those words would cause Imani Evans to smile warmly at me like she did, I would've tape recorded them for her playback pleasure.

"Say, Kid, are you ready to roll?"

Terrance's timing was off. I sensed she was about to say something redeeming, something almost nice to me, but my intrusive house-mate wrecked the set.

Our wait outside was relatively short before a valet rolled the silver Beemer with the personalized plates T-BLACK to the curb.

T. tipped the driver. We hopped in to crawl forward in the line of cars exiting the Capitol City Club's driveway. I glanced in the side view mirror while loosening my tie only to stop at a reflection of the night.

There beneath the awning meant to protect the club's patrons from inclement weather, stood Imani Evans. She seemed small, vulnerable and exposed. Maybe it was my vantage point skewing things. Or was it the way she held that wrap about her bare arms despite the mild night as if shielding herself from something unpleasant? I looked over my shoulder to make sure my perception was real, but then that Nigel character suddenly appeared and put an arm around her so that her expression changed and I lost what I thought I saw.

I faced forward and shook off a crazy rush of . . . what? Didn't know, shouldn't care.

"Let's take the downtown scenic route," T. suggested, pulling me back from troublesome pursuits as the Beemer pulled out into traffic.

We laughed. Unless you like watching crazy people, downtown is about as scenic as a cesspool. Okay, I'm exaggerating. It's not that bad. The city has put a lot of work into its downtown plaza project so it's actually decent. It's not Chicago's magnificent mile, but Sacramento's skyline has its own appeal, especially from the vantage point of the front seat of a convertible.

"What's up with you and that sister at our table? What was her name? Imani! There's either beef between you or some frustrated sexual tension going on."

I could've pissed my pants at T.'s unexpected, and ill-timed observation, but I managed to hold back.

"Man, what're you jawing at?"

"And I saw you watching her in your mirror," T. advised, ignoring my dismissive attitude.

True or not, that sounded like an accusation. "What's your point, T.?"

"Kid, you're guilty until proven innocent. So, really, what's that all about?" he asked, glancing at me. The lawyer wanted to gather his facts.

Scratching my ear, I filled T. in on my office episode with Nia's mom earlier in the week.

"I knew something was up!" he crowed. "She actually threw dental floss at you?" T. found the situation hilarious. Okay, it was slightly funny, but not much.

"Come on, Brax, lighten up or I'm going to think the sister has a hook in you and we don't do women with children, am I right?" my housemate contested, not waiting for my reply. "I know I'm right. Too much drama! You wind up courting their kids who may or may not like you just so they don't feel jealous about you sharing their mother's time and try to sabotage your game," T. asserted as we rolled to a red light. He leaned toward me and pounded my upper arm in sync with each word as he clearly punctuated, "Too much work."

I jerked away from his falling jackhammer and rubbed my bicep.

"You don't have to remind me what's what. My 3B policy is still intact," I maintained, referring to the dating guidelines I'd created in an attempt to weed out the bad seeds. It's like this. I shy away from women with Bebe's, Baggage, or Beer. One: I don't like out of control rugrats passing for children especially if I can't lock them in the closet when their mother's not looking. Two: I can't deal with women nursing emotional scars left by ex-lovers, or tie myself to the bedpost and let a sister beat out her anger on me. And three: I do not date sippers. I'm not sponsoring a sister in AA meetings, and I don't like swapping tongue with a woman who has liquor on her lips. If I want my mouth to feel and taste flammable, I'll drink gasoline.

"Kid, make sure you don't slip."

"Whatever, knuckle. Roll on. The light's green," I announced, indifferently. I leaned back in my seat, kicked off my shoes and, aided by the night breeze and the music pumping through the Beemer's system, focused on enjoying the ride. And I did until T. crashed in on my relaxation ten minutes later.

"Brax, I need a line to Miss Monique St. James," he came at me out of the blue. "Think you can handle that for me?"

My frown was large. "I don't know her."

"She's Imani's cousin. Right?"

"So?"

"So, hook a brother up," T. argued while turning down his stereo volume as if I needed to hear him better. "Put me in touch with her."

"That *ain't* my line of business and even if it were I wouldn't do it. Monique is gone! You see that?" I asked, pointing to an old cemetery engulfing a huge lot at Riverside and Broadway. "Get with that woman and you'll be right up in there on your first date having a séance with dead people."

Chuckling, T. countered, "Come on, Kid, she's not that bad. Just eccentric."

"And she's five short of a six-pack. Just drive man. You're scaring me."

We made it home without further female discussion.

T. restocked his overnight bag, or as he calls it, his Kitty Kit and strolled out to hook up with some sister who left a provocative invitation on his voice mail while he was out.

I was tempted to plop down in the den and watch a video or two, but I missed my trip to the gym to attend the black-tie gig. I owed myself a sweat.

When I reached the gym, the basketball court was brother-free, and hosted a few questionable others who I doubted had much game.

I opted for a swim in the heated pool.

After one lap, I was hungry again. By the end of twelve, I was ready to dab some A-1 on the life preservers and get my munch on. It was time to go.

It wasn't until Pearl and I were cruising close to home that I remembered I'd eaten the last bag of cheese 'corn two nights ago.

There's nothing like munching cheese popcorn, sipping something cold, and falling asleep in front of the TV, so I made a quick detour for one of those open-all-night stores.

I like grocery shopping. No, I'm not soft. But a brother's gotta eat. Besides, it's a holdover from childhood. While Moms was in college, Pops would load up my sisters and me and cart us off to the grocery store to do the food shopping. Pops made a game out of it. My father was frugal so he set a budget each week and it was our job to see how far under that budget we could get. The money we saved went into The Family Bank—an old tin cigar box my father kept hidden in the house—and at the end of each month we used that money for a family outing. Of course my sisters and I made sure we came in under budget every time. We clipped coupons from the Sunday paper and only shopped on double coupon days, and we learned that store brand items were just as good as name brand. My friends laughed and called me Betty Crocker Brax, but that's all right because now I have mad shopping skills and the money I save is deposited in my Tour of Africa fund.

The idea hit me during my last year of grad school. A cohort in the psych program went to Africa one winter break. He returned telling of its amazing beauty. I got to thinking how every person I'd ever known to vacation in Africa was *not* of African descent. I thought about how I had a blood link to the continent, and that in some city or township, an ancestor was born, so if anybody should be visiting, it might as well be me. Besides, I wanted to experience a side of my original birthplace that *National Geographic* cannot provide.

So, anyhow, I'm strolling the drink section looking for something to wash it all down and dreaming of Africa when I glance toward the opposite end of the aisle and see this woman from behind. My heart does this stop, drop, and roll thing in my chest because it looked like Imani Evans. All the swerves and curves, the chocolate skin, and free hair were there.

At first I felt like ignoring her and just letting things be, but then this irrational urge to speak to her again puffs up and has me moving my cart like a bobsled up the aisle trying to reach her before she disappeared. In my hurry my basket nearly careened out of control and into this young couple loading bottled water into their basket. I managed to steer clear of them, but the near collision startled the man so that the bottle he held smashed to the floor, sending broken glass and water everywhere.

"I'm truly sorry," I apologized, faking concern for their welfare while glancing up in search of the mystery woman I pursued. She was long gone. Returning my attention to the couple near me, I asked if they were okay. They assured me it was all good as a voice requested over the amplification system, "Clean up on aisle five." Almost instantly, a young, sleepy looking Asian brother appeared pushing a mop bucket and carrying other cleaning supplies in hand. I apologized again. He yawned. I hurried on.

I didn't look too hard. Or I tried to make it seem that way as I furtively tossed glances here and there, strolling nonchalantly like even Easter could wait on me. She was nowhere to be found. I told myself it didn't matter despite the idiotic sense of disappointment messing with me. Squaring my shoulders like a real man, I rolled my cart toward the express checkout, arriving at the same time as this sister carrying a hand-held basket.

"Ladies first," I said, allowing her to proceed me.

"I know so well," was her offhanded, ungrateful remark. She had the nerve to glance down in my basket and make a quick calculation. She sucked her teeth before adding, not speaking directly to but rather about me, "The sign says twelve items or less. Some folks need to learn to count."

I wanted to laugh. Why this woman was unleashing attitude at my expense was a mystery to me. Evidently, someone somewhere had done her wrong and I was a convenient beating post. Not that I would have been interested in a sister with blue braids and butterfly glasses anyhow, but she and her attitude were prime examples of Clause Two in my 3B policy: no women with baggage.

After her purchases were totaled, I had to stand there and wait for the woman to scrounge through her purse for some change. She was short a quarter. I was tired and ready to go home and eat so despite her nasty attitude toward me, I dug in my pocket and offered her the change she needed. Girlfriend rolled her eyes at my quarter like a booger was hanging from Washington's nose and elected to swipe her card instead. This time I did laugh. Displaced anger is ugly.

*   *   *

When I got home and unloaded my bags, the house was quiet. Terrance was hooching it up with some honey, and wouldn't come home until Sunday. He usually drives to Oakland on Saturdays and stays overnight to attend church with his grandparents. He invites me, but I decline. The way I see it is if I can't get along with God Monday through Saturday, there's no sense in me fronting on Sunday. Besides, I like T.'s grandparents and all, but Skippy, the one-armed monkey freaks me out. So, I finished with the groceries, made myself a bag of microwave 'corn, poured a bottle of strawberry-kiwi spritzer over a glass of ice and tried to watch television.

I couldn't concentrate.

I kept remembering that evil woman, my mad dash, and what I assumed was the sight of Imani Evans at the store. The thoughts swirled in my head as I drifted in and out of sleep in front of the TV until they were a blurred mass of confused images in my sleepy mind and I dreamed of blue-haired imps bouncing quarters off my head.

My ringing telephone jarred me from a disturbed sleep.

I answered the phone. The caller had the wrong number. Stretching and yawning, I got up, turned off the television and called it a night.

Now that it was time to sleep I was wide awake. Even the soft hum of my fish tank didn't lull me over like usual. I lay there rationalizing that I was restless because I'd gone to the gym too late and the release of endorphins was to blame. I refused that other notion that I had more on my mind, namely more Miss Evans, than I cared for. After thirty minutes of futile denial I finally gave into my psyche and let it do what it needed.

I admitted that against my will I considered Nia's mom very attractive. She was enticing. I also considered her an illusion of sorts because my rational, analytical self said there was nothing worth further examination. Any interest on my part would be hazardous . . . just like the spill in the grocery store. Any courtesy I may have been tempted to extend would most likely be tossed back in my face. I had no intention of setting myself up as a candidate for an emotional beat down.

So why are you tripping then, B.? Because!

Rational analyzing aside, the woman is fine! I will never believe in love at first sight, but I've seen this woman twice in one week and both times I felt that little dip above the groin that signals I'm vibing off a delicious sister. My knowledge of her is extremely limited, and I have no encouragement whatsoever to hit a personal note with her. Besides, I saw her hugged up with that Nigel guy at the gig earlier tonight.

I sat straight up in bed. Nigel Evans! It couldn't be coincidental. That had to be Nia's father.

Dag, man! If old Pepsodent perfect was still in the picture then it was all over but the shout.

But all of that aside, I knew something else. I was wrong. I was pissed the day Nia's mom met with me in my office. I was mad at the world as a result of my car being stolen so I vented some of my anger at her expense. Okay, I'm big enough to admit that I was judgmental and harsh, perhaps even antagonistic. Still, she hadn't been a saint.

"Son, two wrongs don't make one right," I recalled Pops telling me time and again.

Yeah, well . . .

Pops had a point. I owed her an apology.

I kicked off my covers and hopped out of bed. Tuning my stereo to the local oldies but goodies station, I opened the blinds at my window to let the moon creep in. The silver lady of the night had a soothing effect so that I got back into bed and dropped off into a sleep free of chocolate goddesses and blue-haired imps with butterfly wings.

IMANI

There was an ocean-like breeze in the valley. It stirred the air with cool, invigorating fingers. Sacramento responded by exposing a soft glory. It was an April day ripe with the lush whispers of spring.

Imani was too preoccupied to notice the wonders of God's world. She was late for her hair appointment.

The westbound traffic on Highway Fifty was as outrageous as a sumo wrestler in stiletto heels. Traffic at a complete stop, Imani drummed her fingernails against the steering wheel while slowly rocking her head from side-to-side in an effort to ease tension from her neck.

"Mom, check this out! According to my social science book isolation can be bad for one's health."

Imani shot Nia a sidelong glance before returning her attention to the roadway ahead.

"It says here," Nia paused to clear her throat before reading, " 'Homo sapiens are communal beings who require direct contact and interaction with other members of the human family. A lack of healthy interaction may lead to a host of disorders that include, but are not limited to, agoraphobia, sensory deprivation, the inability to function properly in society, or an unnatural fear of intimacy.' "

Nia stopped reading and looked at her mother.

"What's agoraphobia?"

"A condition you're going to develop if you don't stop bothering me about being on restriction . . . I mean *isolation.*"

"I didn't say anything about my punishment, Mom. I was just showing love by sharing knowledge from my textbook," Nia innocently proclaimed.

"Mmm-hmm, well show your mother some love and change the radio station before Mariah Scarey gives me a migraine."

Nia complied.

"Oh, Mom, Daddy said when he gets back he'll take a look at my computer to see what's wrong with it."

"When did you talk to your father?" Imani wondered, having had the privilege of not communicating with him since the sorority affair last week. Thoughts of her picture with him appearing in the local newspaper still vexed her to no end.

"I got an e-mail from him yesterday," Nia answered.

"When will he be back?" Imani asked, merging onto the Sixteenth Street off-ramp, glad that she was finally exiting the congested freeway. A drive that normally took less than fifteen minutes from home had tripled in time. Imani had already phoned her stylist to inform her that she would be late, basically forfeiting her scheduled appointment. Hopefully the wait at the shop would not be too bad as it was only Thursday afternoon and the weekend rush had not begun.

"Weekend after next," Nia responded to her mother's question, as she stuffed her textbook in her backpack before tossing the satchel onto the back seat.

Too little time to build up enough muscle so I can beat him down, Imani mused, a throaty giggle escaping her mouth at the thought.

"What's funny?" Nia asked.

Imani shook her head, her dimples flashing with her grin.

"Nothing," she replied as she headed toward G Street, amusing herself with the notion of her ex-husband in traction.

The odors of styling implements and hair products, mixed with the sounds of jovial chatter against a backdrop of piped-in music, provided a warm and familiar greeting as they entered the salon.

Imani glanced about the building's interior. Her parents had spent a pretty penny renovating the old bank into a posh salon featuring rich cherry wood fixtures and furnishings, hardwood floors, recessed lights, and decorative walls that featured ethnic-looking borders on the bottom half and mirrors on top. Two manicure tables, ten styling stations, a bank of hair dryers and shampoo bowls preceded an isolated massage therapy room at the rear. Imani had to give her mother her props. Miss McGee's was inviting and faultlessly arranged. Her mother even possessed the foresight to designate an area in the lobby where children accompanying their parents could read, draw, color or play. Smiling briefly at the two patrons waiting in the lobby, Imani approached the massive reception counter decorated with a humongous terra cotta vase filled with long-stemmed white roses. Serving to separate the lobby from the styling area, the counter stretched across the front of the room and had two passageways on either side of it for traffic flow.

"Hi, Stacey. Sorry I'm late," Imani called as she walked past the currently unmanned front desk and into the styling area.

Her stylist, who appeared to be putting the final touches on a client's hair, glanced up as Imani approached.

"Hey, Imani. Give me a few minutes and I'll be ready for you."

"Don't rush. I'm going back to see my mother. Let me know when you're ready."

"Okay. Hey, Miss Nia. You need to give me those jeans," the stylist cooed, admiring the bead-fringed Capri jeans Nia wore.

"They're cute, huh?" Nia concurred, hopping onto the empty chair in the station next to Stacey's.

"Where'd you get those?"

"My mom got them for me on one of those days when her fashion radar was on hit."

Imani ignored the laughter at her back as she went in search of her mother.

She found her mother sitting at a well-polished mahogany desk eating a tossed green salad. An apple, an orange, a Ziploc bag filled with pretzels and a container of water waited atop a placemat. Eunetta McGee Carmichael was on a diet. Again.

"Okay, Mother, where are you and Ray headed now?"

Eunetta looked up and smiled. She was an older, shorter, fairer version of her daughter. Or as Miss Eunetta would put it, Imani was a younger, taller, chocolate adaptation of herself. Dabbing her mouth with a napkin, Eunetta stood and came from behind her desk to hug her only child.

"Now why do you ask that?"

"Because," Imani replied, returning her mother's hug, "you're eating rabbit food and you only do that before going on vacation or to some event for which you feel compelled to wear some dress two sizes too small."

"Well, you're wrong," Eunetta declared, smoothing her short-cropped salt and pepper hair. Sheepishly she added, "It's not a dress, it's a swimsuit. We're going to Cancun this summer and the suit is *three* sizes too small. So there!"

Imani dropped onto the chair opposite her mother's desk.

"Mother, why don't you just purchase a bathing suit in a size that fits you? And is this all you're eating for dinner?" Imani asked, sizing up her mother's meal before pulling a pretzel from the bag and popping it into her mouth.

"First of all, Miss Missy, I can't find a suit in my size. And second of all, that's not dinner. It's a late lunch."

"Mother, it's almost five o'clock," Imani announced, consulting her watch. "You're just now eating lunch? What in the world have—"

"Don't start with me, little girl," Imani's mother replied, resuming her seat and her meal. "You're as bad as your stepfather. Save all that fussing for Nia Nicole. And where is my granddaughter?"

"Pulling Stacey's ear about one thing or another," Imani supplied. "And, yes, you *can* find a swimsuit in your size. It's not like you're a Venus Hottentot or something."

"A who?"

"Venus Hottentot. It's a carving of an extremely voluptuous and obese African female that served as a fertility symbol in . . . Never mind," Imani abruptly concluded, encountering her mother's perplexed and disinterested frown. "If you'd like I'll go with you to help you select a swimsuit that compliments your shape."

"I'll think about it," was Eunetta's noncommittal reply as she crunched a forkful of salad. "So what's new in Imaniville? You look tired."

"I am," Imani admitted. Sitting there surrounded by proof of her mother's sharp business acumen and success, Imani felt a familiar fluttering within her heart. The sensation was pleasant as it was caused by the ever-present thought and desire to establish her very own boutique. Imani felt the idea pulling at her more and more in the time since her return from Phoenix. It was as if that unwanted journey had somehow sparked a small ember that refused to die, a longing for independence and self-sufficiency. Perhaps it *was* time. As if only now aware that her mother watched her intently, and not wanting to divulge her entrepreneurial plans just yet, Imani hastily supplied, "I've been busy at work."

Her mother nodded her understanding.

"How was your sorority gathering?"

"The Spring Fling was nice," Imani began, giving her mother details of that night's events as she helped herself to more pretzels. As she mentally revisited the festivities Imani's mind paused on one image in particular: Braxton Wade, guidance counselor from hell. Many days had passed since then and still Imani found herself resisting memories of the man. So what if he, daring to be different from the other tuxedo-clad men in attendance, looked lip-smacking good in his black Armani and ecru shirt accentuated by a pale gold silk tie? Still he was, to borrow from the dictionary of Monique, "bootsy." Imani looked off into space. Had she really glimpsed what could have been a tear in his eye after "My Funny Valentine" was performed? And had he actually tried to say something decent about her parenting as they sat at the table just before he left? Imani was unsure, but any man who could get choked up on "Valentine" might deserve a second look.

"So, did you meet any interesting gentlemen?" her mother inquired, snapping Imani from her reverie. Imani shrewdly scrutinized the too innocent look on her mother's face.

Lord, here we go.

"Nope, not a one."

"Hmm," Eunetta murmured and bit her apple. Eunetta was well versed in her daughter's reluctance to date. Imani was a devoted mother. Single parenting consumed the bulk of her time and energy, and what she had left over she gave to her job and sometimes the church. Thinly veiled excuses as far as Eunetta was concerned. She had been a single parent and managed to enjoy romantic liaisons while raising a child. *Mere excuses,* she concluded with a shake of her head. "You shouldn't be single. Maybe if you changed your hair or something."

"Mother," Imani stated, a warning note in her voice, "I like my hair natural."

"So do I," Eunetta quickly amended. "It's just so . . . free."

"You mean wild. Correct me if I'm wrong, but didn't you tell Mo you like her hair when she shampoos and air dries it and wears it loose?"

"Oh, please, Imani. My niece is half-white. Monique's hair is supposed to look crazy."

Imani sat with her mouth open, looking at her mother in disbelief.

"Mother! No, you didn't. I'm telling Mo you said that!"

Eunetta laughed. "You better not. I'll deny every bit of it."

"Deny every bit of what?" Nia asked, entering her grandmother's office.

"Oh, never you mind. Come over here and give your grammy some sugar."

Nia treated her grandmother to her customary greeting. She hopped on her lap and blew a raspberry kiss on her cheek to Eunetta's delight. Imani smiled, her heart warmed by the thought that her daughter still derived satisfaction from "childish" demonstrations of love. If only Nia's innocence would never end.

"How's Grampy?" Nia inquired of her grandfather.

"Just dandy and waiting for your next visit. Heavenly Father in Zion! Nia Nicole what have you been eating?"

"Nothing. Mom's starving me."

"Kill the comedy act, Nia," Imani said, trying to look stern.

"Well, 'nothing' sure is putting something on my grandbaby's skinny bones. What is this?" Eunetta asked, patting Nia's thighs. "And what are these?" she exclaimed, prodding Nia's chest.

"Grammy, stop!" Nia squealed as her grandmother tried to lift her shirt. "Mom, make Grammy stop it!"

Imani suppressed a laugh. "Mother, please don't torment my child."

"Imani, this girl needs a brassiere."

"Nia has plenty of bras."

"I'm wearing one now," Nia proudly informed her grandmother.

"Let me see it."

"Mom," Nia whined.

"Mother!"

"Okay, okay," Eunetta chortled.

"Stacey's ready for you now, Mom."

"Thanks."

Imani stood and turned toward the door.

"Ooh, sweet Jesus, lamb of God! Well, there's no mystery where you got all these hips from, Nia Nicole," Eunetta muttered *sotto voce* in Nia's ear while watching Imani. "Looks like a booty fest is going on over there."

Nia cracked up.

"The apple doesn't fall from the tree," Imani returned, pausing to glance over her shoulder and look pointedly at her mother before switching out of the room.

"Well, go ahead with your good self, Jelly Roll," her mother called as Imani headed down the hall for her stylist's chair.

Imani liked her hair. Stacey had trimmed the ends, deep conditioned then secured her shoulder-length mane, with the aid of a lightly scented pomade, into tiny twists and set the ends on curlers while the hair was damp. After nearly an hour beneath the dryer, her stylist carefully unraveled the twists and styled the hair with her fingers so that it fell in attractive spirals about Imani's face and shoulders.

Very nice, Imani told her reflection as she primped before the mirrors in her walk-in closet. Her raspberry-colored skirt set complimented her deep complexion. The long-sleeved blouse tied at the side, enhancing her waist, and the matching knee-length skirt with its flower-embossed black sheer overlay hugged her hips just right. Imani felt strangely uninhibited. Perhaps it was the hair or the fact that she was going out on a week night instead of sitting in front of the television salivating over some handsome man far removed from her comic affections. Whatever the source of her freedom, she was thankful.

The doorbell rang.

Either Monique was early or Imani was running late as usual.

Imani glanced at her watch. It was the former.

Grabbing her pale pink suede jacket and black Adolfo pumps from the closet, Imani doused the lights and raced to dab perfume behind her ears before slipping her feet into her shoes and running from the room.

"Okay, already, I'm coming!" Imani hollered as the doorbell sounded again. She quickly descended the stairs, wondering why Monique did not use her key to enter, and swung open the front door only to stare at the woman on her doorstep.

True to form, Monique was dressed for bohemian success. She wore a pale orange floppy knit hat that accented the multi-colored, off-the-shoulder peasant blouse that fell from its cinched waist in loose folds over the bright tangerine, ankle-length skirt beneath which peeked the tips of Imani's brown suede boots covering Monique's slender feet.

"Hey, Mani," she sang in her light, soprano voice and stepped through the open doorway. "You look nice. Rather like a capitalistic consumer of overpriced American goods, but nice nonetheless."

"And you look shabby chic," Imani tossed as she closed the door behind her cousin and glanced down at her feet. "I guess this is your way of returning my footwear. Why didn't you use your key?"

"Oops . . . I was lost in my recitation," Monique advised, heading toward the kitchen where she grabbed a bottle of juice from the refrigerator. "I'm nervous about tonight's slam competition."

"Why? Mo, you come alive onstage and give flawless performances."

"Wow, thanks, Mani. I appreciate that." Monique shrugged. "I guess I just have a peculiar sense of my own infinitesimal worth tonight, and how a woman is a dynamic force in the circle of life, but how none of us is really larger than a small cog in the greater sphere of things."

Silence descended on the room.

"Okey dokey then, that's truly special," Imani remarked. "Deep moment over; are you ready?"

"Let's move, girl," Monique sang, turning toward the front door.

Imani followed, pausing to engage the house security system just as the telephone rang. She had recently connected the new answering machine purchased to replace the defunct one, still for a split second Imani hesitated, then disarmed the system and raced toward the kitchen to answer the phone.

"I'll meet you in the car," Monique called as Imani reached the kitchen and saw her parents' number displayed on the caller I.D.

"Hello?"

"Hi, Mom, are you gone yet?"

"Nia, if I were gone could I answer the phone?"

"When are you leaving?"

"Right now. Your godmother's waiting. What did you need, Snookie?" Imani inquired as patiently as possible.

"Did Krista call?"

"No."

"Okay. Oh! You don't have to pick me up on your way home. Daddy's back and he's giving me a ride home in his brand new Porsche!"

Imani was stunned into silence.

"Okay, have fun," Nia cheerfully continued. "Tell Aunt Mo I said 'good luck'."

"Bye," Imani mumbled, slowly disconnecting the call. Nigel had a new sports car and the cretin couldn't even pay child support or alimony? Imani stood there lost in thought when the phone rang a second time.

What now? Did her daughter forget to tell her that Nigel had a new mansion in Malibu as well? Imani snatched the phone off the hook. With annoyance tainting her tone, she half-sang, half-gritted into the phone, "Yes, Nia!"

"Miss Evans? Sorry to interrupt you. This is Braxton Wade, Nia's guidance counselor."

She recovered quickly and stuttered, "Y-yes, hello, Mr. Wade. How can I help you?"

"Sounds as if you're in a hurry. Why don't I phone you later?"

"I am on the way out the door, but it's okay," Imani replied, her tone less than effusive, but her interest piqued. Good Lord. Was Nia in trouble again?

"I'll make this quick. Are you attending the school event tomorrow evening?"

"Yes. Nia and I will be there."

"Is it possible for me to have a few minutes of your time then?"

"I don't see why not," Imani answered.

"What I need to discuss with you shouldn't take long. I'll see you tomorrow."

"Good night, Mr. Wade."

She stood in silent contemplation so that when the phone rang yet again she jumped. Enough was enough. Imani ignored the call and headed for the door, hearing the answer machine click on and the caller state, " 'Sup, Nia. It's Clarence."

She made a mental note to ask Nia about that particular hormonal juvenile who kept calling her house.

Imani finally made it out the door without further interruptions. She hopped into her cousin's Toyota Camry and closed the door, apparently a bit too forcefully.

Monique raised an eyebrow and stared at Imani before turning the key in the ignition. "What's wrong?"

"Nothing," Imani replied. A quick sideways glance confirmed that her cousin sat, watching her intently. She and Monique had always been open and honest with one another so that there was very little one could hide from the other. Imani knew she might as well come clean. "That was Nia who called. She said good luck and that Nigel will be bringing her home in his new Porsche."

Monique's reply was an open-mouthed and incredulous stare followed by a shrill whistle. "Dang, mookie, Nigel is without question a closet sadist who enjoys adding insult to injury. He owes you all kinds of back payments and he has the indescribable audacity to do something like this?" Monique trilled, echoing Imani's own sentiments.

Imani was quiet as Monique reversed out of the driveway and steered her vehicle down the street. What could she do? The same thing she'd done for years: nothing. This would prove another thorn in her side that she would endure for her child's sake. Nigel could be quite vindictive at times. He never failed to amaze Imani in his ability to manipulate their disagreements by either bringing Nia in the middle or insinuating that Imani's "unreasonable" exasperation or expectations would separate him from his daughter. He knew how to play Imani's guilt and fear.

"I loathe that sperm donor," Imani seethed, feeling as if on the verge of tears.

"Don't vex yourself, Mani," Monique cautioned. "Hypertension runs rampant in African American communities. We have to preserve our calm."

Imani shot Monique an irritated look.

"Leave the health care advocate soapbox at home tonight, Mo. Okay?"

"Sorry. I was just trying to lighten the mood. Anyhow, knowing Nigel, that car is probably leased."

"Even so, you have to put a sizeable down payment on a leased vehicle, Mo. You don't drive off the lot based on looks."

"That's true." Monique paused before carefully continuing. "But girl, you gotta give it to him. The man does look good."

Imani stared at Monique as if she had two heads and one tooth. "What? I'm just being truthful," Monique teased with a wink.

"Uh-huh."

"Don't stress, girl. It's going to be okay. Hey, Mani, what do you think about Braxton Wade?" Monique asked, taking Imani completely by surprise and putting a freeze on the bad mood wanting to possess her.

"Huh?" was Imani's only response.

Monique glanced away from the road.

"Braxton Wade, Nia's school counselor. That bald brother who was at your sorority thing last week."

"I know who he is." Imani paused not sure how to respond. "What do *you* think?"

"Honey, someone needs to thank his mama and daddy for doing the wild thang."

They cackled merrily.

"Why'd you ask about him?" Imani questioned, finding her cousin's inquiry odd after the unexpected telephone call she received. Maybe Monique *was* clairvoyant and connected to a hidden, higher power after all.

Monique shrugged.

"No particular reason. I just thought the brother was fine if you like that raw, muscle kind of masculinity, which you do. Hint-hint. Me. I like pretty boys. Plus . . ."

"What?" Imani asked, studying her cousin's profile.

"Oops . . . wait. Forget I even mentioned him because the brother is very handsome and all, but I remember that his aura was discolored."

Imani sucked her teeth. "I was almost ready to give you props for having psychic powers, fraudy."

"I am not a fraud. You're just a nonbeliever," Monique asserted. "Aunt Bill trusted me when she lost her cat and Spirit told her where to find it."

Imani rolled her eyes. "Yes, and Dixie was dead when Aunt Bill found her beneath the house."

"Spirit spoke on Dixie's whereabouts, not her condition. And what about when Spirit warned me Grandpa would fall and break his arm at last year's family picnic?"

"Grandpa's old and has arthritis in his hip and was trying to do The Running Man. I could've predicted that," Imani argued.

Monique remained unflappable. "Spirit revealed that Aunt Eunetta would marry Ray within three months after meeting him."

"Okay, already, all right. You hold the world in your crystal ball," Imani said with a short laugh. "Now back to what you were saying about Nia's counselor having a bad aura. What's that all about?"

"I got a vibe. He could be a psychopath or something."

"Mo, sometimes you're so ridiculous," Imani dryly stated, wondering if there really was anything to Monique's intuited message. She somehow doubted that Braxton Wade was a psychotic killer as Monique insinuated, but what if there lurked beneath his handsome surface something of which to be afraid? Imani hugged herself to suppress the tiny shiver rolling across her flesh.

"Mani, you still haven't told me what you think about the man."

"Does it matter now that you've deemed him a possible serial killer?"

"That's precisely why your opinion does matter," Monique asserted, a mysterious tone clouding her voice as if she knew something that Imani did not. "So?"

"Minus the nasty attitude, he's the kind of brother who makes my breasts itch," Imani answered with a happy shake of her head.

"That's a whole lot of itching," Monique returned.

"He's a whole lot of man."

Their raucous laughter soon faded so that they traveled quietly down a well-lit boulevard until Monique chimed in her bell-like voice, "Mani, I'm thinking of reciting a new piece tonight."

"Really?" was Imani's distracted response.

"It's entitled," Monique paused for dramatic effect, "Ode to O."

Imani gave her cousin her complete attention.

"Ode to O?"

"Yes as in the *big* 'O,' " Monique replied, a queer smile on her lips. "As in *orgasm.* You do remember orgasms don't you, Mani?"

"About as good as you remember what a pork rib tastes like."

BRAX

It's nice seeing so many parents out on a Friday. Parent-Teacher Conference week doesn't officially begin until Monday, but we're setting it off with a school mixer tonight. Yep, that's right: parents, students and school staff all in the auditorium getting their shake on. I say "shake" and not "groove" because the way some of these old timers are moving can only be described that way. I'm checking out this one Latino brother over in the corner with his wife dancing like Muhammad Ali filled with the Holy Ghost. Brother is quaking!

"Yo, handsome, wanna dance?" someone asked, poking me in the side for good measure.

I looked down to find Mrs. Greer, the study lab monitor, standing beside me, a grin spreading across her pleasant face. Now Mrs. Greer is probably older than my mother and slower than frozen molasses, but I was in a good mood.

"Only if you promise not to hurt me, Mrs. G." I grabbed her hand and waltzed her onto the dance floor. Shame on me; Mrs. Greer meant to put a hurting on a brother with all her gyrating and gesticulating as the current song faded into the opening bars of Earth, Wind, and Fire's "Let's Groove."

"Aww, look out now, Mrs. G. This is my era! I'mma have to bust a move on you," I advised as I started doing The Penguin.

"Shake your money maker," she sang, standing back to better appreciate my stride. "Bet you don't have anything on this," she warned and one-upped me by breaking off into The Hustle. I wasn't about to go out like that so I starting Popping and Locking, putting my Fred "Rerun" Berry on her. Man, Mrs. Greer was on a brother because the next thing I knew she was doing The Robot. That did it! I conceded dance defeat and backed up and gave her room.

"Get your groove on, Mrs. Greer, it's your birthday," the students gathered around began chanting so that our beloved study lab monitor worked that Robot until it was out of gas. "Whew! I'm through," she wheezed as the song ended and the kids and their parents cheered. "You young folks have at it." Mrs. Greer returned to a seat on the sidelines.

Someone howled, "The Soul-l-l-l Train," like the theme song back in the day when Don Cornelius was king. Then all these generation X-ers who weren't even a tickle in their father's testicles back then rushed to form a soul train line. The deejay kept the vibe right there and spun some more old school cuts. I made it through the line once, then let the kids take over while I did The Bump with a colleague. By the end of another tune I needed the bathroom, first, and some air, second. I finished in the restroom and made my way out of the gym just as the millennium kicked back into gear with some miscellaneous baby-faced boy band and their canned music.

The night felt good. The air was cool against my sweaty head. My aerobic workout for the night complete, I decided to sit a spell on a park-like bench outside the gym. I grinned, remembering my childhood days when the songs I'd just danced to were hot hits. Then I flashed forward to my junior high and high school days and all the dances and sports I missed out on because of my weight. I was that wall cactus at the dances, goofing around with the other remnants, acting like I didn't care that girls ran the other way when I waddled near. I was that roly poly who flunked P.E. because I couldn't do one of those pull-up/chin-up things or run around the track without stopping to call a cab. But that was then and this is now. Those days were removed enough so that I could laugh into the calm spring air.

After all my cutting a jig on the dance floor I was thirsty so I decided to return indoors and grab some punch from one of the refreshment tables.

Heading back, I rounded a corner leading to the entryway and collided with someone. Hard! I had to grab her to keep us both from crashing to the concrete.

Heaven be my witness I did not mean to grab her *there*. When I righted us both, I had one arm around her back and the other about her waist with a palm on her grip . . . I mean her hip.

Precious Lord, take my hand . . .

"Are you okay?"

Imani Evans—eyes wide as she gripped my shoulder with one hand—patted her chest with the other.

"Y-yes. Whew! That was close," she sighed.

Any closer and we could've been conjoined.

"You sure you're okay?" I inquired again.

She nodded and we released our mutual hold.

"I figured you must have gone outdoors to get some fresh air after all that rump shaking," she said, laughing softly.

She had this low, sultry, velvet voice that I wouldn't mind hearing more of.

"Were you looking for me?"

"Yes, I arrived late and wanted to make sure I got to you before the night was over. You said you needed to speak with me when you called yesterday."

"Of course. You mind if we stay outdoors? It would be hard to talk over the music."

"That's why I'm here, Mr. Wade," she matter-of-factly stated.

Together, we walked back in the direction I had just come from and sat on a bench beneath a lamppost. I couldn't help noticing the easy way she moved, smelling the clean scent of her perfume. And her hair was . . . liberated. I can appreciate a sister who's bold enough to flaunt her natural style with pride. She was dressed casually in black slacks and a white blouse. Still, there was something about Imani Evans that gently screamed grace and style.

"What did you want to discuss?" she asked, crossing her long legs.

I cleared my throat, scratched my ear then spoke as evenly as possible.

"Miss Evans, I owe you an apology."

I knew by her surprised expression and her momentary silence that she was not expecting that.

I saw her relax; her shoulders soften their rigidity.

I continued in her silence.

"When we met in my office regarding Nia, I was rude."

There I'd said it. How would she respond? I proceeded before she could. "I don't mean to offer excuses, but I'd had a bad experience that day and hadn't recovered by the time you arrived."

She nodded and softly stated, "My daughter later told me about your car being stolen. I was sorry to hear that."

It was my turn to be surprised, but I quickly regrouped and continued.

"Thank you. My car was recovered. Anyhow." I paused to clear my throat. "I said some things that were inappropriate, Miss Evans, and I merely wanted to ask your forgiveness."

"Imani," she stated.

"Pardon?"

"Imani is perfectly fine," she said.

I instinctively perceived that this was an olive branch of peace being offered me. I accepted.

"I'll call you Imani if you drop the mister and the Wade and call me Brax."

"I can't call you Mr. B. like the students do?"

Sweetheart, you can call me anything, anytime you want, almost slipped out, but I caught it in time. Where that came from, I wasn't sure. I'd have to analyze that little slip of the lip later.

I chuckled.

"Well, you know, that's a little sumpin' sumpin' for the kiddy kids."

Our laughter floated out into the night.

"Apology accepted . . . Brax. And forgive me if I was offensive in any way, which I probably was knowing how I can overreact about my child."

"Naw, you only cut me with that dental floss toss."

She threw her head back and really laughed then.

"I did do that, didn't I?" she asked, looking at me with beautiful shining almond-shaped eyes.

Dag, sister had dimples deep enough for me to bathe in.

Extracting the very same vial of dental floss from my pocket, I handed it to her.

"I offer evidence."

"That was too uncalled for, wasn't it?" she remarked, taking the floss from my palm, brushing my palm with her fingertips in the process.

"I'm a real man and all," I said, thumping my fist against my chest and ignoring the trail of heat in my hand, "but I was ready to curl up and suck my thumb on that one. Why can't a brother have green onion in his teeth after lunch if he wants?"

It took a moment for her to sober up from laughing. "I guess you're just going to have to hold that over my head."

I liked that idea. Not the hanging the matter over her head, but the notion that there could be future interactions between us.

"I'll let it slide if you go back to this dance with me and show these kids how grown folks do it."

Imani rose to her feet and cast me a dubious look.

"If I'm not mistaken, you were out there getting booted by an old lady doing The Robot. You can't keep up with me."

"I was being merciful, Imani."

"Mmm-hmm."

"Oh, you don't believe I have moves?" I asked, sliding to my feet. "Peep this." I gave Imani a little preview of my dance prowess by doing The Dog. I had one leg out to the side shaking it like crazy.

"You have to come harder than that," she taunted and started doing something that could pass for The Snake, jerking her head and undulating her neck from side-to-side. She even managed to lower herself inch-by-inch with each swivel of her neck until she almost fell flat on the ground, causing me to catch her by the elbow so that she wouldn't.

She laughed and regained her footing, admitting, "I guess mother's a bit rusty."

"Better get the oil out and lube it down," I teased, as we returned to the lively sounds of the Friday night festivities.

The following week was good. Pearl was back in running order with a brand new rear fender and sound system. I had yet to replace the music that was stolen from my car, but I had a check from my insurance company that was just waiting to be cashed on some of my all-time favorites. I'd probably have to search the Internet to replace my Bootsy Collins jams. It's not every day that a brother can walk into a record store, find that piece and hear my man sing "Aww, Bootsilla baby!" Classic.

So, my week was decent, somewhat hectic, but in a good way. During this week of parent conferences I met with nearly forty percent of my parents, which is remarkable considering the number of students on my caseload. I believe last Friday's dance contributed greatly to this successful turnout. Parents seemed more relaxed and amiable, less difficult if and when I had to address a delicate matter regarding their child. Even the parents who were unable to attend the dance expressed appreciation for the concept of their inclusion.

I think that dance was the most carefree fun I've had in a long time. Sometimes adults forget what it feels like to take off our shoes and let our hair down. Doing The Bump and The Penguin and getting spanked by Mrs. Greer's Robot put me in a good mindset and even helped me unwind enough to apologize to Nia's mom. And I'm glad I did. Not just because I like to consider myself a decent person and do the right thing, but because it also broke an unnecessary barrier. There really was no need for beef between us.

I admit that the moment Imani first walked through my office door I promptly and unfairly classified her as uptight and highbrow, and you already know how I feel about "perfect" people. Ain't got no need for 'em. I mean the sister stepped in smelling good and looking like money that I can't spend. So I categorized her, neatly, safely, and that helped me squash that horny-eyed demon that tried to rear its head when I was confronted by all her velvet beauty at that sorority thing. I am glad to report that Imani proved me wrong last Friday. Any woman who can out Penguin me is worth her weight in cheese 'corn.

I had promised some of my kids in the marching band that I would attend a competition before the year was out. Tonight is as good a night as any, especially seeing as how the top three schools from this competition will advance to the northern California finals and possibly to the state championship this summer. So I pulled Pearl into a parking space, got out and engaged her recently installed security system and made my way into the stadium with the rest of the late stragglers.

The place was packed. I tried to search out a familiar face, but couldn't quickly identify anyone so I just looked for an empty seat. Then I heard my name.

"Brax!"

There to my left, about seven rows up, sat Imani Evans waving at me, an inviting dimple drenched smile on her smooth chocolate face.

I waved back and climbed the stairs in her direction. I had to step on several spectators to get to her, but I didn't mind.

"Miss Evans, how are you this evening?"

"I can't complain, Mr. Wade," she replied. "And you?"

"Same here. Have I missed much?"

"No," Imani answered, shaking her head and lowering her voice as she leaned close and continued. "Just some band from hickville line-dancing to country music."

"That's cold," was my remark.

"Like my grandfather says 'the truth ain't always hot.' "

"He has a point. Where are we on the lineup?" I questioned as I discretely appraised her person. Even casually dressed in jeans and a pink silk-blend T-shirt with her hair pulled back, Imani looked good. I was beginning to think the woman didn't know *how* to look bad.

Imani unfolded a program that I'd obviously failed to obtain when entering the stadium and leaned toward me so that we could peruse it together. Her perfume invaded my nostrils with its exotic sweetness, and her fingers tickled my skin where our hands touched as we held the brochure together.

Suddenly, I couldn't care less whether our school band was fifth or fiftieth. I merely wanted to sit next to this woman and get to know her better.

And I did. Our conversation was lighthearted. Nothing deep or world shattering jumped off between us. We didn't debate politics, religion, world peace or Pulitzer prizes, but there was an openness that allowed me to feel as if any possible vestige of a barrier between us was truly eradicated, and I imagined us as friends. Our close proximity to one another tempted my body to imagine us as more. But I didn't go there. Often.

"Oh, wait, we're up!" Imani excitedly exclaimed, grabbing my arm as our school was announced over the PA system. We stood and applauded as our band came onto the field below dressed in their blue and white uniforms, marching to the beat of the drummers' cadence. There was no music, just the steady drum rhythm, as the band assembled on the field. Then, the conductor blew his whistle. The drumming ceased and the flag bearers snapped their flags into position. The whistle sounded again and they broke into the opening bars of Stevie Wonder's "Sir Duke."

You know that was all right by me. Apparently, Imani concurred because she was singing at the top of her voice, "You can feel it all o-o-o-ver." She wasn't America's next idol, but her voice was sweet.

Our band was straight jamming. The horn section was breaking off those riffs like mad. And you know kids can't do anything simple. The student conductor was straight clowning like he was on primetime TV, while the band was out there floor showing. The audience ate it up, and the band marched off to deafening applause.

"Aww, shucky ducky quack-quack," Imani crooned, turning to exchange a high-five with me. "We were good! No, as Nia would say, off the chain!"

I laughed as we reclaimed our seats.

"Speaking of Nia, was your child and her clarinet getting jiggy with it or what?"

Imani shook her head. "Can you say 'ham'?"

I chuckled then sobered.

"You have a decent kid in her, Imani. You did good."

That flowed out of me, unchecked. I knew absolutely nothing about Nia's upbringing or her parents' intimate role in her life, but I somehow felt it safe to assume that Imani was the primary caregiver. I knew she was divorced. I also knew that Nia's father traveled a lot and had been absent from Parent-Teacher Conference week, the school dance, and the initial meeting I'd had with her mother. I could only imagine what else he was missing out on.

A soft, strange and almost vulnerable expression passed over Imani's face. Her mouth opened as if to speak, but she quickly bit her lip and turned to gaze silently across the field below. I sat quietly, curious about her private thoughts.

"Mom! Mr. B.!"

Imani and I were milling about the stadium entrance amid a crowd of others when we heard the piercing shout. Because I'd actually enjoyed our brief time together I found myself prolonging the inevitable good-byes. I'm not sure about Imani's reason for lingering other than waiting on her child and maybe showing mercy on me.

Nia, dressed in street clothes, was moving swiftly toward us, waving and smiling, carrying her band paraphernalia in one hand.

We headed in her direction.

"Hey, Snookie!" Imani chimed as she embraced her daughter, hugging her tightly.

"*Mom,* don't call me that in front of Mr. B.!" Nia protested. "He might write it in my file."

"No, I wouldn't . . . Snookie."

"See!" Nia groaned. "What are you doing out here with my mom anyhow, Mr. B.? I haven't been in detention or in trouble—"

"Relax, shorty. Your mom and I were just showing some school spirit by watching the competition together."

Nia looked back and forth between her mother and me, a vacant look on her face that somehow caused me to think it masked some sort of displeasure.

"Nia, the band was wonderful! How's it feel to come in second place?" her mother asked.

"First would've been the bomb, but second still advances us to the area finals," Nia said with a shrug. "Mom, Krista and I want to go out to eat with some of the band. Mr. Ramirez says it's all right with him if it's all right with you."

"Aren't you on restriction?" I interfered, winking at Imani.

"Mr. B., why do you have to bring up old stuff?" Nia quipped.

"Who's chaperoning?" Imani asked, laughing. I stepped back to allow them to talk. I waved to a few students as they passed through the throng. "And how will you get home? You have money?" I heard Imani ask and Nia respond. "Okay, but I want you home by ten."

"Ten? Mom, there's no school tomorrow. Tomorrow is Saturday," Nia disputed.

"And you'll still be fourteen tomorrow, Saturday or not," her mother countered.

"Come on, Mommy, please just a little later," Nia whined, throwing her arms about her mother's waist and leaning against her chest.

"Ten-thirty," Imani relented. "Not a minute later. Understood?"

Nia kissed her mother's cheek. "Thanks, Mom. Bye, Mr. B.," she chimed and turned to go, stopping suddenly. "Mom, can you take my stuff?"

I grinned as Nia unceremoniously piled her belongings into her mother's arms then hurried off with a backward wave over her shoulder.

"Here, let me take that," I offered. I wasn't trying to score brownie points. My Pops taught me something about chivalry is all. Imani seemed taken aback, but expressed her thanks as I lifted her burden and followed her to her car.

Her Volvo was parked a few rows over from Pearl. I was a bit surprised that she wasn't sporting a Mercedes or a Lexus or some other form of my annual-salary-on-wheels. Imani's Volvo was laid and you had to rub more than two cents together to afford one of those, still it was a practical vehicle. Not pretentious. Once again I had been presumptuous and wrong about her person.

She popped the trunk with her remote, and I transferred the goods into the trunk's confines and lowered the lid.

"Thank you," she offered.

"My pleasure. It was good seeing you again," I said, extending a hand. "Thanks for saving me a seat."

"Saving you a seat?" Imani repeated, one eyebrow cocked as I firmly held the hand she offered. "I wasn't saving anything for anyone. You lucked out because I was on time for a change."

"I'll be sure to say a prayer of thanks in the morning."

She looked at me oddly then snatched her hand back.

"Quit playing."

I wasn't, but I didn't tell her that.

"Hey, are you hungry?" I asked instead.

"Not really," Imani answered rather stiffly before relaxing and amending, "Well, I am thirsty."

"Would you like to go out for a drink? Just coffee or something."

Why did I feel as if I were holding my breath underwater as I waited for her reply?

"Sure."

That one word expelled the wind and worry right out of me.

IMANI

Imani contemplated turning her car around and heading home. Instead, she pressed on telling herself that she was only having coffee with a new acquaintance. Nothing more.

Then why did she feel dizzy as if her world were spinning much too fast?

Stop flipping, she told herself, lowering her car window in hopes that the night air would help clear her mind.

She liked Brax despite their rough start. He appeared to be a good person. He had a warm sense of humor, seemed sincere, and from what she gathered from their conversation, he was passionate about his work and truly cared for his students. And he wasn't stiff or pompous. Not like Nigel. Brax had a certain essence, a calm about him, maybe a maturity that came from life lessons hard learned. And it certainly didn't hurt matters that he looked lip-smacking, toe-tapping, rump-smacking good.

Then why the angst?

Imani turned off the car stereo and drove in silence, allowing her mind to clearly formulate her thoughts.

Nigel was never a true love. She had married him because she was pregnant *and* to please her mother who was adamant that Imani not repeat her own mistake of bringing a child into a fatherless world.

The two-year marriage was a farce from the start. Love was lacking between them so they were left with obligation and resentment.

Unable to handle the load as new mother and student, Imani took a break from college while Nigel moved full speed ahead in his studies. Finding it increasingly difficult to live on her husband's financial aid, Imani found a job, leaving their infant daughter in the school's daycare center. The times Nigel was available to care for Nia, Imani often came home from work to find her baby in heavily soiled diapers, her hair and clothing a mess. Nigel was impatient, self-centered, hollering at Imani to "shut Nia up" if she became fussy or cried when he tried to study. Some nights it took all of her strength not to evict Nigel from the apartment paid for by *her* wages. But the final straw came after Nigel successfully graduated with his degree (without one word of thanks to her) and Imani expressed a desire to resume her post-secondary education.

Nigel laughed in her face, told her she couldn't handle the pressure, and that he wasn't playing Mr. Mom. Besides, he was ready to pursue a career in entertainment with or without her. Imani decided it would be the latter. She knew Nigel's shortcomings, and their precarious marriage had suffered a steady and rapid decline, still his lack of support and indifference toward her desires hurt her deeply. Imani filed for divorce, and prepared for her return to California. Only then did she discover Nigel had emptied their savings. Penniless and bruised, Imani was forced to temporarily live with her mother and stepfather until she could set things in order again.

Imani twirled a lock of hair about a finger and sighed into the night as she drove.

She dated infrequently after her divorce. Her mother told her she was being ridiculous. Her family was quick to remind Imani that she was not getting any younger, or as her grandmother put it, she was "wasting daylight." If she was going to find a man, she had better do it soon. Imani filed their comments away and told herself she would do what she deemed best. She was not about to replicate her own childhood by parading a chain of "uncles" in and out of Nia's life.

Her mother was a God-fearing married woman now, but that had not always been the case.

In her heyday, Eunetta had been a beautiful, popular woman who never lacked male companionship so that Imani's memory blurred with the chain of men who whisked in and out of their lives. Imani remembered feeling as if she had to fight for her mother's attention, as if the men in her mother's world were somehow more important than she. She recalled the instability, the longing for a permanent father figure so that the constant attachment and detachment that occurred after each of her mother's break-ups would cease. After becoming a parent herself, Imani vowed never to subject Nia to anything remotely similar. And if that meant not dating, or sparingly if at all, until Nia was off to college then that was one sacrifice she was willing to make. In the meantime, she could "window shop" and drool over brothers on television or in the streets, remote and safely removed, without compromising her child or violating her developing sense of Christian values. But now there was Brax.

He exuded persuasive magnetism. She felt it drawing on her mind, calling her near. His unrehearsed appeal caused Imani to abandon her normal restraint to laugh openly with him, to sit close as they chatted effortlessly at the stadium. Imani reflected on the brush of her fingers against his palm and the resulting unnerving rush. She remembered crashing into him at last week's school dance so that their bodies molded together indecently. That's when it hit her.

Soon you will stumble into the arms of love.

Her cousin's prediction galloped through her mind at a wild pace. Now was not the time to believe Monique's "messages." If she gave credence to that particular prediction then she'd also have to consider Brax having, in the words of the family psychic, a discolored aura.

Imani shook her head as if to clear it of unwanted ruminations. She was a grown woman who could speak and think on her own, and right now her own inward voice was speaking loud and clear. She was attracted to Braxton Wade. But was the attraction reciprocated? And if so, how should she respond?

"By drinking some coffee and taking your edgy self home," Imani announced in the stillness of her car as she approached the gourmet coffee/sandwich shop they'd agreed upon. Brax was already there leaning against the side of a vintage Mustang looking like something wild she wanted to ride.

Get behind me, Satan! Imani silently rebuked, waving at Brax as she parked. *Lord, am I doing the right thing?* she wondered before taking several deep breaths so that she was relatively calm by the time he walked over to open her car door.

Plus point, she thought, *the man has manners.*

"Is that your car?" Imani asked, pointing to the candy apple red Mustang as she exited her vehicle.

"Yes," Brax answered. "It was my father's, but now it's mine."

"I love classic sports cars! I can't believe your father parted with a vintage 'Stang," Imani incredulously exclaimed.

"Actually, I inherited it when he passed," Brax explained, a shadow passing briefly across his face.

"Oh, I'm sorry," Imani softly intoned, touching his arm briefly.

He nodded, then cleared his throat and waved a hand toward the coffee shop. "Shall we?"

Imani preceded him, pausing as Brax opened the door for her. The atmosphere inside was lively yet cozy. Together, Imani and Brax stood in line and inspected the menu posted high on a wall above a glass-enclosed counter display filled with scrumptious looking desserts.

"What will you have?" he asked.

"I think I'll try the double caramel brownie ice-blended mocha," Imani decided.

"You must not plan on getting any sleep tonight."

Imani smiled.

"Believe me, caffeine and sugar do not bother me. I'll be out like a light as soon as my head touches the pillow. So, what are you having, decaf, no cream or sugar?"

Brax shook his head.

"No, indeed. I don't do coffee."

"Then why did we come here?" Imani asked, concerned that Brax had put himself out on her behalf.

"Because they have the best honey Dijon chicken on focaccia bread sandwich that you'd ever want to eat. You should try it."

"Sounds delicious, but I'd better stick with my calorie-loaded syrup in a cup," Imani responded as they neared the top of the line.

"Ladies first," Brax said, deferring to her as Imani placed her order then opened her purse and pulled out her wallet.

"Put that away. Your money's no good with me," Brax advised.

"But—"

"But nothing. I invited you."

"I know but—"

"Imani, can you let me handle this? Go find us a table, please, before I have to read you up in here."

Imani nodded rather sheepishly before walking off to do as requested.

They sat at a table in a secluded and dimly lit corner chatting amiably.

"So you're the baby of the family, huh?" Imani remarked, sipping her beverage. "That explains a lot."

"Meaning?" Brax inquired, reaching for his peach-pineapple iced tea while waiting on his sandwich to be served.

"You have this cocky little attitude like you know who you are and won't take stuff from nobody. I think that comes from having that position of youngest child," Imani surmised. "You obviously had solid reinforcement and the care and protection of older siblings."

Brax sat back, ran a hand over his head then fingered his goatee.

"That may be true, but I can't say that I've ever been called cocky. Interesting."

"Yeah, right," Imani said, her tone skeptical. "You mean to tell me you made it through high school without someone jocking you about your swagger?"

Brax chuckled.

"Imani, you have no idea," he commented, then proceeded to tell her about his days as an overweight youth. "I wasn't wearing high waters or pocket protectors, but I wasn't far behind. So, believe me, whatever 'swagger' I have came late in life."

"I would have sympathy for you, but it looks like you overcame the battle of the bulge beautifully," she commented, only to become immediately embarrassed by her forthrightness. Maybe there *was* too much caramel in her coffee.

Brax smiled.

"Is that a compliment, Miss Evans?" he asked, his voice deep.

Imani shyly returned his smile before answering, "It is."

"Thank you," he replied.

Imani nodded and they slipped into a comfortable silence.

A server arrived to place the order in front of Brax, and making sure they had everything they needed, disappeared again.

"You sure you don't want to try this?" Brax asked, pointing to the mountain of a sandwich on his plate.

The savory aroma pervaded Imani's senses.

"I ate before the competition but tomorrow *is* Saturday and calories don't count on the weekend. So, sure, I'll have a bite since you insist." Imani accepted the proffered portion, her eyes wide as the flavors flooded her tongue. "Mmm," she purred. "That *is* good."

Brax waved a hand overhead to get the attention of their server.

"What are you doing?" Imani asked.

"Ordering you a sandwich."

"No, really, that's okay. I shouldn't eat that much. I'll just have some of yours."

"Woman, please, I don't know you that well," Brax teased, protectively hovering over his sandwich as he placed the order. He waited for their server to depart before sitting back and asking, "Imani, why are you concerned about calories, if you don't mind my asking? You're not dieting are you?"

"Sort of," she answered, not the least bit annoyed by the inquiry. Usually, Imani tensed whenever Nigel made reference to her "thickness" or a family member failed to hold her peace about Imani's "breast and booty fest." Brax's inquiry lacked ridicule so she responded openly. "I've been struggling with some extra weight for a while now."

Brax passed a napkin over his mouth. "Why?"

His response was unexpected. It gave her pause.

Imani did not consider herself insecure. She accepted the fact that her beauty as a voluptuous African American woman would never be the standard or the norm, and that her body type deviated from mainstream America's ideas of what was good and acceptable. She chuckled to herself recalling an article in some magazine she'd recently read while waiting on Nia at the dentist's office. It heralded the "return of curves" in Hollywood and featured snapshots of notable stick figures with knots and knobs larger than the average waif. Imani had laughed and wondered who "accidentally" omitted the photos of women like Halle Berry or Vivica Fox—women who, in her opinion, better exemplified the article's claims.

She was not an insipid woman and did not assign value to her person based on her physicality. Imani knew that she was more than pieces and parts fabricated for a man's sexual pleasure or objectification. Yet her body image was important to *her*. As was her health.

"I want to be healthy," she replied at last. "If I'm blessed to live long I don't want to be decrepit."

Brax fingered his goatee thoughtfully. "I hear you," he eventually stated. "I have an aunt who's pushing eighty-four and she still polishes her fingernails and wears high heels to church."

"Exactly!" Imani chimed. Just then her meal arrived, and Brax's empty plate was removed and his beverage replenished. Imani placed her napkin on her lap, said grace then proceeded to eat. Swallowing, she continued. "Plus I want my fourteen-year-old daughter to grow up honoring who she is as a Black female, and in my opinion that includes her physical self so I have to provide a good example."

"Looks like you're doing just that," Brax remarked, causing warmth to creep into Imani's cheeks. "So, Imani, have you always worn your hair natural?" he asked as she ate.

Imani paused, swallowing with a smile.

"I went natural two or three years ago."

"What prompted the change?"

"My cousin and a bottle of dye."

"Let me guess. Monique?"

Imani nodded. She told Brax how, after having a fresh relaxer, she allowed Monique to put blond highlights in her hair.

"I must have been temporarily insane to let Monique dye my hair when the girl can't even follow the instructions on a box of Rice-a-Roni. To this day I don't know what my dingy cousin did to that solution, but I woke up the next morning with highlighted hair lying on my pillow. I was walking around with my scalp all patchy, looking like Ray Charles had been up in my head. I tried my *best* to ring Mo's skinny neck."

Brax was doubled over, laughing. "I-I'm-m sor-r-ry," he tried to say.

"Go on and laugh." Imani giggled. "It wasn't funny at the time, but it is now. Besides, served me right. Black women have no business being blond."

Brax used a napkin to wipe tears from his eyes.

"So you went natural as a corrective measure?"

"Yes. My hair was badly damaged so I went to a stylist at my Mom's shop who specializes in natural hair care. Over time she gradually cut what was left of my hair and as new growth occurred she treated it without chemicals so that my hair could repair itself. I loved the look and feel of my *authentic* hair and have been wearing it natural ever since."

"It's very attractive," Brax offered.

"Thanks," Imani stated.

"Do you find that people treat you differently with your hair this way?" Brax inquired.

"You know you're the first person to ask that question," Imani replied, amazed. She placed her sandwich on the plate and wiped her mouth before continuing. "Very insightful." Pausing, Imani looked away as if to collect her thoughts before focusing on Brax. The words spilled out of her. "Let me say it like this: YES! My "old world family," as I like to call the older generation just shake their heads and lament, 'but you have such a pretty face, baby.' My younger kin thinks it's cool, but perhaps a fad. I won't even go into how some of my Anglo coworkers ooh and ahh and want to touch my hair, or just ignore it all together."

"And your daughter?"

Imani smiled, her dimples winking at Brax.

"Nia calls me Warrior Woman and says my hair makes me look strong."

"Hmm." Brax nodded, pondering the idea. "She's right. But I still see your softness."

Imani stared silently for a moment before blurting, in an attempt to diffuse the heat stealing over her, "Okay, see, you're just trying to have a sister get all emotional tonight, aren't you?"

Brax laughed.

"Just speaking the truth as I see it. So your mom owns a beauty salon?"

"Ooh, Lord, no. She is the 'sole proprietor of a unisex style emporium' better known as Miss McGee's."

"You're kidding! My housemate gets his hair cut there."

"Small world," Imani commented and smiled before resuming her meal. Moments passed before she spoke again. "Brax, why did you ask if I was dieting?"

Brax sipped his iced tea and looked directly at her, saying nothing for a moment.

"I didn't think you were being modest and trying to spare my billfold by ordering something to drink, but I didn't think you were dieting either."

Imani raised a brow.

"Or I should say I don't think you *need* to diet. Not that you asked my opinion," he quickly amended.

"Is that a compliment, Mr. Wade?"

He grinned. "Just the precursor to one."

Imani waited for the follow-up, but no further words were forthcoming.

"Must I beg for it?"

"Good things come to those who wait," Brax sagely advised. "Enjoying your sandwich?"

Imani nodded, chewing.

"Can I get a bite?"

She shook her head.

"See how you do," Brax playfully griped. "You ate almost half of mine and I can't even get a sniff of yours."

"Like you said, I don't know you that well," Imani bantered and sipped her drink.

"I'd like to remedy that."

The sumptuous tenor of his voice sent a sudden thrill through her veins, his candid confession jolting something inside of Imani that was dormant, almost extinct.

It was only 8:15 in the morning, but Imani felt energized. She tried to stay in bed as long as possible on Saturdays but not today. She was up and about and even had on her cross-trainers and walking attire. Imani was ready to take on the day.

She tapped lightly on Nia's bedroom door.

"Girls, are you awake?" Imani asked, opening the door and peering into the dark room. "Nia? Krista?"

A grumbled moan was Nia's reply.

Peering at the bed Imani detected the outline of two bodies beneath the rumpled covers. Nia and her best friend, Krista slept at opposite ends of the full-sized bed, their feet in the other's face. Imani entered Nia's domain and walked over to the window to pull back the curtains.

Nia groaned and slapped her pillow over her face.

"Rise and shine, sleepyheads. It's a beautiful day that the Lord has made, let us rejoice and be glad in it."

"Morning, Mrs. Evans," Krista Ramirez slurred, pulling the covers over her head.

Nia removed her own pillow from off of her face and treated her mother to a bleary-eyed stare.

"Mom, what are you doing?" she asked, her voice lethargic. "We're tired."

"That's because you two were up until almost three in the morning giggling and acting silly," Imani practically sang.

Nia stared at her mother before groaning again then flipping over onto her stomach.

"I'm going to walk Miss Pitman. You want to come?"

"Not," Nia slurred.

"Oh, come on, Miss Marching Band. Walk a block with your mom," Imani requested, studying the poster collection lining Nia's walls. Serena and Venus Williams, Mary J. Blige, and India Arie framed one wall with their bright and brilliant youthful beauty. That young model with eyebrows from heaven, Tyson Beckworth, Imani believed was his name, gave attitude from another. Finally, all alone on one wall loomed a reproduction of a group from The Dance Theatre of Harlem, striking lovely poses that accentuated the splendor of the long, artistic lines created by their lean bodies.

"Mom, I'm trying to sleep," Nia answered, her speech heavy, drowsy.

"Krista?"

"I'll pass, Mrs. E."

"See you later," Imani chimed, smacking Nia's bottom as she moved toward the door.

"Ma!" Nia whined.

"Bye, grumpy," Imani teased, closing her daughter's door and heading toward the stairs.

She found Miss Pitman curled up in her dog bed in the laundry room for a change, instead of in her preferred place at the foot of Nia's bed.

"Let's go, girl," Imani called, as she retrieved the dog's leash from a hook on the wall.

The Cocker Spaniel merely stared at Imani without moving.

"I'll give you a graham cracker when we get back," Imani bribed.

Miss Pitman hobbled over to Imani as fast as her antiquated legs could manage. Together they exited the house and entered the bright light of day.

Forty-five minutes later they returned to a still quiet house. There was neither sound nor sign that the girls had gotten out of bed, so Imani set about preparing breakfast.

Within minutes, delicious smells filled the air as turkey sausage and scrambled eggs sizzled on the stovetop grill. Imani poured batter into a waffle iron before placing juice glasses in the freezer to chill. It wasn't long before she heard telltale signs overhead.

Imani grinned. She knew her child. The girl would move for food if for nothing else.

"Hey, Mom."

Imani looked up to find Nia entering the kitchen several minutes later, scratching her temple and stretching.

"Well, it's alive. Where's Krista?"

Nia smacked her lips.

"Her mom picked her up so she could go to some stupid christening party."

"What's so wrong about a christening party?"

"It was for her uncle's cats!"

"Get out of here, Nia."

"I'm serious, Mom. Ask Krista. Her uncle has four cats and he's leaving them in his will and like he's throwing a big catered party for them today," Nia explained as her mother snickered. "Her uncle is 'special'. You want me to set the table?" Nia asked.

Imani nodded, chuckling while checking the meat to ensure it browned evenly before asking, "Do you want grits, Nia?"

"No."

"Good. I don't feel like making any and we already have enough food for three as it is."

"The table's ready," Nia announced shortly thereafter.

"Perfect. Let's eat."

They sat together and held hands as they said grace before partaking in the bounty before them.

"Hey, Mom, can I get my hair braided for the summer?" Nia asked as she buttered then sliced her waffle.

"Braided how?" Imani inquired, sipping orange juice.

"There's a picture in my black hair magazine with the style I want. I'll show it to you after breakfast. It has all these intricate French braids with beads at the ends. It's really cute."

Imani nodded.

"We'd have to check with Stacey to see if it's something she can do."

"She can. I already checked, and Daddy says he'll pay half," Nia assured her mother as she drizzled syrup over her waffle.

How magnanimous of him, Imani thought, remarking instead, "I'll think about it."

"Can you let me know soon 'cause I want to have my hair braided before Daddy and I leave for Nashville to visit Grandma and Grandpa and the gang?"

Imani forgot all about her eggs as she lowered her fork to her plate.

"You're going to Tennessee this summer?"

Nia was ignorant of her mother's displeasure at having been left out of such a decision as she excitedly conveyed, "We leave on July fifteenth and we're staying three weeks." Seeing the look on her mother's face Nia quickly added, "Daddy was supposed to call last night to tell you. I guess he forgot."

Imani took no issue with her child visiting her paternal grandparents. Mr. and Mrs. Evans were loving people who doted on their grandchildren. It was Nigel! Once again he had orchestrated plans involving their daughter without Imani's knowledge or consent. It was irritating to say the least.

"Well, make sure I speak with him the next time he calls, okay?"

"Okay," Nia answered before continuing her breakfast. "So, how was your date last night?" Though her voice was even there was a perplexing look in Nia's eyes.

"It wasn't a date, Nia. Mr. Wade and I merely went out for coffee."

"So how was it?"

"Fine. Now stay out of grown folks' business," Imani advised, playing her parental trump card to avoid discussing the issue. She knew Nia liked her guidance counselor, but Imani had the distinct impression last night that Nia somehow disapproved of or was disturbed by their having sat together. She had been a mere toddler and possessed no recollection of the chaos that led to her parents divorce so Nia held onto a childish fantasy that perhaps her parents would one day reconcile. Looking at her daughter, Imani wished she could spare her the disappointment of that impossibility, but she could not. That chapter of her life was over. Imani had moved on and Nia would one day need to accept the man Imani eventually welcomed into her world.

Is Brax that man? Imani wondered.

She was still trying to process the evening and the unexpected friendship budding between them. Imani welcomed the idea of their developing camaraderie. Whatever aversion she may have initially possessed was gone thanks to Brax and his ability to breach her defenses with his warmth and his lack of pretense, not to mention his penchant for catching her off guard. Imani had a flashback of them at the Capitol City Club and Brax recounting his advice to a pouting Nia, reinforcing Imani's parental role. Then last week he had apologized for his conduct the day they met. And yesterday, as they sat at the band competition, the man nearly brought tears to Imani's eyes by acknowledging her investment in her child's life. No such validation had ever come from Nia's own father. At the coffee house, Imani had found herself speaking and laughing openly and freely without the reserve that served as her usual defense. And, she was certain there was a physical attraction between them. Could there be more?

Imani shook her head as if to clear her thoughts and refocused on her child.

"Before I forget, who is Clarence?"

Nia's expression hovered somewhere between innocence and surprise.

"Huh?"

"You've received some calls from someone named Clarence. Right?"

"Yes-s-s," Nia tentatively answered before hurriedly concluding with studied indifference, "he's just some guy at school."

Imani scrutinized her child's expression, not completely satisfied. If Clarence was more than Nia claimed he was, so help her Holy Ghost, Imani would dust off her grandfather's hunting rifle and—

"How old is he?"

"He's just a friend, Mom—"

"Nia."

"He's in the eleventh grade."

"Then he must be at least sixteen or seventeen," Imani stated, trying to keep her voice as even as possible. "Do you spend time with him alone or in a group with other friends?"

"Mom, I know I can't date for two more years so Clarence is not my *boyfriend* boyfriend. He's just a boy who's also a friend. We're not having sex or anything."

Imani sat in silent assessment of her child, hoping she could effectively prevent Nia from growing up too fast or making choices that she might later regret.

Imani exhaled. She could not recall openly discussing matters of a sexual nature with her own mother. Imani could still remember how embarrassed her mother had been when she began to menstruate for the first time. She called her mother at work to inform her and her mother merely asked Imani, stammering all along, if she had sanitary napkins and a belt. Unsettled by her mother's discomfort, Imani said she did, not even knowing what a sanitary belt was. Imani called her grandmother who picked her up and took her to the store to purchase the items she needed. When her mother came home that night, tired after a day spent on her feet styling hair, she stopped in Imani's bedroom to stroke her daughter's forehead, offer her a cup of hot tea, and warn Imani that she had to be careful now that her "womanly issue" had begun. Such was the extent of sex education between mother and child.

So when, at the age of four, Nia asked where babies came from, Imani started by telling her daughter that God was the creator of life and how babies came from heaven. When Nia asked how babies got from heaven to earth Imani knew she had to take it a step further. So they took a trip the library to find an age-appropriate book then, together, they sat in the park eating ice cream as Imani read aloud to her curious child. When the afternoon was over Nia understood that babies came from the love shared between mommies and daddies. It was a start, and over the years Imani made it a point to keep the lines of communication open and natural. Now that Nia was at an age where sex was a real possibility, Imani hesitated. But hoping that her daughter was willing to be open Imani continued.

"Nia, are you sexually active?"

"Mom, I just told you we're not having sex," Nia exclaimed, irritably. "Not now."

Imani felt a nervous tremor roll over her at her daughter's reply.

Had she been so caught up in her own world that something significant had transpired in Nia's life without her notice?

"Not now," Imani blandly repeated.

"Gotcha!" Nia returned, laughing wickedly.

A relieved calm descended over Imani's rapidly beating heart.

"I'm glad you brought up the subject of Clarence, Mom, because he asked me to the Junior Prom and—"

"Absolutely not!" Imani replied.

"But, Mom, you—"

"Don't 'but Mom' me, Nia. You're too young to attend the prom with some mannish hypersexual boy!"

"Mom, the prom was two weeks ago and I told Clarence I couldn't go because my mother would bust an artery if I even asked."

"Oh," Imani contritely replied. Laughing she said, "You know your mother don't you, Snookie?"

"Yes," Nia replied, folding her arms.

"I'm sorry for going off," Imani apologized, placing a hand on Nia's arm. They resumed their meal until Imani asked, "Want to go to the movies today?"

"Sure," Nia sang. "But please, Mom, none of those sappy chick flicks you and Aunt Mo like to cry over."

"You can choose as long as it's appropriate."

"Cool. Can it be R rated since I'll be accompanied by a parent?"

"No!"

"Mom, I've seen and heard everything they could show."

"Not quite, Nia."

"Dang, I'm fourteen already," Nia sulked.

Imani put down her juice glass and gave her daughter *the look*.

"First of all don't 'dang' me," she warned, pointing a finger in Nia's direction. "Second, I'm thirty-four and I don't need to see or hear some of the mess in these films. And finally, if you want to live as long as I have don't give me grief."

The telephone rang.

Nia pushed back her chair and stalked over to retrieve it from the kitchen counter.

"Hello. Yes, who's calling? Mr. B.! Dang, I can't get in trouble on Saturdays. There's no school." Nia laughed at something he said then returned to the table and handed her mother the phone. "It's for you."

"Good morning, Brax. How are you?" The sound of his voice reminded Imani of his response to her teasing that she did not know him well enough to share her sandwich with him. *I'd like to remedy that* had been his reply. Imani decided the notion was mutual.

"Brax?!" Nia repeated, twisting her mouth and frowning. "Eww!" Imani put a finger to her lips, signaling Nia to be quiet.

"Oh, I'm fine," Imani answered into the phone. "What's that? Yes, I like basketball."

Nia sat across from her mother, exaggerating and imitating Imani's movements and speech.

Imani covered the mouthpiece with her hand and hissed, "Don't make me hurt you," then back into the phone, "no, not you, Brax, Nia," she stated into the phone. "Don't mind her, she's just acting as usual." Imani sat quietly, listening to the voice on the opposite end. "Okay. Was that all you wanted to know?" There was another pause. "Thanks, I enjoyed your company, too. All right. Have a nice day."

"Ooh, bye-bye now, snookums," Nia cooed rather irreverently, batting her eyelashes.

Imani disconnected the call and placed the phone atop the table. Suddenly, she jumped up and ran around to the other side. Nia squealed and ran in the opposite direction, around the table and out of the kitchen. Imani chased her, catching up with her daughter just as Nia reached the stairs. Imani grabbed her and they tumbled onto the stairs together, laughing, as Imani tickled her child until they were both out of breath.

BRAX

I forgot to pop in my contact lenses so now I'm squinting and driving like Mr. Magoo with a hangover.

I can barely make out the addresses as I slowly roll down the street knocking down mail boxes and running over stray cats while searching for Imani's house. Just kidding, I barely tapped that mailbox. Anyhow, I believe I have arrived.

Nice neighborhood. Kind of reminds me of some of the 'hoods back home in Indiana with the wide lawns and older, solid-looking houses. There were even a few kids playing in the street. It was Norman Rockwell meets the 'burbs.

I walked up the driveway and onto the path to the front door feeling apprehensive. Don't ask me why. Maybe it has something to do with the fact that Adam and Eve were prancing around naked at the time of my last date. Or could be that I like this woman even if doing so violates clauses one and two of my 3B Dating policy.

Okay, Imani has a child, but Nia's already past the rugrat stage. Imani has an ex-husband but I am not privy to her feelings toward him so I can only hope she doesn't answer the door with a whip, a fifth of Hennessey and a shot of gin.

I told myself to stop adding conflict to the Kool-Aid and rang the doorbell.

Momentarily it opened and Imani stood on the opposite side look-

ing like a gift I wanted to unwrap, flashing those dimples and welcoming a brother inside, all hospitable like, causing me to relax as we
exchanged pleasantries.

I was just beginning to feel good when this old, swollen-looking
dog came waddling up to me, sniffed around my ankles, then raised a
hind leg like my name was tree bark not Brax.

"Whoa, there!" I yelped, stepping back before Pissy could get its
aim on.

Imani glanced down.

"Miss Pitman, no! Bad girl," she scolded, squatting and picking up
the mannerless mutt. "I'm sorry, she only does that when she first
meets someone, and only if she likes you. I guess it's her way of marking you as territory."

"What would she do if she didn't like me?" I asked, cautiously
scratching the mutt behind the ears.

"Ask my ex-husband."

We laughed.

"Have a seat in the living room," Imani directed, waving toward the
room to our left. "I just need to get my purse and situate Miss Pit and
I'll be ready."

If the rest of the house was remotely similar to the living room then
it was laid. The sister had style and taste, nothing flashy or fancy, just
simple elegance. There was a blue sofa set with an oversized bur-
gundy leather ottoman serving as a table between the two pieces, a
Persian rug with muted colors, a console table behind the sofa on
which sat a vase filled with flowers, artwork on the walls, and a baby
grand piano in the far corner. Nice.

I walked over to the piano to admire the statue on top of it. On a
solid, oval base stood a figure of a Black man—his skin so ebony it was
almost blue—wrapped in white linen from head-to-toe, one muscular
arm escaping from his shroud, the other pulling back a corner of the
linen to expose a proud face. There were tiny crystals spattered on
the inner folds of the garment near his face and his hairless head.
The figure stood in stark relief against the sun affixed to a tall backdrop that rose up from the pedestal—its rays shooting outward like
fingers of light.

"That's part of my Thomas Blackshear collection. That piece is called
"Night in Day," Imani revealed, as she came up behind me. "There's
more on the reverse side."

I leaned forward to see that the opposite side of the backdrop was painted like the midnight sky with silver stars and a quarter moon.

"Very nice," I commented.

"I love Blackshear's work for the way he captures African American beauty and for the strength of character he imparts," Imani fondly stated, running a finger over the figure's muscular arm. "I find it inspiring and reaffirming . . . and if you don't stop me now we'll be late for the game."

"Passion is a good thing. I'd like to see the rest of your collection someday," I requested.

"You've got it," Imani agreed.

"Who plays piano?"

"I did as a child, but gave it up. Thankfully, Nia's starting to tinkle the ivories or this showpiece would be wasted. Are you ready to go?"

"Certainly. Oh, wait one moment." I reached into one of the oversized outer pockets at the thighs of my jeans and pulled out a palm-sized gift box.

"What is this?" Imani asked, smiling brightly, her eyes sparkling as she accepted the box.

"Just a little sumpin', sumpin'."

A huge smile stole across her face as Imani carefully extracted a shiny, red 1970 model Corvette.

I didn't bring flowers or candy because we were only going to a basketball game and I wasn't sure that that qualified as a real date. Still, I had a strong urge to be demonstrative even if doing so violated one of my sub-rules: *nothing* on the first date, not even nookie.

I was pleasantly surprised when Imani actually reached out and hugged me. I didn't leave her hanging. I hugged that body back.

"You said you liked classic sports cars so I thought I'd give you one."

"Thank you," she purred, squeezing me once more. "I'll find the perfect place for it later. And thanks for remembering," she concluded softly while placing the car atop the mantle.

"You're welcome," I returned, feeling cold after her warm softness in my arms.

"I'm ready if you are," she advised. I agreed. She opened the door and stood dead still in her tracks.

"I was just about to ring the bell," the man on the opposite side advised, his picture perfect smile enough to make a horse sick. His eyes roamed over Imani then past her to find me standing there. His smile died like an ant in a cloud of Raid. He sounded shocked when he said, "Oh, I didn't know you had company."

"Brax, this is Nia's dad," Imani introduced us. I wanted to laugh because the brother looked pained at Imani's failing to identify him as *her* former spouse. "Nigel, Braxton Wade."

He gave me some weak noodle kind of handshake as if afraid to soil himself by making contact with me. Dude was a straight trip. He waltzed into the house like someone had died and named him Lord of all. Even his voice was imperial when he demanded, "Where's my daughter?"

"She went skating with her friends," Imani supplied, standing with her arms crossed as if waiting for him to explain his presence. "Nigel, we were just leaving. What do you need?"

For some reason I didn't appreciate the way his eyes slowly raked over her form, or the sly, sardonic smile spreading across his lips.

"Where are you going?" he asked, shooting a glance in my direction.

"Out," was Imani's reply.

"That's obvious, Butter. Where?"

Butter? What was that all about?

I thought Imani's voice sounded rather tight when she responded.

"Nigel, that's really not your business. Again, what do you need and why are you here?"

"I'll make this quick seeing how you're in such a hurry." Can you believe this mess? He actually paused to check his reflection in a mirror on the wall. Old boy was patting his hair and running his tongue over his manufactured teeth like somebody here cared how he looked. "I stopped by to let you and Nia know that I'm moving to LA."

I'm sorry, but I had to laugh at the joy exploding in her voice when Imani hollered, "When?"

Old boy looked at me as if I'd up-chucked on his Italian leather loafers.

"Can we go somewhere private where we can talk?" he asked, shooting me a dismissing look.

"Brax, excuse me please. Make yourself comfortable in the living room and I promise I'll be right with you."

I can't even play a decent rendition of "Chop Sticks," but I sat at the piano tinkling absently with the keys, trying not to be nosey and indulge in an overheard conversation. The house might as well have been an amphitheater because sound carried easily, bouncing off the high ceilings and right into my ears.

Imani's ex was droning on about his soap opera role, influx of fan mail, positive audience response, ad nauseam. I heard something about his part being made permanent. He was moving to the land of angels to be a big star.

"I leave in a few days so I need to store some things in your garage."

Cuddy had nerve. Like he couldn't afford a storage unit with all the bank he was about to make. I shrugged and kept playing and would have missed something but for the sharp tone in Imani's voice that put a pause on the off-brand concerto I was tapping out.

"Nigel, my private life is none of your concern so keep your comments to a minimum."

"Don't think that just because I'm moving you can have some miscellaneous bald heads stomping in and out of my daughter's home," Imani's ex-husband rather viciously retorted. "I don't want her waking up to find your 'friends' at the breakfast table. I will snatch Nia out of here so fast you won't know what hit you."

Homeboy was hanging off the chain there. And whom was he calling a "miscellaneous baldhead"? Next thing I heard was Imani moving swiftly toward the living room.

"Sorry for the delay, Brax. Are you ready?" she asked, her smile not exactly reaching her eyes.

I met her at the door.

Her ex joined us in the entryway.

"Can we finish our discussion?" he demanded.

"We are finished. Good night, Nigel," Imani purred, holding the door open. I had to give babygirl her props. She was smooth, handling the man with a certain grace I found attractive. Without so much as a backward glance, he sauntered past us and out toward a phat black-on-black Porsche parked in the driveway beside Pearl. He got in and sped off, burning rubber in the process as we exited the house. I helped Imani into the car and paused to look at her. On the surface she seemed unruffled, but I was still concerned.

"Is everything okay?"

She exhaled softly before turning to look at me. With a real smile that reached her dimples she nodded and simply said, "It is now."

* * *

When we arrived at the game we went straight to the will-call window. I'd had the presence of mind to order tickets online so we wouldn't waste time at the arena. The Sacramento Kings were taking on the LA Lakers and I didn't want to miss a minute standing in line trying to purchase tickets before the game sold out.

We had center court seats midway up from the floor. Pretty decent, even so there were Jumbotron screens overhead if we wanted a closer view.

"So Nia didn't want to kick-it with the old folks huh?" I inquired as we settled in. I left a message for Imani earlier in the day, inviting Nia to join us. Imani returned my call, appreciating the thoughtfulness, but Nia had other plans.

"Not when she could, and I quote, have 'crazy fun with her girls'."

I chuckled.

"Nia's dad is moving, huh?"

Imani grinned.

"I knew there was a God. He should have moved to Los Angeles when he first landed that recurring role," Imani said, explaining that her ex-husband flew back and forth between Sacramento and Los Angeles for taping on a regular basis. "Praise God his role was made permanent. I'm putting a bottle of Martinelli's sparkling cider on ice when I get home," Imani advised, frowning as her cell phone rang. Retrieving it she glanced at the telephone number displayed and made a sound of annoyance. "Speaking of the fiend. Excuse me a moment," she requested, as she answered the call. "Yes, Nigel?"

I sat back and watched the spectacle about me. The Sacramento Kings' fans are known for their rowdy support, and true to form, they were in full effect, ringing cowbells and beating pots and waving purple and white ribbons in the air.

"Nigel, get a grip," I heard Imani say into the phone. "Is my name Yellow Cab Evans? No!" Imani said, annoyed. "I can not drop you off at the airport tonight. I'm busy. Don't worry about how long I'll be out. I'm grown." There was a pause that ended with Imani sighing heavily into the phone. "Yes, Nigel, you can store some things in my garage. Now, bye already." Imani disconnected the call and looked at me. She shook her head. "The man needs Jesus and a lobotomy."

"That's hard."

"Honey, if you only knew," Imani remarked.

"Imani, if I'm speaking out of turn let me know, but is it routine for your ex to make demands on you? The brother wants to use your garage and he apparently doesn't hesitate to ask you for favors."

A guarded expression passed over her face and I had the feeling that I had trespassed on unholy ground.

"Brax, I do what I have to in order to keep peace in my home," was her candid reply as a voice came over the PA system to welcome all fans to tonight's event and ask that we stand as the "Star Spangled Banner" was sung. Some overdressed duo skipped onto the middle of the court looking like holdovers from the eighties with red, white, and blue sequin and satin jumpsuits. Why did they have to sing the song like they were at some midnight musical in a church filled with folks foaming at the mouth? They reminded me of those crazy characters on *In Living Color* named Cephus and Reecey or something equally ghetto. Imani and I looked at each other, amazed. This had to be a joke. If not, then the talent coordinator responsible for this comic relief act had better start a new job search.

". . . And the h-h-home," the man sang.

"I said the h-h-h-h-h-ome," the woman responded.

". . . of the . . ." he returned.

". . . of the, of the, of the, oh-h-h, of the . . ." she drew out unnecessarily long, then paused. Together the duo ended, "Brav-v-e . . . not the scared, but the brave!"

Imani was biting her lip as the audience thunderously clapped and cheered. We sat and I leaned over and warbled in her ear, "not the *skee-ee-eered*, but the brave," sounding like a wounded moose in heat. We lost it, laughing and gasping for air as tears rolled down our faces.

"Do you see your family often?" Imani asked as we sat munching on the overpriced snacks we'd purchased from the food court concession stands, barely paying attention to the half-time floorshow below. Imani was nibbling on a giant, chocolate-drizzled pretzel and washing it down with a frappucino.

"Is it safe to say you like chocolate?" I asked, watching her obvious enjoyment as she ate.

"Love it," she replied, licking her fingers. "I think I'd even eat chocolate covered bugs if you gave them to me."

"I'll remember that when your birthday comes around," I joked, biting into one of the two jumbo dogs meant to tie me over until after the game.

"Too late. I celebrated my thirty-fourth birthday on March first."

I choked. "Thirty-four?!"

"Yes," she chimed, frowning at my reaction.

"I thought you were twenty-nine, maybe thirty."

"So I had Nia when I was still in diapers myself?" she remarked, smiling.

" 'Ey, it happens," I said with a shoulder shrug. "Well, happy belated birthday, old girl."

"Thanks, I think. And just how old are you, Brax?"

"Thirty-two."

"Lord, I'm out with an infant."

"Is my age a problem?"

"I don't plan to make it one," she replied evenly. "When will you be legal?"

It took me a moment to respond after the veiled promise of her last words.

"My birthday's December twenty-seventh."

"Two days after Christmas? You've probably never had a real birthday party in your life."

I laughed because Imani was right. After exhausting the family funds at Christmas, my parents had little left over for party time. And my birthday gift was usually wrapped in Christmas paper *if* I received a present at all. But I have to give it to Moms; she at least baked a one-layer cake just for me instead of slapping a candle in a leftover piece of sweet potato pie. To this day, I still threaten to celebrate my birthday in August just so I can have a party and get something other than that recycled Christmas soap-on-a-rope or a nut-covered port wine cheese ball.

"I guess I'm going to have to host my own party. And in answer to your earlier question, I see my family twice a year: during school recess in the summer and at Christmas. I usually fly home to see them because there're too many of them to come out here except on occasion," I explained, filling Imani in on my mother, my married sisters, Alondra with her two daughters, and Cassondra whose five-year old triplet boys were paying her back for every mischievous thing she ever thought of doing. Speaking of my family I remembered a recent con-

versation I had with Alondra during which she informed me that I
was missed, my mother was lonely and the house could use a man's
touch. I assured Alondra that I missed them as well, but I wasn't biting
the Bring Brax Back campaign. I was a west coast transplant and liked
my home away from home. Observing Imani, I decided that California
was looking better as the days went by. "My family and I make an effort to stay connected by phone or e-mail or meeting online for live
family chats once a week. But enough about me, what about you? Tell
me something good."

Imani finished her pretzel, balled up her napkin and told me
about her being an only child, her mother's marriage during Imani's
senior year in high school, and her rather large family, who for the
most part live in northern California.

"We're your typical candidates for dysfunctional therapy, but we
have a lot of love to smooth out the kinks," she said with a laugh and
a soft sparkle in her deep eyes. "So, Brax, have you ever been married?"

I almost spewed the tropical fruit smoothie I was sipping.

"Remind me to tell you about me and Brandy and our date at the
altar," I said as the half-time act raced off the floor and a voice
boomed across the speakers announcing that it was game time once
again.

The Kings were up one-ten to the Laker's ninety-nine with three
minutes left on the clock. Unless a miracle was about to occur the
game was over. We decided to leave a few minutes early to avoid the
exit crush. As we walked, I told Imani how I'd planned to elope with
my first girlfriend, but my parents stormed into the chapel, Pops with
his belt in hand, ready to "beat some sense" into my "ig'nant head"
even if I was grown and two inches taller than he was. Moms and the
minister had to hold him down.

"How did your parents know where you were and what you
planned to do?" Imani asked.

"I had a card for unlimited rides because Pops was employed by the
transit system, but I couldn't even afford the fare for my bride-to-be
so I had to ask my sisters for bus fare to the chapel for Brandy," I said,
grinning as old images of that day flashed across my mind. "I was a
straight buster."

"So your sisters told on you," Imani correctly deduced.

"Yep. They were sitting in the back seat of the car laughing their heads off when we exited the chapel. And do you know my parents had the nerve to try and put me on punishment!" I interjected as she laughed, "When I got a job that summer, Pops made me turn over my paychecks to him to make sure I didn't plan another great escape. And if he'd had access to a house arrest anklet a brother would have been shackled."

"Brax, you're hilarious," Imani teased as we walked through the parking lot. "How long have you and Terrance been best friends?"

"Since college. We have our differences but we make it. He has his space and I have mine. T. gets caught up in his work and his life and I do the same, so sometimes we don't see each other for days and that's all good by me . . ."

"What's wrong?" Imani asked suddenly, the look on my face obvious cause for concern.

Not again! Pearl was not where I'd parked her.

"My car," was all I could grind out.

"We didn't park this close, Brax," Imani replied, looking about.

I glanced around for a familiar sight then squinted up at the row marker secured to a light post. Row B-1. Yep, this is where we'd parked. Daggone the devil to hell.

"Brax, stay calm," Imani cautioned, placing a hand on my bicep that was all bunched up beneath my sleeve. I guess she sensed that I was two inches from taking my draws off. "I'm certain we parked further out. Is there a pager button on your remote?"

Thank God she was levelheaded.

We walked up the row with me pushing the siren button on the remote on my key ring, but nothing happened. There was no telltale horn blast signaling my car was near.

"Just humor me, Brax, and let's walk the parking lot a bit."

I calmed down enough to realize Imani was right. We *had* walked a short while before arriving at the entrance of Arco Arena. So I did what Pops always told me to: remembered where I came from.

I took Imani's hand and together we started across the parking lot, doing our best to retrace our steps, me relying on memory more than eyesight since I had rushed out of the house without popping in my contacts and was blind as two bats and a newborn cat without them.

A few minutes later, I heard Pearl's security system holler at a brother and it was all good. There she was sitting peacefully in Row I-8, not B-1. That's what I get for not wearing my emergency horn-rimmed coke bottles that I keep in the glove compartment. Walking around here vain and dyslexic.

"See what teamwork can accomplish?" Imani sang as I opened her door. I had to smile.

I got behind the wheel and inserted the key in the ignition. I glanced at my watch. It was 9:45.

"I don't have to be at work until 10:00 tomorrow, and Nia's spending the night at her girlfriend's so don't worry about the time," Imani advised. "Unless you're tired and want to get rid of me."

"I plan to hold onto you as long as possible."

I think there was a double entendre in that statement that I would eventually have to analyze.

"Then I'm yours for the night," Imani cheerfully piped.

Was babygirl trying to tell me something? If so, I was listening, and I was ready to roll.

Pearl wasn't. She wouldn't start.

I turned the key again.

Nothing.

"What's wrong?" Imani asked.

I scratched my ear.

"I'm not sure."

"Are you out of gas?"

I shook my head and answered, "I filled up this morning."

I tried again, and again nothing. Just a funny little whir as if the battery were dead.

I knew that was impossible because I'd just replaced it two years ago with a Sears Diehard and those things were good for at least five years. Well, maybe not . . . if you left the lights on.

It wasn't totally dark on the drive over. It was a nice April evening with a nice glow in the sky, but again I wasn't wearing my contacts and needed that extra guidance so I turned on the headlights. I must have been caught up in Imani's rapture and failed to turn off the lights once we parked. Shame on me.

I started humming "Fix me Jesus" as if Christ was my personal, on-call mechanic. Hey, it worked. That is, I felt myself grow calm. I sighed and glanced over to see Imani looking at me as if I'd stolen James Brown's pressing comb.

"I hum when I'm stressed," I offered. "I think the battery's drained."

"Let's take a look."

"You know something about cars?" I asked, incredulous.

"No, I'll just keep you company."

We got out of the car. I popped the hood and did my best to see if anything was out of order with my sight-impaired self. Imani was right there beside me looking at the engine like she knew what she was doing. We were both busted.

"Do you have roadside service? Maybe we should call," Imani suggested.

I pulled my wallet from my back pocket and found my automobile insurance card with the telephone number for emergency assistance. I flipped open my cell phone and dialed the toll-free number. I searched for my debit card as I sat on hold and waited for a live body to take my call.

My debit card was gone.

I wanted to cuss, but my mother would have heard me in her sleep and awakened long enough to cast the devil out of my mouth.

"Can you take this for me?" I asked, handing Imani my phone so I could search the car to see if I'd accidentally dropped my card inside. It wasn't there. Man, I was zero-for-two at the free throw line.

Okay, think, Brax, I told myself, scratching my ear and kneading my forehead to help me think.

The tickets! I'd used my debit card to purchase our game tickets online. My card was probably on my computer table right beside my checkbook, which I didn't carry often either because I usually made purchases with the debit card, which I had unfortunately forgotten. And since I preferred using my debit card and always left my credit cards at home for major purchases or big emergencies I'd pay cash for the roadside service . . . if I had some. *Sheesh!* Look at this mess. I left home with a twenty and a five, but after my smoothie and two hot dogs and Imani's pretzel and frappucino, three dollars, a stale condom, and some lint was all that was left in my wallet. Twenty-two dollars ago I was a rich man.

By now the game was well over and people were streaming out of the stadium, passing us up to hop into their nice little cars that started without a hitch while I stood there with a dead Mustang and a souring attitude.

"Hold a moment, please," I heard Imani say. "Brax, there's a rep on the line."

I couldn't think of a way out of this one. I wasn't about to borrow money from Imani. Maybe I could get Terrance to bring me my card and some cash before the service truck arrived.

" 'Sup?" a brother passing through our row slurred at me with an upward nod of his head, saluting me as only we brothers can. He was gaiting—you know smooth-walking, what the old players used to call pimpin'—all geared up in his jeans and Fat Albert jersey, gripping an attractive Latino woman by the hand.

I returned his greeting.

"You need help, bruh?" he asked, all solicitous and stuff.

I was ready to front like I had it all together, but I didn't so I told the truth.

"Looks like my battery's dead. I have cables if you wouldn't mind giving me a jump."

"Give me a minute to pull up and we'll handle it," he promised before gaiting over to a phat Lincoln Navigator. His sound system was enough to scramble my brain as he started his engine and pulled into the now empty space next to us.

"Brax, I still have the rep on line," Imani reminded me.

I took the phone and advised the party on the opposite end that service was no longer needed. I disconnected the call and dropped the phone in my pocket. "Are you cold?"

The air was much cooler than it had been earlier in the evening and Imani was rubbing her arms.

"A little."

I ushered her back into the car, found my leather jacket on the back seat and gave it to her.

"Put this on to keep warm. Hopefully, we'll be out of here soon."

Thanks to the Navigator, Pearl was purring in no time.

"Man, thank you," I told the battery jumping brother, gripping his hand and giving him the Black man shoulder-to-shoulder tap that passes for a hug.

" 'Ey, no thang. You do whatcha gotta do for your people."

"You were my ram in the bush."

He chuckled.

"All you need is a little faith."

"What's that you're listening to?" I asked, liking the sounds of some contemporary gospel choir pumping from his stereo.

Animated and excited, he gave me the name of the choir and song title before asking, "You go to church, bruh?"

I shook my head.

"That's aiight. God knows your address," he said, hopping into his ride. "Me and my wife are out. Peace, bruh, and take care of that woman God blessed you with," he said, nodding his head in Imani's direction.

Imani and I waved and chimed our thanks as the couple drove off. I returned to the car wondering if Imani heard his last comment, wondering if God was trying to get my attention, trying to recall the last time I'd given Him mine.

Imani was rather quiet on the ride home. I was somewhat subdued after my lost car-dead battery-empty wallet episode, so we drove the streets with the sounds from the stereo between us.

It was almost eleven o'clock by the time we pulled up in front of her house. I couldn't even offer to take the sister out for something to eat, not unless she ordered off a ninety-nine cent menu and had a coupon. I felt like a punk buster. Still, I had to give Miss Evans her props. She didn't get her neck rolling, lip smacking, sailor cussing, read-a-brother-his-last-rites evil 'tude on even if she would have been justified in doing so after the way our evening ended. She, unlike some women I'd dated, bypassed an opportunity to emasculate a man. Imani had been right there beside me staring at Pearl's parts in the dark, searching for a fix. Now she sat beside me saying nothing.

I hoped her silence wasn't brooding.

I got out of the car and opened her door and escorted her to the house. I waited as Imani extracted her keys from her purse. Something fell from her purse and onto the ground in the process. Bending, I picked up a small laminated card and returned it to her.

"Thanks," she softly stated, looking at the card. Imani smiled. "My mother had this made for me," she explained, and turned the card so that I could read the bold print against a backdrop of flowers.

Imani: the seventh principle of Kwaanza. Her name means faith.

"Nia has one just like it, except her name is the fifth principle and is defined as "purpose."

"Very nice," I commented, then fell silent as she returned the card to her purse and unlocked her front door and disarmed her security system. Imani turned toward me ready to say something, but I cut her off. I didn't want a polite "good night" without expressing myself first.

I took her free hand and held it firmly.

"Look, Imani, this evening didn't end as I'd hoped."

"What were you hoping for?" she asked.

I scratched my ear and grinned, liking her direct style.

"Well . . . you know . . . I would have rather jump started something other than a car."

"Really now?"

"You're a beautiful, delicious sister, Imani, and I want to know you," was my frank reply that left her momentarily speechless. "Don't hold tonight against me." Imani stood there staring at me. Then she dazzled a brother with those dimples.

"Brax, if you're concerned about my being quiet on the way home, don't be. I merely felt that you were upset and didn't want to invade your space."

Dag, a sensitive sister! That's what I'm talking about. And that's what I want . . . Imani's *who* I want. No use bothering with the analysis, or wasting time trying to prove that what I felt was real. If I felt it then I meant it and if I meant it then I should go with the flow.

All you need is a little faith.

Isn't that what the brother-to-the-rescue told me?

I didn't need to second-guess myself. I just needed to believe. And I had more than a little faith. I had Imani. Or at least I wanted her.

And was she, like the brother had stated, the woman God chose to bless me with?

My pipeline to God was rusty from a lack of use. Maybe it was time to slick it down with prayer so I could hear Him again. Until then I could test the waters.

Still gripping Imani's hand, I stepped to her. She didn't back away. I bent forward and kissed her cheek . . . just in case I still had jumbo dogs on the breath. I ain't crazy! When I do lock hold on her lips I want this woman to remember the touch, the taste of my loving, not the funk of processed meat. So I let my lips linger on her face rather like a promise of things to come. She had the good nerve to slide her arms about my neck and hug me in return. The last time I'd held something warm and soft was when I took my towels out of the dryer last night. Babygirl felt good.

IMANI

Daystar Communications was "restructuring its ranks." Nice little way to say downsizing, which was a quaint euphemism for terminating employees. In light of the nation's recession triggered by a poor economy, unemployment, and recent events threatening the nation's sense of security, a decline in sales would have been plausible. But Daystar's customer base had actually increased over the past year, not decreased. Why then this sudden urgency to mitigate nonexistent losses and keep the company solvent?

"We are taking these measures in an attempt to secure *our* company's continuance," the CEO told the room filled with upper level staff. "We are doing everything within our power to keep your jobs secure, but everyone's cooperation is requested in *our* time of transition." The new Phoenix office was up and running, but a freeze was placed on the opening of future sites until further notice. Who, at the Sacramento office might be affected by possible layoffs was as of yet unknown, but proper notification would be provided and severance packages offered if worse came to worse. "Until then, we must do *our* best to keep employee moral up and ensure *our* company's continuance."

Imani cocked a brow at the CEO's repeated emphasis on "our" as if the news would be better swallowed if a sense of inclusion and responsibility were fostered. The floor was opened for questions that came firing from every direction. Thirty minutes later the meeting adjourned. Queries were answered, but uncertainty lingered.

"This is a bunch of crap," hissed a fellow employee walking with Imani down a wide hall en route back to their respective offices. "How could we be doing so badly if the price of our stocks is still up? They're probably trying to squeeze us old heads out because we cost too much," the other woman angrily accused, her voice rising. "And why all the talk about Phoenix?"

Imani shook her head and rubbed her temples. The beginning of a migraine was knocking at her door.

"I've no idea. All I know is something doesn't sit right with me," Imani admitted, as she reached the Training and Development department to gladly escape into the solitude of her office.

She sat at her desk twirling a pen, praying that there was nothing to fear. She had devoted ten years of her life to Daystar and she wasn't ready to have that devotion unceremoniously tossed back in her face with a severance package and a day-old cake. What if worse came to worse and Daystar did "restructure" her right out of the door? What would she do?

Imani knew her job skills and competence were sound. She could always obtain a position with another company. But was that really her desire? Imani pondered the matter only to conclude it was not. She was unwilling to start all over again. She had no wish to waste another decade working hard only to one day have the carpet pulled out from under her.

"Talk about your job security," she muttered.

Imani had always played it safe. She attended Howard University at her mother's repetitious request. She married Nigel after becoming pregnant rather than face parenting on her own. And when the divorce occurred she allowed her mother to persuade her to return to Sacramento instead of moving to New York. Imani stacked her cards on the side of safety. She lived in a safe neighborhood, drove a safe car, had a safe job. Or so she thought. She even kept men at a safe distance.

Baby, never be afraid to take a risk because even if it doesn't work out, you're young enough to try again.

Imani could not count the number of times her grandfather had given her that tidbit of advice, or how many times she had downplayed or ignored it outright in her attempts to do things perfectly the first time around, sometimes missing the mark.

Imani sat back in her chair and glanced across her desk. Between a framed photograph of Nia and a well-stocked candy jar sat the shiny, red Corvette that was a gift from Brax. Imani picked up the model car and turned it about. As a teenager she had fantasized that her first car would be a sports car, but she couldn't exactly strap an infant seat in a two-seater and go. Parenthood and practicality won out and Imani had driven sedans ever since.

She had backed herself into a corner with her cautious manner of living. Somewhere along the way some of her fire fizzled. Imani was and had always been the dutiful and doting mother making sacrifices for the welfare of her child. She put Nia and her needs first. For this Imani made no apologies, had no regrets. She didn't buy into the rhetoric espoused by many mediums from talk shows to women's rights groups about a woman's happiness being essential above all else and all others. In her experience motherhood was synonymous with sacrifice. Still, Imani was afraid she had wrapped herself so tightly into her child and, yes, her job, that she lost track of the autonomous individual she was.

Or perhaps, she thought, *my responsibilities give me the perfect front behind which to escape and avoid life.*

Placing the tiny car on top of her desk, Imani gently moved it forward and backward with one finger.

Imani wondered if she was, like the toy vehicle, spinning her wheels and getting nowhere fast? What was the use of watching her credit like a hawk and saving money for the purpose of opening a clothing boutique if she never did? Was it a mere fantasy to keep her warm when her world felt cold?

She stopped playing with the car long enough to grab a handful of chocolate kisses from her candy jar, unwrap, and slowly chew them one by one.

This scare with Daystar could be the impetus she needed to shake the dust from her dreams, she thought, suddenly remembering that she was a woman of action. She could not afford to "waste daylight" or be caught one day with her pants down, unready to proceed in life. It was time to shake herself. Immobility was no longer a friend.

That night after dinner, after Nia had gone to bed with the dog curled at her feet, as the old house quietly creaked with the settling of wood Imani sat in the overstuffed chair in her room and plotted a dream.

Her nature CD played in the background, treating her ears to the sounds of rushing water and nocturnal creatures as the scent of lavender candles glowing atop the dresser relaxed her mind. Legal pad and pen in hand, Imani made long- and short-term goals for her business. She made a list of pros and cons, her own strengths and needs, as well as contacts that might prove helpful in her endeavors. She amazed herself with her clarity of vision, and watched as a plan of action manifested before her eyes.

She needed to apply for a fictitious business name and license. She would have to apply for a small business loan. One of her sorority sisters was a loan officer who, at a function last year, mentioned special qualifying programs for businesses owned by minorities and women. Imani made a note to contact her soror. She would need to find a real estate agent, as the agent who sold her house to her was no longer in the area. There was no shortage of agents. Imani simply needed a savvy, reputable one to help her secure a prime site, she thought tapping the paper with her pen, because location could make or break a business.

Jamal Williams: Reina's husband! The business card Imani obtained from him the night of the Spring Fling was in her Rolodex at work. He was a realtor or developer or something along those lines. Imani quickly added Jamal's name under her "To Contact" list.

Then there were legal issues, employee relations, the matter of merchandise and motif, vendors and manufacturers, advertising, competitors, demographics and so much more to consider. Did she want the boutique to reflect an elegant or cozy atmosphere? Should she offer chic, business or evening attire? Would she also offer petite and plus sizes? The thoughts sped through her mind one after the other so that Imani, though exhilarated, was pressed to keep up with them.

Imani paused to glance at the sterling clock on the bedside stand. It was well after midnight. She was surprisingly energized. Still, wisdom got the best of her. Imani safely secured her writing pad in her bedside drawer before slipping into her bathroom to brush her teeth and cleanse, then moisturize her face. Securing a silk scarf about her hair, Imani doused the candles, turned off the lights and got into bed. She felt deliciously languid as she fluffed her pillows and lay down.

Imani was near the threshold of sleep when her eyes snapped open again.

Turning on her lamp she located her writing pad, found a clean sheet of paper and scrawled across the top in bold letters "My Life." It was time to fully rediscover the hidden parts of her heart, to satisfy a latent longing for an ideal mate who was strong, loving, caring, and self-assured. Over and again she retraced the words "My Life" until finally with a flourish she underlined them. Beneath the line she simply wrote "Brax."

"Beloved, I won't stand before you long today. My wife baked a lemon pound cake so I'm trying to get home." The man of God waited for the laughter to subside before reverently intoning, "Let us pray."

Imani bowed her head, closed her eyes and opened her heart.

". . . and merciful Father bless us to hear with our spiritual ears, and receive Your word in our deepest parts. Order our steps that we may walk in Your ways. In the mighty name of Jesus we pray . . . all in agreement say . . ."

The church concluded together, "Amen."

"Please turn with me in your bibles to the second Samuel, chapter twenty-two, verses thirty-one through thirty-seven."

Imani followed along as the pastor read. His rich voice amplified by the tiny microphone attached to his lapel ignited something within her when he reached verse thirty-three:

God is my strength and power; and he maketh my way perfect . . .

She glanced up as the pastor continued, noting the fiery conviction in his tone and the veil of serenity on his amber brown face. He segued into his message, expounding on scripture, examining the issue of the Father's ability to guide His children.

"Beloved, our world is so ripe with uncertainty that we often find ourselves trying to micromanage our lives in our attempts to maintain some degree of control . . . and power. We have our date books and organizers and a schedule for this that and the other; beepers for our mates, our children, and the goldfish and we're still running ragged trying to keep it all together."

"I know that's right, Pastor," someone responded.

"But the scripture tells us today that God is our power and only He can order a perfect path! Some of you have dreams and goals and are ready to launch out into deeper waters in life. I challenge you, beloved, to remember while pursuing your visions that the *power* to realize those very visions comes from God."

That statement was a sweet refrain for Imani—convicting her heart and prompting her to ask God into her entrepreneurial plans as she sat several hours later at her parents' dinner table enjoying a light meal of baked salmon, rice pilaf, steamed vegetables and fruit salad for dessert.

Her mother was still on a diet.

"You look good, Mother. How much weight have you lost?" Imani inquired as they sat at the table on the lanai. It was a beautiful April day. The sun touched the earth with gold fingers, dashing brilliance on the face of the man-made lake fabricated for the express pleasure of the residents within the gated community.

"Ooh, Lord, child I don't know! I'm not getting on that scale until I can see my toes. As of right now I can't see past my kneecaps."

"My vantage point is one hundred percent, sweetheart, and you're ravishing from every angle," Ray Carmichael assured his wife who cooed in return.

"No mushy stuff at the dinner table," Nia exclaimed with a grimace.

"Hush, Nia," Imani chastened, a smile lifting the corners of her mouth as she enjoyed her parents' interaction. A retired contractor, Ray Carmichael was a good man. Imani was ashamed to admit her cool demeanor upon their introduction, thinking he was just another man who would be here today and gone tomorrow. But Ray proved her wrong. Gently, he won Imani's affections in such a non-threatening manner that before she knew it Imani loved her stepfather without reserve.

"Imani, Nia tells us you have a new gentleman friend," Ray casually stated.

Imani could have choked on a grain of rice. She shot a look at her daughter who sat staring innocently into her plate while spearing vegetables with her fork.

"Will we have the pleasure of meeting him anytime soon?" her stepfather asked.

"And what's his name? Brace or Bruce?" Eunetta muttered with a frown.

"Brax, Mother. It's short for Braxton."

"I see. Well, why didn't you invite this . . . Brax . . . to join us for dinner this afternoon?" Eunetta inquired.

"Because it's not like that, Mother," Imani responded as evenly as possible.

"They've only been out a couple of times," Nia confirmed.

"Nia!" Imani gave her daughter a warning look.

"Hmm. We're not important enough for him to meet," her mother stated rather peevishly.

Lord, don't let this woman get started today.

"Now, precious, I don't think that's a fair assessment of the situation. Imani will introduce us to her new beau in her own good time," Ray sagely advised.

"Ray, Brax and I are just friends," Imani explained, wanting to wrap her fingers around Nia's throat for divulging her personal business.

"For now," Nia muttered.

"What did you say, young lady?"

"Nothing," was Nia's rather insolent reply. Imani scrutinized her daughter. She was concerned at the change in her behavior. Lately Nia had been acting different, withdrawn and even sullen. Nia acted as if she resented the new friendship Imani shared with Brax. Much to his credit, Brax showed kind consideration, often inviting Nia on their outings although she always declined. Perhaps with her father living in Los Angeles Nia felt as if both parents were detached from her. Imani decided it was time to have a heart-to-heart talk with her child.

"Well, what's he like? Is he handsome? Does he have a nice body?" Eunetta fired.

"Mother!"

"He's decent for an old man," Nia supplied.

"Nia!"

Eunetta dabbed her mouth with her linen napkin, propped her hands on her hips and fixed Imani with a look of incredulity.

"Imani, you're not serious enough with this man to introduce him to your parents, but you've already exposed him to your daughter?"

How quickly we forget, Imani thought, recalling the miscellaneous array of uncles her mother exposed her to as a child.

"Grammy, Mr. B. is my school counselor," Nia informed her grandmother before Imani could get a word in edgewise.

"You're dating Nia Nicole's counselor?" Eunetta demanded of her daughter.

Imani glanced heavenward for help.

"I'm not *officially* dating anyone, Mother."

"Quibble with semantics if you must. And just how old is this Brax?"

"Mother, please—"

"Don't 'mother please' me, Imani. Does the man need Geritol or not?"

Nia cracked up.

Imani clenched her teeth before slowly gritting out, "He's younger than I am, Mother. Okay?"

"Eww, you're older than Mr. B.? Dang, Mom," Nia commented, a sour look on her face.

Eunetta gasped. "You're robbing the cradle?"

"Sweetheart," Ray cautioned, laying a gentle touch on her arm so that she sat back to catch her breath.

Lord, today! Imani wanted to holler. Instead she closed her eyes, bit her lip and twirled a lock of hair about her finger. The cool finality in her voice was unmistakable when she spoke again.

"Nia, clear the table, please. We'll discuss your mouth later. Mother, Ray, I was going to meet Brax for dessert this evening—"

"Is he paying or are you?"

"Mother, does that matter?"

"Absolutely," Eunetta emphatically insisted. "Back in my day, gentlemen callers treated young women with respect and covered the costs of pleasantries during courtship."

"And you listened to the Victrola by the light of your kerosene lanterns as you sipped fresh squeezed lemonade and pulled homemade taffy while dressed in homespun gingham gowns, right?"

Ray suppressed a chuckle.

Eunetta stared at her daughter a moment before stating, "Don't be flippant, Imani. It's unbecoming."

"We're not courting, Mother," Imani merely returned with an irritated shake of her head. "Okay?"

"Fine," her mother huffed, her head and nose lifted as if she were offended.

"Dandy," Imani retorted. "As I was going to say earlier, I will gladly ask Brax to pick me up here if you'd like to meet him," Imani offered as diplomatically as possible, wondering if Brax would consider such an introduction premature or uncomfortable.

"No, we don't wish to inconvenience you," was Eunetta's regal reply.

"Why don't you invite the young man to join us for dessert here instead of going out," Ray intervened. He laughed, looking at the bowl of fresh fruit on the table. "I can't say it's much, but it's good."

"I'll do that, Ray. If Brax is interested I'll run to the store and purchase some ice cream or something."

Scraping back her chair, Eunetta rose stiffly.

"I'm going to help Nia Nicole with the dishes."

And with that she sashayed away.

Imani rolled her eyes.

Ray played interference, his tone soft and soothing.

"Don't be impatient with your mother, Imani. She comes off a little brusque at times. It's just that she loves you and worries about you, and ultimately she wants to see you happy."

Imani considered Ray's words while watching the sun dip below the lake's shore to blend its yellow haze into the translucent waters. Lovely.

"I know, Ray," she conceded. Standing, Imani came around the table to place a light kiss on her stepfather's brow. Ray was not a big man, barely six feet tall, but he possessed a largeness of spirit and heart that caused him to appear greater than his stature. Imani was thankful for his presence in her life. "Neither of you need worry. I'm grown now," she said, before walking over to stretch out on a chaise lounge where she closed her eyes and her mind and eventually slipped into a light, but peaceful sleep.

Ninety minutes later, Imani stood before the bathroom mirror checking her appearance. To her surprise, Brax was not ill at ease with the idea of sharing dessert with her parents. Her concerns that he might find her invitation the ploy of a desperate woman trying to snare a man were unfounded. His casual acceptance helped her relax.

There was a knock on the door. Imani opened it to find Nia standing on the opposite side.

"Hey, Snookie."

"Hi, Mom. Can I come in?"

Imani stepped back and allowed her daughter to enter. Nia sat on the edge of the tub and watched her mother as she finger-combed her hair and freshened her makeup.

"Mom, I'm sorry about speaking out of turn earlier. I know I'm not supposed to discuss what goes on in our home outside of our home, but I was just talking to Grammy and Grampy about some things and that led to you and Mr. B."

Imani turned and leaned against the sink to face her child.

"Nia, I don't mind Mother and Ray knowing about Brax, but that was my business to tell not yours. Understand?"

Nia nodded, her eyes downcast.

Pushing away from the sink, Imani approached her daughter and knelt in front of her. She lifted Nia's chin so that their eyes met.

"I'm concerned about you, Nia. You've been withdrawn lately. Is there anything wrong at school, with your friends? Are you missing your father?"

Or is it just my seeing Brax that has you edgy? she silently wondered.

Nia glanced away and licked her lips then returned her mother's gaze. She shrugged helplessly before speaking.

"It's nothing I just . . ." Her sigh was heavy. "I might as well tell you before Mr. B. does when he gets here. I have to meet with my Western Civilization teacher and Mrs. Whitston," Nia confessed, referring to the school principal.

"Why?"

"For plagiarism."

Imani was truly shocked. She jumped to her feet, as did Nia.

"What! Plagiarism is the same as stealing."

"Mom, wait, I didn't steal anything . . . exactly," Nia insisted, waving her hands rapidly.

"What exactly *did* you do, Nia?"

"I helped Krista on a Western Civilization paper."

"You helped Krista on a paper," Imani flatly echoed, "and that has you appearing before your school principal."

"Okay, we helped each other. I lifted some material from this homework.com site and we both used different parts in our papers. And it wasn't stealing 'cause the site gives sample topic papers for free. And we didn't write the ideas verbatim, but kinda paraphrased. We thought it would be okay since we have different teachers but I

guess our teachers compared our writings and recognized some simi-
larities," Nia blurted as if it all made absolute sense.

Imani covered her face with her hands and let loose a sound of disgust.

"Nia, this is ridiculous. You know better than to pull a stunt like
this. What is wrong with you?"

"I'm sorry, Mom."

"What happens at this hearing?" Imani asked, overriding her daughter's lame apology.

"I guess we'll either be expelled or flunk Western Civ and have to
repeat the course in summer school. Dang, if that happens I won't be
able to go to Nashville with Daddy."

Imani stared at her child as if she were a pod-like host invaded by
some foreign alien.

"That is the least of your worries, Nia. I will attend this meeting
with you. You will apologize for your deplorable actions and accept
whatever punishment you receive. Furthermore, you and Krista are to
have no further contact with each other until the end of school."

"Mom, that's not fair!"

"Nia, do I look like I care about fair? No contact with Krista.
Understand? I will talk to Mr. and Mrs. Ramirez and I'm sure they will
agree," Imani advised, afraid that this plagiarism fiasco was not the crux
of the matter. There was something else brewing beneath the surface.
But seeing the suddenly closed look on her child's face, Imani knew
whatever it was it would not now be revealed. She could only pray that
God would give them strength to weather the possible pending storm.

Dessert was sweet. And so was Brax. Together, they sauntered along
the paved perimeter of the lake, wrapped in a comfort they effortlessly created. Like a sleepy lover, the waters caressed the shore with
languid fingers and loving lips.

"I enjoyed meeting your parents," Brax stated as they walked. "Mr.
Carmichael reminded me of my father sucking on that unlit cigar."

"Did your father smoke cigars?"

"No, he had this old pipe that his grandfather made. He never
smoked tobacco in it. He just liked sitting there with it hanging from
his mouth."

Imani smiled.

"Did my mother scare you with her twenty million questions?"

Brax chuckled lightly.

"It's all good. If I had a daughter I'd be just as ruthless," Brax admitted.

"Speaking of daughters I'm sure you know about mine being summoned by the principal," Imani said, unable to omit the note of sadness from her voice. She studied Brax, noted his discomfort, and saw him run a nervous hand over his head.

"Yes, I do. This is something beyond my scope of power so there was nothing I could do to intervene. And I was bound by certain counselor-student confidentiality rigmarole that prevented me from telling you," Brax informed Imani, sounding relieved as if a weight had just been lifted from his chest.

Imani shook her head and sighed. Her voice was tinged with defeat when she confided, "Brax, I'm beginning to feel as if I'm failing my child." Imani welcomed the warm strength of his fingers as Brax reached for her hand that slid easily into his.

"Parenting is an underrated job that I don't envy. Give yourself credit, babygirl, for the good you've done."

Imani felt his words pierce her sense of dismay and lift her spirit. They continued in silence, the bellowing of bullfrogs and the chirp of crickets their soft serenade. As they rounded a bend Imani noticed a small object bobbing in the water that, upon closer inspection, proved to be a child's forgotten toy ship. Sight of it triggered a memory.

"I still have that certificate Monique won for a dinner cruise for two," Imani mused aloud. "How would you like to share a romantic dinner with me?"

His voice was serious when Brax responded.

"I want to share more than that, Imani. Do you want more?"

Imani peered sharply at him. Brax boldly returned her gaze. More than his words, his eyes expressed something honest and provoking, some intangible wonder that felt like hunger, deep and raw and pulsing.

"I've already openly admitted that I'm feeling you, but if I'm not who you're looking for let me know now and I'll limp on."

A warm rush invaded Imani's blood.

"Can I have a minute to collect my thoughts so that I can respond intelligently?"

Brax stepped to her, sliding his arms about her waist so that Imani was entangled in sweet surprise.

"Take your time. I intend to take mine," he answered.

Imani felt the warmth of his hand at the small of her back. Space between them disappeared as Brax pressed forward. Their eyes met. Imani witnessed the sensual invitation and welcomed the compelling touch and taste of his mouth slowly capturing her own.

Brax felt like granite wrapped in flesh. Malleable. Impenetrable. Imani imagined that he tasted like . . . brown sugar . . . and heat.

She felt a purr bubble up from the deep, untapped well of her soul. Lord, the man's mouth was marvelous. A sound that was part sigh, part moan fluttered in her throat.

There was a mischievous gleam in his eyes when Brax broke contact and leaned back to gaze down on her.

"Are you okay?" he teased.

Imani fanned her face with her hands.

"Other than the fact I can't remember my name, I'm perfectly fine," she breathed, causing Brax to laugh heartily.

He sobered and drawing her near once again advised, "Imani, I'm not interested in 'kicking it.' Been there done that. I can open my heart if you do the same. Can you take this voyage with me?"

Glancing beyond his shoulder and at the water's hypnotic sheen, Imani perceived Brax made no reference to any dinner cruise aboard some ship, but the journey into the depths and heights, the secret chambers of the heart. Her pulse raced at the thought. Still, she did not hesitate.

"Yes, Brax, I'll take the journey because I find you substantial and I want you in my life," was her heartfelt reply.

Brax would later share that something inside of him moved like a slumbering creature stretching awake. He felt large at the candor of her words. Just then he stroked her cheek and said, "You know you taste like chocolate?"

Imani glanced up at him, stunned by his whispered observation.

"Probably just the dessert sauce," she suggested, feeling a strange sense of elation.

"Maybe. Maybe not," was his deep reply.

WADE IN THE
WATER

I was four-years-old when I learned not to drown.

My family was on summer vacation visiting relatives in Florida who had a kidney-shaped pool in the backyard that was huge in my childish estimation. My older sisters knew how to swim but I didn't, so my mother was paranoid that I would slip and fall into the pool and drown.

"Jesus, keep my baby from falling," Moms murmured every time we went outdoors until Pops—apparently tired of her repeated lament—took matters into his own hands. Literally.

"Come here, Braxton Joshua." I can still remember Pops calling me to him. My father never called me Brax. Said it sounded like a household cleansing product. And he always included my middle name, which was his first name, in matters of importance. Anyhow Pops, dressed in Bermuda shorts only, stepped down into the pool with me clutching him for dear life.

My mother started screaming. My sisters ran to her, fearfully gripping Moms as our relatives looked on, adding their vocalizations to the sudden mayhem.

"Joshua, no, he's too little!" Moms hollered.

Pops kept walking, descending each step slowly with purpose until he stood on the bottom step and looked at me long and hard.

"Do you trust me, Son?"

I nodded, afraid not to.

"I'm going to let go of you, but I promise I won't leave. You won't drown. All right?"

Another wooden nod.

"Okay, hold your breath and take the journey."

With that, he released me . . . and I sank. Down into the watery depths I plummeted, my eyes stinging, my nose filling with the acidic stench of chlorine. Panic had me. Then I remembered my daddy's promise, and I'd never known him to lie. So I believed. And my feet touched bottom.

I felt as if I was flying as I pressed the bottoms of my bare feet against the pool's floor, and with a burst of energy and power, shot back up and out of the water.

Pops was right there with me, a broad smile on his face as he caught me to him.

With me snuggly in his arms, he climbed back out of the pool, and wrapped the beach towel my sister gave him about my dripping form. He walked the few steps to where my mother half-stood, half-sagged against my uncle and handed me into her waiting, worried arms.

"He's okay now, Judith," Pops told Moms before walking into the house, leaving a wet trail in his wake.

And I was. They couldn't keep me out of the pool after that. My mother insisted I wear a life preserver, stay in the shallow end, and never enter the water unless one of my parents was present. But she let me "swim," which was really more my kicking and splashing with all the earnest vigor that only children expend.

My father was one of the most intelligent people I have ever encountered despite his not having "book learning" or college credentials to testify to that fact.

You just don't forget lessons like that.

This was my frame of reference the other night when I asked Imani if she wanted to take *that* voyage with me.

I'll be the first to admit that I've floundered, even sank like a submarine in a bad relationship or two. There was Brandy and the wannabe wedding, Carla the-kids-with-horns and hoofs-having sister, who thought I was her man and built-in babysitter in one, and Vesta my freak-of-the-week, who didn't have a thing to offer other than head-banging, toe-curling, red light district kind of sex. I appreciate sex as much as the next man. It's *all* good, but if it's all a woman has to offer then I need to pass because we need something in common when the lights go on. Then there was the last sister I dated. I don't even know how to describe her. She didn't have children, didn't try to trap a brother at the altar, was intelligent and had much to offer. No baggage, no beer, no bebes. Still, she was the worst of all.

She tried to remodel me.

I was her little dress-up G.I. Joe doll. She wanted to fit me with these high fashion designers as if my FUBU gear wasn't on hit. She wanted me to watch artsy-fartsy French films with subtitles, frequent book readings and art museums, and escort her to wine and cheese tastings and all these boring "mixers" where alarms sounded at the door if you made less than six-figures or wiped your butt with domestic toilet tissue.

There is absolutely nothing wrong, per se, with a little wine tasting and a stroll through an art gallery if that's your bag. I simply object to having some highbred sister treating me as if she's slumming or walking on the wild side by giving me the time of day. I am not an experiment or a taste of taboo.

What I despised most about that relationship was the fact that Polly Perfect couldn't see that I didn't *need* remaking. I'd already been there, done that. I'd lost the fat boy weight, ditched the glasses for contacts, gave my orange double-breasted sweater to the Goodwill and gave up my membership to Nerds 'R Us. I liked then (and still like now) the Braxton J. Wade I became. That is not to say I don't have room for growth or change. I do. I'm not perfect and don't want to be. My point is this: take me as is or don't take me at all.

As I was saying . . .

I've had ample experience that would lend itself to self-doubt or hesitation. I haven't always hit the mark with regards to love. But yet, I'm still here. And I'm willing. I just need to remind myself that I know how to not drown, that it's okay if I inhale and take the journey, get my feet wet, wade in the water. Even if I sink for a split second or two, I'll come up eventually. And when I do, I hope to find Imani in my arms, gripping me tightly in return.

100 STRONG

The fifth annual Brothers Can Cook competition was sizzling. Scintillating aromas filled the large multipurpose room of a south Sacramento community center posthumously named for a former African American city councilman as the men of 100 Strong flexed their cooking skills, their camaraderie sprinkled with much trash talking as they vied to outdo one another.

"You're going down this year, Williams," warned an older gentleman on one side of the humongous kitchen bustling with groups of brothers busy tending their fare. "We've been doing this the Saturday before Mother's Day for five years now and we won every year until you had to get cute with your wife's Jamaican Jerk Chicken and papaya sauce last year. But we're taking back our crown today, Son."

"You'll have to work for it, Papa Mays, because with all due respect, we ain't scared of you," Jamal Williams tossed back, glancing at his team: Chris McCullen, Terrance Blackmon, and Braxton J. Wade. "Right, my brothers?"

"Speak for yourself," Brax replied, evoking laughter.

"There're over three hundred women out there who paid five dollars a ticket for some *real* food, not that frilly mess you kids are cooking over there," the older man goaded. "Try not to break a nail on those crêpe suzettes."

"Don't drop anything in the pot like last year, Papa Mays," Chris tossed as he washed strawberries in a sink before handing them to Brax to slice, whispering something that caused Brax to howl.

"Nobody asked for your commentary, McCullen!" the older man shouted above the chuckles in the room. "Just wash your sissy fruit."

Removing his apron, Brax grabbed a bottle and crossed the room, prompting Mr. Mays to playfully assume a sparring position while warning, "Don't make me call my granddaughter in here."

"Chris wanted you to have this," Brax said, handing the man a jar of honey. "Something sticky just in case your PoliGrip slips like last time."

Laughing, the man wrapped Brax in a bear hug as boisterous cackles erupted in the kitchen brimming with brotherhood and good food.

"You have the touch, babygirl," Brax rumbled as he sat wide-legged across a chair, its back turned foward and his head resting against the table as Imani sat beside him and gently kneaded the muscles in his shoulders. He was whipped after fours hours on his feet in the merry bedlam of the kitchen. He closed his eyes and sighed. "Do you mind me calling you 'babygirl'?"

"I think its sweet," Imani assured him. "The crêpes were wonderful."

"I don't want to see another fancy pancake for as long as Jamal lives. My brother was smoking something to let his wife suggest that recipe."

"Crêpes are easy to make," Imani asserted.

Brax opened one eye wide enough to peer up at her.

"Baby, there's a difference between male and female cooking. If anything is required besides add water and stir it *ain't* easy."

"Did you or did you not win the prize?" Imani reminded Brax as her hands slackened in their ministrations.

Drawing her hand to his mouth Brax gently kissed her palm and answered, "I did when I found you."

Imani gave him a full-dimple grin.

"You can't seduce me without credentials, sir."

Brax sat up and raised a brow at her.

"Whatever you need, Boo, I have it. Take notes: a brother has a job, an advanced degree, a home, and I know how to cook."

"Crêpes," teased Imani.

"I wasn't finished," Brax interjected. "I can tolerate your dog, I believe in God even though we're not on speaking terms, and I have a clean bill of health. No STDs, crabs or critters."

"You need help," Imani commented, giggling softly. "Can you provide medical substantiation as to your critter-less condition?"

"Is that mandatory?"

"Only if you want a taste of my love," Imani replied seductively, causing Brax to stare at her before whipping out his wallet and placing a medical insurance card on the table.

"The 800 number is on the back. You dial while I strip," Brax suggested, tugging at his shirt as Imani laughed and grabbed his hands.

"Keep your clothes on, sweetie. It's not that kind of party."

"Don't foul up a brother's game with all of that bedroom banter," Brax countered. "Speaking of foul, here comes Mother Nature."

"I heard that, crazy bald head!" Monique shrilled, approaching the table.

"You didn't hear anything, Janis Joplin. Sit down before you give me vertigo with all that tie dye," Brax said, shielding his eyes with his arms to block out the sight of Monique's colorful blouse.

"Grow some hair already."

"Calm down before I give you a pork chop."

"You both need Jesus," Imani chided, as a hissing Monique swiped at Brax with her hands curved like claws.

"And eight ball needs to go back to the kitchen and finish cooking. Skeedaddle!"

Brax laughed and rose from the table. He paused to give Imani a quick kiss on the lips.

"Let me wrap things up in the kitchen and we can finish our discussion later when Cousin It ain't around."

Brax was still grinning when he returned to the kitchen.

"Yo, Kid, welcome back to Purgatory."

"T., don't front. You had a good time cooking for these sisters and you know it. Where did Chris and Jamal go?"

"Off to do something with their women," Terrance answered, leaning back against a long, wide counter. "So, Kid, looks like you and Imani are working solid."

Standing beside his best friend and thoughtfully rubbing his goatee Brax agreed, "We're getting there."

Terrance shook his head as if dismayed.

"Kid, I would congratulate you but you know how I feel about women with children. Imani's a lovely sister, but that has to be trouble in the making."

Brax stiffened. Terrance's words were a dreary forecast that hovered like a rain cloud over a parade.

"Listen, Cuddy, I know all that. If it doesn't work, well . . ." Brax ended his thought with a shoulder shrug. "If it does then I benefit from stepping outside my box. I'm willing to take a chance."

Terrance slowly sucked his teeth before offering his fist so that Brax could tap his on top.

"I'll root for you, Kid."

"Thanks."

"So, are you going to hook me up with Monique or not?"

"Hook your own self up. And what happened to Celeste?" Brax asked in reference to his housemate's most recent addition to his "string of pearls" collected for his carnal pleasure.

Terrance shrugged. "I let her go. 'Ey, it's Mother's Day tomorrow," he stated, switching subjects.

"You think!" Brax quipped. "Guess I'd better go home and order Moms her customary bouquet. What are you getting for your mother?"

"What she probably wanted ten kids ago: a one-way ticket to Timbuktu without my father."

Their rich laughter rippled through the kitchen still crowded with men of varying ages, hues, sensibilities and situations who had united to prepare food and tossed love in their pots.

IMANI AND CHILD

"**M**om, can I have a sleepover tonight?"

Imani lowered the book she was reading to gaze through her designer sunglasses at the woman-thing coming toward her, a dog cradled in its arms. Her daughter was becoming, changing. Clad in a sparse pair of cut-offs and a piece of a T-shirt with her belly bare, Nia's long loose limbs gleamed like melted chocolate beneath the sun. Had the girl grown another inch or was Imani's perception askew from her position atop a blanket on the ground, surrounded by books and the Saturday afternoon sun?

"What are you doing?" Nia asked, plopping down onto the blanket.

"Reading," Imani replied, peering at her daughter while petting the dog nuzzling her face.

Nia perused the titles, reading aloud, "*Live Your Dream. Maximize the Moment. Smart Women Finish Rich*—dang, Mom, are you having your own self-empowerment workshop today?"

"Nia, I've asked you not to say 'dang.' "

"Sorry, Mom, I know you don't like that word."

"Did you finish your paper for your western civilization class?" Imani inquired. To her great relief the school principal had been merciful, concluding that Nia had merely borrowed ideas in a manner that they were unable to clearly classify as theft. Plagiarism was a fine line, but one that she'd managed to avoid crossing. Still, Nia's actions were found to be disagreeable. In lieu of expulsion or a failing grade, Nia was required to write a fifteen page essay complete with bibliography in which she was to properly site every source. In addition to her mini thesis, Nia would spend an hour after school assisting in the study lab until the week of finals. That, Imani concluded, should be enough to keep her out of trouble.

"Yep, I just finished my essay and, Mom, my new computer is da bomb diggity!" Nia sang. "And my laser printer can shoot out three pages in the time it took that old thing to print one."

Imani chose not to remind Nia that she had sacrificed and purchased "that old thing" with money from her savings so that her child could compete in this age of modern technology.

It was just like Nigel to floss and front. Maybe it was a guilt gift, Nia's brand new Pentium processor with one year of free Internet access *and* a *color* laser jet printer to boot. Whatever it was, Imani was displeased. Nigel was fully aware of Nia's current problems at school, not to mention her previous detention, and her difficult behavior of late. Still, he found it necessary to reward *his* daughter with expensive toys Imani felt she did not deserve.

Nia's having growing pains, Butter, so ease up on her and give her a break.

The man and his irrational indulgence were too much to bear. It seemed as if Nigel purposefully countermanded her attempts to discipline and steer their daughter on a right path. He reduced Nia's infractions to mere "growing pains," and was bent on being lenient and indulgent even to the point of Nia's detriment. It was a game of good cop-bad cop that Imani was tired of playing.

"Good, Snookie, I'm glad you're enjoying your new PC," Imani finally responded. "And, yes," she exhaled, "I guess you can say I'm empowering myself today."

"What's this?" Nia removed a large post-it note marking a page and read,

God is my strength and power; and he maketh my way perfect.

"That's the verse Pastor Lovett used in last week's sermon," she observed.

"Glad you were listening," Imani teased.

"I always pay attention in church," was Nia's response. "So, Mom, are you doing all of this," Nia indicated the books with a sweep of her hand, "to get ready for your boutique?"

"Yes, Snookie, I am. I needed some fire power."

"I think you'll be a good entrepreneur, Mom," Nia said, returning the post-it note to its page. "The boutique will be off the hook 'cause you got game. You should have a grand opening party and a fashion show. That would be off the chain! I can even be one of the models," Nia said, tossing her head back and striking a ridiculously serious pose.

Imani sat up and patted Nia's leg.

"I'll take that under advisement. Nia, I appreciate your vote of confidence," Imani said, touched by her daughter's sentiments, and feeling as if Nia's usual effervescent self were shining through. She had to admit that Nia had been trying hard to clean up her act. Imani appreciated the effort. "Nia, I've never undertaken a project of this magnitude and I can't promise you it will be easy on either of us, but I will do everything I can to ensure that you and I remain intact and that our home life doesn't suffer."

Nia returned her mother's direct gaze and simply stated, "I trust you."

Imani felt tears well up in her eyes. She exhaled then swallowed to keep them from brimming over.

"So can I have my sleepover?"

"Taking advantage of my emotional state?"

"Just maximizing the moment," Nia chirped.

Imani grinned.

"That's rather short notice, Nia, to have company tonight. And you're still on my bad side after that plagiarism issue. Let's put that on ice until the end of the school year. Maybe then we can do a barbeque party and you can invite Krista and some of your other girlfriends to stay overnight. Deal?"

"Deal. Mom, don't forget that as of next week I have mandatory band practice every Saturday until final competition in July," Nia reminded her mother.

That was another sore spot with Imani. It was her opinion that Nia should step down from band for the remainder of the school year and concentrate on her studies after receiving a C- on a math exam when she normally earned A's and sometimes B's, but again Nigel vetoed her voice, and insisted otherwise. He'd even had the nerve to suggest that maybe Nia's problems were somehow her fault. Perhaps Imani was spending too much time with her new "friend." It was perfectly fine for Nigel to have a honey a week, but Imani was required to stay home with the doors locked and the shades drawn, wasting her life away. Feeling hemmed in by her ex-husband's opposition Imani had gone to Brax to discuss the situation. He was after all Nia's guidance counselor and Imani could definitely use some insight. But his input had actually angered her.

"Baby, speaking off the record, Nia is exhibiting typical behavior for a child her age. But she exacerbates issues by playing on the fact that her parents are on opposite sides of the fence. She has you engaged in parental tug-of-war."

Imani agreed. But his next words in response to her inquiry as to what an appropriate course of action would be angered her, so that she responded with some biting remark about Brax needing to take a refresher course or two in psychology.

"Perhaps," he had cautiously stated, "you should consider allowing Nia to live with her father . . . or at least have extended visits. It's obvious her affections are aligned with him."

The thought enraged her. To think that her daughter, the child she loved day in and day out in word and in deed, would favor a parent who was part-time at best was a wound to Imani's soul. It hurt all the more because Imani grudgingly admitted the words held a degree of truth. After a day or two, she eventually calmed down, apologizing to Brax for her rudeness. True to form, he'd merely wrapped her in his arms and assured her that he understood.

Imani watched Miss Pitman as the dog wandered about the yard, realizing that she had never opened the lines of communication with Nia regarding her relationship with Brax. Perhaps it was time to do so. Fingering the sterling silver floating heart necklace Nia had given her this past Mother's Day, Imani initiated a necessary dialogue between them.

"Nia, we need to discuss something," Imani stated, redirecting her attention to her daughter. "How do you feel about Mr. Wade?"

It was a question she had never asked before. There was no need. Imani was not a recluse, but she had not dated with any real regularity in the past twelve years. Occasionally she went out with a male acquaintance, a friend of a friend's or somebody's relative who was in town for the weekend, etcetera, etcetera. But never, since her marriage, had she been involved in a relationship of any significant length, or depth. So bringing a man home for her child to meet was a rarity. Now, for the first time in years she was embarking upon a relationship that she wanted to be neither brief nor platonic. Imani was not falling in love so much as she was . . . drifting down deep into something that felt incredibly right. Substantial. Imani was not asking her daughter for permission, still she needed to assure herself that Nia would not be negatively impacted by whatever blossomed between she and Brax.

Only the sounds of the spring day were heard as they sat in silence until Imani asked again, "Nia, how do you feel?"

Nia shrugged.

"Mr. B. is cool and all—"

"But?"

Nia shrugged again before answering in a roundabout way that conveyed she understood where her mother's line of questioning was headed.

"My friend Tracey's mom started dating some new guy like two weeks ago and now her mom's never home and when she is her boyfriend's always there, and Tracey even saw him walking through the kitchen in his underwear. Eww!" Nia shivered. "And now it's like Tracey has to compete for her mom's attention."

Oh, Lord, how I remember, Imani thought, knowing too well the sense of vying for a parent's divided attention.

"Do you think that I would ever put a man before you, Nia?" Imani asked, removing her sunglasses and placing them atop her pile of books while carefully considering her daughter's expression.

"It could happen. You could get all caught up in Mr. B. and I won't matter."

Imani was shocked by the candid admission. Based on conversations prior to Imani's ever meeting Brax, Nia had displayed a certain liking for her guidance counselor, calling him "cool" and using other favorable descriptions. But that was before Brax became a personal, romantic part of Imani's life. Now that he was, Imani had the sense that Nia would merely view Brax as a threat.

"Nia, if I were to ask you if you have a problem with my dating Mr. Wade what would you say?"

"Yes," was Nia's forthright reply. "I have Mr. B.'s Career Exploration class so I see him like twice a week, and then I'd have to see him outside of school if he comes here. That would be like having a stepfather for a teacher or something and that's totally gross!" Nia concluded.

Imani was at a loss. She had not anticipated Nia's frank, but disapproving, admissions. She felt numb. Now that Brax was a part of her life, now that she had opened herself to his affections what was Imani to do when her only child was so clearly opposed to that relationship? She needed time and space to process this knowledge and, perhaps, find a solution to this unexpected dilemma.

"Snookie, I want you to know that I have no intention of making you secondary to anyone at anytime in my life. No one can dethrone my baby," Imani stated, lightly stroking her daughter's hair. "Can you trust me in this?"

Nia's gaze was a dark, unfathomable canvas meant to camouflage her feelings. Still, Imani glimpsed some bleak emotion that bothered her. Nia never responded to her question. Instead, she readjusted her long ponytail and hopped to her feet.

Imani pushed herself up off of the ground to stand in front of her daughter. She knew by Nia's stiff body language that they could make no further headway on the matter today. The situation was delicate and had to be handled with kid gloves. Imani told herself not to fret, but to pray that God would grant her divine direction.

"Nia, I'm sorry for any discomfort this has caused you, but all I ask is that you trust me."

Again, Nia ignored her mother's plea for trust. Instead, her arms crossed, her expression indifferent, Nia remarked, "Are you sorry enough to let me have a tattoo?"

Imani shrank back.

"A tattoo? Nia, you're delirious."

Indifference vanished as Nia became a typical, cajoling teenager once again.

"Come on, Mom, I'd get something small. Maybe a butterfly or a heart on my arm."

"Or a two-by-four on your behind. Don't even think about it, Nia."

"What about having my ears pierced?" Nia compromised.

"Your ears are pierced."

"I know, but I want a another piercing at the top in the cartilage so I can wear a tiny diamond."

"The last thing you need is another hole in your head."

"Come on, Mom, pretty please?"

"No. Case closed."

Nia smacked her lips. "You're such a warden."

"Keep it up and you'll be back in solitary confinement," Imani threatened, pinching Nia's nose. A sense of relief washed over her when Nia smiled. In light of Nia's objections, Imani perceived that a long and perhaps difficult road lay ahead for her and Brax. Was she ready for the battle? Was Brax? And just how rough would the battle rage? Imani had no idea. She forced the daunting thoughts from her mind. For now Imani would do what she had to, juggle if necessary motherhood and romance and do her best to keep the two separate. She loved her daughter. Would her daughter interrupt her loving a man? Tenderly, she stroked Nia's cheek. "Hey, little girl, have I ever told you that you're my favorite child?"

Nia rolled her eyes.

"Mom, I'm your only child."

"You're still my favorite. Oh, and Snookie, this *little* outfit you have on," Imani said, glancing at Nia's brief attire, "it's for my eyes only. It doesn't go out of the house with you in it or it on you. Got it?"

Nia nodded.

Imani kissed her daughter's forehead and said, "Good."

SAILING

Much to their regret, the dinner cruise was coming to a close. There, barely visible in the distance, was the San Francisco skyline, its illuminated buildings like bright towers luring the ship closer to its final destination. Hand-in-hand Imani and Brax slowly strolled the deck of the sizeable vessel, teased by the sweet caress of an ocean-scented breeze.

The mood between them was mellow as if in sync with the tranquil night.

"You look lovely," Brax commented, glancing down at the red sleeveless dress that Imani wore to perfection, forcing his eyes up from the lush crests of her breasts peeking above the material holding them in check.

"Thank you," Imani softly replied, her dimples bold but beautiful beneath the deepening sky mirrored in the dancing light of her eyes. "You look rather scrumptious yourself, " Imani complimented, thinking Brax looked exceptionally handsome in navy slacks and matching shirt jacket with a cream colored V-neck beneath. He smelled of patchouli and sandalwood and strength. As a rule Imani did not care for men with earrings, but with that tiny gold hoop glittering in his left earlobe Brax looked wickedly delicious. "Are you enjoying the cruise?" Imani asked, forcing her mind away from carnal considerations.

"Time spent with you can only be enjoyable," Brax answered.

"Careful, Mr. Wade, flattery might get you somewhere."

With a grin and a squeeze of Imani's hand Brax smoothly replied, "I know."

Imani stood still, forcing Brax to do likewise as she peered up at him. "You're not being disingenuous so I can break you off a little something are you?"

She shivered when Brax pushed a windswept lock of hair away from her face before he replied, "I'd lie to the Pope if necessary."

"You're not right," Imani responded, laughing softly as they moved forward into the ocean-kissed evening.

"How's the boutique coming?" Brax questioned, as they paused at the ship's edge. Arms resting atop the banister and leaning slightly forward, Brax fixed Imani with an intent gaze, watching her profile that glowed like smooth satin in the moonlight.

Imani's smile was brilliant.

"Pretty good. I have an appointment with Jamal Williams next week to discuss my game plan before investigating site options. I'm actually toying with the idea of purchasing versus leasing a space. I have to examine my budget first and may have to cut things like my gym membership," Imani said, her palms lifted. "We'll see."

"Sounds exciting," Brax commented.

"It is exciting, but nerve-wracking as well."

"You'll make a properly informed decision, and if you need me I'm here for you."

This unshakable confidence in her ability was just another something Imani admired about Brax. He seemed forever ready to bolster her up, stroking her with his optimism and genuine belief in her ability. His constant confidence was refreshing.

"Thanks, sweetie. So tell me more about not wanting to retire from the school system," Imani requested, segueing into an interrupted conversation from days before.

Brax chuckled before responding, "Don't get me wrong I enjoy my job, but listening to my kids whine and cry day in and day out can be draining. I toyed with the idea of returning to grad school to become a licensed psychologist and go into private practice, but I have my limitations."

"That doesn't appeal to you?" Imani asked as she stood, an arm linked with his.

Brax shook his head.

"It's okay being on a school campus because I'm not stuck in the office all day, and I have other duties that give me a break from counseling. Plus the type of counseling I provide isn't necessarily as intense as in a full-time clinical practice," Brax stated, propping a foot on a lower rail. "I don't want to hear problems day in and day out. I don't want to be on call and I wouldn't relish having to talk someone from jumping off a ledge. And I'm not trying to waste time convincing a patient that Whoopi Goldberg is not *the* antichrist and Cher is not a man."

"I am so through with you," remarked Imani, snickering. "So what do you envision yourself doing ten or fifteen years from now?"

Brax thoughtfully gazed out over the bay.

"I want to work with young men who are struggling to make a positive impact on society, or just struggling period."

Imani listened attentively.

"I feel as if Black men need resuscitation, like we need to breathe life back into each other and our families. I can see myself getting involved with an organization similar to 100 Strong when I've had my fill of guidance counseling because of its emphasis on revitalizing the involvement of Black men in the lives of our youth."

Respect shone in Imani's eyes.

"That's admirable."

Brax shrugged his broad shoulders.

"We have to do what we have to do to regain our communities. So, babygirl, let me get in your business. Do you want more children?"

Throwing her hands upward, Imani pulled away.

"Lord Jesus, thank you, but no! The thought of raising another Nia is enough to make me want a hysterectomy. Besides, by now my eggs are probably scrambled and my ovaries on perpetual hiatus."

Brax laughed full and deep.

"Plus, single parenting is the hardest thing I've ever done," Imani admitted, turning to lean back against the railing. "Rewarding, but hard." She paused, looking up at the star-speckled sky. "Being divorced and raising a child alone was not part of my perfect plan, but I learned that you have to rise to the occasion and do what needs to be done so that this tiny person who is completely dependent on you has a fair chance at the best life possible."

Brax nodded and considered Imani's words before speaking.

"Both of my sisters are married with children and I see that even with two parents in the home they struggle to make it work," he observed. "And I *know* the three of us ran my parents ragged so I commend you, Baby," Brax complimented, lightly stroking Imani's chin with his finger.

Her whispered "thank you" was nearly swallowed by the live music pouring through the speakers on deck.

"Care to dance, beautiful?" Brax asked, extending a hand to Imani.

"Out here on deck?" Imani replied.

"Come on, lovely, take the voyage," Brax enticed.

Her smile was velvet as Imani quietly accepted his embrace. The live band in the dining hall below played an old big band tune, but Imani did not care, for in the close proximity of his warmth the world rang smooth.

"You feel good," Brax breathed in her ear, enticing a shiver to crawl over her spine.

A contented sigh was her only reply as Imani leaned against Brax and welcomed the fullness of his embrace, wondering if it would be too melodramatic to say that being with Brax was her destiny. Or did she merely seek to justify a sudden rousing hunger? Imani could neither deny nor dismiss the overwhelming attraction between them. It was emotional and intellectual, perhaps spiritual. Without question it was physical. They had yet to cross *that* bridge. Their relationship was growing, blossoming into something solid. The time they spent together was a precious thing that they both anticipated with great relish. And although physical intimacy remained uncharted territory, Imani felt as if she were warring between her flesh and her faith and she wanted to resist the craving. But struggling to remember the last time she felt so rich and full and free, Imani gave in and allowed herself to melt beneath the sumptuous heat Brax generated.

"Only to you," Imani finally replied, surprised by the sultry tone of her voice.

"All for me," Brax agreed, branding her neck with a kiss.

"Do you mind if we sit down? My feet are tired," Imani nearly gushed, blaming her three-inch high-heeled red satin sandals when in actuality she needed time to put lust in check.

Reluctantly, Brax loosened his hold.

"Can you make it to that seat over there or shall I play Black Knight and carry you?"

"I'll make it," Imani assured him, turning only to find she was stuck. Glancing down she noticed the heel of her left shoe wedged tightly between the boards of the old-fashioned wooden deck. "I can't move."

Glancing down, Brax noted her predicament and gripped Imani's elbow as she vainly wrestled to free her foot.

"Here, let me," he offered, leaning over and working to resolve the problem, eventually lowering himself on bended knee so as to get a better grip.

"My Brown Sugar Bear to the rescue," purred Imani, causing Brax to smile. "Or are you trying to propose?"

"I might be marriage material but I'm still under construction," Brax asserted with a laugh. "Dag, Boo, did you step into a black hole? It'll be easier if you take your foot out of the shoe," he advised, while unbuckling her sandal and bracing Imani about the waist as she balanced on one foot. "Lean on me. I need both hands for this," Brax informed, gripping and forcefully wrenching the shoe free of its confines. "Boo-yow!" Pleased with himself, Brax handed Imani the upper portion of her strappy red satin sandal. "Huh?"

They glanced down to see the heel remained firmly wedged between the planks.

"Aww, Baby, I'm sorry," Brax apologized with a laugh as their arrival at dock was announced over the speakers. "Guess I'll have to carry you back to the bus."

"Oh, no you don't! My shoe is broken not my leg," Imani protested even as Brax effortlessly scooped her up into his arms. "Brax, put me down!"

"Relax, Babygirl, I have you," Brax assured her as he swiveled in the direction of the exit.

"Brax, this is ridiculous," Imani seethed between clenched teeth as they approached the ramp where the ship's crew was assembled to bid passengers farewell.

"Is everything okay, sir?" a uniformed attendant asked.

"She's a little tipsy," Brax confided, before descending the ramp leading down to solid ground.

"That wasn't funny," Imani advised, squirming slightly.

"Girl, stop protesting. You know you like it here," he said, giving Imani a playful, seductive growl.

"If you're going to carry me at least take me to the correct vehicle." she said, conceding defeat.

"I am," Brax assured her en route to a parking lot and the waiting charter bus that would transport them home.

"No, actually you're not. Look over there," she directed with a nod of her head toward the curb.

There at the curb, next to a sparkling white limousine, stood a uniformed driver bearing a sign on which was printed in large black letters EVANS AND WADE.

"Sir, your carriage awaits," Imani announced with a dramatic sweep of her hand.

A look of pleasure spread across his face as Brax met Imani's gaze to find that her expression clearly reflected her enjoyment in surprising him.

"Woman, what are you up to? Are you trying to abduct a brother?"

"I am," confirmed Imani. "You're mine for the night."

Placing a tender kiss on her cheek Brax replied, "Babygirl, I'm yours for as long as you want me."

The late great Grover Washington Junior serenaded the contented couple via CD, his smooth horn blowing notes of pure mood as they traveled over the highway.

Eyes closed and her head propped against the ultrasoft seat cushion, Imani wiggled her toes in rhythm with the music, her discarded sandal-and-a-half on the carpet beside her tiny evening bag. Imani lightly gripped a half-empty champagne flute in one hand while drawing lazy circles on the back of Brax's head with the other.

"When did you scheme up this limo ride?" Brax questioned.

"Last week. I can't be trusted." Sighing, Imani purred, nearly slurred, "I'm feeling serendipitous."

Brow cocked, Brax opened one eye to peek over at her.

"That sparkling peach juice is nonalcoholic, right?"

"According to the label it is. But maybe drinking a bottle-and-a-half hypes the potency."

Brax sat up.

"Are you getting your buzz on?"

Imani took another sip from her glass, ran her tongue across her top lip and announced, "Yep."

"You just sit back and drink and ride, Boo. It's all good even if you can't pass a Breathalyzer test," Brax teased.

"Now you know why I don't drink. I can't even do sparkling apple cider without getting silly," Imani announced, growing quiet only to start singing the theme song from Mr. Ed a moment later. "A horse is a horse of course of course . . ."

Brax removed the glass from Imani's hand and placed it atop the fully appointed bar in the back of the limousine while commenting, "You need coffee and a cold shower."

Imani laughed and sat up. Wrapping her arms about herself she gazed out the window. The night was deep. A mere sliver of a moon hung in the enchanting sky. Even the stars glowed faintly as if reluctant to rise from their rest above the dark silhouette of distant hills.

"One of the things I love about California is its vast and varied terrain. You can go from beach to valley to snowcapped mountains within this one state, and sometimes within a matter of mere minutes," Imani observed. "And we have some of the most beautiful waterways."

"I hope you're not referring to that muddy pond Sacramento tries to pass off as a river," Brax challenged.

"What's wrong with our river? It's lovely . . . in the dark. I was actually thinking of Lake Tahoe," Imani admitted.

"Never been there," Brax commented.

"Really? Let's go."

"When?"

"Now," Imani said, her eyes sparkling with sudden delight. "I haven't done a spontaneous thing in eons and I'm feeling adventurous."

"You're serious aren't you?"

She nodded.

"I'm not ready to go home alone. Let's take the journey."

Brax detected something subtle yet evocative in Imani's expression, in the silk of her voice, and in the way she held her body as if possessing a secret. But before he could respond she suddenly switched gears and stated, "Tell me more about your dream trip to Africa."

Brax hesitated momentarily, trying to grasp what he felt was an elusive invitation, only to give up and settle back with the comfort of his dream. He would take a sabbatical from work and begin his visit on the Ivory Coast to see the European castles and dungeons that once served as holding places for Africans before they were loaded like inferior chattel aboard cramped slave ships to endure the Middle Passage to the Americas, where they were to be sold into lives of utter peonage.

"I want to visit Ghana, Nigeria, and South Africa to start. I plan to camp out on the savannas, visit townships and cities and villages, and I hear there are some wild game restaurants where you can eat water buffalo and antelope and other wildlife."

"You had me until you inserted dining on the cast of *The Lion King*," Imani remarked, grimacing.

"I thought you were adventurous," Brax challenged.

"That's one thrill I can do without."

Chuckling, Brax stretched his long, muscular legs and reached for Imani's hand to draw her near. She snuggled close in the crook of his arm and laid her head against his chest. Grover Washington's horn gave way to the sounds of the consummate crooner so that the song "Amazing" became their serenade. Brax felt mellow, expansive there in the limousine's confines. He was touched by Imani's generosity, her desire to be with him as demonstrated in her arranging their chauffeured ride home. Inhaling the scent of her perfume, feeling the thickness of her hair against his jaw, loving the warmth of her body beside his, Brax concluded that this woman, *his* woman, as Luther sang, was amazing indeed.

Moved by a wave of tenderness, Brax swept back the hair framing her face to kiss Imani's jaw. She peered up at him, her deep eyes reflecting a wondrous softness of their own. Brax held her gaze while lowering his mouth to communicate in his own smooth and unique way. Her lips were soft beneath his as Brax offered what he had to give. He teased her with his tongue, flicking and tracing the inner flesh of Imani's mouth with a tender motion that made her hum. Imani gave as good as she got, welcoming his touch, savoring the flavor of his mouth like a thirsty woman who had just found drink. Deeper, deeper they probed until the air between them snapped with the energy generated by a surge of mutual hunger.

There was a breathless quality, perhaps a sliver of trepidation in Imani's voice when she spoke.

"I've changed my mind about Lake Tahoe."

Brax raised a brow.

"I'd rather go home." Imani bit her lip nervously and added, "With you."

BRAX AND THE BEAST

Somebody call the law before it gets illegal up in here.

In the time that Imani and I've been dating, we haven't had sex, consummated our relationship, knocked boots, got busy, nothing. *Nada!* Trust me, it's not because a brother doesn't want to stroll that way, but I never had the green light until now, and kicking it on Abstinence Avenue hasn't been easy when I have this dark, luscious, curvy-swervy, banging body boo in my life. But I'm gaitin' now and it's all good.

We made it back to Sacramento before I . . . *lost the victory* in the back of that limo. Imani was doing a number on a brother with all that friction she was causing me, innocently playing with my ears and rubbing the back of my bald head. When an advertisement on Sacramento's premier Old School and R&B station announced an upcoming concert featuring some of my favorite performers and Imani suggested we go, I had a response on my lips, but just then, Imani's wicked fingers hit *the* spot on my neck. I answered her offer by jerking up tight, a hissing sound seeping between my clenched teeth before collapsing into a bar or two of "Bless that Wonderful Name of Jesus."

Holding Imani's hands before she got us both in trouble with the limo company, I looked at her and pointedly asked if she didn't want to go to Tahoe after all, you know to give her one last chance to bow out gracefully. She passed. I did a mental cartwheel. We crossed the Yolo Causeway to enter our capital city. We had another twenty minutes ahead of us before reaching Imani's. By then I would be able to walk again.

Pearl was sitting at the curb looking like she missed me when we rolled up.

Imani wouldn't allow me to pay for the limousine expense, insisting it was her treat. I backed off and waited until her transaction was complete before escorting Imani to her dark house where the porch light appeared to be the sole source of illumination.

Unlocking the front door and stepping indoors long enough to disarm her security system Imani returned to the threshold to quietly, needlessly and nervously remind me, "Nia's staying overnight at my parents'."

I stepped inside and closed the door. Let the freak fest begin.

I knew Imani's crib was tight, but I was only mildly aware of her collection of Black art or the volumes filling the built-in bookcases when I waited for her downstairs. I'd seen it all before. Besides, when she returned after a brief absence wearing some lounging gown looking thing and finally ushered me upstairs, I was much more interested in a new sight—a four-poster bed in the center of her bedroom that had booty time written all over it.

Imani stepped into the room and with an expansive sweep of her arms said, "Welcome to my love." Taking my hands, she drew me further into the room, her smile sweet and suddenly shy. "You like?"

"Very much so," I assured her, noticing that her belongings reeked of quality and care.

"I'm glad," Imani told me, releasing my hands. She grew quiet, appeared hesitant. I felt her uncertainty. I'm not a monk, but I am a gentleman and if babygirl was having second thoughts about becoming intimately involved I could wait a while longer with the help of a daily ice bath and Dr. Ruth. When trying to delay my gratification during lovemaking I conjure up images of the venerable sex therapist. That little gnome with her crazy accent, bizarre behavior and stiff hair is enough to bring me to a standstill. So if Imani wasn't ready I could log onto old Ruth's website and download a pic when I got home.

"Imani, baby, I don't have to be here."

A soft stream of air escaped her mouth. "I want you here. I'm just nervous," she admitted.

I understood. Brothers have it easy in that regard. We don't have to jump juicy in a negligee and get our hair and makeup together before stepping to a woman. All we have to do is drop the draws. Still, if you haven't dropped them in a while there's room for concern because I don't care what anyone says: having sex is not like riding a bike. You can forget how to ride. You just don't hop on after a long absence and start pumping. You have to find your balance and your rhythm, take a trip or two around the block to regain your speed and momentum until you're smooth riding.

Sensitive to the fact that Imani had not been in a relationship in some time I opened my arms and let her step to me so that I could wrap some reassurance about us both. In fact, I planned to be sensitive all night. I made up my mind right then and there that if it was a go I was going to make sure Imani knew my affection was deep, real deep. I was going to be that sensitive brother who made sure she was often satiated before my groove got off. After we'd both climbed the walls and reached the ceiling, I'd even do the cuddle-chat thing and not just fart, scratch my assets and roll over like a dead man.

I felt Imani relax as I held her tightly.

"I'm your man, baby, count on that. If you're not ready it's not a problem. I'm not going anywhere."

She watched me intently before quietly saying, "I'll be back."

I watched Imani disappear into the adjoining bathroom. I wanted to jump in the air and click my heels together like white guys do in movies.

Okay, what to do? How comfortable should I get? I could drop the gear and hop on the bed and let my stuff air out. Or strip to the boxers and strike a pose against the wall. What if I sprawled out on that area rug on the floor at the foot of Imani's bed and just waited for her butt naked with one of those flowers from the vase on her dresser clenched between my teeth? Laughing at myself, I opted for the armchair, clothed minus my jacket I neatly draped over the back of the chair.

Wait! I didn't have toiletries to freshen my tools. No toothpaste or mouthwash. Did I need to hit the pits with deodorant? Were my hands dry or ashy? I sniffed the pits, checked the paws. They passed inspection. But the breath! It wasn't humming, but it wasn't on hit either. Now, I understood why T. carried what he referred to as his Kitty Kit in the trunk of his car so that he was prepared when, in his words, "booty duty called." I was about to take a swig from one of the perfume bottles on Imani's dresser when I remembered there were after dinner mints from the cruise in my jacket pocket.

I fished them out, unwrapped and popped all five in my mouth. Nothing like the blast of cool mint for foul breath.

What about protection?

Fumbling through my wallet, I found an old faithful condom. I whistled my relief. Prophylactics were beautiful things.

Much more at ease, I leaned back in the chair and stretched out my legs. Next to the chair was a small reading table on top of which sat a daily devotional bible for women of color, yet another something crazy by Iyanla Vanzant, and a novel entitled *The Street*. Flipping to the back cover, I scanned the author's photograph. Old girl was clutching a cane and looking dignified and wise like she had something to say. Intrigued, I opened the novel and began reading.

Engrossing. But not so much so that I didn't hear her entry or smell the scent of her perfume. She smelled like warm vanilla and honey, and looked like pure-D seduction, velvet and deep. Gone was the hesitant woman from before. I rubbed my goatee in anticipation as Imani moved toward me, slow and easy.

There was a dim glow, maybe a nightlight gleaming in the bathroom behind Imani, casting a hazy silhouette about her. She seemed ethereal, awe-inspiring in the play of light and shadow; the white robe with large gray flowers she wore was sheer enough to show the curves of her body barely covered by some lacy black bra and short set showcasing her wonders. *Good God,* I thought, *she's a Bad Mamma Jama.*

"Victoria's Secrets have been revealed," I rumbled in admiration. Imani was tight. I'm talking incredibly gorgeous. She sauntered on long, dark, shapely legs that stretched up into thighs and hips that made my palms itch, only to give way to a tapered waist that was outdone by beautiful breasts that made my mouth water. Her hair was soft and loose against her shoulders. Wicked. Wild. Wonderful.

I watched her every move as she dimmed the lights and aimed a remote at a wall-mounted television unit. On the shelving unit beneath the television was one of those streamline compact stereo components, and it filled the room with the sounds of mellow jazz. Speakers were affixed in two corners, giving off surround sound. I raised a brow, impressed.

Glancing at the book in my hands, she smiled.

"That's my favorite novel. It touches home on so many levels. The story was written decades ago and still I identify with the protagonist who does everything in her power to save her small child from the streets," Imani shared as I closed the book and set it on the table.

I wasn't as interested in a fictitious heroine as I was in the woman of flesh and blood before me.

I eased out of the chair and walked the few steps toward her.

"Did you know that the author was the last remaining writer from the Harlem Renaissance?" Imani asked in a rush.

"No, I didn't." The words reverberated in my chest.

"She was a national treasure, the last of a vanguard of—"

Her voice trailed off as I reached for her, drew her to me. She did this little lip nibble-lick thing that I'd noticed her do often. But in this context it was provocative and screaming my name. Thank God for the mints because I was ready to work that mouth overtime.

I swear the woman was lethal. I took my time, told myself to hold my mule and not get carried away. I'd come too close to buck wild now. Still, the beast was hungry. *I* wouldn't have passed a Breathalyzer with all the intoxication going on. I already knew Imani tasted good, but the feel good blew a gasket as I untied the sash at her waist and slipped my arms beneath her robe, slowly sliding my hands over her back to Imani's behind while tracing a path from her mouth down her chin to her throat with the tip of my tongue. Guess I hit a nerve because she dipped her head back and shivered.

"Woooo! Forgive me, Lord, for I am about to sin," Imani nearly whimpered.

I couldn't help laughing.

Kissing her throat again I felt her kind of melt into my arms, melding her body against mine. I thought I had it going on, whipping hunger on her, caressing her hips, stroking my hands up and down Imani's thighs while exploring her neck and shoulders with my mouth. But then Babygirl turned the tide.

I felt her fingers sliding beneath my shirt, creeping and caressing while she moved backward toward the bed with me following like iron to magnet. Her grin was rather impish as she fumbled with my belt buckle.

"Who's running things here?" I teased, easing us both onto her bed.

"We are," was her hushed response.

Studying her, I liked the sparkle in her eyes, the way Imani looked at me with trust despite any trepidation or vulnerability she may have felt. In return I felt protective of her, wanted to convey my care and assure Imani that I wasn't just some miscellaneous knucklehead trying to hit it and quit it. Supporting my weight on my forearms, I stroked her hair, sank my fingers in the thick, soft virgin locks before kissing her temple.

"Do you believe I'll love you right?"

I referred to more than the moment. Oh, I intended to take my time and do it right until we were both satisfied. But I meant more than glass shattering sex. Imani meant more. This woman was loving and passionate and possessed a genuine kindness that emanated from deep within and it was certainly a plus that she was breathlessly beautiful, but I needed her to know that I wasn't looking for a cheap thrill. I wanted Imani: all of her. She had value in my eyes, and I intended for us to maintain something lasting beyond one, two, ten orgasms and a cigarette. Kidding. Neither of us smokes.

"I trust you."

Those three words sealed an unspoken pact between us. It was all good.

AWAKENING

Imani decided that after-sex sleep had to be the sweetest sleep known to womankind. It was still dark in the room when she awakened to find her body twisted in the sheets and Brax lying besides her sleeping soundly, his arm anchoring her about the waist to his side. Shifting to face him, Imani traced his eyebrows with her finger. Her Brown Sugar Bear needed the rest after all *that!* Whew, Lord, did they trip the light funktastic or what? She felt raw with wonder, whipped and wiped out. Had she any inkling loving Brax would send her over the earth she would have stripped him naked long ago.

Imani felt a purr in her throat as she remembered the gentle ways he caressed her flesh, loved her deep and long and strong. Brax was a generous and attentive lover, a man who enjoyed her enjoyment as much as his own. And that was a good thing considering how she had been a hungry little honey whose amorous appetite roared awake with a vengeance of its own.

You're just a little hoochie, Imani told herself, blushing at the sumptuous memory of her experience with the man beside her. Her very nerve endings had been on fire, teasing, torturing her body with overwhelming sensations that left her weak and wanting more. Even now she tingled with the after shock of a loving so complete it frightened her.

Imani peered about the dark room. It seemed odd in the pre-dawn hours. Perhaps it was the presence of a man in her bed that tilted Imani's perspective, but the room, her world felt fresh and new.

She examined her surroundings, noting the vase of flowers that seemed mysterious and full atop her dresser, her eyes adjusting to the dark as Imani looked about. There atop the small circular table near her window sat her favorite novel about a young divorced and loveless Black woman whose struggle to give her child a better life cruelly backfired on her in the end. Imani considered the tale even as her gaze shifted. Despite the dark of night she knew exactly what was resting beneath *The Street*: her daily devotional bible for women of color. Looking at the bible in the dark something fluttered inside of her.

You're a nasty girl on your way to hell.

Even as she laughed inside, Imani resisted a shiver. She had attended enough Saved & Single functions and heard enough sermons to know God's commands concerning sex outside of marriage. Fornication is and was and would always be a sin. All traces of her humor fled as Imani admitted she had violated a basic principle and tenet of Christianity. Breathing deeply, Imani listened as her head told her heart that she was being sanctimonious and overly religious. What she had shared with Brax was pure, unadulterated, and without premeditation. Imani had merely accepted the gift of an unforeseen opportunity, maximized the moment. There was nothing wrong in that.

It was unplanned. Spontaneous. Imani never imagined the evening would end as it had, with she and Brax knocking the life out of her bedsprings. But, good googa mooga, was she glad.

She would have to send a note to the manufacturer to ask what that peach drink really contained. Imani grinned, knowing sparkling peach juice was not to blame for her suddenly becoming uninhibited. Perhaps it was a combination of factors: the lush night, the relaxing cruise and limo ride, the tenderness she felt from and toward Brax. Or maybe she was just an undersexed, overstressed woman suffering sensory deprivation that her brown sugar bear managed to stimulate and satisfy at the same time.

Brax shifted slightly, his arm growing heavier about her waist.

Imani felt secure, wanted, and precious there with Brax. Stroking the smooth skin on his back, she felt a wall of defiance erecting itself in her breast. She refused to be like her novel's protagonist, unloved and alone. Imani was tired of being mother and father, sole provider responsible for everything that concerned herself and her daughter. She wanted to feel something between the sheets other than old cracker crumbs and toe nail clippings. *Wait on the Lord, baby. His timing is everything,* her optimistic, saved and sanctified grandmother told her ten times too many, the same grandmother who told Imani she was wasting daylight by not dating. What a paradox. Wait. Go. Hold on. Turn loose. And then there was Mo with her eerie spirit readings that Brax was the wrong man, not to mention Nia's difficult attitude and clear dislike of their relationship. Imani ignored the voices clamoring to be heard, attempting to dictate her way. And, so, she granted herself permission to indulge and permission granted she would proceed despite fear or vulnerability. Brax was there and he was hers and that's the way she wanted it, the way she wanted him. She had to seize the day.

It's my life. I'll live it as I please, Imani told herself as she kissed his shoulder and stroked his back until Brax stretched himself awake to find her waiting and willing.

The smell of something good coming from the kitchen led Brax to her when he awakened before the burst of dawn to find that he was alone in an empty bed. Sliding out of bed, he slipped into his long discarded boxer briefs, and made a pit stop in the bathroom before going in search of Imani.

He found her moving about the kitchen, arrayed in that sheer robe thing of hers with an apron on top as she removed a cookie sheet from the oven. Cooking in the kitchen never looked so good. Soundlessly Brax eased up behind her to lavish her with his embrace.

"You scared me," Imani breathed, relaxing back against him.

"Do you always bake chocolate chip cookies at five o'clock in the morning?"

"Only when . . . I . . . get . . . a craving," Imani mumbled, arching her back and doing a little shoulder shimmy as Brax nuzzled her neck. "You're going to make me drop these," Imani drawled, using a spatula to remove the oven fresh confections from the baking sheet and onto a plate atop the counter to cool before she would place them in a waiting cookie jar that was a bust of an elderly Black woman with a floppy, flowered hat on her gray head. "Brax . . . stop . . ."

"Have you ever made anything other than cookies in the kitchen?"

Brax suggestively crooned in her ear, relentless in his seductive manipulations as his hands slithered upward to cup and caress her fullness.

"Okay now . . . *wooo* . . . Brax, put one of these in your mouth before you get in trouble," Imani warned, gingerly picking up a warm cookie and turning about to pop the sweet confection in his mouth.

"Ouch, Boo, that's hot!" he protested, chewing cautiously, his brows slithering up in pleasant surprise. "Whatcha say now? Babygirl has other skills." Grinning mischievously, Brax fingered the flimsy robe beneath Imani's apron, which was holding her bosom in check, and asked, "Got milk?"

Imani swatted his arm, screeching, "You're terrible!"

"I know, and you like me that way."

Amused, Imani pried herself free from his embrace to pull a carton of cold milk from the refrigerator and fill a glass that she offered to Brax, who was busy downing his third cookie.

"Did you know that the cacao bean is an aphrodisiac in some cultures?" Imani inquired as Brax sipped his milk, his eyes slowly, wantonly traveling from her face and down her body as if her long apron concealed nothing from his view.

"Oh?"

"Ancient Aztecs used chocolate as a sacred concoction in certain religious ceremonies pertaining to their goddess of fertility," Imani relayed, as Brax grabbed another warm cookie and extended it to Imani so that she could take a bite before he devoured what remained. Melted chocolate on his fingers, Brax drew a path from her chin to her throat.

"It's an opiate," Imani murmured as Brax followed the path of chocolate with his tongue.

He felt raw, rough, like he wanted to dispense with tenderness as Imani wiggled against him as he embraced her, igniting something ancient in him. Preoccupied with conveying the sudden raw hunger he felt Brax seemed oblivious to the ringing telephone. Imani was not. She stiffened.

"It's after five in the morning," she needlessly announced, breaking their embrace to hurry across the kitchen to glance at the caller ID before snatching up the telephone.

"Mother? Oh, Nia . . ." A slight pause elapsed before Imani spoke again, this time concern coloring her tone. "Nia, stop crying. Everything is going to be all right. Nia, are you listening to me?" This pause was longer than before. "I want you to find the telephone directory and look up that animal emergency hospital off of Freeport Boulevard. Call them and explain the situation and tell them we're en route. Can you do that? Okay. I'm on my way."

"What's wrong?" Brax asked when Imani hung up.

"Miss Pitman is throwing up. Ray is out of town and my mother can't find her car keys and Nia's in a tizzy," Imani reported. "Oh, Lord, look at this kitchen. I have flour and sugar all over the place."

"Go get dressed. I'll do this," Brax offered, laying a gentle hand on her arm.

"Thanks, sweetie," she sighed and raced from the room.

Five minutes later Imani returned fully dressed, keys and purse in hand, to find Brax had made good on his promise to straighten her kitchen.

"Thank you, Brax. I'm sorry about all of this," Imani apologized, looking suddenly harried.

"Things happen. You want me to come to the hospital with you?"

She shook her head, wondering how she could possibly explain his presence if he did.

"We'll be okay."

"Are you sure?"

Imani nodded.

"I'll wrap up these "opiates" for you to take home and enjoy," Imani offered, smiling briefly as she found a container in which to place the fresh baked cookies.

"I'll get dressed so you can go," Brax advised, pausing to hug Imani and lend some comfort to an obviously stressful situation. "You know I hate your dog for messing up my game, but I hope she's okay. If you need me call me."

"I will," Imani promised. "Brax?" she called, stepping from the kitchen as Brax reached the stairs.

"Yes?"

"Thank you for being here with me. I appreciate . . . *everything.*"

"Believe me, Boo, I know," Brax assured her with a salacious grin.

IMANI

Imani vacillated between exhilaration and exhaustion. Her weekend had been full of surprises that left her weary and wonderful. The ordeal with Miss Pitman was enough to put hair on her chest. Apparently, Saturday night the greedy old thing knocked over the garbage can in her parent's kitchen to help itself to a forbidden feast of grilled pork chop bones. Unable to properly digest the bones, the shards lacerated her stomach lining and irritated her intestines, causing violent bouts of vomiting in an effort to expel the blockage. It was a most costly meal to the tune of seven hundred and fifty dollars.

It was emergency surgery or inevitable death according to the expensive doctor and his expensive X-rays. But seven hundred and fifty dollars?! Imani did not have that kind of money. Not for a greedy, scavenging canine. She was ready to kiss Miss Pit good-bye, light a candle and say a prayer, but Nia's dismay and heartbreak compelled Imani to find a way to save the day. Of course Nigel could not be found to help with the financial burden so Imani applied for a line of credit at the pet hospital only to be surprised when her request was denied. Credit was rarely granted, the clerk assured her, so Imani was forced to write a check for a portion of the bill and charge the remainder on her credit card.

By the way, Miss Evans, were you aware that we offer a health insurance plan? The Premium Package is only $11.95 a month and could save you up

*to 45% on any future medical expenses for your pet, and bi-annual compre-
hensive exams are free. I'm sure you and Nia want to keep Miss Pitman
around a long time.*

Imani remembered looking at the clerk, her mouth agape, telling
herself not to hop over the desk and beat the man upside his head
with the dog leash she held. Why didn't someone tell her about the
stupid insurance before now? And how much longer did Miss Pit *need*
to live? She was already two-thousand-and-twelve in dog years.

Surgery was performed and Miss Pitman was saved. After keeping
the canine for observation, the dog was released on Sunday night and
came home drugged and sluggish but alive with an arsenal of antibi-
otics, anti-vomiting medication, and toothbrush and chicken-flavored
toothpaste (Miss Pitman had gingivitis) that set Imani back another
fifty dollars and required that she set her alarm clock every three
hours in order to administer the medication. Imani silently accepted
the paraphernalia thinking Miss P. would just have to gum it when
her teeth went because she was not about to brush a dog's grill.

Such was her weary world as Nurse Nightingale.

But Imani the Wonderful bounced into work Monday morning despite a gnawing fatigue.

Her weekend with Brax was like a cassette in her mind that she
wanted to rewind until the tape snapped. Imani had a one-word description for what transpired between them: supercalifragilisticexpi-
alidocious!

Imani laughed at her own sudden silliness as she headed toward
her office. Making love with Brax had done something to her, energized and fueled her in a curious way.

"Good morning, Rachel," Imani sang, waltzing into the anteroom
of her office and greeting the department's administrative assistant.

Rachel glanced away from her computer screen and returned
Imani's infectious grin.

"Well, happy Monday morning to you, too. You're in a good mood."

"Aren't I always?"

"You're not exactly a morning person, but then again, it is after ten
so I guess your joy is legit," the young woman tactfully responded.

"Thank you, Miss Fong. Any messages?"

"No . . . oh, wait. Gladys popped in and asked that you come see
her as soon as you got in."

Imani frowned wondering what urgency the sales and marketing director could possibly have that involved her.

"Don't forget your training session for the new software and database system starts at two."

"Thanks, Rachel," Imani stated, stepping into her office and closing the door.

Securing her purse and briefcase in her desk cabinet, Imani turned on her computer and checked the water pot atop a stand near the desk. It held just enough liquid to nourish the bevy of plants lending an exotic beauty to the small room. Imani set about her task, snapping off dead debris and tossing it into a wastebasket before watering soil and stroking verdant leaves with nurturing fingers.

Her mind drifted.

Like black and white images preserved for all time, reflections spun across Imani's vision at a slow and tantalizing, almost torturous, pace. The sheen of his skin glowed brown sugar sweet as Brax lowered his body on top of hers. Again, Imani saw the hunger and desire in his eyes like a torrential rain that threatened to sweep her away. She imagined she felt his moist mouth, his probing tongue raking her flesh with wanton delight. Imani shivered in the warmth of day recalling the heat of that night.

Smiling, Imani recalled her hectic quest to set the mood. Shortly after their arrival she had raced upstairs to quickly shower, slip on a lounging gown, then scour her closet for something sensual and seductive to wear while Brax waited downstairs in the family room. Imani was disappointed to discover she owned a few silky nightshirts, but nothing guaranteed to set it off. Just when Imani was about to despair, imagining Brax's expression when she appeared in some Moms Mabley cotton panties, she came across the black lace bra and short set she bought herself two Christmases ago. Imani cut off the tags, grabbed her white and gray robe and dashed into her bathroom to hang the garments on the door hook before going downstairs to bring Brax up into her private domain.

Then she panicked. Protection: she did not have any. She was not taking oral contraceptives, she had no diaphragm, and no Norplant she could poke up her arm, no sponge to soak it up. Nothing! Maybe she could just hop up and down or do jumping jacks after intercourse to shake it all loose. Nervously she slipped into the bathroom to finish her preparations, wondering what to do the entire time. And then she stepped from the bathroom, immediately spotting the small plastic wrapped contraceptive Brax had placed on the book table. Imani sighed with relief. Where there was a want there was a way. What ensued was enough to fill several pages in her sexual history annals, volumes one and two.

There was a tap at the door.

"Come in."

Rachel opened the door and stepped inside.

"Sorry to disturb you but . . . Imani!"

"Hmm?"

"There's water dripping all over the place," the woman cautioned.

"Oh, no," Imani yelped, realizing the plant she was watering was overflowing, the run-off dripping onto the floor. She rushed to her desk to find a box of tissues to blot the carpet dry as best she could.

"I'll go get some paper towels," Rachel offered.

"No, that's okay. What gives?"

"Oh, right. HH called," Rachel informed, referring to Daystar's CEO whom she and Imani jokingly called HH, short for Head Honcho. "He wants to see you in his office pronto!"

"I have been summoned," Imani gravely announced. "Rachel, would you mind calling maintenance to see if they have an air blower or wet vac or something they can use to clean up this mess?"

"Will do," Rachel promised.

Imani plopped the soiled tissues in the trash and the box onto her desk and glanced at her computer screen to see her electronic mailbox flashing. She had ten e-mails waiting, one marked urgent. Quickly, she clicked open the box and saw that the message marked urgent was from Gladys. In the subject heading was the word "RESTRUCTURING" typed in capital letters. What now?

Whatever was going on it had to wait. HH rang.

Not until she rushed down the hallway in the direction of the executive offices did Imani consider a correlation between the urgent e-mail from Gladys and the CEO's summoning her. Her pace slowed. Her pulse quickened. Something was going on. What had Gladys stopped by to tell her? *Restructuring.* Imani had a sudden sinking feeling. The hammer was about to fall. The powers that be had deemed her as expendable, surplus goods and she was about to be let go.

Imani just hoped the CEO had the decency to look pained when he did it.

You are not without hope, Imani. Have faith.

The thought drifted peacefully through her mind like falling leaves.

She had a plan, a vision. Imani realized that indeed she had hope. If she was about to receive the boot she had something to fall back on. Her boutique was a plan in progress. It might be rough and tumble for a minute but her entrepreneurial endeavor could and would work. It had to. Besides, getting the ax could prove a blessing in disguise, the final push and impetus she needed to truly delve into her dream.

"Imani! Come on in," Daystar's CEO welcomed her, a bright smile on his face. He proved jovial, asking about her daughter, her department, did she have any suggestions for streamlining or improving Training and Development.

Imani responded to his inquiries feeling as though she was being milked for ideas before the bouncer arrived.

"Well, Imani, you're fully aware of the current state of affairs here at Daystar. The executive board has had to make some painful decisions of late . . ."

Imani tried to stay in tune with what the man was saying, but she couldn't bear to hear his words. Boutique or not it would be hard letting go and leaving an employer to whom she had devoted ten years of her life.

". . . demographics, salary expenditures and cost of living have led us to shift our home base from Sacramento to Phoenix . . ."

Here it comes, she thought. Gladys was right. The old heads had to go.

". . . so we'd like you to consider our offer. We want you to relocate to Phoenix as the Regional Director of Training and Development."

Imani sat speechless.

The CEO rushed on to entice her with a proposed salary double her current earnings. And perks and perks and perks. Plus, the company would pay for temporary housing in Phoenix, as well as provide ten percent toward a down payment on a new home if she chose to purchase in Arizona. They needed an answer as soon as possible, preferably in a matter of days. But understanding that she might need more time, Imani could take a week or two to mull it over.

"A decision today would be optimum, but no pressure," her boss said, chuckling before Imani departed to return to her office where Gladys waited at Rachel's desk.

"I have been waiting for you all morning," Gladys announced, grabbing Imani by the arm and whisking through the office, Rachel on their heels. "HQ is moving to Phoenix," she whispered, closing Imani's door behind them.

"I-I know," Imani muttered. "Sacramento will no longer serve as headquarters."

"I told you *they* were up to something," the other woman exclaimed. "Next thing you know they'll be closing us down."

"That won't happen, will it?" Rachel inquired, appearing afraid.

"I don't know, Rachel," Imani responded, still reeling with the offer she had just received. She needed time to process the offer, to mull it over and decide what she would do. Until then she felt it best to conceal the proposed promotion. "But you'll know the moment I hear anything about this site remaining open or not."

The phone rang.

"I have to get back to my desk," Rachel announced, exiting quickly.

"And I have a meeting with a vendor. Let's chat later," the sales and marketing director suggested and departed as well.

Imani sank into her chair and answered the ringing phone.

"Training and Development, Imani Evans speaking."

"Good morning, lovely."

A tender smile stole across her face.

"Good morning to you, too, handsome. How are you?"

"Missing you," Brax replied, his voice rich and resonant.

"That's the sweetest compliment I've had all day. I miss you, too."

"Yeah, tell a brother anything. I haven't heard from you in, what, two or three hours," Brax joked. "I'm starting to feel insecure as if you just used my body for your personal pleasure."

"You're right, I did and I'll do it again in a heartbeat if you let me. So, how's your day so far? Any students go fifty-one-fifty on you?"

"Not yet, but the day is still young."

There was a knock on Imani's door, halting her reply.

"Brax, hold on for just one moment."

Imani depressed the hold button and went to open her door. Rachel stood on the opposite side with a large decorative gift box in hand.

"Special delivery for you, mademoiselle," she announced, handing Imani the package.

Imani managed to extract the card attached to a lavish bow while balancing the bundle in the crook of her arm. Her eyes grew misty as she read,

You kiss my senses.

—B.

"What does it say and who is it from?"

"Bye, Rachel," Imani chimed, waiting for her assistant to disappear before closing the door and returning to the telephone. "Brax, are you still there?"

"Yes."

"I just received a beautiful gift box," Imani announced.

"From whom?"

"A mysterious admirer."

"What's inside?"

"Let's see." Imani carefully unwrapped the package to find it filled with chocolate kisses and a bottle of sparkling peach juice. "Mmm!" Smiling, she placed the beverage on her desk before opening another box nestled within the larger one. She held up a pair of red satin dress sandals similar to the pair she'd ruined the other night. "Brax, you didn't have to do this. I could've had my shoe repaired."

"I did it because I wanted to. You like?"

Removing the pump she wore, Imani slipped her foot into the sandal and smiled.

"I like them better than the other pair," she declared. "Thanks, sweetie, I'm touched by the drink, and the kisses, and the shoes—"

"Keep looking. There should be something else in that box."

Cradling the phone against her shoulder Imani rummaged through the large box until finding the missing gift. She laughed aloud at the coupon for fifty cents off a twelve-ounce bag of Nestle's Tollhouse morsels.

"Brax, I love it!"

"Good. So when can I get some more cookies?"

"When can I get some more, period?" Imani returned.

Brax coughed into the phone.

"You need a sexorcist. Calling my job talking all nasty and I can't do anything about it."

"You called me," Imani reminded Brax. "And the way I remember it there's plenty you can and do well," Imani crooned suggestively, easing back into her seat and crossing her legs, bobbing her foot slightly.

"So, you had a good time, huh?"

"I'm ready for round two," Imani purred.

"Close the blinds, I'm on my way. Hey, are you available for dinner?"

"Sorry. I came in late today so I'm here until seven, and when I get off I have to take Nia shopping for shoes for band. How about tomorrow? Or Thursday when Nia's at band practice?"

"I'll let you know if I can clear my calendar," Brax answered. "I have an appointment with the sauna room at the gym, the lawn mower and my backyard, and that novel you loaned me. Girl, I'm busy."

"Me and my cookies will make it worth your while."

"I'll get the milk on the way," Brax bantered. "Listen, baby, I have a meeting with a student. Can I call you later?"

"Please do. Have a good day."

Imani disconnected the call and turned her attention to the gift before her. It was a thoughtful gesture, an assurance that Brax shared the wonder of their new world. Their sexual explorations had only just begun. For Imani it was gratifying to know she meant something to the man other than a physical thrill. She cherished that reassurance.

Imani could not believe she was making booty calls. The weeks flew by in a sex-filled rush. She just could not slow her roll. It was a difficult negotiation. She had to synchronize her schedule with Brax's. She attended church on Sundays, worked late on Mondays. Brax was usually at the gym on Tuesdays and occupied by 100 Strong meetings on Wednesdays so that by the time Thursday rolled around Imani was biting nails like bubble gum. She had the itch and she had it bad. Now that her three thousand years of self-imposed celibacy had ended, Imani felt like a candidate for Nymphomaniacs Anonymous. She was off the chain.

It was awkward trying to sustain a relationship when her daughter showed her disapproval in so many subtle yet unmistakable ways. Imani decided it was best to retain a certain degree of privacy. She told herself she was not hiding, merely separating her love life from her home life by keeping Brax out of the house when Nia was home, or by visiting Brax instead. Nia would need to adjust and to help her do so Imani would gradually incorporate Brax deeper into their lives. Until then she had wheels and would travel.

With Nia at band practice, Imani surprised Brax one Thursday by showing up unannounced at his house and—after ensuring that Terrance was not and would not be home any time soon—started the foreplay right there in the entryway, only to back that thing up until they were conjoined in the middle of his bed, the fish tank gurgling softly beneath the sounds of their wild loving. After that Thursdays and weekends were marked for their official Freak Fests.

"You're wearing me down, Babygirl," Brax teased, kissing her out the door one Freak Fest Thursday and into her car so that Imani could race to pick Nia up from band practice.

That was last night. Tonight—after a trip to the gym during which Brax spotted Imani as she attempted circuit weight lifting for the first time, their meal at an Italian café, and a trip to Baskin Robbins—they reclined in Imani's family room, each with a spoon sharing a pint of Jamoca Almond Fudge. Occasionally, they fed each other, elaborately licking spoons and dribbling fudge as part of their private brand of seduction.

The only light was that emanating from the television and the glow of vanilla scented candles strategically placed throughout the room. They sat in the oversized chair-and-a-half, Imani's legs across his lap as Brax sprawled out comfortably, his long muscular legs propped on the ottoman, watching *Daughters of the Dust*.

Imani had lost count of the number of times she had viewed the film. She loved the imagery, the slow camera pans across the Gullah women of a fictitious island. Beautiful black females with intricate braids and natural hairstyles, their white dresses stark against their rich skins, cavorted on a beach, the sparkling ocean a backdrop to their majesty. It was a cinematic wonder showcasing spectacular black women in all of their glory, loving one another and the men who cherished them. It was stunning, visually and emotionally. And despite the often-thick dialect, Imani managed to quote a few lines, tears in her eyes as a wanton and wayward relative who had returned to the island with her female lover in tow greeted her grandmother.

"Baby."

"Hmm?" Imani absentmindedly responded, watching the film and rubbing the back of her man's neck in a slow, tantalizing fashion.

"I hate to break it to you, but I'm having trouble with this movie," Brax admitted. "It's visually appealing and all but the veins in my head are throbbing with all this Geechee language and symbolism."

Imani's expression was one of incredulity.

"You're kidding right?"

"No, I'm not. It takes too much to follow along," Brax stated, licking ice cream from his spoon. "Give me some subtitles or *Daughters of the Dust for Dummies* or something, please."

Imani smacked her lips in annoyance.

"You're worse than Nia."

Brax cocked a brow at her.

"So I have the sensibilities and sophistication of a teenager?"

"I didn't say that, sweetie," Imani amended while gently kneading his ear. "I had difficulties understanding the first time, too. I suggest you watch the film at least twice to grasp the thematic idealism and—"

"Twice would be two times too many," Brax replied.

Imani stared at him briefly before cramming her spoon in the ice cream, hopping from the chair and walking over to the television to eject the disc from the DVD player.

"What would *you* like to watch?" she asked tightly, rifling through the movies neatly organized in a cabinet within the entertainment center. "I have Samuel L.'s *Shaft*. No, that's probably too deep as well. Here we are! *Kindergarten Cop* and some old Disney." Turning toward Brax she offered, "You're my guest. It's your choice."

Imani watched as Brax fingered his goatee. He appeared amused. Setting the ice cream container on a nearby table Brax inquired, "No *Monster's Ball*?"

"No," Imani replied, crossing her arms. "I can't have all those naked butts in my house."

"Can I have yours?"

Imani smiled almost grudgingly.

"Come on, Babygirl. Come see me," Brax invited with a pat on his thighs. "Put anything on. I won't be paying attention."

Imani took her time inserting a new disc into the DVD player before casually easing herself back into their chair to focus on the screen ahead.

" 'Ey, you mad at me for dogging your movie?" Brax breathed into her ear.

"No," was her somewhat petulant reply. Imani admitted to herself that she had overacted to Brax's comments about the film. She was on edge and she knew why.

Imani's boss wanted her to fly to Arizona again to spend a few days at the Phoenix sight. Sensing her uncertainty, he was relentless, court-ing and flattering Imani with the benefits of relocating. She should, he suggested, reacquaint herself with the infrastructure there—the other employees, the flow of business, the vibe, etcetera. Imani consid-ered his suggestion a wise idea as her prior visit had been consumed by her training assignment. Still, Imani was uncomfortable, not with the return to Phoenix, but with the knowledge that she was actually considering the offer.

She vacillated.

Moving to Phoenix might prove beneficial. The promotion would provide a certain financial security, a change of scenery, and perhaps it was God's way of giving her a second chance to move away and ex-perience a different life, as she had never fulfilled her desire of living in New York. But there was Nia, the plans for her boutique, and now Brax to consider. Imani did not want to uproot her child or push the realization of the boutique further away. And her relationship with Brax merited time and energy that she could not give hundreds of miles away. Torn, Imani decided not to broach the subject with Brax until she had made a definite decision one way or the other. The stress had upset her stomach for days on end.

Imani tried to play aloof as Brax brushed her hair from her neck to nuzzle her throat, nibbling her skin so that she wanted to purr.

"I think you're mad at me," he whispered, running his bare foot up her leg.

"I would appreciate it if you wouldn't scrape your rusty hoof across my flesh. That is not sensual," Imani instructed, suppressing a smile.

"The woman wants sensual," Brax remarked, slipping a hand be-neath her T-shirt, his wandering fingers pausing suddenly in their journey. "What is this?"

"What?"

"This," Brax returned, pulling the elastic band of Imani's sports bra so that it snapped back against her ribs.

"Ouch!" she yelped, jerking away.

"Sorry, Boo. That contraption is a little on the binding side, don't you think? What happened to the easy access hook things?"

"I accidentally dropped my other "contraption" in the shower at the gym and had to put this one back on. Where there's a will there's a way," Imani challenged.

"My Lord knows the way through the wilderness," Brax sang before burrowing his head beneath Imani's shirt, causing her to scream and wildly squirm so that they both fell onto the floor where they proceeded to wrestle until Imani managed to wiggle out of his grasp and sit on top of him.

"You're on my stomach, babygirl," Brax informed.

"Yes . . . and?"

"I just ate."

"Oh," Imani replied, bouncing slightly. Throwing his head back, Brax painfully grimaced as Imani continued her torment. "Watch my movie with me and I'll get up," she wagered.

"Get a bucket 'cause either way I'm going to heave. Now get off of me." Before Imani could react, Brax grabbed her about the waist and quickly inverted their positions so that he, having the upper hand, could resume his earlier exploration. Imani screamed as Brax manipulated her bra until he gained access to pleasure. In between her own encouraging coos and the sound of the television Imani thought she detected something else. A soft click then voices in the distance?

". . . I think Mom has one but I'm not sure. Mom!"

"Nia!" Imani hissed, readjusting her breasts in her bra as Brax got to his feet and helped her up. She frantically glanced about the room as if to ensure there were no obvious signs of their foreplay, then grabbed one of the burning scented candles and slowly pivoted with it as if to freshen the air, fanning the room with her free hand all the while. Repositioned in the overstuffed armchair Brax scratched his ear and laughed as Imani replaced the candle then rushed across the room to plop down beside him. Thinking better of it, Imani jumped up from the chair and hopped over onto the sofa, smoothing her shirt only to discover two telltale signs of arousal pressing against the fabric. Brax laughed uproariously as Imani folded her arms across her chest just as Nia entered the room.

"Hey, Mom," Nia cheerfully called. "Oh, hey Mr. B.," she said with far less enthusiasm. "I didn't see your car."

" 'Ey, shorty, wassup?"

"Hi, Snookie," Imani greeted her child, displeased by Nia's response to Brax being there. "We had to park up the street because of a dinner party next door."

"Why are you guys watching cartoons?" Nia asked, looking from Imani to Brax as if she found their actions weird. "Mom, I thought you said Walt Disney was a racist, sexist propagandist?"

"He was, but I like Sebastian the Crab. Let me see your hair. Very nice, Nia," Imani admired, stroking and examining the intricate braids with decorative wooden beads Nia wore. "I thought you were going to call me when Stacey finished."

"I was, but Grampy was at the shop so he gave me a ride home."

As if summoned by the mention of his name, Ray Carmichael entered the room chewing on a banana.

"Imani, hope you don't mind, but I grabbed myself a snack. Oh, well, now it's your young gentleman friend."

Imani frowned as Brax rose awkwardly from his seat and tugged down his oversized T-shirt before extending a hand toward her stepfather. She wanted to howl when realizing that his discomfort was the result of his attempts to shield his own waning evidence of their sex play.

"How are you, Mr. Carmichael?" he politely inquired.

"Just fine, young man. It's nice to see you again. Oh, Imani I came in because I need another ice cooler for my fishing trip tomorrow. Do you have one I can use?"

"You fish, Mr. Carmichael?"

"Oh, yeah, all the time," he informed Brax, who had quickly resumed his seat. "My buddies and I go up to Clear Lake and come home with all kinds of catfish and perch. And the best part about it," Ray said, finishing his banana, "there're no ladies allowed. You should come with us."

"Imani and I have plans this weekend but I just might take you up on that offer later," Brax advised.

"You do that, young man."

"Imani, I'm going to pull up now and head out," Brax announced, cautiously easing out of his chair, causing her to snicker. "Peep you later, shorty. Enjoy your trip, Mr. Carmichael."

"There's an ice chest in the garage, Ray. I'll get it for you after I see

Brax out," Imani promised, taking his hand and escorting Brax to the front door, neither one missing Ray's stating "now that's a nice young man" or Nia's sucking her teeth in reply.

"You have my stepfather's seal of approval," Imani stated, hoping Brax would ignore Nia's petulance. Time to put her daughter in check.

"That's a good thing," Brax remarked, hugging her close.

"And what plans do we have this weekend that would prevent you from going fishing?"

"I'll let you figure that out," answered Brax, rubbing her thigh for good measure.

Her smile became a grimace.

"What's wrong?"

"My stomach hurts. Probably too much ice cream," Imani suggested. "It'll pass."

They kissed goodnight, and Imani waved as Brax got into his car and drove away. She closed the door wondering if she could fill up enough on Brax during this weekend's love fest to hold her over until she returned from Phoenix.

WHEN MOM IS AWAY . . .

Kicking it came easy. With her mother in Phoenix, Nia had the whole house to herself. And it was about time. She was fourteen and old enough not to need a babysitter. One day Imani would realize that. Until then, Nia would do what she had to. Like now for example. Her grandparents had arranged to pick her up after school so she could spend the time with them until her mother returned. Nia found a crafty way out. She told her grandparent's she'd decided to stay at her godmother's instead. She told Monique the exact opposite. Nia did neither. She stayed home. And knowing how her mother was prone to call and check on her in her absence, Nia was sure to beat her mother to the punch and call Imani on a daily basis. Slick.

It was cool kicking it with her friends after her hour-long penance in the study lab, just chilling and vibing on whatever they wanted. But Nia did *not* need to vibe off of *that.*

"Clarence, what are you doing?" she screeched.

Her friend lay back on the grass and inhaled.

"You're going to get me in trouble," Nia shouted above the din of the music blasting from the portable stereo she'd moved outdoors for their enjoyment.

"It's only a cigarette, Nia," Krista Ramirez pointed out, snapping her fingers and dancing provocatively with her own male companion.

"Yeah, a funny herb-filled cigarette," Nia retorted, choking on smoky air.

"Chill, Boo, your mama's away so let the shorties play," Clarence sang, blowing smoke rings into the air. "Here, hit this."

Nia scowled and pushed away the offensive smelling object.

"Just give me a drink," Nia retorted, attempting to save face. She accepted a wine cooler and found she actually liked the fruity concoction. It was one, two, and by the time she started in on her third one, Nia was singing at the top of her lungs, and creating a human sandwich with Krista and her male friend as they danced.

Clarence jumped up and ran from the backyard hollering over his shoulder, "I gotta get somethin' outta my brother's trunk." A few moments later he returned, hiding something behind his back.

"W-h-hat's that-t-t?" Nia asked, her speech rather slurred.

"It's for you, Boo," Clarence said, producing a plastic plant with bright yellow flowers. Handing it to Nia he grabbed her from behind and started in on his own peculiar version of bump and grind.

"Isn't that Mrs. Greer's stupid singing plant?" Krista asked. Walking over to Nia she took the pot, turned it over and flipped a switch that set the yellow blossoms into action.

"Daisies, daisies, it's a wonderful day," the animated blossoms began to sing.

"Ooooooo! Are you guys the ones who broke into the study lab?" Nia shrieked, suddenly sober.

Clarence and his friend exchanged looks and laughed.

"We went for a ride that day in a red hottie, too," Clarence bragged.

Nia felt Krista's fingers digging into her arm.

"No! Tell me you did not steal Mr. B.'s car," Krista screamed, giggling and jumping up and down.

"Shhh!" Clarence hissed, suddenly cautious. "We didn't steal anything. We borrowed his car is all."

"Ohmygosh," Nia panted repeatedly. "You guys are crazy stupid."

"And you're crazy fine, Boo. Let me get at you," Clarence said, rubbing her bare belly. Nia shrugged him off.

"Hey, Nia, when're we gonna finally do this?"

"Do what, Krista?"

"This," her best friend responded, rubbing her own stomach and playing with her navel while giving Nia a pointed, conspiratorial look. "A butterfly would be cute."

"Y'all getting' tattoos?" Clarence wanted to know. "You should. It's crazy sexy."

"Come on, Nia. Let's do it so it can heal before your Mom gets back," Krista urged.

Nia looked from Clarence and back at Krista and said with a shrug, "Why not?"

HELL AND HIGH

WATER

Can someone tell me how I went from falling in love to being fouled out all in a day? Either I'm trapped in a nightmare or God doesn't like me anymore. Either way my world is jacked!

It started yesterday.

There I was at work, cleaning up my office, setting my files in order and taking care of my business when the bottom started falling out.

Summer vacation was a week away and a brother was jumping with joy. One of the perks I love most in my job is having a ten-month work year. September through May I get my slave on. In June I usually work half days just to get my stuff straight and squared away, tightening up loose threads while preparing for the upcoming school year. July through August I'm outtie five-hundred.

I was looking forward to my trip home to Indiana, looking forward to being with Imani tomorrow night. She said she had a surprise for me. I had no idea what it could be but I couldn't care less. All I wanted was a taste of the chocolate. Thoughts of Imani brought me to a task I didn't relish. I had to dump Nia.

I felt it was unethical to continue as her counselor. My dating her mother constituted a definite conflict of interest. Fortunately for me my grading policy in my Career Choice class was qualitative and not subjective. Student grades were based on attendance, the computer modules they completed, and the assessment of the instructors they personally selected to act as on-site supervisors. The "supervisors" reviewed the student's "job" applications, evaluated their mock interviews, and reported to me on the student's fulfillment or failure of job duties which merely amounted to daily punching in and out on a time clock, and meeting with the supervisor once a week. According to her supervisor Nia had earned an A fair and square. So I gave it to her, relieved that in this regard Nia's enrollment in my class was not problematic. But I felt bad sitting at my computer addressing a mandatory "Dear Jane" letter to her mother, informing Imani that I had reassigned Nia to a different guidance counselor for the upcoming school year.

I like Nia. I always thought she was a good little shorty. I acknowledge that my dating her mother hasn't been easy on her, and her attitude leads me to believe that Nia wishes her parents were still together. I understand that. But the thing is: *they* aren't and *we* are. Honestly, I think Nia's a sweet kid despite her showing some subtle hostilities toward me. I know she's conveniently failed to give her mother some of my phone messages, and she takes pleasure in inserting her father into conversations whenever I'm around. But the strange thing is that at school, in my Career Exploration class, Nia is as she always was: lively and outgoing. She's very ambitious and wants to be a veterinarian and applies herself in class. It's only off campus, after hours, when I'm with her mother that she acts like she wants to shoot me with poison darts. Still, I'm careful to invite her on outings with Imani and me out of respect for them both, wanting them to know that I value Nia's person and that I do not view her as an intrusion.

"Mr. B., you have a minute?"

I looked up to find the study lab monitor, Mrs. Greer, standing in my doorway.

"I have *two* minutes for you young lady." The look on her face suddenly wiped the smile from mine. "What's wrong?" I asked, rising from my chair and moving toward her, noticing the plastic potted daisies in her hands. "Hey, you found your singing flowers. Where were they?" I questioned, remembering that Mrs. Greer's battery operated plant was the only item missing from the study lab when it was vandalized three months ago.

Stepping into my office, Mrs. Greer closed the door behind her and placing the plant on my desk she started crying.

"I found it this morning in a locked supply cabinet in the study lab." She paused, pulling a tissue from her dress pocket to dab at her teary eyes. "No one else has access to that cabinet . . . except Nia Evans," she sobbed. "Since N-Nia s-s-started helping me I give her the key whenever she needs it. And I thought she was such a nice girl." And with that Mrs. Greer broke down and wailed.

Having seen us at the annual Dixieland Jazz Jubilee in Old Sacramento last month, Mrs. Greer was the only member of school personnel who knew about the relationship between Imani and me. So, I was not surprised that she brought this matter to my attention. But I was surprised at Nia. What did she want with some crazy annoying plastic flowers . . . ? Another, more disturbing thought with far-reaching implications rose above the former. Had Nia been involved in the vandalism incident?

Mrs. Greer and I talked for a while in hushed tones until she eventually left, a sad look on her face, her little plant in her hands.

Damn! I hate daisies!

An hour later, I sat in the principal's office facing Nia, Krista Ramirez, Clarence Johnson, and his partner in crime. It was obvious from the onset that Nia had not been in this alone, and although confronted by the evidence she had a sudden case of lockjaw. But it didn't take long to put two and two together until things added up to the rag-tag crew of juvenile delinquents sitting across from me who, once confronted with the evidence, admitted to their crimes.

Mrs. Whitston, the school principal was fit to be tied.

"What, pray tell, do you have to say for yourselves? This is an upstanding school, one of the finest in the district and I expect you to behave like upstanding students. How could you commit such atrocities?"

Clarence Johnson was shooting Molotov cocktails at Nia with his eyes. Unless my hearing had checked out on me, I could've sworn he'd hissed something at her about her being a punk—a female dog who needed her tongue cut out.

"Excuse me, young brother, but what did you say?"

Before I knew it I was up in his face ready to check him.

Principal Whitston jumped between us.

"Mr. Wade, take a seat. Clarence, you do the same."

"Naw!" he yelled. "You wanna lock us up? Go 'head. I ain't scared. I know how this game works. Nia'll walk 'cause her mother's banging him," he said, tossing a finger in my direction, "and the rest of us will take the rap. That's aiight. She'll get hers," Clarence threatened.

"I didn't say a thing to anyone about anything," Nia shouted in return, momentarily taking the heat off of me. I knew by the puzzled expression on Mrs. Whitston's face that she was curious about Clarence's reference to Imani and me.

"Then how the hell did they find out?" Clarence spat.

"I put the plant back!" Nia screamed, close to tears. "I was just trying to do the right thing. I swear I didn't say a word about the plant or the car . . ."

"What car?" Mrs. Whitston looked like a wolf tracking prey.

There was absolute silence in the room.

"I will repeat myself one time only. To what car are you referring, Nia?"

Nia glanced quickly at me before looking out the window. Her shoulders slumped and she picked at her cuticles. She was a closed book.

"Tell her!" It was Krista Ramirez this time. "This is so stupid. Nia and I didn't do anything and we're being treated like criminals with these two scrubs," she said, pointing at their male companions. "Tell 'em about Mr. B.'s car, Clarence, since you're the man and you can do your time." Her voice continued to rise in volume and pitch. "Tell 'em how you stole his car to go joyriding and backed into a telephone pole and knocked off his bumper, you stupid no-driving punk!"

And that's when the bedlam broke out. Kids were shouting and cussing and posturing on one another, threatening each other with bodily harm. And I was right there in the middle of it all, vainly trying to regulate and restore order. And poor old Mrs. Whitston, two years away from retirement, sat there looking as if she wished she'd never gotten out of bed.

That was yesterday, and it was mild in comparison with the craziness that jumped off today.

I was stuck between a rock and a hard place. Imani said she would pick me at six o'clock for my surprise. For the first time since the beginning of our relationship, I wasn't looking forward to getting together. After evicting the wild ruckus from her office yesterday, Mrs. Whitston grilled me on the obvious dangers of dating a student's parent. Even after I informed her of Nia's being transferred to a fellow counselor, the principal was still clearly displeased. So was I. I knew Nia's involvement in this latest nonsense would somehow rear its ugly head between Imani and me. I was still governed by counselor-student privilege so I could say nothing to Imani about what had occurred, but I knew the school principal would inform her fully. Still, knowing Imani like I did, I wondered how she would react. I found out in quick time.

When I answered the front door she walked in without a word.

"Hey, babygirl."

I tried to greet her with a hug and a kiss, but she pushed me away. The battle royal had begun.

"Where do you get off concealing information from me?"

I didn't bother playing ignorant. I knew what this was all about.

"Baby, let's talk," was all I could get out before she took over.

"You knew Nia was implicated in this school vandalism mess and you didn't have the decency to tell me!"

"Baby," I sighed, "let me finish getting dressed and we can talk about this on the way out," I offered, hoping that a change of scenery or a neutral locale would help diffuse the situation.

"I highly doubt that you and I will be going anywhere or doing anything this night," Imani tossed as she marched into my living room and flung her purse on my couch. Placing her hands on her luscious hips she glared at me. "I want an explanation and I want it now. Why didn't you tell me about this?"

I remember Pops telling me that a man should never argue with a woman on an empty stomach, and I was hungry so I offered Imani something to eat just to be polite so I could refuel my tank. Judging by the way Imani looked at me, as if I were the ghost of Christmas past, I couldn't get through this one on empty.

"I don't want anything except an answer to my question, Brax."

"Listen, Imani, this thing with Nia is unfortunate but let's keep things in perspective between us and not blow this out of proportion. She met with the principal and—"

"Duhh," she scoffed, belligerently. "I'm fully aware of the fact that Nia met with the principal. Who do *you* think informed *me?* And don't talk to me about proper perspective as if I'm emotionally unhinged."

She was well on her way, but I knew better than to convey that. Instead, I went to her and wrapped my arms about Imani's waist, wanting to connect with her so we could work this out. Folding her arms beneath her breasts she leaned back and stared up at me as if I was three seconds from a beat down. I got the message. I released her and sat on the arm of my couch out of her reach.

"Imani, you do understand that there is a thing called counselor-student privilege involved here. Right? What I heard, I heard in confidence. The matter has been handled by the proper authorities, and they have obviously informed you so what's the problem?"

She laughed, but she was not humored.

"What's the problem? The problem, mister counselor, is that *you* withheld vital and potentially detrimental information from *me* that involved *my* child. I was under the impression that you and I were somehow involved in a relationship in which communication and honesty are essential."

"Come on, baby, you just heard me explain that—"

"What I heard was," Imani began, propping her palm in the air and looking off to one side as if she could not be bothered with my ignorance, "your technically correct excuse for being the east end of a west-bound mule."

Under normal circumstances I might have laughed, but this was not normal.

"The east end of a west-bound mule," I repeated, knowing I'd better proceed with caution. So I scratched my ear then rubbed a hand over my goatee in an attempt to collect my thoughts.

"If that thing bothers you shave it off because I'm sick of you playing with it."

Babygirl was truly off the hizook tonight!

"Imani, is there anything else about me that annoys the hell out of you?"

Whoomp! Didn't intend to go there, but I did.

"Believe me, Brax, the list is too long and time is too short."

I walked right into that one so all I could do was hum a hymn which I didn't feel like doing so I tried to reel it in and act the mature part instead.

"Imani, what's really going on here?"

Was there something other than this mess with Nia that I didn't know about? I reached for her hand. She pulled away like I was trying to tag her with a communicable disease.

Okay, I'm an easy kind of man. I don't make many waves. I handle my business; live my life as harmoniously as I can. But there was only so much I could take and my crap quotient was almost at capacity.

"I can't seem to win with you, Imani. You ask my opinion on issues with Nia then you bite my head off and act as if I'm intruding if you don't like what I have to say." I scratched my head instead of my goatee. "I try to explain to you the ethics governing my job and you treat me as if I'm lying or using it as a smoke screen. Bottom line: it's a sore spot with you for someone else to know something about your child that you don't."

"You bet your black . . ." She caught herself in the knick of time. Imani stopped cutting me with her dagger eyes long enough to sit down opposite me. When she looked at me again her eyes were wet and bright. "I don't appreciate being in the dark where my child is concerned. I raised her by myself. I'm the one who got up in the middle of the night when she was teething or sick or had a nightmare. I'm the one who has fed and clothed and loved, nurtured and taught her what it means to be a strong Black woman in today's society so I am entitled to information where she is concerned. Not you."

Putting a pause on this conversation would have been best, but best was out and Brax was in. Blame it on hunger. Blame it on the tension growing at the back of my eyeballs. Blame it on I did not appreciate being blamed.

"Listen, Imani, I concede your point, but maybe you should have taught *your* child something about honesty in the process of all that wonderful rearing you single-handedly accomplished. If you had, we wouldn't be having this conversation." Her eyebrows slithered upward. The daggers were back with missiles and Uzis in tow, but I didn't care. "Don't transfer blame onto me. I did not hook Nia up with that knucklehead crowd she was running with. Better yet I am not responsible for your child. You are. So don't make this my problem because it's not. It's yours."

The firearms disappeared behind the tears. Dag, I'm a sucker for a woman with water in her eyes. I told myself to exercise objectivity and stop the madness marching in on us. This argument wasn't about me or whatever deception I was accused of. Imani knew it. I knew it. I had to squash this and now. But Imani swallowed her tears and squared her shoulders.

"You are absolutely right, *Braxton.*" Imani's voice was so low and lethal she sounded like James Earl Jones with a head cold as she stood. "This isn't your fault. And it's not your affair. It's my daughter's and mine. After all, you are not her father so consider yourself exonerated and dismissed."

Dismissed? Girlfriend was sniffing industrial strength Pine-sol if she thought she could come into *my* house and dismiss *me.*

"Dismissed?" The echo rumbled out of me. "Who the hell do you think . . . Naw! It's time for you to roll. Take your high-priced prissy—"

"*Prissy?* Who the freak are you calling prissy? I'm more real than any woman you've ever drooled over," Imani flung.

"Yeah, you're more expensive, too. Step! The door is waiting," I said, standing and pointing toward the front of *my* house.

"Just because I don't, unlike *some* folks I know, slouch around in jeans and jerseys all day that does not make me prissy," Imani defended, her voice rising. "Don't hate me because I like something other than combed cotton and a hot dog on a stick. I earn my silk."

"Yeah, whatever. Still you better bounce your pampered, silk panty wearing—"

Imani kind of growled and bared her teeth before grabbing a pillow off my couch. Now I know why they're called throw pillows. Imani proceed to beat me with that pillow, just beating and fussing, knocking me over onto the couch. All I could do was put up a block and let her work it out because my phone was too far away for me to dial the local chapter of the NAACP to report that a brother was getting stomped.

"You . . . don't . . . know nothing . . . about me." She was pounding and punctuating her words like Moms did that day she had to beat me when I put my turtle on a hot plate to see if it would crawl out of its shell. "I bought my car . . . less than retail . . . at an auction. And my parents . . . loaned me . . . the down . . . payment on my house . . . *hater!*"

I guess she was tired because Imani hit me one last time then tossed the pillow at my head. But when she snatched her purse and reached into it, I grabbed a couch cushion and pulled it over me just in case she was packing.

When I didn't hear the click of a trigger, I peeked around the cushion to see she had extracted two tickets from her purse. Standing over me, Imani wagged them in my face.

"Here's your surprise! Enjoy the concert, you insensitive, cockeyed . . . Clydesdale!" And with that she ripped the tickets and tossed the pieces in my face before marching toward the door.

Something sane told me to get up and go after her, not let her walk out like that, but I wasn't about to move. Imani's the one who came in my house insulting me, accusing me of things of which I was not guilty. I didn't punch her with a pillow or tear up treasured Ashford and Simpson concert tickets. She was the one proving that a mind was a terrible thing to waste. Instead, I reassembled the torn ticket pieces. Let her come back and grovel at my feet. And she did: come back at least.

"I can't find my car keys," Imani announced, as if that were an invitation for me to help her find them.

"Imani, can we talk like civilized adults?" I asked, regaining my footing. Okay, I admit it. I'm sprung. Soft. The girl has me wrapped. I've grown with this woman, shared intimate secrets and dreams with her and she with me. What we had was brief, but real. It could stand above high water if we could just hold it together now and not let it unravel like a cheap swap meet sweater. The counselor, the mediator in me told me to make amends. "Let's not go out like this."

Sistergirl was untouched by my attempts at civility. "Where are my stupid keys?" she spat, looking about.

I was worn out.

"They're on the floor. Listen, Imani, we've both said some irrational things here tonight. You're upset. So am I. But you know this is not all about Nia. There's something else bothering you." How does a man say "you've been edgy, moody, and attitudinal" without getting cut? "And let's not forget that I've suffered a loss here as well. My car was stolen by these same—"

"You know what? Don't ever mention that car to me again. You act as if driving it is some kind of connection with your father. Why don't you just go ahead and deal with his death already!"

Game over! I was through.

"I understand that *you* don't understand that connection seeing as how *you've* never had a father yourself," I bounced back. "And don't talk to me about hanging on seeing as you can't extract yourself from your ex-husband's funk," I hollered, remembering the times Imani buckled. She had allowed her ex to use her garage like a storage facility and even picked up his dry cleaning and watered his plants before he moved. Even now she let him interrupt our time with his telephone calls and demands. Maybe I was completely off, but some insecure notion at the back of my head told me that part of Imani's discontent was due to his absence. Was she still in love with the old boy? "And furthermore," I said, gesturing with a finger in her face, "if you need some PMS pills I suggest you pick up a bottle on your way out 'cause you gotta go before I do or say something criminal."

I sensed that Imani was wounded, but so was I, and the Rhett Butler in me didn't give a good damn.

"Take your finger out of my face," Imani warned.

"Who died and crowned you queen? Raise up out of my . . . *Yeow!*"

Can you believe this crap? This crazy woman bit me! She actually bit my finger like it was a link on a bun. I need a tetanus shot. I wanted to bite her back but she was busy scooping up her keys and rushing toward the front door, opening it just as my housemate stepped in.

"Hey, Imani—"

"Screw you, too, Terrance!" she spat, catching T. by surprise. Then she hurled back at me, "I should have stayed in Phoenix. And I don't need Pamprin, Midol, or Tylenol as you've insinuated because I'm not premenstrual. Thanks to you I haven't *had* a period since last month . . . you sperm dropping . . . platypus!"

And with that Imani stormed out the door. I heard the screech of tires and smelled burning rubber as she peeled off down the street. I remained where I was unable to move.

Imani hasn't returned my calls, my e-mails, my page, nothing. She refuses to acknowledge my attempts to reach her. Imani missed a period. I've, as she so crassly put it, dropped plenty seed, but that should have been blocked by the condoms we used. But then again some of those condoms were from my old stash. Can latex expire?

Four or five hours have passed since Imani blew out of here, and I'm not sure what to do. I've considered revving up Pearl and going over to the house in the event that she's home but not answering the phone to avoid me. But then I keep thinking about what she said about me driving my father's car and I get pissed all over again until I remember that she might be pregnant with my child and my heart melts. I always planned to be married before having children and I wasn't going to do that until age forty, but I guess this is what happens when you put the cart before the horse and knock boots on the steady. But I am a real man and a real man takes care of his responsibilities, so over the past few hours I have come to terms with the fact that I may be a baby's daddy.

I want to be active in my child's life, not some weekend-holiday father. I want to experience all the things a father experiences. I have nieces and nephews so I know how to change diapers, bathe, hold, and rock a child to sleep. But that real-time day in, day out kind of parent-child relationship is not mine. I need to contact my financial planner and set up an educational IRA and a trust fund and do whatever I have to do to ensure my child's welfare so that he or she grows up loved and secure, seeing his or her parents in a bonded relationship . . .

That thought slowed my mental roll. The bond between Imani and I was in serious jeopardy after this evening's fiasco. I should have remained levelheaded and let her blow off steam, but her accusations stung causing me to feel as if I'd purposefully deceived her, provoking me to hurl my own unfair ammunition in her face. Didn't the woman know what she meant to me? She was my lover, had become my confidante, but Imani was also my friend. I valued the time we spent in or out of bed, at the Jazz Jubilee, cultural events, on the phone, in the park; it didn't matter. I'd do anything, go anywhere with her . . . except church. I still wasn't ready for that despite Imani's gentle invitations.

Still, call me a fool, but I love this woman. I'm mad as hell at her right now, but I do love her. And what's with Phoenix? Was she planning to move? And why has she walked around without telling me her period was late? I could wring her long neck. At least I know now why Imani's been difficult. I'd be difficult, too, if I had a rugrat in my womb. Thank God I don't have a uterus, but that rugrat is *my* rugrat and I'll be a day late fool if I don't get this thing right. So, fragments of the Ashford and Simpson concert tickets in my hand, my heart pounding in my chest I jumped up, put my shoes on and would have headed out the door except the phone rang.

I snatched it up thinking it was Imani.

"Brax! Oh my God! Mama's in the hospital."

It was my sister Alondra wailing in the phone.

"What do you mean Mama's in the hospital?" I asked, my blood running cold.

"Cassondra went by the house an hour ago because Mama called her saying she was having chest pains. And when Cassi got there . . ."

My sister was unable to continue she was bawling so. I hadn't heard her cry like that since our father's funeral.

"Alondra, where's Edwin?"

"R-r-right here," she stammered putting her husband on the phone. "Brax, man, I'm sorry about this."

"Where's Mama and how is she?"

"She's in the emergency room at St. Joseph's. The whole family is here. I don't know, bruh, Mother Wade is in a lot pain," my brother-in-law sadly informed me.

"Look, I have to call the airlines. Tell everyone to hold tight. I'm out of here on the first thing smoking." I hung up the phone and did something I haven't done in years. I dropped to my knees and prayed.

"Don't worry about anything here, Kid, I've got your back," T. assured me, as we did that quick shoulder-to-shoulder, clap-on-the-back Black man hug. "Tell your family I'm praying."

"Thanks, Cuddy. I'll call you when I get there and know what's what," I promised, hopping into my car and reversing out of my driveway. I made it to the end of the block when my cellular rang.

"Imani?"

"Mr. B."

I didn't recognize the voice trembling on the opposite end.

"Who is this and how did you get this number?"

"It's Nia. I got your number off of my mom's Palm Pilot."

"Nia, what's up?"

"Mr. B., can you come get me?" There was a sniffle and a slight pause. "I'm at the bus station."

"Nia, I hate to sound cruel, but can you take a Regional Transit home? I have—"

"I'm not at the local station. I'm at Greyhound. I was leaving, but I can't do it."

I pulled over to the curb. "Nia. Are you running away from home?"

Her only answer was a choked cry.

Glancing at my watch I saw that I had exactly seventy minutes until flight time.

"Nia, don't move. I'm on my way."

What I was going to do with a fourteen-year-old wannabe runaway I had no idea. Maybe I could call T. and ask him to meet me at the bus station so that he could take Nia home. Whatever I did, I had to do it fast. Time was ticking.

I made it from my house in the Pocket area all the way downtown to the bus station in eight minutes flat. Pearl knows how to haul. She's my girl.

I found Nia looking like a scared child on a bench inside the terminal, out of place in her surroundings. When she looked up and saw me she actually ran to me, her backpack across her shoulders, and hugged me so hard she almost toppled us both.

"Are you okay, Nia?"

She nodded, wiping fresh tears from her eyes.

"I need you to come with me," I instructed. "I'm in a hurry, but I'm here for you."

The summer night was dark. My eyes were feeling suddenly tired and the rest of me felt drained. First Imani, then Moms, now shorty over here was in need. I listened as Nia told me about the fight she had with her mother that resulted in her sneaking out of the house and making her way downtown to the Greyhound station. It wasn't until she got there that Nia realized she didn't have enough cash to purchase a ticket to LA. When she called her father's house some woman answered the phone, told Nia she was interrupting her sleep then disconnected the call. Shorty was having it hard.

"Nia, I'm not defending any of her actions, but I want you to understand that your mother is experiencing some difficulties right now that have nothing to do with you," I cautioned, careful to omit the fact that Imani could be pregnant, deciding that was something mother and child should discuss. "You know better than me that your mother loves you so don't do something drastic like this. You owe it to the both of you to work this out."

"I know, Mr. B., but I'm so mad. Everything's crazy! My dad's in southern California with some new trick and my mom is with—"

She cut off her words and glanced at me before quickly averting her gaze.

"It's okay, Nia, you can be honest about your feelings regarding my relationship with your mother. You're going through, shorty. Do you feel abandoned or alone?"

She looked at me again before putting her face in her hands and sobbing.

Reaching over I gently squeezed Nia's shoulder. I didn't say anything. I just let her purge her pain. When she finally quieted and looked up Nia gave me a weak smile.

"I'm sorry, Mr. B., for everything," she said, sweeping all of her less than benevolent behavior toward me into one apology. "Thank you for coming to get me. I didn't know who else to call. My grandparents are on vacation. I couldn't find my Aunt Mo so—"

"So you're stuck with old-head Mr. B. I feel for you, shorty."

I glanced over to see a real smile playing at Nia's mouth only to see that smile suddenly replaced by a look of sheer terror. Shaking, she managed to scream.

"Mr. B., look out!"

I glanced to my left to see a set of headlights coming toward us.

I found a serious traffic jam on northbound I-5 after retrieving Nia from the bus station. Trying to make good time and get to the airport, I decided to take the surface streets as far down the I-5 corridor as possible before reentering the freeway. It was a choice I wasn't sure I'd live to regret.

TRIAL BY FIRE

She could check herself in. She was not too far from the mental health hospital on Stockton Boulevard. She could do a fifty-one-fifty and be done with it, have a nice three-day vacation compliments of the county. But she could not afford to slow down now. If she did she might really crack and once that happened there would be no turning back.

Imani pushed these morbid thoughts from her mind. Concentration was imperative so she had to remain focused.

Her daughter was missing.

How had things come to such an ugly head?

Imani knew exactly how and when and where and why.

Just hours ago Nia—her only child, the child who distorted *her* body with pregnancy, the child whose watermelon-sized head she spent ten hours laboring to push through a birth canal the size of a quarter, that ungrateful daughter she struggled to raise—stood in Imani's face, her fourteen-year-old behind grown enough to tell Imani she was leaving. Imani would pack Nia's bags and give her cab fare. Defiance was not an option in her house. Now, she wished she had taken Nia's threat seriously.

Imani was at work when the first call came through.

It was her mother thanking her for the souvenir she'd dropped off as a thank you gift for taking care of Nia during Imani's recent trip to

Phoenix. Her mother appreciated the gesture, but Nia had not stayed with her grandparents, going over her godmother's instead. A call to Monique blew the cover off of Nia's lie.

Imani was ready to storm out of her office and march onto the school campus, but a second call came through that left her alternating between chewing on a pencil and stabbing a letter opener through a piece of paper as the school principal relayed the sordid facts of Nia's involvement in school vandalism. The principal was certain that Nia had not been involved in the actual deed; she had merely failed to come forward with the information regarding the suspects who, subsequently, admitted to the crime. The culprits were suspended from the first week of school when classes resumed in fall, and the case was being sent to juvenile court. As for Nia, the principal merely wanted to inform Imani of what had transpired. She was proud of Nia, as prompted by her guidance counselor, for admitting her own involvement.

How noble, Imani silently mused, thanking the woman and disconnecting the call. Grabbing her purse, Imani raced out of her office informing her assistant that she had a family emergency and would return in two hours. Imani never made it back to the office.

She went directly to Brax. Somewhere deep inside Imani knew she erred. She should not have vented her anger and despair at him. Brax was not to blame. Her rational mind understood counselor-student privilege. But her emotional self was in control. And so she had made a mess of the relationship with a man she truly cared about before speeding home with Nia on her mind.

"Nia!" she hollered, entering the house and tossing her purse at the foot of the stairs. The music in Nia's room was so loud that Imani could not be heard. She rushed up the stairs and into her daughter's room.

At the sound of her mother's entrance Nia, telephone in hand, whirled. Imani stared. Wearing a midriff tank top and low riding shorts, Nia's decorated belly was fully exposed.

"Nia Nicole Evans! *What the hell is that?*" Imani grabbed her daughter by the arm and peered closely at her belly. A tiny silver hoop rested in the center of a colorful butterfly decorating Nia's navel. Imani covered her face with her hands before shouting, "Hang up the phone, Nia. Now!"

"Krista, I'll call you back later," Nia informed the party on the other end and disconnected.

"No, you won't," Imani contradicted, turning off the stereo. "Your telephone privileges are revoked until further notice."

Nia's defiance was unmistakable when she spoke.

"Daddy said—"

"Do yourself a favor, Nia, and don't mention your father right now."

"Daddy said it was okay if I got a tattoo," Nia brazenly insisted.

"Then he can pay to have it removed because the last time I checked I was the mother up in here and I clearly recall telling you a tattoo was off limits so don't play with me, Nia!" Imani announced, feeling disgusted and undermined. "My name is on the deed to this house so I will dictate what goes within these four walls. Are we clear on that?"

Nia's answer was a silent glare.

"And I thought I was real clear about no new piercings so what are you doing with an earring in your navel?"

"You said I couldn't pierce my ear. You didn't say nothing about my navel."

Imani unconsciously clenched and unclenched her fists, her heart beating a mile a minute in her chest as she grit her teeth and told herself not to pop a blood vessel.

"You just insist on defying me, don't you, Nia?" Imani remarked, waving at her daughter's colorful, jewel-adorned stomach. She shook her head in disgust before continuing, "And I know you pulled a fast one on your grandparents and Mo while I was away. I'm curious about what you did in my absence. We'll get to that, but first, Mrs. Whitston called me today." That was enough to knock the sail from Nia's wings. She glanced at the floor and nervously bit her lower lip. "Is there anything you'd like to tell me?" Imani asked, tapping her shoe on the carpet.

"No, you obviously already know everything," Nia replied after an awkward silence.

"Yes, I do," Imani confirmed, irked by Nia's tone. "Why did Mrs. Whitston have to call me, Nia? You're my child and we live in this house together—"

"When you're home," Nia muttered.

"Excuse you?"

"Nothing," Nia petulantly replied, folding her arms and looking at anything, everything except her mother.

"No, is there something you want to say to me, Nia?" Imani insisted.

Still sulking, Nia finally looked at her mother. Her face, her mouth was tight. Closed.

"Never mind," was Nia's offhanded response.

Imani's jaw worked rapidly before she spoke.

"Your principal was gracious enough not to exact a punishment, but as for me grace is long gone."

"Mom, it's not my fault those imbeciles trashed the study lab. I had nothing to do with that! And I'm not the only one who knew. They bragged in front of me and Krista—"

"Nia, your friends are not my concern. You are."

"Since when?"

Imani felt her muscles twitch and her hands itch. She told herself to breathe. Deep. She rubbed her scalp and did her best to recollect her calm while reminding herself that infanticide was a crime. She wondered if there was such a thing as "adolescenticide?"

"Nia, you're two inches away from getting snatched. I don't appreciate your tone of voice or your sarcasm. Understand?"

Nia's response was a venomous glare.

"Nia, this is the third time you've been in trouble at school this year, and each time you exercised terrible judgment and deceit. Deceit is a character flaw, but lack of judgment is a matter of immaturity. Neither one is good or acceptable in this house. So until I see you demonstrate better—"

"I'm so sick of this!" Nia cried, unfolding her arms and dropping them at her sides with a loud huff. "Every time I do something wrong I get a lecture *and* I have to hear about all of *my* faults. What about yours, Mom? You're not all that."

Imani told herself not to reach out and touch her child because if she did Nia's cute little braids with beads and things would be swinging in the wind. Instead, she walked slowly, purposefully, over to sit at Nia's desk. Slowly, she counted backward from ten in an effort to pull herself together. She knew she should never let Nia stand toe-to-toe with her, should not reduce herself to a peer and answer her daughter's emotionally driven accusations, but Imani was tired of conflict. She wanted peace.

"Nia, sit down. Please." Imani watched her daughter sulk over and drop onto her bed as if she preferred to be any place else in the world than in a room with her. Imani swallowed. "No, I'm not flawless. But I've been fourteen. You've never been thirty-four, so I know some things you don't. Now, talk to me, Nia, and tell me what *you* want me to know. What's wrong?"

Nia's body was tense, her arms folded across her chest. It appeared as if she would say nothing, would sit and pout, but then she softly sniffed and looked at her mother.

"Mom, why are you so dang hard on me?" Nia blurted, angrily. "I can't do nothing because you watch me like a hawk and trip out on every little thing I do or say." Nia paused, grinding her teeth before exhaling and continuing. "I can't wear what I want to wear. I can't go where I want to go or see the people I want to see. Most of my friends have boyfriends and some are having sex, but I can barely talk to boys on the phone without you doing back flips." Nia looked at the ceiling as if the sight of her mother was too much. Puffing out her cheeks, she returned her attention to her mother. "Okay, I stayed home when you went to Phoenix because I'm sick of being treated like a baby. I can take care of myself. And so what if I didn't snitch on my friends—"

"That's just it, Nia. How can you call them friends when they willingly incriminate and implicate you by leaving you with the evidence of a crime?" Imani asked, her hands extended toward her daughter in an imploring gesture.

"Clarence was going to put it in a random locker but I didn't want another student to get in trouble so I took the plant to return it to Mrs. Greer!" Nia insisted.

Imani watched her daughter carefully.

"Nia, how involved are you with Clarence?"

"It's nothing serious. We just kick it." Nia quickly amended.

"Nia, if I find out that you and your juvenile delinquent homeboy are doing more than kicking it—"

"We're not!" Nia screamed.

Imani glanced about her as if the *Candid Camera* crew would jump out of hiding at any moment because what she was experiencing was unreal and ready for TV. Her voice was dangerous when she continued.

"Don't you *ever* raise your voice at me like that again! I will . . ." Imani paused, slowed her breathing, and told herself she was in control. She leaned toward her daughter. "Nia, do you understand that as your mother it is my duty to protect you? I am trying to teach you responsibility and integrity. I don't want you to make the same mistakes I did—"

"But I'm not you, Mom," Nia asserted, her voice breaking. "I have to make my own mistakes."

Imani slowly shook her head back and forth.

"No, sweetheart, that's what I'm trying to tell you. You don't have to make the same mistakes I made. That's what wisdom and maturity are all about. I don't want to see your life ruined—"

"Is that how you see me? Did I ruin your life?"

The question took Imani's breath away. She sat, her mouth open, stunned.

"Do you regret having me?"

The strident anger and helpless pain in Nia's voice brought tears to Imani's eyes.

"Snookie, that is not what I'm insinuating—"

"Well, that's the way I'm hearing it. I'm sorry that you got pregnant and had to marry my father, but I did not ask to be conceived. And I'm sorry that you wrecked your marriage by dissin' Daddy, but that was your choice."

Imani's stomach turned. She felt sick.

Several moments passed before she was able to speak and when she did Imani's voice was hollow.

"You're absolutely right, Nia. You were conceived out of wedlock because I was young and stupid and away from home and fell for the first man who showed an interest in me. I got pregnant when I should have been gaining an education. Instead, I was retching over a toilet bowl and getting fatter by the month. And I had my baby because I wanted her. I didn't abort her. I didn't abandon her. I raised my child," Imani said, pointing directly at Nia. "*That* was my choice. And I've no idea the lies your father has told you about our divorce, but if my working to put food on the table and keep a roof over our heads 'dissed' him then so be it!"

Nia began clapping.

"You deserve an award for not sucking me into a bucket or dropping me off at the nearest orphanage. But don't think that you did me any favors. Growing up with you and Daddy and all of your drama has not been cute."

Like a frozen pond experiencing the spring thaw, Imani's barriers cracked and flowed. Her vision turned red. She saw lightning flash. Thought she heard thunder roll. But when the haze cleared from her mind she realized the summer sun was still high in the clear sky.

She rose, slowly as if vertebrae by vertebrae, stepping away from the desk and toward her daughter, who, seeing the look on Imani's face, stood quickly and squared her shoulders as if preparing for war.

"You can forget about having your barbeque party. It is as of now officially canceled . . ."

Nia stomped her foot.

"Mom, that's not fair!"

". . . and the only way you'll get to the state marching band competition is if you can stowaway in your clarinet case," Imani continued as if Nia had never spoken. "You will need to call your grandparents and apologize because you are not going to Nashville. Kiss it all good-bye."

"I hate you!"

Imani grit her teeth, steeling herself against the hurt caused by Nia's vehement, emotion-driven barb before painfully concluding, "I love you so much that you have three seconds to go in the bathroom, remove that earring from your gut, and disinfect the hole 'cause it's closing up as of now. And if I had the right chemicals you'd be scrubbing that paint off, too. Go. Get out of my sight!"

"I'm getting as far out of your sight as possible," Nia hurled. "I'm moving to Los Angeles with my father."

Imani stepped closer to Nia and asked, "You're going where and doing what with whom? Nia, go do as I said before I knock the taste out of your mouth and the sight from your eyes!"

Nia flinched, but stood her ground.

"You should be glad I'll be out of your hair so you can do whatever you want without sneaking," Nia spat.

I am going to need the best defense attorney in the country because I am about to choke a child, Imani thought.

"Maybe it would be best if you stayed with your father for a while." Her own words were enough to pierce Imani's heart.

"Believe me I will. I need to be with someone who loves me and has time for me," Nia countered.

"I'm sure you'll fit into your father's life somewhere in between his career and his women."

"At least he gives me things!" was Nia's immature response.

"Things, Nia? Is that what you want?"

"He bought me a new computer when that old thing you bought me flipped out," Nia sobbed.

"And how was he able to do that, Nia? I'll tell you how: with your child support money. Your father can afford to toss trinkets in your lap with all the money that rightfully belongs in my pocket for your benefit, but that he fails to contribute. So, sure he has extra money. But it's *your* money."

"My dad does pay child support!"

"Nia, do you really want to know how many child support payments I've received from your father? Four! Count them, sweetheart, four in the twelve years since our divorce. That's one for every three years. So I guess we can expect another one when you turn seventeen. So don't talk to me about *things* and who does what for whom."

"Daddy remembers my birthday and allowances," Nia tossed lamely, tears in her eyes.

"No, Nia, he doesn't. I give you your allowance so you can go out and get your cute little braids and anything else you fixate on. I buy your birthday and Christmas presents and sign your *loving* father's name to the cards—" Imani stopped suddenly. She knew she had gone too far.

Nia's eyes narrowed. Her lips quivered as she glared at Imani with a look that bordered on hatred. Her voice was unnatural.

"I'm out of here as soon as Daddy can come get me. Have fun with your man without me in your way."

"Be careful, Nia," Imani warned.

A queer smile passed over Nia's face as she bolted to retrieve something from her near empty backpack hanging on a peg in the closet.

"You dropped this on the stairs," she snidely returned. "Maybe you're the one who needs to be careful, Mom."

Nia violently flung a tiny package at Imani. It ricocheted off of her arm and hit the ground so that Imani stood there staring at a wrapped condom near her feet.

She snapped.

The sound of her palm making impact with her child's face ripped the air like lightning. Then all was still.

Imani stood with her hands covering her mouth. She was too shocked to cry. Never had she struck her child. She felt sick with a pain beyond the physical that exploded in her gut.

"Nia," it was a plaintive whisper, guttural and bewildered.

Nia, who had been standing as if frozen, sprang to life. She raced for the phone and depressed a button that dialed a stored number. She began crying hysterically, screaming into the receiver.

"Daddy! Daddy, are you home? Pick up the phone if you're there! Please," she begged.

God, what have I done? Help us, please, Imani silently prayed.

"Nia, I'm sorry."

Imani reached for her daughter only for her to jerk away and throw the phone against the wall. It split on impact. Nia began to sob as if something within her very soul were crushed.

"Get out! Get out of my room and out of my life!"

Slowly, heavily Imani backed away. Nia slammed the door so that the walls shook. Imani felt her energy seep right out of her until she was limp. She leaned against the closed door, feeling as if the world was tumbling down, caving in on her and her only defense was to hide. But there was no place to turn, nowhere to run. She was without shelter. Exposed. Imani shivered as if cold. She was alone. Wrapping her arms about her body, Imani began to cry.

"All I have on me is a ten and a five," Imani said, handing the bill to her cousin who sat in the front passenger's seat of her Volvo.

"What do I want with that?" Monique questioned.

"Go inside and get it for me," Imani requested. She was drained. Her face was drawn and her eyes sunken. "I can't do this right now."

Monique studied Imani a moment before snatching the money from her hand and unlatching her seatbelt. "Didn't I warn you that man was dangerous?" she fussed in her soprano voice, slamming the car door as she exited.

"Mo!"

"What?" she hollered as she walked away, not bothering to look back.

"Bring me some M&Ms . . . with peanuts!" Imani added as her cousin disappeared into the store.

Imani sat in the car nervously tugging and twirling a lock of hair. After falling asleep on the family room sofa curled in a fetal position and sleeping like the dead for three hours, Imani awakened to a quiet house feeling as if her body and emotions had been trampled. Imani was exhausted mentally, physically, and emotionally. She felt an over-whelming need to escape. So before caution could get the best of her

Imani phoned her boss. She would take the job. Obviously delighted, he asked Imani to stop by his office so they could discuss the details. Imani promised to be there bright and early Monday morning.

Now she sat waiting for Monique to return with a pregnancy test kit second-guessing the wisdom of her decision. But a steel-like resolve fortified her choice, caused Imani to sit higher in her seat and cease the nervous twirling of her hair. She needed to leave. She was drained. And she had no need to worry about uprooting her child since Nia was moving to Los Angeles with her father. It hurt Imani's heart to admit that a separation might prove to be what both she and Nia needed right then as things had come to an ugly head between them and perhaps outside intervention was needed. She felt as if she had lost her child.

Imani was losing one and about to confirm the presence of another. *When did I down an extra dose of stupid pills?* Imani wondered, thinking that being single and pregnant at the age of thirty-four had to qualify as one of the stupidest things she had ever done. Her menstrual cycle was late and she had recently experienced bouts of queasiness but she had, in her denial, chalked it up to stress. It wasn't until yesterday morning when Imani, en route to work, was forced to rush back into the house to vomit that the scare of pregnancy loomed large. She had dropped Nia at school then took the long route to work and cried a river of tears. She could not go through this alone, again.

After today's altercation with Brax, Imani concluded that their relationship was a thing of the past. And to think she actually believed she was in falling in love with the man. But despite the shattered state of their affairs would Brax want to be a part of their child's life? Or would he abdicate his parental responsibility and leave Imani to bear the burden of raising another child on her own? As unfair as it might be to the child, Imani hoped Brax would opt out of fatherhood. She did not want to bother with another baby's daddy. Nigel was already one too many. But something inside told Imani that eradicating Brax from their child's life would not be easy. She knew him. He would stake his claim, declare his right to be a part of their child's world if she attempted to revoke those rights. Imani sighed, imagining being embroiled in legalities over parental rights. The thought was unsettling. She cautioned herself to take one step at a time. First things first: she had to confirm her pregnancy. The rest would follow.

* * *

Ten minutes later they stood in Monique's bathroom reading the instructions.

"Okay, you have to pee in this little cup and then we pour some on this indictor stick and wait for the results," Monique surmised, sneezing.

"Bless you," Imani returned. "Okay, I'm ready." Imani inhaled deeply, and filled her lungs. With shaky hands, she picked up the box and slid the cup into her palm. Then she looked at her cousin and waited.

"What?" Monique intoned.

"Get out so I can use the restroom."

"Get real, Mani. You came over my house, busting down the door acting like somebody died. I'm staying for this," Monique announced, propping herself on the sink ledge. "Besides, I've seen your natural naked butt before."

For the first time since locking horns with Nia, Imani grinned thinking of how she panicked when she arrived and there was no answer to her knock. Monique's Camry was parked in the driveway of her condo, and the stereo was on inside the dwelling. After all Imani had experienced that day her emotions were raw and she imagined the worst, flashing back on Monique's breast cancer scare and thinking for some inexplicable reason that Monique had had a relapse of some sort and was, perhaps, sprawled out unconscious on the floor in need of medical attention. Imani unlocked the door with her copy of Monique's house key only to find her cousin in the living room, the stereo at full volume, singing while vacuuming, topless *and* braless with some grass hula skirt looking thing tied about her waist as if someone had crowned her Josephine Baker's successor.

Looking at Monique, Imani pulled down her bottoms and sat on the pristine white commode and waited for something to happen.

"Stop staring at me. You're blocking the flow," Imani told her cousin.

Monique sneezed.

"Just pee already."

"Turn the water on or do something to help."

Monique complied, letting water stream from the sink faucet. Again, she sneezed.

"You should have bought some cold medicine at the store. By the way where's my change?" Imani asked.

"You ate it. A king-sized bag of M&Ms is not free," Monique retorted, shivering as if cold.

"What's wrong with you?" Imani asked.

"I'm not pregnant that's for sure," Monique said, laughing. "There's a virus or summer cold or something going around. That's why I stayed home tonight instead of going to my poetry circle."

"Oh. Mo, I can't urinate."

"You want some water? I have some sassafrass tea," Monique offered, hopping down from the counter. "I could make some for you."

"Umm, no, that's quite all right. Wait . . . okay . . . here it comes!" Imani excitedly announced. "Whew!"

"I read a pamphlet at work the other day that said some cultures believe urine can improve the quality of the skin if one bathes in it," Monique announced as the elimination process continued.

Imani finished her business and carefully placed the test indicator atop its box before washing and drying her hands and saying, "Mo, save all that nasty medical 4-1-1 for your 9-to-5 at the hospital because it works a nerve."

"Did you know that the central nervous system—"

"Mo, be quiet already! You're disturbing my test results."

Together they stood, their heads bent over the device watching and waiting until finally the symbol appeared. They silently regarded each other until a mutual scream ripped the air. Holding hands they hopped about the room.

"*I have the flu,*" Imani repeated over and over in a singsong ditty.

"You're not pregnant. You're just a skoochie," Monique trilled in reply.

When finally they calmed themselves, Imani sat on the edge of the tub and sighed.

"The vomiting and nausea is flu related," she mused aloud. "But my period is late."

"Hasn't that happened before?" Monique asked.

"Only twice. Once when I was pregnant with Nia and again when I . . . went . . . through my divorce," Imani stated, remembering the physiological effects caused by that particularly stressful event. And she recalled how her cycle had not been interrupted but simply off-track during other times of stress such as during college final exams week or when waiting to close escrow on her house. Her body reacted sensitively to the pressures in her world.

Relieved, Imani closed her eyes and said a prayer of thanks.

Rising, Imani walked into Monique's living room and looked around. There were framed photos of Monique, her two younger brothers and Monique's parents; another of their grandparents; Monique and Imani in their teens clowning at Santa Cruz Beach Boardwalk; and Imani's favorite—a black and white portrait of Nia when she was three, licking a rapidly melting ice cream cone. Vanilla cream trickled down Nia's chubby little hand; her eyes were big and brown and her face reflected the pleasure of her task. Precious.

Imani choked back sudden tears as she lovingly stroked the cool glass in the wood frame.

"I knocked on Nia's door before I left. I knew she was in there but she wouldn't answer so I told her where I was going and left. I figured we still needed space from each other," Imani sadly admitted. Turning toward her cousin she added, "I'm losing my baby, Mo."

"Mani, Nia's not a baby and hasn't been for a while," Monique gently replied as she dropped into an armchair with a colorful Aztec design throw cover. "When's the last time you really looked at your child, Mani? The girl's boobs are almost as big as mine," Monique stated, pulling at her shirt to peek down at her breasts. "They may be bigger than mine, but that's not the point."

"What is your point, Mo?"

"My point is you may have idealized your child and pigeonholed her at least in your mind to some nebulous place where she grows up perfect. It's unfair and unrealistic to assign her that role. Granted, I plan to help you beat her after today's drama, but Nia's a fourteen-year-old girl, not a woman. And she's human. She makes mistakes and you can't hold that against her."

"I don't think I do that, Mo," Imani returned, as she moved on to finger CD cases stacked neatly on a wall shelf. The works of artists from Jill Scott to Angie Stone, and other such musicians of elevated genius comprised Monique's collection. Imani paused to look about. Monique's condo looked like a sixties' revival with its incense burners, framed posters of Monique's poetry, earth colored bean bag cushions, myriad potted plants, and the curtain made of beads on strings that separated the living room from the kitchen. There was even a lava lamp on the fireplace mantel. Imani knew their relatives teased Monique for her eclectic preferences and eccentric behavior, but Monique took it all in stride, appearing undaunted by the critiques. Imani had to admit that she admired her cousin's free spirit and ease of living without all the pomp.

"So you're saying that you never have unrealistic expectations or standards that Nia is incapable of reaching?"

"No . . . yes . . . look, Mo, I want the best for Nia. I want her to have what I didn't. I want her to be secure, to know she's loved, to have a father—"

"Nia has a father. Good or bad, Nigel *is* Nia's father and if he ever walks away from her that's not your doing. It's his. Stop trying to over-compensate for the fact that you don't have a father, Mani. That's not your fault. His failure to be in your life is due to some moral fault of his own not because of something you failed to be. There's nothing you need to do or become to prove yourself worthy of love. So give up your little idealistic quests because this is real life and we're real people," Monique exclaimed, hopping from her seat and crossing the distance to stand before her cousin. Laying a hand on Imani's shoulder she softly continued. "You don't need to micromanage Nia to ensure she's never abandoned."

Imani considered Monique's words before reaching out to hug her cousin.

"Every now and then you reach past your blond roots and strike a wise woman's pose."

"Yeah, well you're welcome, whoremonger. Speaking of which what are you going to do about Brax?"

Imani released Monique and went to sit on the floor, her back against the sofa. Imani laid her head on Monique's shoulder as she sat down beside her.

"Mo, I can't do this anymore. I cannot afford to get pregnant again. I just can't."

"Hello, but you're not pregnant so what does that mean?"

Raising her head, Imani stared at the far wall.

"It means I have to do what I have to do to avoid that possibility, and as we know the only true fail proof contraception that exists is abstinence. So—"

"So, there's going to be one hungry brother stomping around on a rampage because you've pulled the plug on his pleasure," Monique remarked as if tickled. "Can I ask you something, Mani? You usually put a brother through a ten year probation period before giving up the goods so why did you get physical with Brax so quickly in the first place?"

Because I was lonely and stagnant and tired of acting as if I was content playing the strong sisterwoman role and because Brax moved me for the first time in forever, Imani mused, articulating her thoughts to her cousin. She had felt immobile and suspended for too long. Nia was growing up and would be college bound in a matter of mere years. Lord knew she was glad Nigel moved to southern California, but his ability to come and go as he pleased over the years highlighted her static condition. Even Imani's parents moved and flowed with life, traveling and enjoying the company of others. Being with Brax enticed Imani to feel life again . . . in every conceivable way. So she reached for pleasure only to find pain.

"Brax was wonderful and I was weak and reckless and maybe even defiant," Imani admitted, thinking of how she repeatedly ignored her spirit to indulge in her flesh.

"And you almost paid the piper," Monique commented.

Imani frowned but her cellular phone rang before she could reply. Imani searched her purse until she found it.

"Hello? Nigel, hold on, I can't hear you," Imani hollered into the phone, depressing the volume control for better reception. "Okay, now what? What do you mean Nia's on her way to LA? What! No, I'll call you later, bye." Imani sprang to her feet and pulled her keys from her pocket.

"What's going on?" Monique demanded.

"Nia called Nigel and left a message with his live-in that she was taking the bus to Los Angeles."

"What!" Monique shrieked.

"I am about to kill me a fourteen-year-old she-thing."

"If you don't, I will," Monique shrilled as they raced out the door.

And that is how Imani came to frantically race through the streets of Sacramento in search of her runaway child.

After checking her parents' home and the salon in the hopes that Nia had elected to hide there in her grandparents' absence, they searched Imani's house only to find some of Nia's clothes were missing. Imani's heart sank with thoughts of her child alone in some seedy, dank bus station surrounded by the dregs of society, feeling unloved and confused. After confirming that Nia was not with her friends, Imani broke speed limits rushing across town to the bus station only to find that Nia was not there. Yes, a security guard and a ticket agent remembered her when Imani showed them a picture but, no, she did not purchase a ticket. If the ticket agent remembered correctly she left with a man in a red mustang.

Brax! If Nia was with Brax then she was safe, Imani thought as she and Monique hopped back into her car.

Their progress was impeded by a four-car pile up on I-5 affecting both north and south bound traffic as the big rig involved had crashed through the center divider, affecting both sides of the highway. Imani whipped a quick right on Third so she could wrap back to J Street and take the surface streets from there. But she never made it. The sight in the road brought her heart to a standstill.

There surrounded by emergency response units was what remained of a classic candy apple red Mustang.

SHADOW OF DEATH

They raced through the hospital corridors toward the emergency room. All about them was the hustle and bustle of medical personnel attending to the wounded and afflicted, and the impatience of those waiting to be seen. The smells of sickness and disease, crisis and conflict filled the air, making Imani's head thick with the stench.

"Excuse me, ladies, that area is off limits to you. Only emergency room staff is admitted beyond that door," a voice called.

Imani and Monique paused to find a uniformed security guard hurrying toward them.

"I'm an employee," Monique advised, flashing her badge "I'm a community liaison in Patient Care."

"I'm sorry, ma'am, you're still not allowed back there."

"I'm looking for my daughter," Imani announced, feeling as if she would fall apart at any moment. "My daughter was in a—" Unable to complete her sentence, Monique took over, gripping Imani's hand while informing the officer that they were looking for the victims of a car accident. The officer led them to a nurses' station.

"Maggie, these ladies here need some help."

"I'm sorry. They'll have to wait. I'll be with them as soon as I can," the harried clerk announced, racing back behind a closed door, leaving Imani and Monique to stand there, tense and afraid.

Imani could not stand still. She released Monique's hand and paced back and forth.

"Ma'am, Maggie or one of the other clerks will be right with you," the security guard advised. "Sorry, but summer is injury season and every summer it's like this here. Just stay calm, okay?"

Imani looked at him, but she could not respond. If anything happened to Nia her world would never be right again. Images of that red Mustang smashed and twisted into a heap of metal flared up in her mind. Imani recalled the stains on the asphalt that glared at her, mocking her fear. She could not tell, in the dark of night, whether it was blood or fluid from the vehicles tangled around each other like coiled serpents. The Mustang was totaled. There was no way on earth anyone could have survived that wreckage unscathed. No way on earth they could still be . . .

Her breathing jagged, Imani leaned against a wall for support and tried not to sink to the floor as a sob tore at her throat. Covering her face with her hands she sobbed all the pain, the sorrow, the hurt, the frustration of her days, the terror she had witnessed with her own eyes that night. Her baby was hurt. Gone beyond Imani's access and embrace. The tears rolled down Imani's chocolate brown cheeks, huge and full. She began to pray, to plead, and bargain with God.

Lord, if you just let my baby live I'll do whatever you ask of me . . .

"Miss Evans."

Imani looked up to see a nurse hurrying toward her, Monique in tow.

"Are you Nia Evans's mother?"

Imani wiped her eyes, her heart hammering in her chest.

"Yes."

"Come with me," the nurse instructed, swinging about and hurrying off in the opposite direction. The double doors at the end of a corridor opened as the nurse swiped a card attached to an elastic cord about her wrist through a slot in a wall. She led them down a series of short walkways until they arrived at what was little more than an examination space surrounded by a curtain. The nurse pulled the curtain aside. Imani froze. There on the bed lay Nia, wan and still. She looked so small, so helpless that Imani could not move.

"Nia?"

It was Monique who called her name.

Nothing happened.

Monique called again, her voice louder but shaking with dread.

Nia stirred slightly. Realizing she was not alone, Nia slowly attempted to sit up, moving as if it pained her to do so.

"Aunt Mo," she cried, tears welling up in her deep brown eyes large with relief.

Monique ran to her and, wrapping Nia in her arms, rocked her goddaughter back and forth as the tears spilled down her own butterscotch-colored cheeks.

"Nia, are you okay?" she asked, brushing Nia's braids behind her ears, peering into Nia's eyes for an answer.

Nia nodded and hugged her godmother again. Peering over Monique's shoulder she saw her mother.

Mother and child beheld one another, searched each other's eyes, their faces wet with the release of contrite tears that purged their pain. In that moment contention ceased.

"Mom."

It was a soft plea, a call for forgiveness and a pardon all in one.

Imani never felt anything as sweet as the warmth of her child in her arms as she sat on the hospital bed and stroked her daughter's hair, kissed her face, rubbed her back over and over again.

"I'm so sorry, Snookie," she whispered, tears clouding her voice as Imani held Nia's face in her palms. "If anything ever happened to you—"

She said no more. She clutched her child to her breast as they both cried. It took several inhalations before Imani could collect herself enough to speak again. And then her words tumbled out in a rush.

"Snookie, what happened? How hurt are you? What injuries did you sustain? Where's the doctor?"

"I'm right here, Miss Evans," a tiny woman of East Indian descent announced as she parted the curtain to enter the small space. Extending a hand she introduced herself. "I'm Dr. Sanjit," she said, her voice and accent lyrical. "I take it that you are Nia's mother."

"Yes, ma'am, Doctor. I am," Imani confirmed. Rising from the bed she shook the doctor's hand before returning to Nia.

"Your daughter is a very lucky young lady," the doctor pronounced. "She has little more than a serious headache and some muscle soreness. I have prescribed some pain medication for her. I am releasing

Nia, as there is no need for her to remain overnight. I do however ask, Miss Evans, that you watch her carefully and if there are any signs of complications bring her in at once."

"I will," Imani promised. "Thank you for everything."

"Nia, if you didn't have finals next week I'd keep you here so you could miss a couple of days of school," the doctor offered with a wink, causing Nia to giggle. Nia winced from the pain and clutched her sides.

Imani was immediately there, gently touching her child's body, concern causing her heart to lurch yet again.

"I'm okay," Nia assured her mother.

"Mothers do that, Nia. We're overprotective that way," Dr. Sanjit explained, before handing Nia's prescription to Imani. With a pat on Nia's arm and a smile at the two women in the room the doctor departed reminding Imani to bring Nia back if she experienced any undue pain.

Exhaling noisily, Imani turned to Nia and shook her head. Only God deserved all praise. There was no way that Nia or Brax could have walked away from that accident without life-threatening injuries or permanent damage or worse.

"Brax! Oh Lord, Nia, what happened to Brax?"

Fear came over Nia so heavily that she began to tremble.

"I don't know," she choked out. "The last thing I remember was seeing the other car coming at us," Nia said, sobbing, "and Mr. B., k-k-k-ind of thr-r-owing himself over m-m-m-e to protect me. Mom, you have to find him."

"Mo, help Nia get dressed please. But don't leave here. If they have to use this area then wait for me in the lobby. I'll be back as soon as possible." And with that Imani took off running, praying over and again that Brax was somehow, miraculously alive.

Brax was in surgery, Imani learned. No, there was no word on his condition. When he came out of surgery only immediate family would be allowed access to the patient. Was she immediate family?

No, just almost his baby's mama, Imani thought as she sat with Monique and Nia in the waiting room. Nia had refused to let Monique take her home, insisting instead that she wait with her mother until Brax's condition was known. Another hour passed before they received word that Brax was out of surgery. It was against hospital policy but upon learning that they were there he asked that they be allowed to see him.

"He's a little groggy from the anesthesia, but I think it will be okay if you spend a few minutes with him," a nurse informed them as she directed the trio back to Recovery.

Monique and Nia went ahead of Imani, who lagged behind steeling her nerves for whatever awaited her. She had gone from being possibly pregnant to thinking she had lost her daughter all in a day. Now Brax lay in Recovery having suffered only God knew what trauma as a result of an automobile accident in which his vehicle had been utterly crushed. God help her heart, she didn't think she could take any more. But then Imani found strength somewhere inside. She remembered Monique's words from their earlier conversation. Life was real. It was not perfect. And neither was she. Imani quietly asked God for strength, realizing she needed it right then and there. And she needed, she wanted Brax. She had been given another chance. Her daughter was alive. So was the man she loved. Whatever the state of his body or mind he was alive.

Willing herself to go on, Imani entered the quiet sterile room.

Monique sat in a chair while Nia stood at the bedside holding his hand. Brax lay connected to a series of machines via various tubes, a smile lighting his tired face when Imani entered the room. His voice was thick and hoarse, and his words were slow in coming.

"Hey, babygirl. Happy to see me?"

Imani started crying as if a waterfall in her soul was unplugged.

"Mom, Mr. B. is going to be all right," Nia said, putting her arms around her mother.

"Your mother has to be the biggest crybaby this side of Georgia," Monique fussed.

"Come on, Mom, stop crying. Please. You're gonna rust my shoulder."

Imani lifted her head and, accepting the tissue Monique offered, she proceeded to blot tears from her eyes. She saw that Brax reached out to her. She accepted his hand and drew near. Gently, Imani stroked his head. "How are you?" she asked.

The effects of the ordeal were clear. Brax seemed weary, but he made a brave attempt to smile.

"I've been better, but I'll be back to normal in a matter of weeks."

"That's too bad," Monique quipped.

"Don't start with me, gypsy. I have a concussion, muscle tissue injuries, a busted shoulder and a cracked foot," Brax said, nodding toward his heavily bandaged appendage that was propped on a pillow. "But I will raise up and kick you with my good leg."

Imani laughed, thankful for the miracle worker responsible for two very alive people in that hospital room who could have been casualties of a truly horrendous accident. Chance had nothing to do with that.

"I have a couple of pins in my foot and in my big toe and depending on how things look in a day or two I may need another one in my heel. I also have some cuts that were hell to clean because of broken glass imbedded in them," Brax advised, pulling back his hospital gown to expose a bloodstained bandage covering his right shoulder. Imani winced at the sight of it. "Other than that and the fact that I can't see straight, I'm straight. Thank God for big tough rusty hoofs, huh, babygirl?"

Imani's lips trembled.

"Oh, Lord, girl come here," Brax invited, gingerly easing over on the hospital bed so that Imani could climb up beside him to lay her head on his chest and fight back tears. "Who's supposed to be comforting whom?" he asked. "It's okay, baby. She's a wittle harmonic," he told Nia and Monique, while stroking Imani's arm.

"I think you mean a *little hormonal*," Monique offered.

"Dat's what I thaid," Brax asserted, his head drooping slightly against the pillow.

"Must be the anesthesia," Nia said, giggling. Nia suddenly sobered as she reached over to hug Brax, including her mother in the embrace. "Mr. B., you saved our lives. I love you," Nia said, burrowing her face against her mother.

"Dag, I love you, too, forty," Brax answered, taken aback by Nia's sudden change of heart.

"That's shorty!" Nia corrected.

"I'm about to hurl with all this syrup floating around in here. Just give me love, baldy," Monique said, extending a fist across the distance for Brax to top with his, which was not easy to do considering both Nia and Imani were wrapped about him in varying degrees. "Nia, let's step outside for a minute so your mom can have some time alone with musclehead." As they reached the door Monique turned back and looking at Brax stated, "I take back almost every mean thing I've ever said about you. You're all right by me, B. W."

Brax just smiled, not knowing what to make of Monique's declaration.

He closed his eyes and leaned back against the pillows propped behind his head. Knife-like pain shot through his body. He felt stiff and sore and drugged. But thank God he felt. He could be in a morgue somewhere with a tag hanging from his toe, a cold cadaver waiting to be identified. The thought sent a shiver down his spine.

"Are you cold? Do you want another blanket?"

Her soft, low voice nearly startled him. Brax peered to his left to find Imani sitting on the bed beside him.

"What are you doing here?"

"You invited me here."

"I did?"

She nodded.

"Must be the drugs because I would remember welcoming a sexy siren into my bed." Noticing the somber expression on Imani's face Brax sobered. He ran a finger across her chin. "What is it?"

"Brax, I'm not pregnant. I took a pregnancy test and the results were negative."

Despite his drug-induced state Brax felt a mix of emotions that ranged from relief to disappointment. He had mentally, if not emotionally, prepared for the eventuality of Imani's having their child. Brax remembered the utter sense of protection he felt toward Nia in that split second it took for him to reach across the vehicle and shield her body with his own at the moment of impact. It was a fierce and pure kind of rush that he imagined all loving parents experienced at one time or another in life. He was ready to offer that loyalty to Imani and their child. Oddly excited, Brax had even toyed with the idea of informing his family when he arrived . . .

He sat straight up in the bed.

"I was en route to the airport," he murmured as if remembering. "My mother was taken to the hospital. I have to get in touch with my family!"

Imani jumped from the bed and raced outside to retrieve her cell phone from her purse that was in Monique's possession.

"What are you doing?" Brax inquired as she returned. "I can use the phone in here."

"This is Recovery, sweetie. There are no phones in this room," she said. "What number should I dial?"

His mind was clouded. Try though Brax would he could not remember the numbers to reach either of his sisters on their cell phones. Nor could he recall the name of the hospital back home where his mother had been admitted. Frustrated, Brax rubbed his temples. His head hurt and he muttered miserably, "I don't know."

"Are the numbers stored in your cell phone?" Imani questioned, stroking his arm in a soothing manner.

His countenance suddenly brightened.

"Yes! Where's my cell?" he asked, looking about. "Dag, it's in the car."

"What about Terrance?" Imani asked. "Does he have access to your telephone book?"

"My address book is electronic. It's on my computer."

Imani quickly dialed the home telephone number, knowing Terrance had his own line, but praying that he would answer Brax's. He did on the first ring.

"Terrance, it's Imani."

"Where are you? Where's Brax?"

Imani explained what occurred as quickly and as simply as she could. After reassuring Terrance that Brax would recover she asked him to pull up the data.

"It's password secure," Terrance announced when his attempt failed.

"Brax, your PC is locked. Terrance needs the password."

Brax smiled.

"That I can not forget. It's 'babygirl.' "

Imani smiled briefly before passing the information to Terrance. Hurriedly, she scribbled the data on a meal selection card left behind on the bedside stand in the room.

"Thanks, Terrance. Oh, and T., will you forgive me for my ugly ways and for hollering at you earlier?"

"I guess so seeing as you're in the family way," Terrance joked.

"Well, actually I'm not but—"

"Imani, hold on, the other line is beeping."

Imani sat in silence, rubbing soft circles on Brax's skull as she waited for Terrance to return. Shortly, he did.

"Imani, put B. on the phone please."

"Yeah," Brax said, giving his best friend his customary greeting. "Naw, I'm straight, Cuddy. Just a little banged up. What? You're kidding." Suddenly Brax laughed a full kind of sound that made Imani smile. "Father God, I thank you!" he shouted. "All right, man. Naw, they're keeping me overnight so the house is all yours. Don't tear up nothing or it's coming out of your paycheck. Peace."

Brax leaned back. Looking at Imani he announced, "My mother's fine." He breathed a sigh of immense relief. Brax handed the telephone back to Imani as his hands shook. "Can you dial my sisters for me, Boo? You're still my boo, my babygirl, right?"

"That's affirmative, Mr. Wade."

Moments later, a nurse appeared to announce that the patient needed his rest.

"I'm leaving," Imani politely replied, "but may I have just a few more minutes please."

The nurse looked at them then turned stiffly on her heel and left, a tight smile tugging at her mouth.

"So it was angina and not a stroke or heart attack?"

"Yes," Brax answered. "Guess Moms has got to lay off the fat back and greens for a while." He shook his head. "Losing one parent was hard enough. I could not imagine losing two like that." Brax scratched his ear. All of sudden, without warning, he felt an overwhelming relief rise in his chest so that he lurched forward, and wrapped his arms about his knees. The motion panged his injured shoulder as well as his foot, forcing him to relax backward again as his eyes grew misty. Imani was there, holding his hand as he exhaled loudly, feeling as if the world had been turned upside down only to be flipped right side up once more. "Whew!" he breathed. "What a play, what a play."

Imani kissed his cheek.

"That's 'day', sweetie. I have to leave so you can rest. I'll be back tomorrow."

Brax nodded, feeling the effects of the drugs in his system. He inched down in the bed and made himself more comfortable.

"Good night, Brax." Imani stroked his head one last time before softly murmuring, "I love you."

Brax mumbled something unintelligible.

Imani exited the room. Finding her family not far away, Imani wrapped an arm about her daughter, and with Monique on Nia's opposite side, the three walked away.

Just before floating down into a dreamless, peaceful sleep Brax whispered to the empty room, "I love you, too, Imani."

BRAX

I couldn't let Pearl go out all by herself so I made a point to be there when the insurance inspector paid a visit to the yard where Pearl was laid up like a smashed can ready for the recycle bin. Poor girl was a jacked up, banged up heap of scrap metal, and not even a fragment of the car Pops had purchased so many years ago new off the showroom floor. I felt sad looking on as the inspector assessed my ride while jotting notes on his clipboard.

"Mr. Wade, it's amazing you're standing here considering the impact your vehicle sustained." He paused as if afraid he'd said too much then sadly shook his head. "Another classic bites the dust," he mused, nodding at Pearl. His nostalgia past, he stood up tall. "I'll submit my report to your claims adjuster and she'll be in contact with you soon."

"And what's your conclusion?" I asked, knowing that there was only one possible verdict, but needing to hear it just the same.

"It's a total loss," the inspector announced, his tone surprisingly reverent as if he understood the importance of the moment. "I'm sorry. The personal affects that were recovered, your CDs and what have you, are at the front office. You can take a quick look in the vehicle yourself just to see if there's anything I missed."

If you think breaking up is hard to do, letting go is more difficult still. I nodded, unable to speak.

Imani was right there, holding my hand, lending support in my time of need.

I knew I didn't have to be there to witness this, but I needed to be. Something told me it was required. So I steeled my will and did what I had to do. I glanced down at Imani's reassuring smile before easing my hand from her grip to take that first step—cane in hand, cast on foot—toward what used to be Pearl.

Pearl smelled bad, like rancid fuel, charred matter and mildew. I vividly remembered the engine fire that erupted once the EMT pulled Nia and me to safety. That day had been filled with divine delays and deliverance. If I had made a left turn onto Fifth Street as I initially planned we would have been facing that drunk driver head-on. Thank God it was a side impact and not a head-on collision. I shivered, as I touched what was left of Pearl's hood, knowing I would not have walked away had that been the case.

I checked the car. There wasn't much to see, just remnants of a side window that shattered on impact, and a road map that lay on the floor, soggy and destroyed by the water used to douse the engine fire. Both the trunk and the glove box were open and empty. The inspector had been quite thorough.

I hobbled back to where Imani and the insurance inspector waited. My cast would be removed in a few days. The healing process was nearly complete. I'd stomped about for weeks with this contraption on my foot and knew how to get around so my slow gait wasn't due to my being encumbered by the cast. There was something else hanging heavily on me.

I thanked the inspector. Before walking away, he shook my hand and assured me the claim would be handled expeditiously.

Imani was quiet. She merely held my arm, rubbing little circles on my skin in her attempt to offer comfort. I appreciated and needed her presence.

We've had several in-depth, heart-deep discussions since the accident. Of course we had to start off apologizing seeing as how we both went off the hook, babygirl more so than me, talking trash and flexing stupid on one another that fateful day. Taking the time to reexamine our relationship, Imani and I have concluded that it's what we both want, that the connection is more than physical that it's spiritual and we belong together.

I admit that at first I had doubt gnawing at the back of my mind thinking that Imani felt obligated to me in light of the fact that my actions in a life-threatening crisis helped save her child. But the thought passed and I allowed my instincts to overrule the misgiving: Imani was not playing with a man's mind. She is not with me out of gratitude. I'm determined to be with her despite fear.

I have to finally confess I've been afraid of loving another somebody who could hurt me by leaving me suddenly, without notice or fanfare. I went through that with Pops and I guess I put up a blockade that guaranteed that I wouldn't have to go through it again by remaining distant and disconnected. Thus my deliberate attempts to keep love at arm's length with all my policies and principles. Make no mistake: a man should exercise prudence when it comes to matters of the heart and deciding who gets a pass to his love and who gets the boot. But it is highly likely that I've buried my head and my heart in the sand to keep myself safe . . . until Imani.

Babygirl burst through my barricades with the ease of the wind, laying me flat with her gentle charm. Let's not floss and front like feet don't stink, the woman *ain't* perfect. Then again neither am I. But at least I don't get attitudinal just because she doesn't want to watch ice skating videos or eat a burger instead of watching some joint that needs subtitles or tossing back Lobster Newburg at some posh place that I can't afford to burp in. Still, despite our unique differences and idiosyncrasies I believe I am right where I'm supposed to be: with Imani. And like Pops used to tell me when I got frustrated with something or someone, including myself, perfect ain't always possible.

Son, perfect ain't always possible. Sometimes you have to opt for good.

"Are you okay, sweetie?"

Looking at Imani I decided that she was lovely and loving, caring and kind, and she could do some things with chocolate chip cookies that had to be outlawed in forty-one states. And I loved her as she was, beautiful and bodacious and wonderful and that was all together good.

"I'm straight," I told her, believing that I was.

"Why don't I wait in the car and give you a few minutes alone," she offered as if sensing my need for privacy.

I accepted and bent toward Imani as she stretched to place a soft kiss on my cheek, softly touching the place on my right shoulder injured in the accident. She left me there but I did not feel alone. Someone was with me.

I moved forward.

In the heat of the August sun I stood beside my ride and thanked Pearl for seeing me through the years. She was a real hoopty and I hated to see her out for the count, but I had to let her go.

The truth of that conclusion hit me square in the stomach.

I had to let go.

My baggage was weighing me down.

Right then and there something opened in me, something that I closed long ago, and it was suddenly inescapable and staring me in my face.

An admission began . . .

Braxton, for years you've harbored an anger at God that was a seething thing, like a pot of water on a stove subject to continuous heat. But like a pot under such conditions, the water long ago boiled and evaporated into nothing leaving you, the vessel, cracked and dry and on the brink of destruction. Let go of anger and live. It's time.

I wasn't delusional. The August heat was not frying my brain. My father's voice was felt more than heard and that was on the inside of me. I was left with bitter sadness caused by my resentment toward my heavenly Father, and the sense that my liberation had always been a word away.

Unconsciously, I passed a palm over my head while collecting my strength. A response was required. There was no denial. All I could think as I stood there fighting wet tears on a dry hot day was, *Pops, you're right.*

Finally admitting that God did not take my father away from me as some punitive or vengeful act of a cruel deity far removed from the concerns of man was hard. Not because it was untrue, but because the admission destroyed my cover-up. Truth rolled through me, liberating but draining: my father wrote his own obituary by his own hand. He was his own cause of death. My anger, all these years directed at God, was truly toward him.

"Pops, why?"

The question hung in the still air, heavy like lead.

No answer came, but I knew that if I never had insight or understanding concerning my father's actions, or his failure to act by not following his physician's instructions, I had to go on. I could not postpone my living. It was my turn to speak.

"Pops, I'm mad at you." That admission was so difficult I had to pause before I could continue. "You left me. I wanted you to see me grown and good, see my wife and my children, but you let something . . . stubbornness or indifference or . . . I don't know . . . but it stole your life from me, Mom, the twins . . . from all of us."

There's something about emotions long held—when they break, they break and there is nothing you can do to check their flow.

"You and I both know you were wrong. I was your only son. You were my only father. I needed you."

I wasn't aware of the tears until they jumped from my chin down through my shirt and onto my chest.

"And I still need you. Who's going to kick my butt if I try to elope again? Dag, Pops, I miss you and love you, but I can move forward."

I had to stop and catch my strength.

"And Pops . . . I forgive you."

It was finished. I felt the farewell somewhere deep. It was both bitter and sweet. But it was necessary. I could leave Pearl in her final resting place knowing that I no longer needed her as a tangible link to or reminder of my father. I did not need to hold onto his vehicle or the past to feel close to him. At last I had the courage to speak my heart, release my pain and anger, and in the process I sensed a connection with an ever-living spirit that perhaps my chaotic and wounded soul had somehow prevented me from knowing.

See! I *knew* I should have never gone to church with Imani. I should have gone to Friday night poker with 100 Strong or rolled to Hot August Nights in Vegas with T. like I started to. I actually gave up seeing a parade of classic cars in sin city to sit here and have some preacher talking up under my sheets.

After my farewell to my father, I was feeling expansive and was ready to atone for my sins, so when Imani invited me to some singles' shindig at church I agreed to attend despite the fact that I haven't stepped into the Lord's house in so long I wouldn't be surprised if angels fainted at the sight of me. But Nia was in Los Angeles. Apparently, if things go well there's a possibility that Nia might relocate to live with her father and that had Imani a little down so I caved. Besides, according to Imani the second Friday of every month was social night for the Saved & Single ministry at her church. What Imani failed to tell me was that this food fellowship would be interrupted by a roundtable discussion featuring her Singles' minister who was this tall, lanky brother with a good sense of humor and a bad habit of messing in other folks' business.

"Boo, I thought you said tonight was social night?" I whispered in Imani's ear as her minister pushed away his plate and picked up his bible and called for a cessation of the jovial noise in the church's dining hall.

Swallowing the chocolate cheesecake she was eating, Imani looked at me and innocently replied, "It is, but we always have a roundtable forum on social night. We have a box in which we can anonymously deposit cards on which are written issues that we may be dealing with and our minister pulls the cards so we can discuss them."

"I owe you a spanking," I whispered back, feeling a little quickening down below at the thought. I ended up having to wear my cast longer than anticipated so it was removed only last week. I was only too glad to see it go because that thing restricted more than my foot. Nurse Evans apparently thought sexual deprivation was part of my healing process. She was not crawling into bed with me and, I quote, "knocking that poor foot out of alignment." Knock it out, poor or not. The foot would mend and if it didn't I had another one. But I think it's more than concern for my injuries because since the accident Imani has been different. She's become a little reserved, more reflective as if she's searching inward for a higher understanding or something. I'm more "aware" of life, too, since the accident, but that hasn't put my libido on lockdown. So being able to count on two fingers the number of times we've had sex since my accident, I'm starving.

"Okay, who put this in the box?" the minister asked, before reading the card aloud. " 'Is it okay if a man has a woman for a roommate as long as she's a Christian, too?' " Looking over the top of his eyeglasses Imani's minister answered, "Only if you want a Christian baby nine months from now."

I had to laugh and as I did I felt Imani stiffen beside me only to remember how close we'd come to encountering the predicament of pregnancy ourselves. I looked at her, but she stared straight ahead.

"Okay, next," the minister chimed, tossing the card over his shoulder before reaching into the box to grab another one as we laughed.

" 'I'm a single, saved woman and I'm attracted to a brother in this ministry who seems interested in me but I'm tired of waiting for his approach. Would I be wrong if I asked him out on a date?' " Pausing to place the card atop the table the Singles' minister nodded and commented, "This is good. Let's open up the floor. What say ye all?"

It was quiet until this Tyra Banks knock-off—extreme forehead and all—offered her point of view.

"Why not? I think women have the right to make their interests known, and our doing so might be the opening some men need, especially shy men."

"I agree," another woman called out. "I think it's okay as long as you pray first and ask God's direction and permission."

That triggered a volley of responses and opinions from the audience until someone finally asked, "What's your opinion, Minister Reed?"

"Let's revisit a basic principle. What, does our pastor teach, is the purpose of dating?"

"Marriage," someone answered.

"So, we don't just randomly date as something to do. We date for courtship and we court to marry," he explained, causing me to think Pops would have liked this young preacherman with his old fashioned values. "Now who initiates marriage, the man or the woman?"

"All four of my ex-wives did," hollered a man in the back, sparking laughter.

"Okay, Brother Pruitt, you're out of control as usual. Seriously now, I have to turn to the bible on this. Genesis two tells us that the *man* leaves his father and mother and cleaves to his wife. Brothers do the leaving and the cleaving."

"Okay!" a sister chimed.

"Then Proverbs eighteen verse twenty-two informs us that the *man* who finds a good wife obtains favor of the Lord. So, my sisters I'm sorry, but you need to cancel that his and hers wedding ring set you have on layaway. Let the brother step up and pay to marry you," he concluded to a sprinkled round of applause. "I'm on a roll now. Let's go for broke," he said, pulling another card, his smile fading as he read, then removed his glasses to sit and stare at nothing. "This is real, saints," he finally intoned, holding the card and reading, " 'I was single for a long time and finally met this nice brother several months ago. I'm ashamed to admit it but we fell into sin and I became pregnant.' " The minister paused to clear his throat. " 'Things got chaotic be-

tween us and we broke up so . . . I had an abortion.' " There was dead
silence in the room as he read. " 'Now I'm so wracked with shame that
I've contemplated suicide. I don't know what to do.' "

Imani shuddered.

I reached for her hand. It felt cold to the touch. I saw that she had
tears in her eyes, and my heart plummeted thinking that that
woman's story could have been hers. I prayed that it wasn't as she returned my gaze and shook her head as if to assure me it was not.

"I'm a man," the minister began, "so I can never truly understand
the agony this woman is feeling about her terminated pregnancy or
her relationship with this man. But—and I don't mean to sound pa-
tronizing or condescending—every person in this room, myself included, has fallen short of the glory of God. But love covers a
multitude of sins." Pushing back his chair he stood and said, "The sister who submitted this card could be here right now. I'm not going to
embarrass her by asking her to reveal herself. Instead, I'm asking
every woman in this room to get up now and go to the sister nearest
her and embrace her, love on her, because that one you touch may be
the life you save."

I have never witnessed anything as moving as the women in that
place reaching out, crying for, praying over one another until the dining hall reverberated with the sounds of their heart-speak.

"Brothers, I want you to link hands and form a perimeter around
these sisters so they are safe and protected as they reach deep and get
their healing," the minister instructed.

I stood there, a link in a human chain of brotherly protection, realizing I yet harbored a hurt of my own. I'd dealt with my anger toward
my father. I had yet to confess and repent for my anger toward God. It
was a transparent moment, a time for open honesty so I bowed my
head and opened my heart and spoke to my maker like I hadn't done
in years. When I finished and looked up it took a moment before I
saw that Imani had moved off to a quiet corner to sit with an older
woman who held Imani's hands as they bowed their heads in prayer.
The translucent tears flowing down their chocolate and vanilla
cheeks dripped a steady stream of cleansing.

The preacher began to pray, all of his earlier jesting gone as he
called on the powers of heaven to heal the hurts and wounds in this
place.

". . . and, Father, *nothing* can separate us from Your love. So when the enemy comes to remind of us our transgressions we'll remind him of Your blood that takes away the sins of the world. May we always exchange our shortcomings for Your glory. In the mighty name of the Father, the Son, and the Holy Ghost we pray, amen."

Amen and it was all good.

Imani was quiet on the ride home in my rented vehicle. I hadn't decided what kind of car to purchase in place of Pearl so I was sporting a rental courtesy of the other driver's insurance carrier. Admittedly, after my accident I was in no hurry to get behind the wheel of a car again but with my foot healed and my psyche mended I've researched the market for a new vehicle. Pearl was old and her Blue Book value barely covers the cost of a tank of gas so I'll need to dip into my savings and put down some ducats with the damage settlement in order to have a decent down payment on a new vehicle. Or I can wait until the entire claim is settled. But who knows how long that will take? And I'm not going to ride the bus to work with my students.

My claims adjuster settled the damage portion of my claim in July and began subrogation against the insurance carrier of the at-fault driver in an effort to recoup the payout. The only matter that remains unsettled is the bodily injury issue. Apparently in California there is a three-year statute of limitations on bodily injury claims so even if my foot is healed I can submit any medical or related expenses incurred as a result of my accident within that time frame. And there is a punitive factor involved as the other driver was under the influence. I'm entitled to compensation for pain and suffering. I'm not trying to be a growth on the couch watching *Maury Povich* and eating Fritos pretending like my toe is aching, but it's good to know I have recourse if needed.

So . . . anyhow . . . as I was saying, when we rolled up to Imani's she placed a hand on mine and asked if I would come in. Heck yeah! Tonight could be the night we resumed some long overdue loving. That hope was squashed when she announced that we needed to talk.

That was a guaranteed farewell to the freak fest. My high came down. Any time a woman says "we need to talk" she's either 1) pregnant, 2) wants something you can't give, or 3) is seeing someone else. We've already endured the pregnancy scare. Imani already knows I'm committed to her and a monogamous relationship that will, who knows, one day lead to something permanent between us. So, exiting the vehicle I surmised that it was three strikes I'm out. Some marshmallow-coated knucklehead like Nigel had moved in and eased a man out. What if it was Nigel? What if Imani had decided to reconcile with her ex for Nia's sake? I'd have to saw the caps off of his teeth and . . .

"Brax, make yourself comfortable," Imani called as she climbed the stairs, promising to return shortly. I have to admit that I forgot all about my visit to the church and living saved and single while anticipating Imani returning with her gorgeous goods packaged in some flimsy enticement that would make a brother slobber and a nun blush.

I may have been drooling when I slid into the family room to stroke the beats. Turning on the stereo system the sounds of Kirk Franklin's *Hosana* filled the room. Not exactly booty music so I pulled the plug.

Thumbing through Imani's collection, I noticed some new additions beefing up her gospel suite and found a CD cover featuring a sister holding a saxophone. Gospel or not I had to hear what the woman was blowing so I made the exchange and was rather impressed.

"She's good isn't she?"

I turned to find Imani entering the room dressed much more comfortably than when she departed, as in something that looked like a muumuu with legs kind of comfortable.

Okay, I could work with her. I had imagination and memory to recall that what was beneath the Mrs. Roper get-up would have me up and going in a minute. Besides, I was so pleasure starved that Imani could have entered the room sporting a barrel and that would have been sexy, splinters and all.

So I didn't trip. I crossed the distance and wrapped her in a flesh-on-flesh kind of embrace while kissing that mouth to convey all the hunger I could.

Imani pulled away and pressed my chest back gently but firmly. "Brax, we need to talk."

"I'll be all ears afterwards," I promised, reaching for her mouth again.

"Brax, please," Imani urged, her look of intense concern pulling me up. So I sighed and took her hand and headed for the couch to sit beside her and watch Imani struggle to find the words she needed to convey what was on her mind. "How did you enjoy Singles' ministry tonight?"

"It was powerful." But she was there and already knew this.

"It *was* awesome," Imani concurred, a curious glow spreading across her face. "Brax, I know you've noticed a certain . . . hesitation on my part . . . with regards to our being intimate after your accident."

Okay, here it comes. Get ready, B., I told myself. Don't start slinging CDs or breaking up stuff in here. Stay calm.

"Yes, I've noticed," I honestly admitted, remembering the times I'd approached her only to have her tense up and do her best to distract me with something else as if I could forget about wanting the chocolate.

"Something happened tonight that ended the struggle I've been having since then." She paused a bit too long for me. "Brax . . . I can no longer be intimate with you . . . or anyone else outside of marriage."

Whoa doggie! Talk about knocking me over with a feather.

At first I felt relief that another brother, especially Nigel, was not my problem. But then . . .

"I'm sorry, but could you elaborate that point please?" I ignorantly requested. What part of no more nookie did I not understand?

I was not feeling Imani, and she would have made more sense talking like the unseen adults in Charlie Brown cartoons, *waa waa waa waah!* Okay, so I was able to decipher a few key points as she spoke.

Both Nia and I could have been taken from her in the accident. *She* felt as if she'd been given a second chance. And that meant drawing closer to God. *Waa waa waa waah!*

I guess drawing closer to the Creator meant putting physical distance between us. Couldn't we all three just get along?

"Wait, Boo, hold the phone! What exactly are you saying here?" I asked like a glutton for punishment.

"I can't continue a sexual relationship with you," Imani reiterated, holding my hands. "Brax, I did something tonight that I wish I'd done long ago." That curious glow warmed her face again. Imani was all serene smile and bright dimples when she continued. "I gave my heart to the Lord."

Did I notice her sitting with a blond haired older woman during the prayer in the dining hall? Well, that woman was the singles' ministry co-pastor to whom Imani confided that she was involved in a sexual relationship. The minister had listened without judgment and spoken such words of God's love and His wanting the best for Imani's life so that right then and there, Imani prayed with the minister and asked the Lord to be her savior. Blah blah blah blah!

I extracted my hands from hers and sat back so I could stare some sense into her.

"Okay, Imani, you got a spiritual fill tonight but what does that have to do with us?"

"I knew this wouldn't be easy." She sighed. "This really is my fault and it wouldn't be an issue if we had never become sexually intimate—"

"Are you implying that you regret our relationship?" I asked, jumping to angry conclusions.

Imani shook her head.

"I didn't say that, Brax. I just—"

"You what, Imani? It sounds like you just had an itch that you needed scratched and now that I've done my booty duty it's all good and I can bounce because you're satisfied, in the name of the Lord, and ready to hibernate until your appetite thaws again."

Imani bit her bottom lip, a habit I used to find alluring. But right then there wasn't nothing nice about it.

"I know this isn't easy, Brax," she calmly began as if placating me, "but, please, I'd like it if we could discuss this—"

"*You'd* like? Imani, please, I'm trying not to hear this."

"Brax, you have to hear it."

The woman was serious. She had just informed me that she wanted to rewind our relationship back to the beginning when handholding and polite pecks on the cheeks were standard displays of affection, back before we started screwing like runaways from a chastity camp. Aww, hell no, I won't go!

"Sorry, babygirl, we've passed kindergarten and moved on to graduate studies of the anatomical kind. You can't flunk me now."

She actually laughed.

Humored I was not.

Imani shifted away from me so that she could prop her legs beneath her and face me directly.

"Brax, you have every right to be angry with me. I take full responsibility for my actions," Imani stated, as if being with me had been immoral or reprehensible. "I allowed things to move too quickly and I'm guilty of indulgence and not exercising self-control."

"You say that as if I'm a bad habit that needs to be kicked," I retorted.

Imani glanced down before looking at me again.

"No, Brax, you're the best thing to happen to me in a long time," she answered softly, looking at me with all this sincerity gushing out of her big brown eyes. I wanted to spit. "But when I heard about the sister who had an abortion I realized that could have been me feeling so trapped that—"

"Was that you, Imani? Did you abort my child?"

The question took her breath away so that we sat observing each other.

"Brax, how could you accuse me of something like that?"

There was real pain in her voice but I didn't care.

"You're the one reducing our relationship to something expendable and if you feel that I'm expendable then you could feel the same about my child."

Imani got up from the couch and went to lean against the fireplace so that her back was to me. I didn't need to see her face to know that there were tears in her eyes when she said, "I'm sorry that you think so little of me, Brax, but I never lied. I wasn't pregnant. I only feared I was."

"Feared? Oh, I see! That shook you and now you're backpedaling. You don't want to take a chance on getting pregnant and traipsing up into the house of God and face ridicule," I chimed, as if I'd solved a mystery, my blood rushing with anger.

"Ridicule doesn't scare me," Imani replied, turning to face me, her cheeks damp with tears. "I know what that feels like because I faced that when I got pregnant with Nia. And speaking of Nia, Brax—and this is an entirely different matter—my child needs me. She's at a crucial crossroad in her life and whether or not she stays in LA or returns home I am still her mother," Imani said, watching me intently as I glared back at her.

I was between a rock and a mountain. It was a no-win situation. This brother was down for the count.

"What do you want me to say? Do you want me to act a fool and try to fight God and your parenting responsibilities, to try and convince you that I can somehow fit in?" I angrily demanded, feeling rejected and used.

"No, but I want you to understand that this isn't just about tonight. I've been feeling divided and torn for awhile now."

I would have never known for all the moaning and clawing up my back that was her response during our last two wild rides.

"I promised God that if He spared my child's life in that accident that I would do whatever He wanted me to. And this is it, Brax. I have to . . . I *want* to live for Him."

My laugh was a humorless thing.

"Well, dag, you know, Boo, I'm not trying to be reduced to a mere distraction. So let me bounce up out of here," I snapped, getting up and striding quickly out of the room. Imani followed me and laid a hand on my arm. I jerked free of her touch. "You have serious issues that you need to work out. Do it on your own time and not mine."

"Brax, please, don't be this way."

"How should I be, Imani? Did you even bother to think this through? Do you want me in or out of your life?"

"In," she responded without hesitation.

"But on your terms, right?"

"I'm not trying to create rules as I go along, but my life has changed for the best. I've entered a relationship that supercedes even the pleasure I've known with you, and I want to please my heavenly Father more than my flesh."

I just stared at her and shook my head.

"Imani, you've been saved all of a minute, and now you want to capsize my world with some newfound holiness." My laughter was dry. "Do you think we can have some infantile little platonic relationship now? Or should I just stick it out and masturbate until you have *another* change of heart?"

I was ruthless and I knew it. Still, I loathed the hurt in her eyes. I did not want to see her vulnerability when my own anger and sense of rejection was staring me in the face. I despised the imploring tone in her voice when she continued.

"Brax, please don't belittle my experience—"

"And don't you belittle me!" I hurled. "I'm a man, Imani, not a toy." I felt like kicking something. Where was that old fat dog of hers when I needed it? "You can't bend me as you please. Your stuff is problematic and I can't be bothered with it or you," I yelled, sprinkling my tirade with a few profane words before walking out of her house and into the crazy, cold world for comfort.

I went to the gym. Big mistake. Any rockhead knows that strenuous exercise releases endorphins and endorphins fuel stamina and stamina can lead to an increased libido and if my libido increases I might blow a kidney. I'm not a prude but I ain't a pervert either. Still, all I've been able to think about since bouncing out on Imani is sex. There's a principle of psychology called free association. The mind fixates on an idea and freely associates images or occurrences with that idea, sometimes obsessively so. For example when I started driving again after losing Pearl it seemed as if I constantly saw Mustangs— classic or red—on a daily basis. Another example: I've been a member of this gym since I moved to Sacramento and I've never seen so many chocolate-skinned, voluptuous sisters getting their sweat on as there are tonight. That's the way the mind does you: just flaunts friction up in your face.

In my anti-social state, I didn't feel like participating in team sports so I passed on the nightly basketball game and opted for the weights. I was lifting like a maniac, straining muscles and popping veins, growling at my image reflected in the mirror like I had done myself wrong. I was three beats from a hernia and my form was foul but I didn't care. I was trying to work out my own soul salvation. But after two sets of reps I got tired of mean-mugging myself in the mirror and decided to go ahead and join the b-ball game already in progress so I could take out my aggressions on the innocent.

The moon must have been full and some beds empty because brothers were getting all violent, slamming and fouling and sweating all over each other and the ball as if we were playing an NBA championship game. En route to the shower I wondered how many of us had received walking papers from women.

When I exited the shower this guy I'd noticed at the gym several times before was at the sink brushing his teeth. I noticed him before because dude was a psychiatric case study waiting to happen. He was fascinating: probably five-four, one-hundred-and-fifty pounds dripping wet and he was always weighing himself and scowling at the scale. One night I timed him doing crunches for forty minutes before he followed that up with another twenty minutes on the calf press. His lower body deserved a medal but above the waist he was an A-cup stuffed with tissue. Can we say compulsive disorder and improper balance? Basket Case Bill was out of control.

Anyhow, a towel wrapped about his midsection, his hair freshly shampooed, dude stood at the sink using one of those electric toothbrushes that beeped every thirty seconds signaling time to move to the next quadrant. When he finished, he gargled with mouthwash for exactly thirty seconds before bopping over to use a courtesy hair dryer secured to the wall to dry his wet hair.

I casually eyed this while getting dressed myself until I lost interest and began smearing lotion on my body so that the gray ghost wouldn't creep up on me. Ashy skin is not sexy, or so my sisters always told me and I am inclined to agree. I don't know why I bothered because when on a love lockdown a brother can be so ashy that he looks like he's been rolling in cornstarch and it won't matter. Still, I sprayed on a touch of smell good for old times sake. That's when I looked up in time to see Basket Case Bill, the compulsive wonder, aim the hair dryer at one underarm and then the other. I almost laughed until he, finished with his pits, pointed the dryer in a southerly direction. I mean *way* down south.

I stood there in my red boxers with my mouth hanging open just staring. Homeskillet, his towel in a heap at his feet, was actually drying his daggone stank nasty pubic hair with the gym-issued courtesy hair dryer!

Noticing my disbelieving stare he gave me an apologetic smile.

"I didn't mean to hog it up. You can have it now," he announced in a booming voice better suited for a man twice his size, extending that hand-held apparatus in my direction.

Stick me like a pincushion but I wasn't feeling that! That was one locker room routine, one male bonding ritual I could do without.

I hooked up with T. at this comedy club downtown to celebrate my last weekend of freedom before school resumed. I had T. rolling, recounting the bizarre encounter with homeskillet at the gym as we sat at a table waiting for the show to start.

"Kid, you should have stayed around long enough to see if he whipped out a comb and brush," he finally managed to state.

"Yeah, and some Dixie Peach hair grease," I offered, causing T. to laugh harder still.

"Hey, what did you decide about the jokers who stole your car?" he eventually asked.

I told T. I'd actually decided on his suggestion that I not press charges against them. Knowing his own past as a troubled youth and how one judge's faith in him helped turn his life around, he'd asked me to consider some alternative action other than the penal system. There were, as he reminded me, enough young men of color flooding the system as it was. So I recommended to the courts that the two who stole my car be assigned to the mentoring program with 100 Strong. It would entail community service, financial restitution, adopting a younger brother as well as being adopted by one of the members of the network.

"That's what I'm talking about, bruh," T. said, tapping his knuckles to mine. "Save these young brothers from themselves."

"Yo, Cuddy, on another note Imani and I broke up."

"What? When?"

"Tonight."

"Why? I thought you two were tight."

"Obviously a little too tight for her," I replied, giving T. the details of what happened between Imani and I.

T. fingered the thin scar on his cheek. Suddenly he reached for his drink but paused before taking a sip to say, "Kid, I feel for you."

What deep words of comfort from a friend.

"*You feel for me?* I don't need your sympathy. I need some legal advice. Can I sue Imani for breach of affection?"

Terrance Blackmon, attorney at law, chuckled as if something was funny.

"I'm serious, Cuddy," I protested. "Is there a small claims court for copulation crises?"

"Kid, get real," T. responded, humored.

"Okay, what about that Waiver and Estoppels thing," I contended, alluding to a legal principle T. long ago explained to me, an argument that once a pattern or behavior was established and continued over a period of time it could not be suddenly breached or interrupted without penalty. By the look on T.'s face my legal eagle was a fried chicken.

"You're going to have to tough this one out on your own. But you know, B., you have to give Imani credit for standing up for her principles."

I was not about to celebrate this thing.

"She should have stood up for her precious principles *before* she laid down on them."

"Ouch! That may be true, B., but sometimes we make choices that we later regret or we have a change of conscience that interferes with established behaviors. And I'm sorry, man, but you can't fight the fact that Imani's elected to adhere to what she considers biblical commandments by abstaining from sex. Are you going to hold that against her?"

I looked at T. like he was crazy, which he was.

"*Hell, yeah!*"

"Come on, Kid, you're up against a higher opponent here. You better bow down before you lose."

I'd attended my share of church services as a child. I knew a little something about God and His Word. So I really did not need a sermon from the not right reverend who had more women switching in and out of his life than Star Jones has wigs.

"I'm trying not to hear you with your Friday through Friday fornicating self."

T. laughed and took another sip of his mixed drink.

" 'Ey, Kid, this is your issue and Imani's convictions not mine. I am a neutral party merely assessing and trying to mitigate the damage as any good lawyer should."

"Yeah, well you can fly that mess out the window because you don't know my plight," I returned, before grabbing a handful of peanuts from the bowl in the center of our table and popping them in my mouth. I chewed like a mad cow as the house lights dimmed and the emcee took center stage. Now what am I supposed to do with all of this? I can't fight God and I'm not going to take cold showers until Jesus comes back. I popped more nuts in my mouth and angrily concluded that I'd better send Doctor Ruth a plane ticket and invite her to move in because I needed a strong deterrent to desire.

SECOND TIME AROUND

Imani's bed was crowded. Between Monique, Nia, and even Miss Pitman at the foot of the bed Imani had just enough room to breathe. One of Nia's elbows was pressed almost painfully against Imani's ribcage, but Imani was only mildly conscious of the discomfort as she gazed on her daughter's sleeping face.

Nia appeared so sweet and innocent just as she had last night amid the hustle and bustle of travelers and traffic at the Sacramento airport. From her vantage point on the main floor, Imani watched her daughter descend from the second floor via escalator, an air of bravado about her as if Nia were a seasoned jet-setter accustomed to organized chaos. But the moment their eyes met and Imani smiled the false bravado melted away. Nia waved and rushed forward.

After the turmoil that erupted between them, precipitating Nia's escape to her father nearly two months before, Imani felt an indescribable joy as she embraced her child. Nia wiped the tears from Imani's cheeks in an effort not to cry herself.

"Mom, if you embarrass me I'm going to leave you bawling here in the middle of the airport and go call Grammy to come and get me," Nia teased, hugging Imani who released her long enough to step back and examine her child.

"Turn around and let me look at you. You've grown taller, Nia, and you lost a little weight."

"That's because Carmen can't cook," Nia answered with a scowl, referring to her father's live-in lover. "She gets all excited if her Jello sets."

Imani laughed, relieved that her daughter had elected to return home rather than remain in southern California with her ex-husband and his shack-up. The idea of Nia living in that situation concerned Imani so that she dropped on her knees and asked God to intervene. He did. Her baby was home.

Imani shifted onto her side so that her face was in close proximity to Nia's.

Thoughts of Nigel and his current situation led Imani to reflect on her relationship with Brax and to wonder exactly how much Nia knew about the level of their involvement. She had taken every possible precaution to keep their intimacies secret: Brax never stayed the night at Imani's and vice versa unless Nia was away. And she was careful to be discreet or avoid sex altogether when Nia was home. Still, Nia had found that unused condom on the stairs and the child was anything but stupid. Nia had to know. Imani felt as if she had lived a double and deceitful life.

How often had she counseled Nia against being prematurely intimate, even going so far as to allude to the fact that it might be best if Nia waited until marriage? Imani was aware of societal pressures and social norms that imposed no such strictures, making it perfectly acceptable and permissible for children to experiment with their bodies before their minds and emotions were fully developed and mature. Nia could walk into the school nurse's office and leave with contraceptives if she chose and Imani would be none the wiser. So, she made it a point to communicate with her daughter, to be aware of what occurred in Nia's world. And there she was having sexual intercourse with a man to whom she wasn't married. The rationalizing arguments were many: she and Brax were consenting and responsible adults involved in a committed and monogamous relationship built on more than mere physical attraction. Or so Imani thought until Brax withdrew from her world.

Nia stirred as Imani brushed twisted hair away from her daughter's eyes. Nia had exchanged her braids for cute little double-strand arrangements called Sister Twists. Imani felt oddly rewarded that Nia had begun experimenting with styling her long hair without the aid of regular chemical processes. Imani smiled, glad for a new common bond between them.

"Mom, stop staring at me, please," Nia requested, her eyes still closed.

"Oh, it's alive. Good morning, Snookie."

"Morning," Nia mumbled.

"And how do you know I'm looking at you?" Imani inquired.

"I can feel your laser eyes boring into my skull and I smell your . . . *fragrant* . . . morning breath." Nia squealed as her mother grabbed her face and blew into her nose then proceeded to repeatedly kiss Nia on the mouth. "Mom! You're melting the enamel off my teeth."

Imani laughed.

"Oh, quit acting up before you wake your lazy godmother."

"Her butt is all up in my back," Nia complained, shifting uncomfortably, causing Monique to mumble something incoherently before burrowing deeper beneath the lightweight covers.

Imani missed the occasional slumber parties she once shared with Nia and Monique. Fondly, she remembered how it had been customary for them to get together at either home and stay up late watching movies, painting toenails, listening to music or Monique's poetry, and eating any forbidden food their hearts desired. Imani could not even recall their last sleepover, so much time and so many occurrences had since transpired. She was glad Nia had suggested it en route home from the airport, and that Monique made it over after her reading circle meeting. Imani felt divine in the company of those she loved.

Nia's voice interrupted her musings.

"Mom?"

"Hmm?"

"Do you think you and Mr. B. will get back together?"

Imani propped herself up on one elbow and looked into her child's eyes.

"I don't think so, Snookie," Imani answered, attempting to keep the sadness from her voice. She had informed Nia last night that she and Brax were no longer together. Nia's disappointment had been genuine, even touching. Imani knew an incredible emptiness that still plagued her despite her joy at her child's return. Brax had somehow crawled into her bones.

Imani was certain that she did the right thing by choosing to end the physical intimacy but she had not anticipated the utterly painful disillusionment of their relationship.

What did you expect, Imani? she asked herself for the first time. *Did you expect the man to be content playing Scrabble with you after you gave up the goods?*

Imani smiled for Nia's benefit, but she didn't feel joy.

It proved wishful thinking on her part. Imani had hoped that Brax would understand and support her, and somehow manage to continue loving her, to stay with her despite the sudden overturn of their sexual relationship. Imani admitted that she had played with fire and burned them both. Quenching the driving desire that Brax kindled in her had not been easy. She was left with an aching hollowness that she now understood went deeper than sex.

But Imani planned to fill that void by refocusing on her renewed bond with her daughter and their relocation to Phoenix on a trial basis about which, surprisingly, Nia was only mildly unhappy. If things panned out and Phoenix proved fruitful Imani would withdraw her business loan application and put her plans for a boutique on the back burner yet again. In her opinion, that was a fair exchange for a way out of the mess she had made. Imani had found an out but what about Brax?

What about him? she silently argued.

Brax would survive.

Imani knew it was unfair to do so but as she lay there she found herself lumping Brax into a category. He proved no different from her ex-husband . . . or her father. The two men who should have treated her right—the father who should have loved her first and the first man she almost loved—left Imani to fend for herself and reclaim the broken pieces of her scattered heart. Imani bit back tears and reminded herself that she was *not* damaged goods. Her father, Nigel, and now Brax forfeited *her* affection. *She* was not defective.

"Mom, I'm sorry. You and Mr. B. could have been good together. I think your break up is partially my fault."

Imani was amazed at the confession.

"Why is that, Nia?"

"Because I was a brat, and I kinda sabotaged things," Nia quietly admitted. "I was difficult, and I kept getting into trouble and being rude and stuff. I just didn't know how to share you and . . . I was jealous of Mr. B. and I . . ." She lapsed into silence.

"Yes, Nia?"

Her voice trembled.

"I did want you and Daddy to get back together."

Imani waited as Nia struggled to continue.

"Some of my friends have parents who are still married, but most don't. Even so the ones who don't at least got to live in the house with both parents before things fell apart. I didn't have that." Nia played with her hair. "You know what's really sad? The only picture I have of you and Daddy together is from your sorority party five months ago so I don't even know what you two really look like happy together. But I wish I did."

A stab of pain pierced Imani's heart. She proceeded with caution.

"Nia, I grew up without my father so I understand your hurt more than you know. But, Snookie, you have to accept the fact that your father and I are not and never will be in love with each other," Imani simply stated. "Baby, we're not going to reconcile because there is nothing to reconcile or reclaim. That's just the way it is," she added as gently as she could. "As your parents we both love and adore you, Nia. You are the beauty our marriage couldn't be."

Nia swallowed a sudden gathering of unshed tears.

"Mom, that was the corniest line I ever heard."

Imani laughed.

"Sorry. But you do understand what I'm saying, right?"

Nia nodded.

"I know. I have a stack of Daddy's media clippings and whenever there's a photo at some function he's always hugged up with some new skank."

Imani clenched her teeth so as to not to reprimand her daughter for the use of such an ugly word. Nia was being open and honest, which is exactly what Imani wanted. Then Nia made an amazing statement.

"It's been a long time since you and Daddy divorced and I think you put your life on hold for me. I didn't see it before but I think it's unfair how Daddy never slowed his roll for anyone or anything while you raised me alone all these years," Nia stated, shocking Imani with her observation. "Mom, living with Dad was not what I expected. I was mad at you and wanted to be with him thinking things would be better there. But they weren't." Imani listened as Nia recounted her experience.

Upon arriving in Hollywood Nia had been dazzled by the glitz and glamour of her surroundings and her father's new status as a popular figure. But the fizzle faded fast and reality set in. Nigel was rarely home, always on the set, or out on the town promoting his show leaving Nia in the care of his lady friend or alone. As if feeling guilty for not spending time with his daughter Nigel doled out money for his girlfriend to take Nia shopping, to buy her anything and everything she wanted. But that thrill could last only for a while. Nia got the point: she was an intrusion. "I wanted to be there because I never had the chance to live with Daddy. But Mom, Dad acted like a doting father in front of his friends but when we were alone it was as if he didn't know what to do with me. We were almost strangers."

"I'm sorry to hear that, Nia," Imani offered, stroking her daughter's cheek.

"Mom, you tried to warn me but I wasn't trying to hear you. I'm sorry."

Imani merely wrinkled her nose at her child and smiled.

"I forgive you, Snookie. And Nia, you need to know that you are not the cause of my breakup with Brax. Lord *knows* you were a challenge but you're not the reason. Okay?"

Nia nodded.

"Dang, Aunt Mo, get your booty off of me," Nia suddenly fussed, interrupting the flow of their sentiments as she turned toward her still sleeping godmother to gently push her toward the edge of Imani's king size bed.

"I'll let you two work that out," Imani announced as she eased from the bed, thankful that her daughter had arrived at a mature understanding regarding her father and his shortcomings. She had never tried to denigrate Nigel in front of Nia, hoping that in time Nia would see for herself the man her father was.

Imani padded toward the bathroom, her bare feet sinking into the plush pile of the soft carpet. As she reached the bathroom Imani heard the outgoing message on the answering machine being activated. Only then did she remember that she had turned off the ringer on her telephone before going to bed last night so that the threesome could sleep without being awakened by early calls on a Saturday morning.

"Nia, turn the ringer back on please," Imani called as she closed the bathroom door. The outgoing message ended and was followed by a high-pitched beep and then his voice, dark and sweet. Imani whirled, snatching open the bathroom door to listen.

Imani suddenly forgot her less than benevolent musings of mere moments before.

His voice conjured up precious memories. They had not seen or spoken to one another since the middle of August. That was two weeks too long. Imani realized that she missed his voice, his broad smile, his gentle touch and strong hands, his sense of humor and loving ways. Imani missed the man.

She stood in the doorway unable to move, and watched as Nia snatched the phone off the hook.

"Yo, Mr. B., wassup? No, I got home last night. It was pretty cool. How ya livin'? Really! Aww, snap, that's krunk. When can I see it?" Nia sat listening quietly to the party on the other end. "Can I drive it?" Nia laughed. "That's cold, Mr. B. How's your foot? That's good. Yes, she's available. Okay. See you at school." Covering the mouthpiece with her hand Nia whispered unnecessarily, "Mom, it's Mr. B."

Imani stood there as if roots had taken hold of her feet, anchoring her to the floor.

"Mom, come on," Nia urged, shaking the phone at her mother who was still unable to move, forcing Nia to scramble out of bed and bring the phone to her.

"Thanks," Imani breathed as she accepted the phone. Her voice sounded peculiar when she spoke. "Hi, Brax. How are you?"

"I'm good." She closed her eyes and nibbled her bottom lip at the sound of his voice and its sweet caress she had nearly forgotten during their exile. "I miss you," he added, causing rippling sensations to flutter in her stomach with the softness of butterfly wings. Imani looked up to find Nia still standing there, grinning mischievously. Imani stuck her tongue out at her daughter before closing the bathroom door in Nia's face. "I miss you, too, sweetie," Imani softly concurred.

Brax chuckled.

"Oh, so I'm still your sweetie?"

"I don't know, Brax, but I pray that you are," Imani replied in a rush. His response seemed too long in coming and Imani was conscious of holding her breath.

"Are you busy? Can we go out for breakfast and talk?"

It wasn't the response Imani wanted, but at least Brax did not shut her down. It was a beginning.

"Actually, Nia and Monique and I are having breakfast this morning. Can we get together for lunch?"

"How's one o'clock?"

"I can't wait that long," Imani practically purred. "How's noon?"

"I'll pick you up if that's okay."

"That would be wonderful," Imani answered. When she disconnected the call she sagged against the sink. Closing her eyes she smiled and said, "Thank you, Lord!"

When the doorbell chimed many hours later Imani felt as if her heart were in her throat.

"Mom, Mr. B.'s here!" Nia hollered from downstairs as Imani flitted about her bedroom preparing for her lunch with Brax as if it were their first date. It took Imani twenty minutes just to decide what to wear and—as testimony to her frenzied search for the perfect outfit—a pile of clothing was strewn across her bed. Finally, she was ready.

"Okay, you're sure this looks fine?" Imani asked, slowly pivoting for the benefit of her audience.

"You look lovely, Mani," Monique complimented, as she stood in the bathroom securing her abundant auburn locks into a loose knot at the nape of her neck. "Even your butt looks tame."

"What do you mean?" Imani felt a new panic. She twisted and turned before the bathroom mirrors trying to assess the girth of her behind in a sarong skirt with an ethnic-looking print in soft hues of orange, red, and gold. "Oh, Lord, don't tell me I look like I'm carting two pigs in a blanket."

Monique laughed.

"I was only playing, Mani. Your butt looks decent."

"Decent? What kind of veiled insult is that? I'm taking this off—"

"No!" Monique yelled. "I do not have the patience to endure another round of the Ivana Trump fashion show. Besides, I was only kidding, Mani. I'm just hating because I don't have a booty on my back."

"Remind me to cut you later," Imani dryly quipped, rushing to her dresser to dab perfume behind her ears and scrutinize her flawlessly applied makeup. With trembling fingers Imani donned crystal earrings and a matching choker. She was ready . . . come what may. "It's show time at the Apollo," she said, smiling nervously before heading out the door.

Their conversation floated up to her.

". . . I get my permit next year. Come on, Mr. B., let me drive it around the block."

"Naw, Hollywood, that's not the way we roll here in the valley. When you obtain your driver's license and a suit of armor for me I'll let you sport the wheels."

"Hollywood?"

Nia and Brax glanced up to find Imani descending the stairs.

"I've graduated from shorty to Hollywood since my trip to LA . . ." Nia explained, pausing. "Wow, Mom, you look nice."

"Thanks, Nia," Imani replied with a shy smile. "Hello, Brax." Her voice felt so low in her throat that Imani wondered if Brax even heard her. Her own ears were filled with the hammering of her heart and a rush of blood as Imani waited at the bottom of the steps and watched Brax who stood in the entryway studying her intently. He said nothing but hesitated only slightly before crossing the distance. Imani thought she detected something like longing in his face as he reached for her hand. "Babygirl," was all that Brax said as he pulled her forward into his embrace.

The strength and power and tenderness of that embrace was a sweet and heady thing that made Imani feel she was right where she belonged.

"Break all this up," Monique sang, bouncing down the stairs clad in loose-flowing pants and an off-the-shoulder cotton blouse.

"Wassup, earth mother?" Brax called.

"Nothing much, Lucifer," Monique replied, surprising Imani and, by the look on his face apparently Brax, by giving him a quick hug.

Imani laughed.

"You two need help."

"And I need an extra forty dollars, Mom," Nia announced.

"For what?"

"Another pair of jeans."

"Nia, don't make me discuss your business in front of Brax, but we both know I just purchased four new pairs of jeans for you. Did they go out of style overnight?"

"Mom, school starts in three days and I need one pair of jeans for each day of the week," Nia explained as if it all made perfect sense.

"You need to get an every-day-of-the-week-J-O-B and earn some scrilla up in here, girlie."

"Scrilla?" Nia laughed uproariously. "Mom thinks she's vibing with the slang. You go, Mother. Now can I get forty? Come on, Mr. B., you know the pressures of my peers. Can I get some help here?"

"Please, I'm trying to get back in your mother's good graces," Brax stated, backing up.

"Bye, Nia. Go to the mall with your godmother already," Imani advised. "Are you ready, Brax?"

"Yes, ma'am," Brax replied, opening the front door.

Imani stepped outside and stopped at the sight of a brand new Cadillac Escalade the color of rich mocha parked curbside in front of her house. "*Whew!*" she whistled, turning to look over her shoulder. "Brax, is that yours?"

He nodded affirmatively.

"Whatcha got?" Monique asked, stepping from the house. "Nice little over priced capitalistic commodity for consumption you've bought into there."

"Yeah, whatever. I don't see you flying around on a rented carpet."

"Truce people," Imani urged. "Nia, your godmother's waiting on you. Here, you can have another twenty but that's it. Your well has run dry," Imani advised as she handed Nia a bill. "Do you want to check your savings account to see if your father deposited the money for your school clothes?"

Nia smacked her lips and answered, "That's really okay," her tone implying that her fantasies regarding her father's shortcomings had truly come to an end.

Imani waved as Nia climbed into Monique's car and the two ventured on into the hot September day.

Brax held open the passenger door and assisted Imani as she climbed into the sport utility vehicle, commenting, "I haven't smelled brand new leather in a long time."

"There're some things I haven't done in too long as well," Brax said, leaning into the open space. "Would I incur the wrath of God by kissing you?"

Grinning, Imani advised, "Just keep your tongue out of it."

"Shoot, forget that," Brax said, closing the door and walking around to the opposite side of the vehicle as Imani laughed as if the world were hers.

* * *

"So, do you forgive me?" Imani asked as they sat at an outdoor café off Broadway. Traffic whizzed by in a constant stream as pedestrians sauntered up and down the walkways creating a buzz of human activity, some pausing to enter the busy record store across the street. But Imani was oblivious to the activity about her as she waited for a reply. She watched Brax, admiring the strength of his hands, the breadth of his shoulders, the sweet brown sugar of his complexion. Nervously, she nibbled her bottom lip as Brax considered her. Imani felt exposed, naked before his intense stare.

Suddenly, Brax cleared his throat and passed a hand over his clean-shaven pate.

"I want to, but let me be honest. I'm struggling with all of this."

Imani nodded her understanding, but said nothing, allowing Brax to continue.

Brax flashed back on a particularly lonely night during their separation. He lay in bed staring at the ceiling, nearly soothed by the sounds of the water in his aquarium as he grappled to understand the turn of events that served to separate them. Since that turbulent encounter months before, a series of upheavals seemed to plague their lives, his life. Brax had gone from one day expecting to be a child's father to thinking he was about to lose his mother, only to be confronted with a danger that could have taken his very life. His vehicle had been destroyed and he was later confronted with his clinging to the ghost of his father only to realize that his affections belonged in the land of the living. Just when it appeared that life had regained its rhythm, Imani pulled the rug out from beneath his size twelves by announcing her need to revoke their pleasure principle.

He tried to, needed to reject love. He argued with himself, insisting that whatever he felt for Imani was sheer infatuation and could be squashed because it lacked substance or depth. It was the fickle outcome of a fast relationship. But the more Brax struggled the heavier his heart felt until, tired and restless, he turned on his stereo. His classic soul collection soothed his mind and nearly put him to sleep until Marvin Gaye began to sing. The words of Gaye's "I Want You" were so timeless and so apropos that Brax felt as if someone were stomping across his chest.

What Brax had felt but been unable to express the last time he saw Imani was a sense of rejection and disregard. He found the words now. Brax did want Imani, as Gaye sang, the right way. But he needed to be wanted as well.

"I told myself that you were crazy and that I should just walk and be done with this," Brax admitted. "I didn't need this kind of rejection, Imani. Let me admit something that you may never hear me admit again: I felt helpless. You made a self-serving decision that involved me without my input or regard for my perspective or how *your* decision would affect *me*."

Imani had to take several deep breaths before she was able to speak.

"Brax," Imani softly stated, "my intent was never to hurt or reject or violate you. Your feelings are extremely important to me."

"Why extremely, Imani, and why now?"

"You're feelings were always important, Brax," she insisted. "My decision was difficult *because* I care for you and don't consider you some miscellaneous man that I want to play with."

Brax sat back and contemplated her words, thinking that that was exactly how he felt, as if he had been taunted and teased and trivialized as if he were nothing more than a random, rutting, disposable male.

"Truth be told, I do feel as if you think I'm some easily disposable automaton instead of flesh and blood with feelings. You have an unrealistic expectation if you think I can be content with things as is. Wait, let me finish," Brax said, lifting a hand to halt Imani's attempt to interject. "You tried to cut me out cold turkey, Imani. And I'm not just referring to sex. All of a sudden your home life is too busy, and your stuff is falling apart so I'm the one who gets shafted. Did you ever stop to think that I might be made of something strong enough for you to lean on?"

The silence between them was thick.

"May I say something?" Imani finally requested.

"Absolutely."

"I never cut you out, Brax. You left of your own accord."

"It was my only option at the time," Brax defended. "I can't fight God. I'm glad for your spiritual conversion and accepting Christ is probably the best thing anyone can do, but still you have to admit you came at me hard."

Imani looked away, gathered strength.

"I wouldn't pit you against the Lord. We know who'd win," Imani said without apology. "But you have an extremely vital point in what you said," Imani painfully admitted. "I *am* accustomed to fending for myself and my child. I'm accustomed to being alone without a man to care or comfort me or be there when the chips fall. I won't retract my stance on wanting to please God, but yes, perhaps it was partially out of habit that I retreated from you. Maybe that's all I know to do," Imani confessed, pausing to choke back a sudden rush of emotion. "But, Brax, I need you to know that you mean something to me. I meant it when I said I love you—"

"When have you ever admitted to loving me," Brax questioned with a sardonic chuckle.

Imani stared at him, brows furrowed.

"You were in Recovery . . . after the accident."

"Oh, so, were you feeling grateful that Nia was okay—"

"Brax, please, that's so completely—"

"What, Imani? Unfair? Unfounded?"

Imani said nothing, her frustration mounting.

They sat in silent observation of one another until Imani spoke again, feeling as if her soul was raw.

"I had really hoped for resolution of the riff between us, Brax, but—"

"So now everything should be legit because you apologized?"

"Brax, would you please stop being difficult!" The heat in her raised voice startled even Imani. Glancing about, she saw she'd gained the unwanted attention of several onlookers. She sipped her water and gave herself a moment to calm down. "I don't know if we're at a place where repair can occur. And I think you've concluded that I don't truly care about you and that's part of our problem. But I do, and I want you to know that I fell harder in love with you than you know. I'm not toying with you, Brax. I love you . . ." Her voice trailed off.

His fingers drummed the table in a steady staccato.

"Would that be a Christ-like sister-brother, platonic kind of heavenly affection or are you really capable of loving me like a grown woman loves a man?" was his biting retort.

Imani's lip trembled. She opened her mouth to speak but no sound came out. Instead she rose so suddenly that the water glasses on the table wobbled.

To Brax the scraping sound of her chair legs against the stone patio floor was like fingernails dragging across a chalkboard. He watched

Imani rush toward the cool indoors but he remained seated as stubborn pride anchored him in place.

Imani was nowhere to be found.

She was not in the telephone booth or on any other part of the restaurant premises. Confirming that Imani had not gone out to wait at his vehicle, Brax dashed across the street to the record store. He had noticed her regarding it a few times during their conversation. But after a quick but thorough check Brax concluded she was not there.

Brax dialed her cellular phone as he crossed the street back to his SUV sitting beneath the hot September sun. There was no answer. His call rolled to voice mail. He did not bother to leave a message, rather disconnecting as he started the engine and shifted the Escalade into gear.

There were plenty of people strolling along Broadway but not one fit the description of a long, dark, lovely woman who could wreck his world. Brax made a U-turn at Broadway and Twenty-first Street to return in the direction from which he had just come. Making a left onto South Land Park Drive he felt defeated, thinking Imani had probably found a taxi to take her home. He decided to ride a while before doing the same.

He turned on the stereo and was treated to Barry White's "My Everything." Brax rapidly depressed the button to change CDs, and was gratified when Sugar Hill Gang's "Rapper's Delight" kicked in. He did not need *any* kind of love song just now.

"Aw, yeah!" he chimed, drumming his fingers on the steering wheel and bobbing his head, wondering whatever happened to the innocent age of rap before black-on-black violence, misogyny, and a ghettocentric ethos flooded the genre.

Cruising down South Land Park Drive with its stately brick houses, wide lawns and lush appeal, Brax tried to resist replaying the afternoon's conversation with Imani in his mind. He tried to avoid recalling the sincerity in her words, her tone. He grappled to hold onto anger but it was elusive and slick and slipped through his fingers so that Brax was left with much needed emptiness. He already knew the dangers of failing to forgive. After weeks of feeling congested with anger and hurt a cleansing began.

Driving, Brax did a quick double take. A man on the right side of the street was jogging in his direction at high speed, his form stiff and erect and hypercontrolled. It was the happy hair drying obsessive-compulsive guy from the gym, his lower body fit and fabulous, his torso and above looking like the underbelly of a sick whale. He flew past the Escalade oblivious to his surroundings. Brax glanced at him in the rearview mirror and shook his head. Homeskillet needed an overhaul. He needed to get himself in check and strike a balance.

Even too much of a good thing could be bad.

Balance.

Proper discipline.

Isn't that what Imani was attempting to achieve?

Brax did not consider himself unreasonable. He might have been able to consider Imani's need for abstinence had she only invited him into the discussion, or made that choice *before* physical intimacy erupted between them. But then again, her surrender to God had not been an issue back when they first crossed that ocean. If only they had left things status quo and not become involved from jump street.

"Yeah, but we did, so enough of the 'if only' syndrome," Brax said aloud, pausing to consider that had he not become involved with Imani he might have, he grudgingly admitted, missed out on one of the sweetest blessings of his life. "Call me crazy, but I love the woman," he confessed in the solitude of his Escalade. "So now what?"

The answer lay ahead.

There she was, walking at a modest pace, the motion of her hips stirring immodest memories in him.

Brax sped up only to pull the SUV to a halt alongside Imani with a quick stomp on the brake pedal and a screech of tires.

Imani looked up startled, stopping in her tracks until recognizing Brax. Her face hardened and she continued her journey.

"It's a long walk home, Miss Evans."

She ignored him and kept moving, quickening her pace.

"You want a ride?

"No, thank you," she tonelessly replied.

"So you're going to make me talk to you through the open window of a moving vehicle?"

"That's your prerogative, Mr. Wade."

"Come on, Imani, quit playing. Get in the car."

Imani merely lifted her head and kept her stride.

"Fine. I have mad driving skills so I can do this," Brax tossed. "Okay, woman, listen up. I love you and I respect your decision. I don't *appreciate* the fact that your decision means a change in the dynamics of our relationship but like I said I respect you."

"Whatever," Imani replied, a dismissive note in her tone.

"That's all you have to say?"

"That and have a nice life."

Brax accelerated his vehicle, made a sudden and sharp turn of the steering wheel to the right and brought the Escalade to a complete stop in front of Imani. Exiting, he stalked onto the sidewalk and came face to face with her.

Imani moved to step around him.

Brax blocked her progress.

"You don't get the final say, Imani. It's my turn to talk and your turn to listen and you're not walking away from me."

"Why not? Isn't that what you did two weeks ago?" Imani returned, fire flashing in her eyes.

"Yes, and look where that got us. So can I have a minute of your time?"

Imani glanced at the second hand on her watch.

"You have one minute exactly. Time begins . . . now. Go."

Brax suppressed a chuckle.

"You drive a hard bargain."

"Fifty-nine . . . fifty-eight . . ."

"I swear! Listen, I said I love you and I mean that, Imani. That doesn't mean I'm not challenged by all of this—"

"Brax, I recognize that. I understand that. I want us to have the opportunity to work through this," Imani declared, exasperated.

"Hush, it's my turn. Can a man have the floor? Huh?"

A reluctant smile tugged at her mouth, and her dimples peeked out of the dark chocolate of her face.

"Fine. Go ahead, sir."

"As a man was trying to say," Brax paused, groaning loudly, "we . . . *I* have to struggle with this. I don't know what it means to love a woman who can't love me back . . . completely. But I'm more than an erection, Babygirl. You know that. And I know that."

Her touch was gentle as Imani laid a hand against his jaw.

"Brax, if enjoying you physically . . . sexually weren't a violation against what I've found with God, I'd do it in a heartbeat. But it is, so I can't, and I'll need to find other ways to express what I know."

Brax considered her several moments before scratching his ear and quipping, "Yeah, all right. Just don't stitch me any quilts. And I don't wear home-knitted draws so don't even bother. But really, Boo," he grew serious, "I honestly have no idea how to negotiate this. I may have to check in to a Betty Ford clinic for the sexually obsessed before it's all over with."

Imani stifled a laugh, but amusement was written all over her face.

"I was straight and good, doing my thing without a woman in my life until you came along wrecking stuff," Brax stated, his humor and good nature restored much to Imani's relief and delight. "Still, your self control and commitment are admirable but you didn't hear that from me, okay?"

"Okay," she replied.

"Imani," Brax began, laying a gentle hand at her waist, "I'm here because I choose to be. I'm not going anywhere. You can lean on me when you need. I'll just take cold baths for the rest of the century."

"It might not be that bad. We'll just have to be careful in our conduct and not do things that lead us into temptation."

Brax shot Imani a dubious look.

"Are you for real? Right about now you could pluck a rooster and I'd get aroused."

Imani laughed. Brax leaned in and drew her near.

"Seriously, I respect you, Imani. You believe that?"

She nodded.

"I cherish that respect but I'm only doing what I think is right, Brax. I'm not trying to win a morality prize," Imani offered. "God knows I don't deserve one." Imani glanced toward the yard of the house in front of which they stood. Flowering bushes filled with bright pink blossoms lined the path leading to the front door. She allowed their beauty to fill her senses as she made a confession. "Brax, my life was imbalanced. I sort of lost myself in Nia so that in a sense she served as a buffer, an excuse for me to hide from myself and my desires," Imani quietly admitted, confirming a suspicion Brax had considered long ago. "I guess I flipped the script upside down when you came into my life. I kind of overindulged without allowing time for a firm foundation to be established between us. I just wanted and needed to feel real in my less than rosy world."

Brax kissed her cheek.

"Can I tell you like my father used to tell me? Perfect ain't always possible. Sometimes you have to go for good."

Imani considered his statement before nodding.

"That's very wise advice. So . . . can I call you mine?" she asked.

Brax stalled unnecessarily long before asking, "Can I have a kiss and do I have to keep my tongue out of it?"

Laughing, Imani purred, "Just kiss me already."

GOT CREDIT?

M onday was Labor Day: the last day of summer vacation and the California State Fair. The Cal Expo fairgrounds were swamped with revelers trying to wrest every possible vestige of enjoyment from the season. The air was thick with the scents of cotton candy, jumbo corn dogs, hot buttered corn-on-a-stick, sugary desserts, and the sweat of human flesh. The relentless heat of the sun had long ago faded into tolerable warmth kissed by an occasional breeze.

Imani was dizzy. One ride on the tilt-a-whirl was more than sufficient for her, but the pressure was great and she was not about to prove them right. She was not a buster.

Nia, Monique, Brax, and Terrance were already in line waiting for the opportunity to be strapped within a tall, circular, cage-like conveyance in a standing position only to be spun about for sixty seconds too long at high speed as the ride dipped and swayed at vomit-inducing angles. They were gluttons for pleasure.

Imani started screaming before the ride was even in motion.

"Dang, babygirl, we're not even moving yet," Brax commented, laughing at Imani's antics.

"Mom, why does Mr. B. get to say 'dang' when I can't say 'dang'. I don't think that's 'dang' fair," Nia protested from her place in the cage.

"Because, Hollywood, I'mma grown a—"

"Brax!" Imani interrupted.

Monique started laughing. "You're foul."

"What? I was only going to say that I was a grown African American man."

"Yeah, right, Kid," Terrance interjected. "Aiight, this party is about to get started," he remarked as the sound of motors shifting into gear whirled above their heads.

"Mom, if you don't make it out of here can I have the car?"

"Nia, if I do make it out of here will you get a job? Oh Lord, here we go-o-o-o," Imani cried into the warm evening as the world rocked and twirled beneath their feet.

"Girl, you need to get your sea legs," Brax teased, holding Imani's hand as the ride ended and they dismounted from the platform putting them back on solid ground. "I guess you can't go fishing with me and your Dad."

"Fishing is one thing. Flying around in the middle of the air fast enough to break my neck is another," Imani returned. "But I don't do worms so you'd have to bait my hook."

"That's what I know," remarked Brax. "Is anyone hungry besides me? Imani's screaming worked up my appetite." The sly reference was lost on the others but Imani pinched his arm.

"Obviously, bottomless pit," Monique quipped.

"Don't start with me, grass guzzler."

"I saw a veggie kabob stand back that way," Monique announced pointing east.

The others quickly exchanged glances before turning west.

"Fine! Go ahead and gorge on grease and transfatty acid. If you clog an artery don't call me," Monique warned, hurrying to fall in step with her party.

"Mom, can I still meet up with Krista?" Nia asked, remembering that she had agreed to meet her best friend near the entrance at an appointed time. "It's still okay, right?"

"Mister and Missus Ramirez are bringing you home?"

"Yes."

"Fine. We'll walk you to the gate but your curfew is 9:00. School starts tomorrow."

Having safely delivered Nia to her destination where her friend Krista and a few other young ladies from their school awaited, the remaining foursome sat at a picnic bench in a grassy area eating their selected fare when Imani's cell phone rang. Recognizing the telephone number displayed she quickly answered the call.

"Debra! I was supposed to call you last week," she told her fellow soror and loan officer who was assisting Imani in securing a small business loan for her boutique. Phoenix was no more. Imani realized that escapism had been her primary motivating factor in considering relocating. She forced herself to buckle down and rise above the storm and finally, at long last, truly pursue her dream. "What? I'm sorry but what do you mean?" Imani pushed back her plate and rose from the table, leaving Brax, Monique, and Terrance to look after her as she walked away. When she returned several minutes later her expression was strained.

"What's wrong?" Brax asked, reaching for her hand.

"My business loan was denied due to a negative rating on my credit report. Debra's going to stop by the house later tonight and provide me a copy so I can review and dispute anything erroneous," Imani stated woodenly. "I've always been careful with my credit. I don't know what happened."

"There's a plausible explanation," Brax soothed, "just review the document and don't panic."

She didn't. She went off.

Imani could not believe her eyes. The last time she really paid attention to her credit report was when purchasing her car a few years ago and at that time it was in good standing, and she made a concerted effort to keep it that way.

Now, here she stood in the middle of her kitchen calling on Jesus before she cut someone. Imani understood now why her application for credit was denied when her dog needed emergency surgery. Her credit was a mess.

Credit lines were opened in her name that Imani knew she had never established. Most were extremely delinquent; many had already been assigned to collection agencies. Accounts existed with jewelers, men's clothing stores, a dentist's office and an electronic goods store just to name a few. She might as well have purchased Nia's new computer seeing as how the credit line was established with Imani as a co-applicant. But most egregious of all was the fact that an automobile dealer listed Imani as a co-signer for a recently leased vehicle. Reading the name of the Sacramento Porsche dealer Imani screamed.

"Nigel!"

IT NEVER RAINS IN
SOUTHERN
CALIFORNIA

Dear Mr. Evans,
We have elected to redistribute the advertisement in which you are
featured. Your signed consent form is on file permitting us to do so,
but if for any reason you wish to be omitted from our upcoming cir-
culation please sign and return the enclosed postcard by the date
indicated below.

By the time Nigel received the document the reply date was three weeks past. The letter had gone to Imani's address and was forwarded to him. He would have Carmen call the clinic and update his mailing address for future correspondence, as well as ensure that his photo was not included in the upcoming ad.

Nigel took a break from the set. He had been up since four o'clock that morning rehearsing lines for his on-screen part that day. The drama was intensifying and so were the ratings. His character, Dr. Chance Montgomery, was a big hit with female viewers, and being stopped on the street with requests for autographs had become commonplace. So when the young, pretty Filipino woman approached him with a smile as he walked down the long boulevard to stretch his legs and get a breath of fresh air, Nigel pulled an ever-present pen from his pocket.

"Wow! I saw you on—"

"Heart of Angels," Nigel supplied. "I play Doctor Montgomery. I have the pen if you have the paper."

The young lady wore a quizzical expression.

"Paper for what?" she questioned.

"My autograph," Nigel responded.

"Why would I want your autograph? I detest soap operas. I only recognized you because I just saw you back there at the bus stop," the young woman advised, pointing over her shoulder in the direction from which she had just come.

"The bus stop?"

"Yes, on some hair ad." She jumped aside in the nick of time as Nigel took off at a fast trot up the block. He stopped, out of breath, staring in disbelief at the humongous vividly detailed poster plastered across the bus stop bench. There he was in living color for all of LA to see: Nigel Evans before and after his trip to the Hair Doctor . . . and the dentist.

Imani held the phone inches away from her ear and still she heard his every raving word.

"Do you know what it's like driving around town these days? That ad is every damn where! If I wanted everyone in Hollywood to know my business I would've told 'em my damn self! I have a reputation to uphold and thanks to you it's raining crap on my parade."

Imani hated to admit it but she found the situation amusing.

"Oh, that's terrible. I thought the Hair Doctor was only in Oregon."

"Well, it's obvious that they've expanded their damn territory to California, isn't it?"

Imani stifled a laugh.

"Nigel, this was avoidable. I asked you many times in the past to stop using my mailing address. This wouldn't have happened if your mail was delivered directly to—"

"No, this would not be a damn issue if you had simply forwarded my damn mail before the damn response date!" Nigel raged.

"So your early male pattern baldness and bad teeth are somehow my fault?" Imani inquired, thinking back on how shortly before their divorce Nigel began losing his hair and manifested a progressive dental condition that made him prone to gingivitis and calcium deposits so that his teeth began to decay. Good looks being imperative to his chosen profession, after graduation Nigel had agreed to be a test candidate at a hair treatment clinic in Oregon. By using the monetary stipend he received from the clinic combined with the money he secretly drained from their modest savings account, Nigel was able to afford cosmetic and corrective dental care. Imani bit her lip to keep from laughing as a mental image of the old Hair Doctor advertisement loomed in her mind. Nigel had looked like a partially plucked chicken with dominoes for teeth. Priceless!

"Don't play stupid on me. You *know* this is your damn fault. I should file charges against you for mail fraud. Tampering with mail is a damn federal offense!"

"Nigel, cut the irate act and all the *damn* profanity. I get your *damn* point. Lord, forgive me," Imani added, casting her voice upward.

"No, you obviously think I'm something to play with. Don't try me, girl. I'll have you in court so fast your nappy head will spin."

Imani grit her teeth at the intended insult before replying, "Speaking of the legal system, did you know identity theft is a federal offense?"

There was absolute silence on the opposite end.

"Nigel, do you have an attorney?"

His voice was oddly calm when he responded.

"Why?"

"If you don't I advise you to obtain one because I received my credit report a few weeks ago and it had some very interesting activity on it."

Nigel coughed nervously into the phone.

"Do you know anyone who shops at Zale's Jewelry or Gianni Brother's Men's Fashions? And my dentist is Dr. Yasuda, not Dr. Tompkins," Imani stated, walking about her bedroom. "Any idea how these accounts were opened using my social security number and name? And the last time I checked I did not have a spouse for whom I am a co-creditor."

"Listen, Butter, we can work that out," Nigel meekly replied, sounding nothing like the irate, self-righteous man of a moment before. "I'm only behind on a couple of accounts. If you pay them off for me I can make payments to you—"

Imani laughed as she paused before her dresser to wipe a thin film of dust with her finger.

"Like your child support and alimony payments, right Nigel?" She laughed again. "I don't think so. I don't know what crazy woman was dumb enough to forge my signature on your stupid credit applications but when I find out who she is she'll be taking a county jail vacation with you."

"Wait . . . wait . . . wait . . . now! Come on, Butter, let's not get bent out of shape and do anything stupid here. I told you I'd pay you back. Just keep this on the down low. I have a career—"

Imani sighed almost painfully.

"Yes, Nigel, I know. You've always had a career even at the expense of our family. You made choices then that were detrimental to us, but the choices you've made here will only be detrimental to you. You have to atone for what you've done."

"Butter, girl, come on now sweetheart. You don't want to see your baby's daddy on lock down do you?" Nigel asked with a false chuckle that rang hollow and empty in Imani's ears.

She made no reply.

"Butter? Hello? *Butter!*"

"Nigel, my name is and has been Imani since the day I was born. Act like you know." And with that she disconnected the call.

Her call rolled over to voice mail.

You have reached the office of attorney Terrance Blackmon. I am unable to take your call at this time. Please leave a message and reference the case or file number if appropriate. Thank you.

"Terrance, it's Imani. I need to take you up on your offer," she advised, recalling Terrance's offer that last night of the fair. "I need some legal assistance. Call me, please," Imani requested, leaving her home, cell, and work telephone numbers. It was the hardest call she had ever made, but it was so very necessary. Nigel had crossed the line with her so many times and she had failed to put him in proper check, allowing his abuse to continue for years. But his most recent transgression was one of the worst yet. Imani felt like a first-class fool. She knew a sense of utter betrayal and disgust. Nigel had made painstakingly clear his lack of respect and utter contempt for her. He did not care about the far-reaching ill effects his actions caused. He sabotaged Imani's credit with utter disregard for her livelihood or Nia's, and once again sabotaged her plans for her future.

Imani remembered crying all night upon discovering the betrayal. Because of Nia, she made concession after concession with Nigel only to have contempt instead of grace tossed back into her face. Imani was tired of rolling over and playing the fool just so she would not be guilty of isolating Nia from her father. But after her trip to southern California, even Nia had begun to see Nigel for the self-centered, pompous individual he truly was. Imani prayed that she had not done more harm than good by fostering the relationship between the two.

Opening the curtains, the autumn sun seeped into her bedroom like warm liquid against Imani's skin. Imani looked at the yard below. Fallen leaves were everywhere. The yard needed raking and the gutters would have to be cleaned and drained before the rainy season began. Imani realized that like those gutters she, too, needing cleansing. She had to release her ex-husband and the debilitating debris of the unhealthy relationship between them.

Imani knew it was time to cut her losses and be free. Over Nigel Evans she would cry no more.

BACK IN LOVE
AGAIN

"I can't see with this blindfold on," Brax complained three months later, feeling as if his equilibrium were off-center as the car traveled across the roadway.

"That's the whole point. It's a surprise and I don't want it spoiled."

"How much longer before we arrive at our destination?"

"Another hour," Imani answered.

"An hour? Oh, heck no. Pull over 'cause riding blindfolding is making me sick."

"I'm only kidding, precious," Imani said, reaching over to pat his hand. "We have another five or less minutes before we get there. You want a peppermint to settle your stomach?"

"No, I want a steak. I'm starving," Brax griped, thinking how on Imani's strict orders he had had nothing to eat since lunch because he was not to 'spoil his appetite' in any way. Now his stomach was growling like a tiger in a cage. "Can we stop and get a burger?"

"Brax, I promise we're almost there."

"You said that twenty minutes ago, babygirl. What's wrong with your watch?"

"Nothing, grumpy. See! We're here."

Brax felt the vehicle slow as Imani pulled his SUV into a parking lot. When the Escalade was finally parked Imani reached over and waved a hand in front of his face.

"Are you sure you can't see anything?"

"I can see stars flashing in my eyes because of hunger."

Imani laughed and disconnected her seatbelt, removed the key from the ignition then exited the vehicle to walk around to the passenger's side. Opening the door, she helped Brax unbuckle his own seatbelt and step down from the automobile.

"Okay, hold my hand. I'll guide us safely indoors."

"Yes, Mommy," Brax dutifully responded. Brax tried to estimate their time on the highway and follow the direction they had traveled but Imani had taken so many twists and turns that he had no idea of their whereabouts. Slowly, cautiously, he moved forward as she led the way.

"We're approaching a set of stairs. Okay? Ready?"

"All right," Brax replied, stepping up only to find his foot suspended in air with nothing solid on which to land. He stumbled slightly, causing Imani to catch him about the waist so that they both teetered precariously until she was able to right their footing again.

"I should have clarified step down and not up," she said, laughing.

"That would have been helpful. We have the blind leading the blind here. May I step *down* now without you dropping me to my death?"

"Yes, you may. Here, place one hand on this railing and hold my hand with the other," Imani instructed. "Let's go."

Brax breathed a sigh of relief when they made it to the bottom landing without incident.

"Okay, walk straight ahead. No, Brax, straight. You're veering to the left. You're about to run into a . . . wall," Imani concluded, as Brax made contact with the solid wall in front of them. Thankfully his shoe hit first and absorbed the impact.

"Woman, you have one minute to take this blindfold off of me," Brax threatened.

"All I need is two seconds," Imani responded, moving behind him to untie the cloth about his face. Quickly she did so. It took a moment for Brax to regain clear vision and when he did Brax jumped at the roar.

"SURPRISE!"

"Whoa!" he hollered, grabbing his chest and wobbling back, widelegged in a perfect Fred Sanford pantomime as a vision of friends and coworkers materialized. It was a beautiful sight to behold.

"What is going on here?"

"Happy Birthday, sweetie. Welcome to your first birthday party."

Brax stared at Imani in disbelief before glancing about at the gathered assembly. Terrance, Imani's relatives, Mrs. Greer and her husband, and a slew of other school staff, as well as a few of his basketball playing buddies, and a smattering of the 100 Strong brothers and their companions were there waving ribbons or tossing confetti and wearing crazy looking party hats to celebrate the occasion.

Brax was clearly overwhelmed.

"Thank you, babygirl," he whispered in Imani's ear, hugging her to his side. "Where are we?"

"The banquet room at The Set," Imani answered, referring to a marina front jazz club off of Garden Highway. "And don't thank me yet. There's more."

As if on cue the crowd parted straight down the center to reveal a group clustered at the very back of the room.

"Happy Birthday, Son!"

His mouth dropped open as Brax watched his mother approach, flanked by his sisters, their husbands, his nieces and nephews. He lost himself in his family's embrace; their joyful reunion jarring tears from the eyes of the onlookers until the room resounded with sniffles.

"Now you know why I insisted that you not come home for Christmas," Judith Wade explained. "We were coming to you."

Speechless, Brax could only shake his head in amazement, remembering the sadness he felt two days ago when Christmas came and went without his customary trip home. Spending the day with Imani and her family helped ease the longing. Still, it seemed especially difficult, his feelings exacerbated by the fact that, due to his car accident and subsequent convalescence, Brax had been unable to go home this past summer. His mother was adamant about flying out in July to make sure Brax was well. But because of her bout with severe angina Brax and his sisters agreed it was best that she not interrupt her own recuperation period, but remain in Indiana until she was fully recovered. By then Brax was up and about and promised to be home for Christmas so his mother could baby him proper. Now there she was: holding her baby boy, praising God that all was well.

"Kid, your Mother and Imani have been a little too tight since your family arrived yesterday. That means trouble," Terrance warned.

"You'd better watch out or your mother will have you humming the wedding march."

"Nothing wrong with that," Brax replied before tasting his birthday cake. Imani had gone all out. The soul food dinner, catered by Nedra's Place—a five star Black owned restaurant in north Sacramento—had been excellent and elegant.

"Kid, are you getting soft on me?"

Brax looked out across the room to where Imani was dancing with all three of his six-year old triplet nephews—Joshua, Justin, and Jordan—forming a circle and twirling with them until they were dizzy with delight. Brax smiled. The woman was priceless. Imani was his heart. Three months ago in September things seemed bleak between them but thank God He snatched them from stupid and tossed some sense back into their heads before it was too late. Brax had found his woman for life. Turning back to his housemate, Brax looked at Terrance long and hard before emitting a simple answer, "Maybe. Maybe not."

"Brax, she's beautiful," his sister Cassondra remarked several minutes later as he went to sit with his family as Terrance coaxed Mrs. Wade onto the dance floor. He glanced at his sister to see her gaze was locked on Imani who was still out there thrilling the triplets. "I see why we can't get you back to Gary."

"I could use a new sister, Brax. Hint, hint," Alondra remarked, nudging her brother with an elbow.

"Man, you better run for the border," one of his brothers-in-law cautioned.

"What's wrong with me?" Cassondra demanded of her sister, hands on her hips, before Brax could respond.

"Nothing, Cassi. But I've been looking at you since the womb. I need a new face," her twin commented.

"See if I ever let you share a uterus with me again!"

Laughing, Brax stood and grabbed his youngest niece from Alondra's lap.

"Y'all Wade girls work that out. Come on, pudding cup, let's go get our groove back," he sang, waltzing onto the dance floor with the small child in his arms. "You want to dance with us, Mrs. Greer?" he called to the older woman sitting at a table enjoying her dessert.

"Oh, no, sugar. I'm not trying to hurt your feelings in front of your family," she returned.

"That's too kind of you. Come on, pudding cup, let's show these folks how to party." And with that Brax broke into the Bankhead Bounce, doing a little dip that caused his niece to squeal with glee, which only served to draw the attention of his nephews and Alondra's oldest daughter so that they ran to join in the fun. Two of the triplets stood on one of their uncle's feet and clung to his leg while the other two youngsters took hold of the other.

"Wait just one minute. Were we not dancing here?" Imani inquired, pretending that her feelings were injured.

"Yes, Miss Imani, but you can dance with us here with Uncle Brax," Jordan offered.

"Yeah," his niece added, "Uncle Brax has big feet."

Laughing, Imani joined in the fun, dancing and cavorting with the children as Brax struggled to move with the added weight of his tiny human appendages.

"Wait, now, you can't leave me out."

Nia approached, relieving Brax of Justin's weight and spinning him about in her arms.

"Nia, be careful," Imani cautioned.

"Girl, please, that child has a head of steel!" Cassondra called out. "Nia can drop him and he won't break."

"Don't talk about my nephew like that," Brax returned above the music. "The Wade men are built Ford tough. Come on, Nia, let's do the bump."

"I can't. You have too many kids on you."

"Here, let me drop them off—"

"No!" the children yelled in unison.

"Keep dancing, Uncle Brax."

"I'm tired," he asserted, heaving dramatically.

"That's because you're old," Nia tossed.

"Old? Who you calling old, Hollywood? That did it. It's on now!" Brax began shaking and gyrating so that the children screeched their delight until—to his great relief the song ended.

There was applause as Brax freed himself of his tiny partners.

"Nia, can you hold on a moment?" Brax quietly requested before she could move away. Taking Nia's hand, Brax signaled the deejay to prevent any further music. "May I have everyone's attention?"

The jovial chatter throughout the room dwindled into a pleasant silence.

"First of all I have to thank everyone for coming out and sharing this evening with me."

A round of applause rippled soundly through the room.

"This has been a truly special night," Brax continued. "I have my friends, my family. I'm blessed." Brax paused to collect his thoughts. "Seeing as how this event was a surprise to me I didn't plan to do this here," he quietly stated, looking at those around him. "But I know better than to pass up a moment when it's presented." A puff of air softly escaped his pursed lips. "If there's one thing that's missing from my life it's this." Still gripping Nia's hand, Brax turned to her. "Hollywood, I feel a sense of responsibility toward you," he began. "You're a good little shorty and we've been through some things together. I just want to say thank you for allowing me into your world and for sharing your mother's love with me."

Standing at the inner perimeter of the crowd, Imani's heart thrilled at the sight of Nia and Brax together.

"I'm not trying to be your father or take his place, but I want you to know that you have the care of this Black man. Again, this evening took me by surprise so I don't have my gear with me and I'm a little ill prepared but," Brax slowly lowered himself to one knee, "will you be my daughter? May I have your mother's hand in marriage?"

A thick hush enveloped the room.

Nia gasped. She stood holding his hand and peering at Brax through a haze of sudden, unshed tears.

"Well, Hollywood, what's the word?"

"My mom and I w-would be very b-blessed to have you in our lives," Nia answered, her voice halting and catching with emotion.

Standing, Brax hugged Nia. Over Nia's head Brax looked for Imani. Finding her, Brax held Imani's gaze and directed his words to her even while embracing her child.

"Nia, I promise to love, honor, and cherish your mother like the exceedingly beautiful Black woman she is. I want to show her a lifetime of goodness. I want to be that rock that she can rely on, her shelter from the storm. I am far from perfect and I don't have it all together, but my love for her is pure. I want your mother to be my wife." He paused to swallow nervously. "Imani? Will you marry me?"

Imani stood frozen, trying her best to silently communicate her own love across the distance.

She knew such a tremendous regard for her man. She honored his struggle as they negotiated the new constructs of their relationship over the past few months. Brax had proven himself to be a man of his word. And though at times it proved a strain, he did not buckle or press her for intimacy that she could not give. It was a challenge, but together they discovered new ways to express their sentiments, their passion, without compromising Imani's accountability to God, and in the process delved into deeper places, broadening the span of their bond while growing in their esteem of one another. There were shared walks in the park, spontaneous excursions to South Lake Tahoe and Monterey, brunch aboard the Napa Valley Wine Train, as well as their frequenting various concerts and plays, art and cultural exhibits. Brax even talked Imani into hang gliding on a jaunt to Calistoga, where they journeyed with Nia, for a little pampering at a deluxe day spa. Imani had not particularly cared for the thrill of free-floating miles above the earth, but the memory of the adventure was pleasant.

More rewarding still was a new pastime she and Brax developed. On a recent trip to Culture Corner, Imani stumbled upon a collection of beautifully illustrated journals depicting various facets of life, love, and family. Partial to one journal whose cover showed an African American couple gazing down at their reflections cast in a pool of water as the woman stood sheltered in the embrace of the man behind her, his strong arms wrapped about her, Imani purchased two. She gave one to Brax and kept the other for herself. To her delight, Brax was the one to suggest that they use the journals as an outlet and opportunity, a recorder of sentiments regarding their relationship perhaps difficult to express only to then share its content. And so once a week they laid themselves bare and came together to disclose what was written that they might appreciate their individual perspectives and enhance their bond. But one entry in particular provided a most precious revelation. The entry was dated November eleventh, and it had set her heart on fire.

There in the festive vibe of The Set, watching Brax through tear-swept eyes, Imani remembered it word for word.

My mother has been saved all of my life, so I know what a virtuous woman looks like. Now here I am faced with that kind of woman all over again. I've been privileged to witness Imani's ongoing spiritual transformation with my own eyes, and her metamorphosis has encouraged me to unlock the door of my own heart and ask God to dwell within. That is an invaluable exchange.

And he's priceless to me, Imani thought, her dimpled smile confirming the pleasure she found in the notion of a life with the man gazing at her as if the world existed for their love alone. Distance melted, apprehensions dissipated as Imani beheld her beloved. She relished every inch, every pound and ounce of the man watching her, his strong and oh so handsome face burning sweet like brown sugar. And, admittedly, saved or not, she craved him, too.

Lord, help me to hold out, 'cause I love me some him!

Imani felt a slight nudge at her back.

"Child, go get that man before you melt in place," her mother whispered at her ear.

Smiling at her parents, who stood near, Imani muttered a breathy "Oh" as if awaking from a precious dream. Shaking herself and squaring her shoulders, Imani walked the short distance with her head lifted high until she was there in her perfect place knowing that a dream could never compare to the reality of his wonder. Nia gave her mother a quick hug before moving discreetly to the side as Brax took Imani's hands.

"You know this night caught me off guard, and I originally planned to do this on New Year's Eve, but baby, here I am," Brax stated, his voice low and resonant in Imani's ears. "Will you marry me? Can I be yours for life?"

"For life and a day," Imani answered, sealing her promise with a kiss as the room swelled with uproarious applause and cheers. Many wanting to convey warm wishes and emotional embraces immediately surrounded them.

Monique was there, her long arms locking a stranglehold about his neck as Brax struggled to breathe and Monique cried, "Welcome to the family, cousin."

Standing beside Monique, Imani whispered, amused, "What happened to his foul aura?"

"Must have been a bad mushroom," Monique admitted before collapsing into tears.

* * *

Imani's house, the site of an impromptu after party, was swarming with folks. Boisterous chatter, a blaring television, and equally loud music coming from indoors was loud enough that it could be heard outside as Imani and Brax made one last trip to his SUV under the ruse of retrieving something. They were truly more interested in a moment alone. Holding hands, legs swinging, they sat comfortably on the lowered tailgate despite the December chill.

"You're a slick one, Miss Evans," Brax remarked, gazing lovingly at her.

"What do you mean?"

"This whole surprise party business."

"Your surprise engagement upstaged my little attempts altogether."

"Your attempts were not little, and I appreciate everything about them . . . and you," Brax concluded, kissing her briefly. "Can we skip all that wedding madness and go straight to the honeymoon?"

"Only if you want us to go to hell," Imani teased.

"I hear the devil likes Black folks."

"Ooo, you better stop!" she chimed, squeezing his hand as Brax chuckled. "Pastor won't even consider marrying us until we've had a year's courtship," Imani reminded her fiancé.

"That's retroactive, from the moment you first walked into my office right? I ain't counting a year forward from today just to get my conjugal rights," warned Brax.

Imani leaned back and fixed Brax with a dubious stare.

"Are you marrying me for sex?"

"Absolutely! I say let's just have Pastor marry us in a hotel room. You be naked between the sheets because as soon as we both say 'I Do' I'll toss Pastor over the balcony."

Their laughter tinkled warmly in the cold December air.

"Seriously, sweetie, could we consider honeymooning in Africa? It won't be your two-year dream tour, but it would be a start," Imani suggested.

"I'd like that very much," Brax concurred. "Do we need to have your ring resized?"

Imani inspected the lustrous silver band with its pear-shaped diamond sparkling white against her long, dark finger. En route home after the party Brax made a quick detour, stopping at his house to retrieve the slender silver "promise ring" he purchased for Nia, and

Imani's engagement ring—slipping it onto her finger there in the quiet privacy of his home.

"Actually, it fits very nicely. You did good, Mr. Wade."

"I know," he agreed, kissing her once more. "Man, you should have seen your parents when I asked them for your hand in marriage last week. I did it early because I couldn't wait until New Year's Eve. Your mother was wild, asking me what I could do for her daughter. Even your Dad put me through. But I limped out all right."

"That you did," Imani agreed, caressing her ring.

"I forgot to ask you about the judgment. How did that go?"

Shaking her head, a mirthless laugh escaped her lips as Imani explained, "Nigel's wages are being garnished for the child support and alimony in arrears, and he was "sentenced" to community service and has to make restitution for the damage to my credit."

"That's it? Old boy merely has to spend an afternoon in a soup kitchen and that's all she wrote! I thought identity theft was a federal offense."

Imani shrugged.

"There's one law for Hollywood and another for the rest of the country. It may take a while to clean up my credit but I'm not giving up on my boutique and I'm not worried. Nigel will get his. There's a higher power than Hollywood."

"Preach, sister." Brax hopped down from his perch atop the tailgate and extended a hand to help Imani do likewise. "It's getting cold. Let's go back inside." He began securing the vehicle only to stop suddenly, remembering the presence of a large envelope in the cargo space. Retrieving the already opened envelope, he handed it to Imani, explaining, "My personalized plates arrived today."

Imani extracted the vehicle license plates and smiled as she read: CHCL8T

"Chocolate, huh? Sounds delicious."

"She is," Brax answered, pulling her to him.

Brax prepared for what he hoped would be a long and lingering kiss but the front door opened and Nia appeared on the doorstep, the dog in her arms.

"Mom, telephone!" she hollered above the din within.

Imani sighed.

"Who is it, Nia?"

"I don't know."

"Why you interrupting grown folks' business, Hollywood? That's why we're shipping you and Toto off to boarding school when your mother and I get married."

Nia rushed down the steps toward them.

"Mr. B., you're falsifying right? Hey," she paused, "I guess I need to find a new name for you when you become my mama's baby's step-daddy. How about B-Papa?"

Brax frowned.

"Let's let that marinate a while."

"Mom, are you really sending me to boarding school?"

"Stop being ridiculous, Nia," Imani said, shooting Brax a look.

"Whew! I want to stay here and work both of your nerves."

"You're doing a good job right now," Brax stated.

Nia laughed and turned to leave, reminding her mother that she had a call waiting.

"Nia, ask whoever it is to call back."

"Okay," Nia agreed, closing the front door behind her.

"That child is a mess, but she's my mess and I love her."

"Hey, I just thought of something," Brax intoned. "Here I come whisking you off into matrimony just when your alimony's about to kick in. You want to postpone our 'I Do's'?"

"Sweetie, *I* would pay Nigel in a New Jersey minute if it meant being free so I can spend the rest of my days with my Brown Sugar Bear," Imani sweetly stated, gently grabbing Brax by the ears and easing him forward.

"Babygirl, that's a 'New York' minute. "

"Mmm-hmmm," she purred, sinking into the comfort of his embrace. "Come on and kiss me California Christian style."

"Can I put some tongue in it?"

"Just kiss me already."

WHEN PERFECT AIN'T POSSIBLE

Suzette D. Harrison

ABOUT THIS GUIDE

The following questions and topics of discussion are especially designed to enhance your group's reading of WHEN PERFECT AIN'T POSSIBLE. We hope they prove thought provoking and foster richer, fuller conversations about this heartwarming story.

DISCUSSION QUESTIONS

1. Imani Evans is described as a voluptuous, chocolate-skinned woman with unprocessed virgin hair. Physically speaking, is she a "likely" heroine, or does her "brand of beauty" break with mainstream notions of that which is lovely and desirable?

2. Braxton Wade is a man who takes sabbaticals from the dating scene, stating that he is not a "woman a week kind of brother". In this regard, how does his character challenge widespread depictions of African American men?

3. When Imani and Brax first meet sparks fly, but not of the romantic kind. What helps turn their combative relationship around? Is forgiveness a factor?

4. Teased by her family for her "breast and booty fest" and having endured snide commentary from her ex-husband about her "thickness", Imani must come to accept and appreciate her "sisterish" physique. Do you think she has done so fully, or is she transitioning into full acceptance?

5. Do you feel as if Brax is hiding from life by not dating, saving for his trip to Africa, and "testing his longevity gene" before parking his slippers beneath the marriage bed? If so, why? Does grief over his father's passing have anything to do with this?

6. How do single/divorced parents manage to enjoy healthy romance without jeopardizing/compromising their children and their home life? In your opinion does Imani do this effectively? If not, what are her challenges?

7A. Before becoming a devout Christian, Imani's mother, Eunetta, was a promiscuous teen who had Imani out of wedlock. Oddly enough, Eunetta shied away from openly discussing sexuality with her daughter. Why is this?

7B. Imani grew up with a "string of uncles" and no father. How does this shape her life with respect to dating and parenting her child?

8. *"Son, perfect ain't always possible. Sometimes you have to opt for good,"* is the sage advice Brax received from his father, as well as a variation of the book's title. What does this mean to you? Are these words a caution against idealizing life or a justification not to strive for more?

9. How is the automobile accident in which Brax and Nia are injured a crossroads for Brax? For Nia? For Imani?

10. After becoming romantically/physically involved with Brax, Imani undergoes a spiritual metamorphosis. How does this impact their relationship? Should Imani have severed her relationship with Brax entirely? Was she presumptuous in thinking the relationship could continue?

11. Nigel Evans, Imani's ex, is a villain of sorts ruining her credit and devaluing her privacy, while her questionably psychic cousin, Monique, is a harbinger of doom raining psychic cautions against Brax on Imani's head. Terrance Blackmon, Brax's best friend, reminds Brax that they "don't do women with children." Here these three characters represent oppositional voices that serve to warn, challenge, or possibly direct and influence our lives. Take a moment to reflect on your dreams, passions and desires. Are important persons/influences in your life sidetracking or directing you away from achieving goals? What will you do differently from this day forward to reassert your right to achieve your god-given destiny?

12. Grace, mercy, and forgiveness of self or others as well as letting go of the past are constant threads throughout this book. How does holding onto the past affect Brax? Imani? How can we extend grace, mercy, and forgiveness to those who have wounded us, and obtain the same from those we have wounded?

Dear Readers:

Thank you for joining me on yet another journey of love and faith with this my sophomore novel, *When Perfect Ain't Possible*. I pray that your hearts have been uplifted, that you've laughed and perhaps even cried until you felt good. It is my aim to continually provide thought-provoking, heartwarming stories that affirm our struggle to live well. Again, may your faith be affirmed and spirit enlarged with God's greatness.

You are invited to share your comments with the author via email at: sdhbooks@aol.com.

ABOUT THE AUTHOR

Suzette D. Harrison is an honors graduate of the University of California at Santa Barbara, where she obtained a Bachelor of Arts degree in Black Studies. An aspiring gospel singer whose vocals have been featured on numerous recordings, Harrison frequently acts as a motivational speaker, sharing messages of hope with underprivileged youth, church groups, and university students. A west coast native, Harrison resides with her husband and their two small children, and is currently writing novel number three. The best-selling author is a member of the Black Writers Alliance, the Golden Key National Honors Society, as well as the president and founder of the Literary Ladies Alliance.